DRONES OVER SEATTLE
Wade's People

R.W. Clark

Second Root
——
Seattle

Dedicated to the memory of Howard Pease

Contents

OPPORTUNITY AND CHALLENGE

"No interview?" said Sean Moran groggily. Wade's assignment didn't sound remarkable. On the other hand, neither had Wade's other contracts that eventually revealed complex design issues he loved to escape into. But still, those all started with an interview.

"Sean," said Wade Jarvis. "Wake up. I said they asked for you by name. This is your specialty in hardware design. Are you on board for this contract?"

"Yeah, sure." Sean absently worked out a kink in his neck. "Of course." Timing was good. Any short assignment coming from Wade, his job-shop guru, promised to keep him out of trouble. It offered Sean a safe path back from last night's temptations in hacking.

"Good. They want you right away," said Wade. "From my office, you walk your contract papers directly to their HR. Follow their lead from there on. You will also be getting the higher rate."

"Thanks." Sean thought Wade's last touch was familiarly suspicious icing on the cake, but he decided he could be tempted.

"Great. See you here in, what? Half an hour?" said Wade.

"I'm on my way."

Sean slipped his phone into his pocket and wondered what he was about to get into. The higher rate, he felt, probably indicated an assignment with a company on the ragged edge. Past assignments with those places left him unsettled with troubled people. Sean had been through this with Wade before, and that discussion found Sean backed into a corner.

"So, what is it you want?" would come Wade's clincher.

1

Wade had the knack of drilling down to find motivation. Wade generally did it with a soft hand until he met Sean's resistance to going deeper.

Instead of facing his conflicts in Wade's question, Sean chose to silently take on the assignments as they came. The troubles with the sometimes melodramatic client settings were offset by their extravagant pay. Wade was a master at mining the opportunities found in client cultural shifts that came in their turmoil with market threats or expansions.

What was it Sean wanted, indeed? He lived for the challenge of solving the client's design problems. He wanted the money for doing it. What he didn't want was witnessing the grief of the client twisting in torment.

There! He thought that should answer it—but he never said it out loud.

Some clients had painfully intimate, and ultimately unsolvable personal situations. It was the dark part of the challenging opportunity that came with the all or nothing deal.

Sean's conflict was forged in his mid-teens when he had engaged in black hat activities. Hacking web sites with other black hats fed his need to solve problems he could prove to himself that he could master. These hackers hung together in chat groups and his participation there drew admirers of his work.

There used to be a pleasurable sense of the hacker community that filled the empty space left by his parents' breakup. But that pleasure faded. To his credit during this time, even if he could crack into a web site, he never pushed the button to empty loosely secured accounts.

It would have been easy money.

The white hats who cleaned up his hacks couldn't connect

the dots to him without that last transaction that Sean refused to complete. Sean knew this because he would watch them secretly, in real time over the web, as they browsed along the trail of his recent visits back then. So far, this was a nasty secret he hoped he had kept buried deep from everyone. He rubbed the knot in his neck as he recalled how he felt like he was being stalked on the web last night. It was an unfortunately familiar feeling.

He shuddered over the close attention from too curious fellow black-hatters back before he shifted out of that field. It was better to stick with his first love of building electronics circuits. There was a new wave of modular components hitting the market. They were affordable and exquisitely sophisticated. He felt he could discover new challenges to dominate.

He soon found a more positive group of hardware hackers who preferred robotics. They had taken up spaces in an old, repurposed government building. They called their lab, a maker-space, *Beyond the CyberDome*. No one hid behind masks of anonymity there. He recalled how good he felt making a presentation to them recently.

"Sean?" his mother, Melissa, called through the door she opened upstairs. "Was that the call we were expecting from your counselor? Are things back on track at the University?"

The smell of Mom's cooking drifted down from the kitchen. Satisfying hunger would have its pleasurable side, but the knot tightened in his neck again. Her question was one that Sean didn't want to go into either, but Mom was not to be denied.

"Yes and no."

"Tell me the yes part then," she said.

Her question pressed him into a corner. "It has to do with

another work assignment from Wade, Mom." She stirred above, as if only half occupied with her question.

What he said was true as far as it went. Wade was a counselor of sorts. He could tell her Wade brought opportunity, but Sean fended her question off because he didn't like being crowded.

With Wade Jarvis' assignments, he could at least contribute some money to maintaining their household. If he could put together a good enough story to tell her how much he got, then he could do more.

He heard the floor creak above. Was this the right time for it?

Offering that story might reveal his hidden sin in that discussion. His income, he hinted in the past, came from odd jobs. Wade, to Melissa, was a tall, solid built older man who was something of a general contractor.

In his two years working on Wade's contracts, he had hidden away a small bankroll. As his account had grown, so had his guilt over his diverting effort away from what his mother considered to be important studies. Sean's sins were compounding. Perhaps he took after his dad who put more stock in experience than in the promises of school. But Dad wasn't here to stand by his choice.

He heard steps above to the head of the stairs.

"So, when are you going to finish your incomplete classes at school, then?" Melissa's work in the kitchen above had ceased to distract her.

"I'm working on it Mom."

He strained, expecting to hear her follow-up questions, but she seemed satisfied. She walked back to the kitchen.

He felt humiliation. Sean was stalled in his degree work

and still living at home in the basement. He wished he could just chuck the illusion of finishing school.

When would she get it? With those tuition costs, why rush headlong into an expensive hole in her bank account? He couldn't ask her to pay for something he wouldn't pay for himself.

He turned to his keyboard to contemplate last night's design problem. Its challenge quickly drew him in and his mother's expectations dimmed. The knot in his neck settled as he submerged into the calming work.

Sean knew if he could keep his current focus in doing hardware sensor integration, that this work would keep him safely away from darker hacks' temptations in the late hours of night. This thought held its own against the prospects of sitting through another Summer quarter in finishing an incomplete in college English.

"I already know a dozen languages," he challenged aloud.

"Why am I haunted by Shakespeare, Milton, and the rest of those dead white Englishmen? How about Walter Mosely instead?"

The floor creaked at the head of the stairs and his mother joined in what he thought was his single-sided conversation.

"Computer languages do not count and professors don't test you for reading trash novels," she called down to him. "You haven't even returned to any of your favorite Latin classics since last year."

Sean couldn't answer that, but he could escape before his neck knotted up again. "Right now I need to get to the office."

He gathered his devices, stuck them into his bag and bounded up the stairs. Melissa watched him with amusement when he stalled at the door. She joined him and they both watched the rain dance on the sidewalk leading to the back gate.

"Need an umbrella?" she asked her son. Melissa didn't like damp weather. She complained it made her eat more, and added weight was something she found hard to shed.

"I'm good." Sean pulled his hood over his head, tucked his bag under his arm, and lunged out toward the shelter of the open garage.

Steady rain bounced off the pavement of the rough alley. The aged ruts filled with water that drained downhill. Normally the weather only shrouded them in an eternal drab mist. They had been living here in Seattle for a few years, and the general pattern of light but seemingly constant drizzle was becoming familiar. Still, there were times when he expected it to let up after twenty minutes. That would have been normal for Colorado. This wasn't the high plains. To his family's shock, their first exposure to Seattle's heaviest rain had come when they arrived in the opening week of twenty seven days of rain—unfailingly everyday. The streak broke one day, revealed a glint from the sun the next, and then a new streak of rainy days followed.

Today's rain lightened up. Luck continued with Sean at the bus stop. Both he and north Ballard's number 45 bus arrived at it at the same time. The bus was empty of passengers. It usually was this close to the beginning of the route.

He knew that the bus would fill as it moved towards the university district, but until the distraction of new riders came, Sean was left to reflect on past assignments through Wade.

His first assignment from Wade was a remarkable stint in a paper mill helping get the kinks out of a process controller.

Then the roller coaster plunged. Some of the five or six contracts that followed were an emotion strained ride—but still well paid. Those assignments were reasonably long. They were not like the three day knock-offs that larger, soulless agencies had sent him on for starvation wages.

Those clients that were suspiciously generous lacked a necessary hungry dog tenacity. They timidly paid ransom for their lost sense of mission. Eventually, over several of these contracts, Sean could recognize these signs as the minor temblors to the disaster that loomed in each of those assignments.

In his own life, their caution mirrored his parent's tentative, safe relationship fixes that stumbled to failure. Both in these offices, and at the supper table with his parents, there was always the tension of something not being faced in the open.

To deaden the heavy pain deep in his heart both on the job, or at home, he hunkered down and worked harder on his task. Employers saw him as a good worker, his parents described him as a strong soldier. He couldn't agree less, but never said anything.

At any job, he took his place in an isolated corner where as a temp he often found himself placed. That was fine. People distractions were minimized. The task flowed without interference. At home, he rushed down to his basement bedroom and hole up at his workbench, or at the keyboard to solve one of his own design's glitches. Mom and Dad's fruitless discussions were left behind.

Wade's new client would probably present Sean with a similar, troubled story. The pattern would be played out again. There would be their nebulous goals and slow change. Taking their money while they agonized would unsettle him as if he were paid the wages of despair.

In that pattern, the project collapsed soon after his arrival. At that point roles switched and managers swapped out. Sean's role became obscure and he was left adrift in the storm surge that swept through. Eventually, fear subsided and he realized he had survived it. This moment's hollow euphoria was soon whisked aside by the next shift in the current.

The project's re-boot would find its way and carry him along a flood tide of audacious new design. Even then, when he was cresting, he had an equally hard time with the money as coming too easily on top of the adrenaline rush this burst of work brought him. The excitement of finding solutions to the technical problem replaced his need for nourishment or company. Unfortunately, after the buzz of delicious activity faded, the old anxiety with a new face returned.

"Are you going to say hi back?"

Aurora stood in the aisle next to his seat, head tilted in that manner that says *I'm waiting, make your move.* Sean was surprised to see that, now, most of the bus had seats occupied by at least one person. He looked back to Aurora, and she tilted her head to the other side as if to emphasize his slowness in response. Her green eyes fixed on him. Did she want to sit next to him?

"Hi Aurora. On your way to classes?" Even though there was already room for her, he slid closer to the window. She joined him.

"I'm on my way to an interview with Wade." Aurora pressed her lips and looked at him, her face framed by her long wavy red hair. "Summer quarter is about to begin, but you were never one to pay attention to college schedules, were you?"

Did her smile mean to sting him, or to draw him? He decided it was a nearby lightning strike and luckily he wasn't in the direct path. "Contract opportunities got Aurora out of her saffron bed?"

"Still in your own dreams, Virgil?" Aurora said. "I think our Latin class was the only one you showed up for consistently."

She theatrically raised one finger to the side of her mouth. She manufactured a pout. "Hmm, let me guess, you're going to see Wade too."

"I'm on my way there, yes."

They had spent time together on a couple of assignments from Wade. It was how Sean had come to know Aurora better. This was beyond the superficial socializing in the few college classes they shared. But the tall red-head noticed that he did make it to Latin quite often. Why didn't Mom acknowledge his language skill here, outside of the dozen computer dialects he was fluent in?

"What does Wade have for you this time, Aurora?"

"You know he doesn't show his hand during a call. I just hope it isn't another burn from the client like our last outing together."

He knew what she felt, but this was the nature of the game, he thought. "Contracts are offered when times are chaotic and businesses need someone to help flex through painful shifts in direction." He smiled at the irony of his more balanced perspective where he had been earlier gnawing with anxiety like her.

Aurora's brow drew down. "You're being uncharacteristically understanding of that last volcano eruption we went through."

She adjusted uncomfortably next to him. Sean

considered that she might have lost some weight. This was something not too easy for her as she had shared with him in the past. It seemed to Sean that they might move on to talking about something more personal. Instead, Aurora pulled out her phone. She started checking her messages, flicking some away as nuisances, and busily responding to others. He recognized the purpose driven side of her and turned his attention to the view outside.

They were both headed for the University District, and in the district, Wade. They left Crown Hill behind and passed through an assortment of communities before pausing near the fringe coffee shops at the north end of Green Lake. There, he caught glimpse of customers who sat in pools of low light, or nearer to a window where the heavy clouds subdued the light. They seemed so detached from his and Aurora's cares.

Sean had gotten on at the route's start where the homes varied between new high-end mansions with a commanding view of Puget Sound, and tucked away shingle mill-worker homes built a century ago. Sean and his mother lived in a home that fell somewhere between that range in North Beach, but Aurora's family lived in the more upscale Blue Ridge.

In the scheme of life, he thought, he and Aurora both enjoyed a good place. However, Aurora still had her complete family. His mother and father divorced some years before when the economy tanked. Dad was the one who moved away out of shame for not being a good provider. Mom wasn't in any better position after Dad's choice was made, but logic was not his strength.

Yes, Aurora, even in anticipation of her fear over their future assignment, had both her parents to return home to. Sean's mother tried to look after him during his low moods, but he kept to himself and tried not to expose his insecurity concerning their thin resources. Or her's rather.

His hidden bank account might boost their prospects, but he hadn't opened up because he felt like he wouldn't be able to keep it up. Contract work was so temporary, and so temperamental. He needed to share more money with Mom, but would it be a trap for them both? He couldn't even enjoy that money for himself.

A painful strap tightened in Sean's chest. In the same down economy where Dad faltered, Sean was rising. But was this an illusion? Could his field wither and leave him struggling for survival? Could the fickle economy ravage him like Dad?

"Sean," said Aurora. "You OK?"

"Just things at home," he said.

"Sorry," she said. "Concentrate on one of Wade's mantras. Or count your breaths."

He was thankful that Aurora was there for him. He smiled and nodded at her suggestion and started the count.

* * *

Sean and Aurora got off the bus to walk the short distance to the Roosevelt Courtyard in the U district where Wade's small office was. The rain had stopped and the sky had become a mild gray that brightened the white of nearby buildings in contrast. In the distance there was a hint of a brief clearing. Pedestrians had emerged from their workplaces to begin their trek out to lunch.

Aurora walked along the drying sidewalk slightly ahead of Sean. Her long stride was measured and talking would have been difficult. For him, his conversations either ran on, mining detail, or ran out of steam. Neither of them had any notion of Wade's prospective assignments, so that conversation had no where to go.

"Aurora. Could you slow down a bit? It's like you're running interference on the field." Sean figured it was shadows from the last assignment that were still chasing her.

"Pick up your feet, Sean, if you want to keep up. I meet at noon with Wade. Are you still working on the drop-in principle, or do we have the same appointment time?"

"Plus or minus. It's already after noon, and we may as well be comfortably late." Sean's noticed his forced, casual manner inspired Aurora to step out more briskly. She started to weave through the thickening crowd on the sidewalk— Sean fell behind the wall of walkers that opened magically for her—but closed on her heels and pressed him back.

However, at the end of the day, thought Sean as he caught a glimpse of the Roosevelt Courtyard's off-street entry, we will arrive at Wade's office only moments apart. He stepped into the courtyard, and it brought a feeling of calm that grew with every visit.

Wade, his guru, seemed to live above the storm here in this classic building. If he had been a student of Greek instead of Latin, he might have called this Olympus. But Wade wasn't majestic, even given his sturdy frame and mop of salt and pepper hair. Rather, Sean imagined him more like a Buddhist monk sitting in the opening of a high mountain cave, and each meeting with him added to that feeling.

The foyer's decoration always captured his heart with its art deco motif that felt energetic. Sean wandered over to a box display on a wall that framed a selection of stamps that memorialized a distant time. Among them were those quite evidently celebrating technology. There was an airplane in a triangular stamp, and what looked like a closeup side view of an enormous dirigible in a square stamp. Sean drew that conclusion from his impression of the classic Led Zeppelin album. He smiled and pondered why he considered the album cover to be the older association.

Sean breathed in the calm, drew in new strength, and climbed the stairs with a renewed optimism that he could catch up with Aurora's elevator ride. When he stepped into the hall upstairs where Wade's office was, he glimpsed Aurora going in. He caught the door, against her closing pressure until she sensed him there.

"Learned to pick up your pace, I see," she said to him quietly.

Wade, seated on his cushion next to a low lacquered tea table, looked over Aurora's shoulder and waved him in. There were empty chairs nearby, but they were for strangers. Sean smiled at this. He had sat in one chair only once, during his interview on their first meeting. Sean and Aurora took up positions on Wade's oriental rugs scattered over the carpet.

Wade returned to what had been occupying him, and held up one hand to indicate he would be with them shortly. Sean began to trace the arabesque pattern on his rug with his finger. Aurora watched, for a while, looping a heavy lock of hair, but turned her gaze back to Wade as he stirred.

"Sean, you are early—or I should say according to your habits, nearly on time. Aurora, is this due to your influence?"

If it seemed like Aurora could blush at this, and hide it well, then Sean's face lit in a flame. However well she managed to cover her first reaction, annoyance easily dawned on her brow, knitting her auburn eyebrows together. "Did you intend to rope us together on an assignment?"

Wade smiled. "How would that make you feel?"

Aurora shifted her gaze between Wade and Sean several times. Her mood got darker. "Not good, if it's like last time."

Sean wondered if their last assignment together still gave her that much of a burn? He knew how rough it was on him, generally. His soul was getting calloused if he had never thought of how Aurora had handled it at the time. He didn't really know her. If he didn't know her, did he know himself?

"All that bad, Aurora?" asked Wade. His voice was deep and caring.

"C'mon Wade, you know the hassle we had!" offered Sean in her support.

Wade took their statements in and pursed his lips. He leaned back to the small table, picked up his tea and took a sip. "Where are my manners? Would either of you like some tea?"

They shook their heads, no.

Wade glanced out the window at the skyline in the distance. "Looks like rain."

Aurora crossed her arms. "Rain? I can take the rain. I was born here. Are you going to say anything about those clowns you set us up with?"

"The client pays your way generously, and my assignments go to those who can handle rough weather. That is our understanding, in a nutshell."

"I'm not for sale," bridled Aurora.

Sean knew where this could go. He uneasily embraced the validity that Wade's assignments were sometimes difficult going. And, yes, the money was good. It began to gnaw on him that his mother thought his work was merely a form of a paid hobby that had grown out of his teen years.

14

"I started out good this morning—" Aurora moved her hand down to calm her stomach.

Wade rocked back and touched his lips with a light stroke. "I'm sorry if I lay out the cards with a snap. It's a guy thing that is hard to unlearn. What can I do to help you?"

Aurora calmed some and the darkness left her eyes, but not her mouth. "I like the work. I didn't like the customer."

Aurora shifted her weight. "The work is rough and can be impenetrable. The pay certainly matches the effort to unravel their knots. But that last customer, it seems, couldn't, or wouldn't untwist."

Wade nodded. "Be careful of characterizations, Aurora, even if what you say is close. There is only one truth in a successful business: give value for value. In our relationship —you, Sean, and me—that is what I try to achieve. It should be your truth, too."

Wade picked up a string of prayer beads, what Sean had heard him call his Mala, and hummed a short chant before he returned to the discussion. Sean was used to these spiritual excursions now. He watched Aurora relax her shoulders. They both knew a story was coming.

"Some—what?—forty years ago when I was trying to find the ropes, I think I felt like you two did on your last assignment. Sorry about that for you. Aurora. Sean." He looked at their faces trying to read if they were taking this in. "It was during the war. I was in the Navy. You might say my customer, uncle Sam, was difficult to live with. However, I couldn't walk away without someone chasing me down— hauling me off to the Brig. I couldn't even quit without disgrace dogging after me for years."

"Was it that bad?" said Aurora. She leaned her firm frame toward him, but she seemed petite in comparison to his solid

200 pounds.

"My buds called it a world of hurt," he said. "We were given million dollar educations, worked on hundred million dollar systems—"

"—but?" said Sean.

"Thick headed officers treated us like inferiors and insisted that every night we be in bed, on board ship, for their head-count at lights out."

Aurora wrinkled her freckled nose. "I've had curfew—it sucks. But then I demanded that my folks cut me some slack. I deserved it."

Sean wanted more, too. "I'm home each night too. No big deal, Wade. Where's the pain?"

"This may sound strange, but you both have enjoyed positive surroundings that allow you to earn and make your choices—good or bad as they may be."

"OK," said Sean.

Wade nodded and set aside his Mala. "So, consider my times, then, where my complaint would be called insubordination, and it could land me behind bars if I pressed harder."

"Yeah," said Aurora and she leaned back with a sigh. "Sounds like my A-list bozos." She straightened back up. "Why'd you go in the Navy in the first place if it sucked?"

Wade smiled and waved the question away. "I'm not trying to dismiss your troubles with my own story of struggle with lame bosses, Aurora, ask me that question again later. It bears examination." Wade reached again for his tea and pondered them as he took a sip.

Sean noticed that Aurora wasn't relaxing from her rigid posture. Wade seemed aware of this too and he put his tea back down.

"I guess this is the time," said Wade. "… We had a Draft back then. Uncle Sam would oblige young men to join the Army or the Marines for a two year contract. You accepted this choice or you explained to the judge why you didn't. Judges weren't very sympathetic."

Aurora mopped back her auburn hair. "Wade, this doesn't explain you joining the Navy—and you were in longer than two years, weren't you?"

Wade smiled, but there wasn't any happiness in it. "My parents' expectations were a big part of it, dear. The starkness of war and the social struggles came at us in terms of black and white. I stepped out of the world of my schoolmates. They rebelled against authority—I didn't."

Sean felt sad for Wade, but confused, too. "You aren't a black and white kind of guy." Sean noticed as he said this that Aurora was following his words. She turned to watch Wade.

"Not even then. The issues were very nuanced. My parents brooded about my lack of enthusiasm, my former friends treated me as a tool. It felt like I lived between two worlds, alone. I spotted the flaws on both sides—but I didn't rebel."

"Why?" said Aurora.

"Aurora," said Wade. "I needed support that was missing early on. Mom had her hands full with my younger sisters and brother when Dad was at sea. Granddad lived in the Mariner's home, down in 'Frisco."

"I'm sorry, Wade," she said. She lost the tightness that had kept her erect.

Sean felt uncomfortable, but he had to ask. "What kind of

support?"

Wade pursed his lips for a moment. Then he lifted one eyebrow as he returned his attention on Sean and Aurora. "Same thing you are looking for is what I would suspect. Unfortunately, last time, I hadn't mixed you both in with my older crew. I am sorry now that I didn't, because you could have used their advice, their watching your back. Keep close to me on this assignment—if you accept it. I will keep you from harm if you find the client abusive."

Aurora and Sean took a breath together. Some of the original tension was gone now. But Wade's last statement suggested that the problems they had had would be a variation on what was in front of them. Wade had promised help, but not solutions.

Sean filled the gap. "What about this assignment?"

"It's doing tech through account managers downtown in the Pioneer Square area. They are upscale for that neighborhood. The Square is drifting in transition between skid-road and software campus."

Sean brightened. "Workin' for a Dot.Com?"

"Sorry, no buffet of Cheetos and Coke around the Foosball tables," said Wade. "Sean, you and Aurora really need to study the history of your industry to realize what was truly twisted."

Sean caught Aurora's glance, and her shrug pushing back at Wade's sermon.

Sean pressed on. "Who is this assignment with? What are they like. You say this is about accounting? Literally?"

"*Pribylov Investment* by name. Handling money by game. They are account managers for Angel investors funding the next hot item. As far as the tech story goes, that is still a blank page."

Aurora said, "You know more than that." Sean felt a bite in her question and considered that her compassion might at times slow to a trickle.

Wade nodded. "A close friend of mine who lives in this building says they know their game. She trusts them with her money, and I trust her read of these guys, the managers. What is certain is that they have a problem that needs fixing, and they can pay for it. That I can stand behind. Personally."

Aurora challenged Wade again. "And what in our resumes suggests us compared to anyone else?"

Sean leaned forward to pick up on this.

"My reading of the situation is they need fresh perspectives and the determination of youth. You two suit that to a T. And, curiously, one other fact."

Sean noticed Wade's attention on him and dipped his toe back into the conversation. "And that fact is?"

"They asked for you, Sean, by name," said Wade. "I don't know how you came up on their radar, but there you are."

A quiet descended upon them all. Aurora hedged between running hot and cold, but she wasn't grilling Wade anymore. Sean was digesting this last piece of news. Wade simply reached back for his tea and left them alone. Outside, rain pattered against the windows and blurred the view of the distant cityscape that peeked over the shoulder of Capitol Hill.

Sean broke the silence. "So, what's next? You said something about signing papers and …"

Wade took a folder off the floor next to him, drew out two copies of his standard contract, and handed them around.

"You know this part, nothing new, you are paid for billed hours, no benefits. Get the customer's signature before you turn in your time-sheets on Friday."

As they signed the contracts without reading them, Wade continued, "You can go immediately to their offices. The address is on the contract, so take note and see their HR. Sean, nose around and ask how and why they chose you and get back to me on that. I don't like the client being ahead of me."

Sean smiled. "You mean you might have been able to charge more if you had known?"

"Sean, understanding isn't always about money.

"Last thing." Wade straightened. "Are you both up on my interview exercise?"

Sean felt perplexed, but Aurora nodded. "Mindful breathing."

"It looks like Sean needs a refresher," said Wade.

Aurora nodded. "The zen of Wade tells us to take in a quick breath and let it out slowly as we approach those offering opportunity and challenging questions."

Sean took a gulp of air as his recall caught up.

Wade simply nodded. "You got it—now—you're ready."

THE GAUNTLET

Sean and Aurora walked back to the bus stop. Almost any bus heading south would get them close to the Pioneer Square district. Heavy clouds marked the distance between here and there like mileposts. Aurora seemed distracted as did Sean as he followed behind.

The roads were filled with the rough sounds of traffic at the nearby intersection. Along with the din came their exhaust's lingering distinct smell of gasohol additives. Sean felt the hunger he dismissed earlier and yearned to walk a few blocks south where some of the restaurants' cooking smells would be drifting out of their sidewalk service windows. There would be food after they visited the client.

The remnants of the last rain found its way behind his collar in slow drips from the edge of a building's marquee overhead. He looked up and caught a drop on his cheek that found its way to the corner of his mouth. It was hard to identify the taste, but it must have been uniquely associated with the University. That drop broke through the haze.

Pribylov Investment, the client, knew him. How did that happen? They asked specifically for him. Sean didn't need Wade to prompt him to find out why. Sean was so engrossed by this puzzle that he nearly walked into Aurora.

She was standing at the bus stop in line next to an old woman.

Turning, and then staring intently at him, she said, "Who are you?"

"What do you mean?"

"You know what I mean." She bore down on him. "They know your name, and you're just a kid. How does an investment business know your name?"

This was unusual. Aurora seemed to be taking his

21

celebrity personally—if he could call it celebrity. These thoughts quickly passed as his anger emerged from beneath them.

"Just a kid," he said. "Who are you then, Missy?"

That wasn't going to work very well. Missy was a name his dad used to call Mom in anger, and that didn't work out very well either.

"Jeez, that was stupid," he said. "I'm sorry I went there."

He wanted Aurora on his side—especially when it came to understanding girls—the impenetrable mystery that was out of his reach.

Aurora, too, had given his angry snap some thought. "Sorry, Sean about that kid thing. But it seems that you guys have things just mysteriously drop into your lap. I am frustrated trying to figure that out."

"It's a mystery to Wade and me, both, too. I'm not sure I like things just dropping, as you say, into my lap." Sean shuddered. "No, not at all."

The arrival of a bus quelled the chance of mysteries being sorted out. As usual, Aurora found a way to slip in quickly, where he got caught behind the slow older woman who fumbled through her knitting bag to find her bus pass.

The interior of the bus was humid with wet jackets. Claustrophobia steamed the windows. Sean wormed between shoulders pushing their way to the exit. The tinny sound of a nearby earbud whistled the opening riff from Ziggy Stardust. He took the open seat next to the old lady who was now browsing for something else in her knitting bag. He was also across the aisle from Aurora.

Sean tried to turn his thoughts to the next job. However hard he tried, there was very little about his nature, his interests, or his past work for Wade that seemed to fit into performing on an assignment in an investment office. He glanced across the aisle to where Aurora was sitting. Her dark mood was gone, but she must be as deeply in thought about the client as he was.

Sean decided he didn't know Aurora all that well. Did she have a boyfriend? Had she had a boyfriend? Did she want a boyfriend?

Would he be attractive to her?

"Be careful with where that can go," he muttered to himself.

"Sorry." Sean's seat mate shifted to give him more room. "I hope my knitting needle didn't stick you."

Sean moved closer to the aisle in response to this unexpected conversation. He looked at the woman sitting next to him. It was the first time he noticed her busily knitting. It added to an incomplete pattern that was emerging.

"You going to see the game?" she offered with a brief look up from her flashing needles.

Sean guessed she was, what, 60, 70, 80? How can you possible guess beyond a certain age? She was impeccably dressed. Even her knitting seemed to be picture perfect. It was like looking at a picture from one of grandmother's old fashioned magazines. His pattern of her was becoming richer in content.

"Game? Aren't we between seasons?" Pioneer Square was near enough to the sports arenas for him to offer that suggestion. It was a long shot for her to mean other games. They were heading for Seattle's tourist trap, after all. Sean wondered if she had all her marbles.

"There's no season for pool. But, I guess most of your generation isn't very interested in that game." She put her needles down.

The bus hugged around a corner and hopped the curb slightly. Sean wondered was this going to turn into a long conversation? "Pool? Like billiards? You are going to play in a game of pool?"

"No, that was my dear husband's game. I still watch now that he is gone. So, you haven't heard about the big game."

"Like, the pool room on Broadway near Madison? This bus is going closer to Pioneer Square."

Sean's seat mate frowned at his presumption. "Not that yuppie Disneyland." In a sudden turn away from Sean's faux pas, she smiled at a memory.

"Wimpy Lassiter came in from Gastown up in Vancouver, on his way to Frisco's Tenderloin."

Sean asked, "Tenderloin?"

"The Downtown Bowl," she said. "Wimpy was mostly an East coast guy. When he passed through, Jack had to take me to see him. Jack knew him when he was in the Coast Guard about 10 years before that, when hustling brought in a lot of money."

"How much money is a lot of money?" said Sean.

His seat mate put her knitting into a bag, closed it neatly and put her hands on it as she leaned into her story. "Usually $1000 for a money game, maybe $10,000 for a big challenge match—not that any were played here."

Sean nodded. "$10,000 would be a lot for me."

His seat mate laughed brightly. "That was 60 years ago when our first small house cost that much."

Sean noticed that Aurora was getting up. He looked through the foggy window and could see the smudgy block shapes of older buildings typical of Pioneer square. His seat mate also appeared to be getting ready to get off too, but he had to close her story. "I don't suppose they are playing for $10,000 a game any more."

"They better be," she said. "That's why I came to town! It's not like it's all that much money. Look, dear, if you want to see the real action, go a couple blocks down First. On the west side look for a sign that says *Snooker* with an arrow pointed upstairs."

"Thanks, that sounds like a nice idea, but I have to go to kind of a job interview thing."

"That's nice. What do you want?"

Sean was hit with the question he managed to avoid with Wade. But having dodged that one so often meant he could do it again. "Computer stuff."

"There are lots of those outfits popping up near where I'm going. Is this a small computer business?"

"Strangely enough, no. It is called *Pribylov Investment.*"

His seat mate took this in and let it digest. As she buttoned up her raincoat, she seemed to be weighing her words. "I know investments. That's how I parlayed Jack's winnings into our retirement. If Pribylov doesn't work out for you, drop by the money game."

Sean smile at her invitation. "Shall I say Jack sent me?" He thought his line from an old gangster movie would amuse her.

"You might get noticed with that." She smiled at something in the distance. Then her focus fell back on him. "They remember Jack. But if you say Betty sent you, you will probably get better treatment." With that, she stepped out into the crowded aisle with him. She slipped off the bus before either he or Aurora could navigate through the damp crowd shuffling towards the exits.

"Got a girlfriend?" Aurora slily winked. "Maybe I have misjudged you. You certainly seem to be known well beyond my small world."

Sean watched his former seat mate, Betty, move through the mist in the street and out of sight around the corner ahead of them. "Betty's her name."

"She looks like an ambassador's wife," said Aurora as she watched. "What's she off to, a shoe store?"

"Not as she described it."

"OK, international man of mystery, I'm not going to drag it out of you." With that, Aurora took up her usual pace and lead the way to where they turned the same corner Betty had already disappeared around.

* * *

The weather and Aurora's steady march kept them from continuing their conversation. Mist cloaked the trees and muffled the sound of traffic through the shrouded avenue. In short order they entered a doorway that opened immediately to a stairway in front of them.

Sean glanced around them. No obvious business sign announced who occupied the building. In fact there was nothing to indicate there was any businesses at the top of the climb. But climb they did.

Office doors lined the corridor in both directions. Some were fitted with old-fashioned wavy glass in the top panel. Most doors had solid panels. Odd numbers were to the left and even numbers to the right, as indicated by a functional sign on the wall above a table holding a spray of fresh flowers. The sign was a nod to city fire codes; the flowers were a bow to the anonymous wealth behind those doors.

Aurora consulted her notes and swung left.

The dark paneled woodwork was hand buffed. The walls had an immaculate coat of a rose tint. The pearl white carpet swallowed the sound of their progress down the corridor. Sean sniffed the air expecting the musty smell of Seattle's old money.

Aurora signaled their arrival by unceremoniously walking through a door—one of those with the wavy glass—boldly branded as *Pribylov Investment*. Their arrival was met with the instant attention of a goth outfitted receptionist sitting at a desk between two interior office doors. She laced her fingers together, looked over Aurora's shoulder, and offered Sean a smile. "Can I help you?"

Aurora asserted "We are supposed to report to HR." She looked at one door, and then to the next as if neither door could lead to any such department.

The dark, bobbed haired receptionist kept her smile on Sean. Sean was both attracted by it, and put off. It seemed she was doing it simply to annoy Aurora. Apparently to prove this, she turned her attention to Aurora and said "I'm HR. You are my vacation replacement," and turning her gaze back to Sean, "You are Mr. Moran, I assume. You can go into Mr. Andrew Dearborn's office." She indicated the office to her right. "Mr. Dearborn will be back from lunch very soon. He's a man of strict scheduling."

She turned to look at Aurora. "Aurora? Yes. Keep that in mind. He's not difficult to get along with if you do."

"M-hmm," was Aurora's only response.

The receptionist echoed her. "M-hmm." And then she

brightened to cool-white fluorescent as her focus shifted to the corridor door opening behind them. "Have a nice lunch Mr. Dearborn? Your tech expert is here."

Andrew Dearborn was a thin man in his indistinct 30s. He wore a conventional, but tailored suit with an open neck shirt. His tie was probably tucked into one of his pockets. Sean was not impressed if he was supposed to be an investor. However, he didn't know what investors looked like. He reached to offer a handshake. Mr. Dearborn's eyes seemed to be surveying the upper wall for some reason, and his hand sprang out as if fulfilling an ill-learned social script.

They shook hands mechanically. The obligation behind him, Mr. Dearborn blurted out, "let's go to my office." He didn't wait for Sean to respond, and almost walked over him to get to the door behind the receptionist's desk.

On his way in, Sean noticed that the short, slim receptionist and Aurora were coming to terms on their own. They must have noticed Mr. Dearborn's behavior because Sean caught the receptionist's whisper to Aurora. "Asperger's ..."

Mr. Dearborn's office didn't reveal any personal touches. Still, to that alone it was painfully familiar. For Sean's few short term contracts through the body shops, he had been in corporate offices that were hot-desked. That is, desks were assigned to office workers in the order they walked through the door that day. Sean could live with that for an assignment because he mostly telecommuted, but there was a saddening gloom closing in. This impersonal office looked perfect for holding an employee's execution.

Sean waited while Mr. Dearborn settled behind his desk. If mechanical introductions were any indicator, he should find his own chair rather than wait politely to be offered a seat.

But there was no other chair. In fact, it wasn't even a desk. It had the lines of an old-fashion desk, but without drawer pedestals. There wasn't any file cabinet in the room either, and no computer. Mr. Dearborn's gaze occupied the upper wall behind Sean. Moments threatened to become minutes, but Mr. Dearborn appeared to turn the page of the social script and took up the next phase.

"You are here to help us recover from a problem an investment of ours has."

"What is that problem?" asked Sean.

"Our holding is experiencing a cultural shift, and a technical short-fall."

"I don't know about culture, I do know about tech."

"You are going to upset the culture even more, but we have to live with that." Mr. Dearborn folded his hands together.

"What about the tech?"

"You are going to upset that too. And we are going to have to live with that."

"How?" Sean was content to wait this out. Too often in other interviews or project meetings he had encountered less definition. At least Mr. Dearborn could give as well as take in this dialog.

"That is up to you. You do know that don't you? We chose you because your work fits into their scope."

Sean had a problem here. One was personal, and the other professional. Who did they think he was, and what did they think he could do? He decided to start personal.

"Are you sure I'm the right guy?"

"Why are you here if you are not?" Mr. Dearborn braced

himself, and appeared to do a mental recalibration. His gaze hunted the room and found the familiar wall behind Sean again. "Your friends call you Sean. That is your name isn't it? Sean Moran? We were interested in your achievements at a place nearby called *Beyond the CyberDome*."

That answered a lot, but it left a lot unsaid. Sean did mix it up with other hardware hackers at the old Immigration building several blocks away from here, but ... "What does that have to do with what you want me to do?"

"If I knew that, we wouldn't need you. We invest in the culture. Some of that culture infects us here and ..." Mr. Dearborn placed his hands flat on the table and slid them apart as if they were going to help him rise. He started to rock forward and back slightly before settling down and removing his hands from the desk. "Let's not get distracted with that."

"OK." Sean sought a bridge for their conversation and rustled through his mind for something to connect the other side of the bridge to. "My work at *Beyond the CyberDome*, the maker-space you visited, is group hardware hacking."

"Exactly. So, I will give you our holding's address." He pulled out a small notebook, flipped it open, carefully removed a leaf, took a pen from the same pocket, wrote on that leaf, and handed it to Sean. With the choreography reversed, he replaced the pen, the notebook, he stood, and he extended his hand.

Their palms briefly touched and the choreography finished with his hand drawing back, him taking his seat, and his gaze pulling somewhere within the infinite of his mind.

Sean left Mr. Dearborn's office and found Aurora seated at the receptionist's desk hanging up from a call. "I couldn't quit," she said.

Understatement seemed to be the word for day as his mother would say. "You couldn't quit." He was still stuck in the cadence of his last conversation. Hopefully, Aurora's hand wouldn't spring out like an ejected DVD.

"Aurora, you've quit every job before you've ever started."

"Yes I have."

"And you were always there the next day, on time. The only difference here is it seems the next day was five minutes later. You're at work already?"

"Du-uhh!" Aurora's mocking seemed to announce a shift away from her earlier tension.

Sean didn't find this line of conversation any more useful than the last with Mr. Dearborn. Mr. Dearborn was right about a cultural infection, and whatever the bug was, it was certainly viral.

Aurora slipped into an explanation. "Megan's vacation started within moments of us coming through the door it seems. What my dad would have called an Australian Tag-Team thing."

Sean took out Mr. Dearborn's note and handed it to her. She took it, glanced at the tight scribble and handed it back.

"Back to your *CyberDome* stuff I see. Better you than me. What a circus you're heading into."

Aurora threatened to know far more than Sean about this, and a world more than he could ever expect to draw out of Mr. Dearborn, now. How could so much wicked chemistry neutralize between the girls while he was in Mr. Dearborn's antiseptic office?

"Whaddayamean?"

Aurora's eyebrows rose. "You haven't heard the buzz about *GyroNautica*? They missed a design milestone, went

31

through a meltdown when they dismissed a designer, and their angels held back a progress payment."

"Angels? This must not only be the cultural thing, but a religious thing." Sean searched his memory for the odd phrasing and gave up. Stick with what he knew, he thought, and it would carry him through. "What is it they're trying to do, and how do you connect it to me and the *CyberDome*?"

Aurora pursed her lips and looked at Sean while she seemed to weigh the next words. "Wade said you might need a lifeboat—and here I am floating within your grasp. You going to give me a slice of your pay?"

"Can you fix *GyroNautica*'s problem?"

Aurora shook her head, not to answer his question, but as a sign of Sean failing to acknowledge her contribution. "So, you weren't told anything at all?"

"You saw it on paper, you filled in the blank of culture, all I need to know is what the tech problem is."

"This is all from Megan. *GyroNautica*'s mission is with robotics. Their market is public service—police, fire fighters. There's something about their 'bot doing accident investigations in hot zones and searches in disaster sites. Anything familiar there?"

When Aurora finished, a gust of breath escaped from Sean. It was like he had been underwater searching for a pearl at the bottom of the murky ocean. "Thanks. That does connect some dots. Where did things collapse?"

Aurora had shifted away from the confrontational mood she had carried into their office visit with Wade. Now she appeared to be reflective. "Megan had little time to pass her job over to me, but she did want to touch on your assignment." She searched for words. "Remember about my problem with twisted clients?"

"Yes. You seemed to carry it here and—Megan is it?—caught your bug."

"This twist is the same … but different." She paused. "This looks dark. I can't give you anything more. Even if Megan wasn't specific, I could feel her feeling. She's got this goth thing going, but she's not the bleak type, so this must be heavy, deep, and real."

"How long was I in there with Mr. Dearborn?"

"Andrew?" said Aurora. "Didn't notice, particularly. Why?"

"Andrew, is it?" He continued to tick off the cascade of highlights. "Megan is not the dark type. Angels. And things are heavy, deep, and real." Sean mused on the transition that occurred in the short time he had been in the inner office. "Between you two, you've all but written the eulogy for *GyroNautica*, sung the dirge, and put me on the path to the—"

"—please don't say redemption, Sean." Aurora shook her head. "You shoe-horned into the martyr is so … Don't go there."

"And this from Aurora Vesuvius." Sean recognized she could read him, but he was more interested in a reading about her and Megan. "I was with Mr. Dearborn for a short time, and when I went in, it seemed you two were standing on the edge of a glacier."

Aurora shrugged indifferently. "It was about you, not me."

How had become the focus? He decided not to follow that deflection. "That doesn't explain the thaw," he said. Even here, he was on a precipice by pushing into the unfamiliar territory of how relationships start, shift, and endure.

Aurora shook her head. "Give your analysis a rest, Sean.

I'm not going to talk to you about this until you stop thinking."

He was slammed up against the velvet wall with that. Still, he felt better now that he had, at least, asked about the mysteries of Women. She showed she was willing to help— on her own terms.

Aurora was picking up an amazing amount of investment information, lingo, and backstage drama. Sean needed to move on and root out the guts of this assignment.

* * *

Sean headed out, leaving Aurora at her post. They agreed to meet after work to talk about how things were going on their assignments.

Outside, it was overcast with the occasional mist. He consulted Mr. Dearborn's note for the location of *GyroNautica*. The address looked familiar. As he returned to their last bus stop, he looked up the street in the direction of the address.

It was the Elliot Tower. How was it that the investment managers worked in what could only be charitably called genteel anonymity and their investment was housed in Seattle's classic landmark office building? Yes, he and Aurora were going to have things to discuss. The prospects were brightening.

As he stepped into the lobby, it was also a step back in time—something like 100 years? The bank of elegant elevators were arrayed before him. The old operator standing at his post looked at Sean. He looked like he could tell Sean wasn't a tourist.

The elevator operator smiled and offered, "Can I help you with your destination?"

Sean pulled the note out again, and handed it across.

The operator glanced and handed it back.

"Step in. You looked like you were going there."

Again, it seemed the whole world knew more about his assignment than he did. "So I do, do I? What do I look like?"

"Sorry if that sounded bad. We've seen our share of hackers up and down these elevators. More in the dot.com boom, less now years after the bust. The tide is rising again. You're a hacker, or at least you dress like one."

"Close enough," said Sean. "Do you know much about this outfit?"

The operator shrugged. "Not them specifically. In general, some occupants are self described white hats, but not the white hat that I was. But there's no telling about slang these days."

"You were in the Navy, then?"

"Yup. Good catch." The operator moved the lever. They rose smoothly. "So you know both meanings of the white hat, I take it."

"Some experience in my own way on the web." Sean thought he would skip his story. "Sailor's hat, white hat. My boss is ex-Navy. His grandfather was a merchant ship captain between the world wars."

The elevator operator pulled the lever back as they slowed to a stop. He looked at Sean with an appraising eye. "Your boss will, then, recognize intelligence and dedication." He opened the door to a hallway of doors.

Sean stepped into the hall and glanced both ways.

"To the left. All the way. They have a grand view," said the operator. As the door was sliding shut, he offered, "We'll see more of each other."

Sean walked down a corridor that was brighter than the corridor at Pribylov's. The door to his destination used to have another name on it, but that had been removed. Only a feint apparition of that logo remained. He hesitated in what to do next. Knock? It was clearly the right number even if no longer branded with its logo. He stepped through into an open bay office that was a conversion of the century-old floor plan. Windows wrapped two sides looking west and north. Right now, there was little general lighting except what came through the dapple sky. The various workstations had a variety of period table lamps and modern LED fixtures on goose-neck booms. They cast pools of light that varied from butter yellow to a violet tinged white.

He was interrupted from his musings by a voice calling from across the large room. "You here from Andrew?"

Well, that solved roughly half the introductions. "Yes. I'm– "

"Sean Moran. Yes. Brandon's the name here." After setting aside a laptop, Brandon got up from a couch against the dark wall to Sean's far right. "I told Andrew to get you here if you could be found. Andrew is good at making things happen."

He took Brandon's hand in a heartier handshake than Mr. Dearborn—Andrew—had offered. Brandon was as tall as Wade, and carried as much weight, but Brandon had softer edges and thinner joints. "Nice to meet you, Brandon. Now, before we get any further, how did my name come up in casual conversation between you and your investor Mr. Dearborn?"

Brandon paused a moment to choose his words. "Andrew Dearborn, my brother, is an account manager for investors. We Dearborns aren't investors, ourselves. We help opportunity along with the lubrication of someone else's money." Brandon smiled at that particular phrase. "I told him that you were a solution. We saw you give a demo nearby at *Beyond the CyberDome*. You've done things that need to be done here."

Sean was wondering which presentation Brandon was talking about when three more people, two of them women, came through the door behind him. Brandon perked up and began making introductions.

"This is Sean, our new platform man."

Sean noticed that his introduction was not met with universal approval. Mr. Dearborn's—Andrew's—comment about culture problems was his first thought about their cool reaction.

"Sophia–Sean. Ashley–Sean. Teodor–Sean."

Sean knew something about manners and so it seemed did Brandon. The introductions were a nice start from him. However, Sophia and Teodor offered only the hint of a grip and a suggestion of greeting. Ashley, small with active dark eyes scanning him, nodded at him from a distance. Sean wondered why they weren't warming up to him yet.

Maybe it was because he was younger than them. But, except for Brandon, that wasn't by much. Sophia and Ashley seemed as old as Aurora. Sophia was similar in size to Aurora—with the promise of a dimpled smile. Teodor, taller at six-five and heavier than himself, was somewhere in his late 20s. Brandon was the old man of the group at, probably, 35ish.

Sean was drawn by their movement toward a large table littered with take-out coffee cups. Uptown Espresso seemed to dominate, which surprised him. For some reason he thought they should have been Starbucks. Was he already culturally misaligned with the wrong coffee? These were cups from northern parts of the city where they lived, no doubt, carried in on the tide of their morning commute.

Again, it seemed unlikely that he would be invited to take a seat. But, here, there were at least more chairs than people. Sean grabbed one from an apparently unused workstation area and it drew attention. The way they consciously stared at the seat, there must've been a ghost already sitting in it thought Sean.

"How many of you are superstitious?" He thought the question might break the ice.

Brandon smiled while Ashley scowled. Ashley threw out a comment. "That was Jason's chair." That didn't seem to satisfy her need to press a barb in. "What are you doing here?"

Sean wondered too. So far they exhibited nothing that seemed to match his abilities, much less his interest. He had been the new kid on the block too often these past few years. He got her assertion of pecking order. Knowing what was going on, and knowing what to do were separated by a vast gulf.

Ashley's hair was cut short on one side, and she wore a long curl over her right eye. She twirled that curl nervously. Ashley was not going to be won soon. The others were holding off. It seemed they could wait on her decision. This was as soothing as watching a fuse burn down to this small bundle of dynamite.

Wade cautioned him about facing an unsympathetic crew. *They have a need you might fill. Both sides have to know what that need is before the tension will fade.* Sean recognized he had already rehearsed this earlier with Aurora in some small way.

"What are the odds?" he said in a low voice. He took a breath and let it out slowly. "People asked me to come here. Ashley, I don't know why. It sounds like you four want to take care of yourselves. You've invited me to move on, and that is becoming increasingly more attractive."

Sean thought he had to push more. "Or is there more to the story?"

Teodor smacked the table heavily and stood to full height. "We're running on fumes right now. That's the story! The investors are holding back on last month's installment, and if we fold up, they will get our work for next to nothing."

Sean was shaken by Teodor's eruption. His reading of this tall fellow was that he was normally slow to explode, but clearly that time had arrived. Sean needed to keep close to Aurora's short profile on the company which amply revealed they had exhausted their funds. The other fact of one of their crew being ushered out had to be churning beneath the surface. That could be the significant aspect of the freeze he was feeling.

Brandon stirred now that part of the first meeting's steam had escaped from Teodor. "We missed a milestone. In fact we missed several, but investment money kept feeding the group until last month."

The strap tightened across Sean's chest with Brandon's stake-in-the-heart end to what seemed like a fable. For investment money to return might pivot on Sean being accepted by Teodor. Brandon would follow. Sophia was a cypher. Ashley was another matter.

Right now it was time to draw out more detail. "Milestones," said Sean.

Teodor jut his chin. "Milestones. Then Jason disappeared. Cut out. Left us hanging. Those were his milestones."

Sean saw that Teodor needed a cohesive group. Sean felt the same need and warmed to him. They shared the wound of being abandoned. He wanted to help Teodor.

Brandon held up a hand like a referee. "Our milestones, Teodor. Jason was certainly our key man. It was his idea that attracted Pribylov, and Pribylov found the money."

Teodor renewed his storm. "And Pribylov leaned, nudged, and pushed him out. That's what happened! And Pribylov knew that we would fold without him."

Sophia and Ashley were sympathetic towards Teodor. They leaned forward and held their attention on his turn in the conversation. Ashley moved as if to offer more of the story, but she slumped back into a personal shadow. Sophia moved with her, but not as completely back.

"Teodor has a point, Brandon," said Sophia. "You always favor Andrew in these things." She completely joined in Ashley's mood as she sat defiantly back.

As much as Sean sympathized with their plight, it threatened in coming too close to his own problems with his folks. Without the narcotic of work to tamp that down, Sean couldn't see what he could do. Their story glared with contradictions. Jason jumped or Jason was jettisoned.

He wanted to help Teodor find stability, but Sophia had unleveled things by joining Ashley in her dark corner. He was familiar with where they were in this painful shift, but they were stalled in self paralysis.

Stepping back from the drama, Sean could see the professional side was in shambles. He guessed a group this small was operating on Scrum principles. Brandon was the Product Owner—given the nature of his concerns. Teodor appeared to be the Scrum Master—running interference to make sure the ball got to the goal. But the ball wasn't moving. Overall, they didn't have the energy for a sprint.

It was time for him to step back into this. "I don't know about missed installments. I don't know Jason or his work. But right now I do know that I was wrong thinking you could take care of yourselves."

As he stood, big Teodor stumbled back in defense. Sean tried to ignore his distress. "I'm going to take the elevator back to earth."

* * *

Sean discovered a text from Aurora on his phone. She wanted to meet nearby the offices of Pribylov. Aurora promised to fill in some gaps, but Sean texted back that there was no point.

`had to quit`

`still want to see u`

Sean found that curious. Aurora seemed to have turned on a dime after her truce with Megan.

Reluctantly, he ambled back through the Pioneer Square area to a bakery she picked for their meeting. The aroma was great, but not great enough to overcome his disappointment. Instead he ordered tea and chose a small table to wait for Aurora. He was doing re-runs of the *GyroNautica* fiasco when he felt the presence of someone nearby.

He looked up and saw her smiling. "Hi Betty."

"Hello—I didn't catch your name."

Sean flushed. "Sorry, it's Sean. Is your money game over? Would you like to join me?" He was now in good manners overdrive.

41

Betty sat down. "Hello Sean. Nice to meet you. Where is your girlfriend? The one across the aisle on the bus?"

"She will be here soon." Sean had slipped into script mode so quickly that now that he thought about his answer, it felt awkward to try to go back and explain about his relationship—none—to Aurora. At least none in the sense of boyfriend or girlfriend.

"Pretty girl." Betty smiled at him and adjusted a white curl away from her face. "The game never came off. That's why I have time to sit with you. There were some small money games that came up, but they don't offer the better performances of good shooting."

Betty fussed with her coffee and creamer and finally settled back. "How about you? How did your job interview go? Is your girlfriend employed?"

"You know, Betty, I think she is. Surprises me. But that is why she will be meeting me here. She wants to talk about work."

Betty took a sip of her coffee and waited for a moment. "That doesn't say anything about your interview. Went bad, did it?"

"I don't know what *GyroNautica* wants or needs, but they are certainly rudderless," he said.

He ran his hand through his hair. "I was thinking this through, just this morning. There are certain indicators I've seen in the past that make me want to back out now. Instead, I used to take the beating for the money."

Betty showed some care for him when he got deeper into his musings. "*GyroNautica* you say." She reached for her bag, but changed her mind. "Interesting, they are part of my investment portfolio."

"I don't know investment from tacos. And I know more about tacos than I do about *GyroNautica*," said Sean. "Do they have stock, or are they a stock?"

"They aren't that kind of investment," said Betty. "They aren't likely to be in the stock market. No, their best bet is to be bought out. That's where my money would return as an investment."

Sean was now perplexed on several fronts about *GyroNautica*. "How can you invest without buying stock?"

"How could you interview with them without knowing who they are?"

Betty's question hit hard.

"A fair question. It's part of a chain of situations that lead me there through my boss to an investment office near here. That is where Aurora seems to have stuck it out."

"Good for her. Let me guess. *Pribylov Investment*?"

The walls of coincidence closed in around him. "How is it you can make such a good guess?" he said.

"How is it I know who to bet on in a money game? I watch the players. There are short stops. There are hustlers. They both manage to feed themselves. But a good road player with the shadow of a hustler feeds me too."

Betty sat with that last memory for a moment and then came back to the present. "I came to know Pribylov through my god-daughter who is their assistant. Megan can read players like I can, even if she doesn't share all of my DNA. She only works part time with them because she is supposed to be in school."

Sean, immersed in this new material, was thinking about the web of relationships when another voice broke in.

"Hi Sean. You going to introduce me to your girlfriend?"

Aurora slipped into the available chair at the table. She stirred her coffee as she smiled at his discomfort. She relieved that by introducing herself. "Hi, I'm Aurora. Sorry if I joked about that girlfriend thing, but Sean needs a push in growing up."

"Hi Aurora, I'm Betty and the thought that this young man could be confused as my boyfriend is charming. But let's face it, a little strained—don't you think?"

Betty's age worn face smoothed into a smile. "From what he says, I can piece together that you have taken over for Megan at Pribylov. Megan's my god-daughter and I know the job is cramping her school schedule."

"Oh! Megan is great. We hit it off well. I like her. I'm sorry we won't be working together. She did say I was her vacation replacement."

"I just don't get it," said Sean. "And you brushed me off when I asked how you two thawed after that first meeting."

"Competition," she said to Betty instead of to Sean.

Betty nodded as she finished up the last of her coffee. "Megan goes after what she wants, and the devil takes those who stand in the way."

"Are you both doubling down?" said Sean.

"I'm interested to hear you know something about gambling, Sean," said Betty.

"You both seem to be talking past me, talking plenty, and I don't get it."

Aurora sighed. "Guys are so thick. Sean, doubling down is something you should never do in a bet." She turned to Betty. "Do I have to explain?"

Betty looked from her to Sean and then back. "Your question reveals the answer. Don't toy with the boy."

Aurora's face softened in response. "I guess so. Sorry, Sean. The story is simple. Megan asked if you and I had a thing going. I hope I don't have to explain that."

Sean felt overwhelmed. If there wasn't color in his face, it wasn't for the lack of heat that filled him from embarrassment. The noise of the coffee shop's crowd around them seemed to fade behind the pulse that thumped in him.

Betty rummaged her belongings together. "Well, I'm sorry dears, but I've got a bus to catch back to the U district. Aurora, Megan's vacation you mentioned is her going back to school. She needs a couple of weeks to get into the groove before she gets bored and needs to return to help research investments for the twins." With that, Betty sighed at that disclosure, then rose, adjusted her jacket, and shook their hands goodby. She lifted one eyebrow and offered a parting comment. "You two probably have a lot to talk about."

Betty, just as she had on the bus, moved fluidly through the crowd in the bakery. Sean thought about her being an investor in *GyroNautica* through Pribylov. This news quickly blurred into Betty's thumbnail description of Megan.

It was as if Betty had added about as much mystery as she had added fact. There were still the personal mysteries about him and Aurora as a pair that arrived out of the blue.

"Megan is great. That is your story, Aurora? And the devil takes those in the way is Betty's?" Sean was compelled to pursue this instead of what should have been their focus on work.

"You think you can read people?" asked Aurora dryly. "Tell me how the meeting with the *GyroNautica* crew went. Something tells me that your powers of reading were just as powerful there too."

That cut deep. Aurora could do that. She probably thought she was being honest—like the burns from other honest girls he tried to get close to. Then he thought about Megan's smile, and how he had parked that in a cold spot. Was Aurora right about his inability to fend for himself socially?

"You already know I walked away from that."

Aurora meshed her fingers together and rested her chin on them. Her face was almost even with his, framed by the wild flame of red hair. Her eyes softened as she seemed to rummage through thoughts about her next question.

"Yes. You told me that much. Sounds like it hurt. Was it you who left, or were you pushed?"

"There was some push, but, ultimately I walked."

"What is it you wanted?" she said.

Sean momentarily drew a blank on that familiar question. Then it gelled. "Answers."

"What kind of answers?"

"Like why they wanted me there."

"No one said anything about that?" she said.

"A guy named Brandon said he saw me do a presentation at *Beyond the CyberDome*. Where that leads, I haven't a clue. They lost it in what Mr. Dearborn would probably call a culture meltdown. So I escaped with scalds, yes."

"Brandon is Mr. Dearborn's brother."

"So I've heard. Hard to believe."

"Fraternal twin if that helps fill your skills with reading people," she said.

Aurora leaned back into her business mode of sitting with

a problem. "And if Megan's notes are any indication—she is quite informed about you and your work—it was about your presentation, just as you said. Feel free to bask in the glow of acclaim."

Sean sifted through his memory of all the presentations he'd made. Only a few drew outsiders, but he never paid attention to them unless they asked questions. People skills made a poor showing again. "Can you give me a clue?"

Aurora sighed. "The price I pay for having signed on as your intel barista."

She brushed the flame of hair back. "Megan's notes were cryptic there. Something about that guy show called Mr. Who."

"Dr Who."

"Dr Who—whatever. Her notes offered only that, and the fact that Brandon asked her to search for a way to contact you through *CyberDome*."

"The TARDIS Stabilization Problem," Sean said to himself. It came together finally. He now knew why Brandon had introduced him as their platform man. "*GyroNautica* is in a world of hurt."

"Using one of Wade's expressions?" she said.

"Yeh. World of hurt. It works. Let's stick to the subject. They want me because, let me guess, *GyroNautica* is all about controlling something that flies."

He shifted in his seat. "No, you've already said they were working on ground based robots." Sean juggled thoughts, but order failed to appear. "Their lead designer was the key player for that. He's gone, the game has changed. What they want is something I demonstrated in front of their investor."

"Their investment account manager." Aurora corrected.

"Yes. And curiously looping in Betty."

"One of their Angel Investors," added Aurora.

"Angel Investor." Sean chewed on this for a while. "You know this investment stuff?"

"I'm getting an education in Megan's notes alone. Andrew has filled in some gaps. He's nice too."

Sean refused to follow that lead. "Can you fill in another gap over missed installments? It seems to have them knotted up."

She shook her head. "Only as a bullet point in a checklist. I think it means one of several payments in a schedule. Each of the bullet points had a specific delivery—deliverable. A milestone kind of thing."

"Click, click, click. The lock tumblers are falling into place. Well, you are the one with the job. Shall we get back to Wade and check in?"

"Let's," said Aurora.

* * *

Wade was unperturbed. Sean had never seen him upset, but shouldn't he have been with Sean's walking away from *GyroNautica*?

"I trust it isn't the last word," Wade said. "So, what was your problem with them?"

"They are paralyzed," said Sean. "You've dropped me into some assignments like that."

"So you describe, but it's not that bad. They don't have a focus, and that can change. That is their problem. What I asked is what is your problem with them?" Wade studied Sean as he reached deep for that answer.

48

"It scares me." Sean could see the risk of no money, and, worse, nothing to buffer that anxiety through interesting work.

"Because you might have to step up front?" Wade asked mildly. He still watched Sean, but his attention was not the harsh dress-down Sean expected when they arrived.

"Is that were you think this is going?" said Sean.

"That is where this is going, but you've been there before. What you describe in Teodor and specifically Ashley, is them sitting under the volcano. Your reaction shows that you've caught their fear."

"They, the investors, are waiting for me to step up?" Sean could feel his heart racing. Even Aurora appeared to be a sympathetic witness.

"You are being handed the opportunity, Sean, you will have to fight to keep it. It is very evident that no one else is stepping up, but that doesn't mean they won't give you push-back."

Sean's warmth drained out of him. "But Teodor, Brandon, and the girls have more at stake." He tried to shake off the chill. "Besides, I walked. It's over."

"You aren't the first to talk to me about this, Sean. Andrew and Brandon have already put in their two cents worth. Brandon isn't a full-fledged coder. Right now he is merely minding the investment as they go through a culture shift— his words. The crew knows they either give it a go, or they are removed from life support. This isn't a welcome situation, but they understand it. Brandon says you have the chops to fill the empty chair left behind by Jason."

Aurora shifted forward and offered her own spin. "Sean, you've been doing this particular line of work since you began high school. This guy Jason was a wiz, their boy

49

wonder as Andrew calls him, but his ego held back key design elements."

Wade was interested in this. "Held back? Was he trying to hold onto IP?"

Aurora paused for a moment to find her answer. "IP meaning Intellectual Property? Megan's notes say he was hiding what she describes as the secret sauce."

Wade waved his muscular arm. "Same thing. Look, ego being what it is, Jason might have simply figured what he did was obvious to everyone and didn't need explaining. We can agree that is innocent. On the other hand, he could have been using funds from investors to boot-strap himself into starting a spin-off. I won't label that."

Wade paused to let that sink in. "Let's simply focus on what we are there for. Aurora, you, and Megan appear to mesh nicely. If the past has any capacity to forecast the future, she will be returning. Pribylov is growing, so the question to you is do you want to keep employed there? You like it there—is that a correct reading?"

Aurora nodded. "Yes, her notes are like reading about a world I never knew about. I want to be in that world."

Wade, satisfied, continued "Sean, notice that Aurora knows what she wants. Now we come to you. They want you to do what you already enjoy. I haven't offered you an assignment any closer to your enjoyment of *CyberDome* stuff than this. Simple question, simple answer. Yes?"

The chill filled Sean to the core. Wade's question sounded like it was coming through layers of dense fabric covering his ears. His mother needed his income. However, he would have to face an angry, older crew and show initiative. There were no more questions he could use to stall here.

"Yes."

And suddenly, warmth began to flow back in. The sounds around him became more distinct. He recognized the patter of rain hitting the office window behind Wade and Aurora releasing her breath. That reminded him to breath again.

Wade smiled and patted him on the arm. "Then back at it. There's no off-the-clock time in this brave new world of start ups."

Aurora smiled as Sean rose. He struggled to remember how to straighten his legs and to use his arms to get up. As he moved more, his muscles needed no more attention.

Sean recalled his presentation, and he reviewed what he had said then. This was who he was, this is what he liked, and he had done it for years. The unseen ghost of Jason may have been good at it, but there was room for Sean to do it better.

BRAVE NEW WORLD

The elevator operator glanced at Sean coming through the lobby towards him. "Going to stay this time?"

"You been reading my texts?" Sean said in jest that surprised him. The operator seemed like a nice, old guy. Sean thought he could detect the familiar smell of Old Spice. It was what his dad would put on when they went to a ball game on Saturday.

The operator pulled the door close, leaving the bustle of lobby sounds behind. "Call it second sight with all the years of raising and dropping coders."

As the elevator's quick climb tightened Sean's calves, he wondered aloud, "You've been in a lot of cultures, haven't you?"

"In and around," admitted the operator. "It used to be simpler when it was men only. The gals that are working with you bring something new to my experience. It's been a slow change, and an unexpected change."

"What did you find unexpected?"

"They are doing these new things because they really like to, not because they need to, or that it brings more money. Some even like it more than the guys—I guess that is what surprises me most." He gave an appraising glance at Sean, and went a step farther. "Mind what you want, they'll take it if they want it more than you do."

The operator moved the lever to slow the car to a stop, and drew the door open. "Here's your floor. You know your way now."

It took a moment longer for Sean to realize he hadn't told him which floor. Before the operator could close the car door, he stepped back and extended his hand "Name's Sean. Thanks."

"Good evening Sean, mine's Jim." Jim's hand took Sean's in a firm grip. "However, the night man, Bill, will be coming on soon, and service will be slower. Hoofing it down stairs will be quicker than waiting for him to roll out of the cot."

Sean waved, turned, and then thought about his entry when he got to the door. He didn't want to freeze at the door like he had to have permission to go in. At this time of day, almost evening, who would still be there? That question almost threw him off balance. A grand entry to an empty office?

Going through the door answered that. They were all still there. There were new empty coffee cups on the table, along with some food cartons exhibiting various stages of consumption.

Brandon, acting as their social buffer, was quick to shift gears and give Sean his attention. "OK, so things were a little stiff before. C'mon Ashley, Sophia, Teodor. Gather round for our engineering review."

Teodor scribbled a reminder on a sticky note and put it on his screen. Sophia merely moved in her chair from her work area to the large open table. Ashley joined them late, with a deliberate slow, final touch to a code masterpiece; a formal closing of her lap top; and added creamer to her coffee cup.

Brandon knew how to assemble and lead the discussion, but it was apparently his only major contribution to the direct effort. "I suppose it's up to me to introduce our mission to you, Sean. We are here to commercialize robotic technology for emergency services."

Sean took this in and asked, "Aren't there enough 'bot builders already?"

Brandon smiled at this question. "Market competition.

Good question. Most, if not all as best we can tell, are doing designs for cataclysmic events, like wars and earthquakes. Our investment opportunity is in the high middle end of market."

Sean looked at the others. They were indifferent to the current discussion, waiting in place for things to begin. "So what does *GyroNautica* have that the rest don't?"

Brandon twisted on the hook of that question. Teodor appeared to shrink. Sean could tell that Jason's ghost was about to make an appearance. As Brandon took his time to respond, Sean recalled similar situations. They were struggling at the core of their product.

Brandon sucked in a breath and offered his confession. "We had a principle member in our start-up, Jason, who brought a novel idea. I and the others here," he indicated them with a sweep of his hand, "know only the general outline. Jason pitched the idea, showed its feasibility, and promised that concept could get to reality quickly."

"And we performed well through the first three milestones," said Sophia. "Our simulations were rock solid."

"Simulations, but not physical models," Sean offered as a judgment, not as a question.

Ashley said, "We don't have the resources for hardware."

Teodor was drawn in with that and grew to his full size. "We aren't going anywhere without it. Jason wanted more time to do the math. More time to tune the code to it."

Ashley threw Teodor a dark look. Sean remembered Aurora's admonition about his people reading skills, so he tucked that away for the moment. He wanted to make a point, and make it hard felt.

"You can't tune code to code," he said. "If I'm here to do

platform stabilization, then the first thing to get is a physical platform to stabilize."

Brandon ran his hand over his head. "We've been there and have moved beyond. Anything more's going to take money."

Sean could feel himself out front, but the team was still going in four directions. Wade was right—there was a lack of focus—but Sean didn't feel he was the center of invention in this group.

There was something burning brighter in someone here. He recalled the elevator operator's, Jim's, point about wanting it more. Who, within this group, wanted it most? It had to be the one closest to the volcano.

Sean focused on Teodor. "What do you want?"

"I want to see this thing fly," Teodor offered in a seemingly unspecific, but animated way.

Sean thought that was a rather shallow goal, but it would do for now. As for the rest, "How about you, Ashley?"

"I insure we can navigate across difficult terrain, I want a platform I can rely on," she pouted.

Sophia didn't wait for Sean to ask. "I'm here to make software and hardware fit together." There was a dimple in her cheek that appeared—and then disappeared. "So far, it has been like stitching shadows together. If things don't turn around soon, there are other places I could be."

Sean was glad that Ashley and Sophia, at least, had expressed their problems in terms of their work toward the common goal. Teodor could come through given his dedication. But anyone's personal mission was still hidden beneath the surface.

"I don't think you heard me," said Teodor.

"I'm sorry," said Sean. "You said you want to see this start-up fly. Everyone seems to be on board, there, Teodor." Sean wondered about Teodor's return to the issue of dedication. Was he trying to tell him something?

"Yeah, yeah, yeah. No. I–want–to–see–this–fly." Teodor stood and rocked in place from one foot to the other. Brandon nodded as if he were in on this curious turn.

"You mean like fly through the air?" said Sean.

"Exactly."

Sean found this remarkable. Where was the focus going now? Brandon hadn't objected, but the girls looked stunned. Sean's skin began to prickle.

Teodor turned to Brandon to cement his plea. "We've talked about this. You know how the project can realign and still put past lessons to work."

Brandon's face flushed at being put on the spot. "That's why you took us to Sean's presentation, yes."

"And it's why you brought him on board," continued Teodor.

"Was this before, or after Jason was shown out?" said Ashley. She stood up too. Her diminutive frame competed in nervous energy against the advantage of Teodor's height.

Sean wondered about his shorthand formula for reading people. There could only be one successful point of focus, but two seemed to be laying claim. His new formula was coming out with a zero-sum game. That wasn't going to propel the team any further than off the edge.

Brandon was now caught between two paths, a new way, and the old way. Sean recognized this and could see how it had colored everything in their conversation until now. Sean knew it was up to him to keep their motivation aligned. It was the cultural equivalent of platform stabilization and that could be the bigger job of this assignment.

Now his being there was relevant, at least as far as Teodor and Brandon's silent conspiracy went. His presentation at *CyberDome* made far more sense in terms of using it for flying over, rather than for crawling through ruins. However, was Teodor's fire enough to ignite the group into taking this shift?

Brandon recovered his equilibrium and faced Ashley's thinly veiled charge. "Ashley, Jason was leaving, not being pushed."

"That's not the way it looked," she said. Her long curl danced to the snap of her head.

Sophia, although larger than Ashley, seemed to shrink in her chair as the uncomfortable drama played out with her caught between them.

Brandon nodded and began to pace off his tension. "Maybe so. Perhaps that was my fault for not pushing him out earlier."

"How is that supposed to make any difference?" she said.

"Letting a problem linger on is not good. I let Jason hang on beyond the time he should've moved on."

"Who's choice is that? He started this company!" Ashley was not letting go.

Brandon raised his eyebrows. "It was his choice. Did you see him fight to stay? Did you see him put his shoulder to the wheel to get us past these last missed milestones?"

Ashley's descent into silence admitted the truth to much of this. However, her attitude, sitting there with folded arms, showed everyone that darkness from deep within was not satisfied. Teodor's fire would have to fill that void for her to stay. She pulled back, but not so much to indicate she was out of the group. Sean understood that much, she had committed to the others as well as Jason. His limited people skills were rewarded when Sophia offered a wan smile.

Teodor's idea sat on the table, out in the open. Nothing was going to change now, but things had changed nonetheless. The missing logo off the office front door had already announced that silently.

Calm settled on Sean now that he could see things in this frame. "Show me Jason's workstation." He noticed this question didn't bring the same upset, but neither were they settled with the idea that Sean was aboard. Teodor pointed out a table with a tower sitting on the floor and several screens arranged around a common work surface. Sean glanced over, but stayed with them.

"OK, what's the story with this Jason?" And having asked that, a chill returned to Sean. Whatever the reason for the separation, he felt he would find himself on the same path— eventually.

"I met him at this hackathon last summer," said Sophia. "We started work on a robot model that climbed obstacles."

"Interesting, who brought the robot? I presume it was a kit of some sort. True?"

Sophia brushed back her frizzy hair out of her eyes. "For sure. But we hacked it so much you wouldn't recognize it as a kit."

Ashley invested herself in this. "I saw it long ago. After I joined Sophia and Jason."

"Is that 'bot useful for where Teodor's new design focus might be going now?" Sean's pulse quickened now that the conversation grounded itself to his first love with hardware.

Ashley and Sophia looked at each other searchingly. It was a complex mix of the new direction being considered, and the remnant of the old design that dimmed out long ago. Sean could see that their drift through the recent months had disoriented them.

Ashley was the first to respond with a shrug of her thin shoulders. "For me, as far as navigating goes, it is somewhat the same design problem." She was warming to the design problem. "However, climbing or scrambling as they say in the Mountaineers, is not like hovering. Hovering is more your problem."

"In what way is hovering my problem?"

"Jason insisted it was more than XYZs."

"True." Sean could see that Jason's engineering first principles were at work. "So, what, according to Jason, is it that is beyond XYZ coordinate control?" Sean wondered how this hovering aspect crept into Jason's more prosaic crawler design. It was as if Jason and Ashley were one page ahead of the rest.

Brandon, who had been fidgeting, broke in. "It's getting late for me, and unlike you geeks, I have a family waiting at home."

Sean glanced at the time, it was still early evening, but definitely outside of the 9 to 5 culture. Brandon was, apparently, a visitor from that culture.

Sean still had nervous energy to work off. "I'm going to rummage around to get an idea of where things stand." No one else showed any indication that their discussion was over for the day.

Brandon assembled some papers into a portfolio and glanced around for a rain jacket he eventually found. "I can see you guys are exploring new options. I will be in at my usual time, early tomorrow. I will want to catch up on your plans Teodor, Ashley, Sophia, Sean, then. Goodnight."

Sophia threw a kiss. "That is for your dog, spike."

Ashley nodded as Brandon headed out, and big Teodor heavily waved his goodnight. Slowly, all reassembled their thoughts and returned to the comment put on pause.

Sean prompted, "So, issues that go beyond the XYZs."

Sophia's brow wrinkled. "It was an edgy place. This stuff he was working with was something he didn't share. I caught a glimpse once, and he got angry."

Ashley and Teodor were taken by surprise. Teodor pressed her. "What do you mean Sophie? Jason is a straight-up guy."

Sophia's gaze dropped. "With the way things have gone, I don't know anymore."

Teodor, drew the conversation away from Sophia. In his evenly paced, baritone, he said, "I came in late last year after Jason, Ashley, and Sophie had finish their last hackathon and gotten investor notice."

Sean nodded at this, but took it back to Ashley. "You joined him and Sophia earlier last year?"

She flicked her dark curl back. "They had a different pitch than the one that brought Jason and Sophia together. They weren't supposed to use earlier work for that hackathon, so Jason searched me out to build a navigation wire frame. Even then, Jason put the effort to roughly the same goal."

Sophia filled in some gaps. "We didn't place in that contest. But we didn't need to. Investor types got super interested about our pitch and our models."

Teodor rang in again. "Brandon brought me in soon after that. He had seen me shepherding several groups through

rough patches in other events."

Finally, Sean thought, the ice was breaking all around. "What did Brandon set you to do? Wait, before you go into that, tell me about Brandon."

Teodor lifted his large hands noncommittally. "Brandon and his brother do some sponsoring of these hackathon events. They aren't the only ones, so it is something like a cheap ticket to cutting edge previews. You can find a number of law and accounting offices footing the bills too."

Sean bobbed his head to acknowledge Teodor. "Maker events don't draw those types, so you did good to take your robot there." He smiled and crossed one leg over his knee. "So, for them, a hackathon is a talent show."

Teodor smiled broadly. "And we like to strut our stuff."

"Word," said Sophia.

Teodor's gaze lifted into the darkening ceiling. The light was fading outside and the pools of table lamps did little for general illumination. "Yeah, it all gelled and the money men were suddenly there."

Sean cautiously turned Teodor back to here and now. "But I get the sense that Brandon can code."

"Some. But not enough. He's a manager, and managers go home at night." Teodor punctuated that with a heavy sweep toward the door.

"And take a break for haircuts," muttered Ashley.

"How's he otherwise?" said Sean.

"He's OK for a guy his age." Sophia offered with glances around to others for support. No one disputed her left handed compliment for Brandon.

And with that, Sean knew he was part of them, and

everyone else were outsiders. But he knew that his status was still marginal.

* * *

The rest had gone hours before. Teodor had given him a spare key to the office. Sean had locked the door on Teodor's way out after checking the key's fit.

Those hours before, the crew had all talked about the project and their climb up the learning curve. They spoke about how hard it was to turn that last hackathon's pitch into a proof of concept. However, with night upon them they were all fading. At the end of their strength for raking over old coals, the best they had to offer was that Sean should look at their improved wire frame and browse Jason's files.

Now, Sean pondered whether to go onto the office server with his laptop, or to simply use Jason's computer. But, no, even here he held to his nature of staying secure and standing clear of any possible infection. Sean's black hat past had taught him of dangers that lie beneath the placid appearance of security. So he fired up the tower at Jason's old workstation. One of his jobs in the next day would be a security scan of this machine. Right now he would simply browse.

Outwardly, Jason appeared to be an orderly, structured worker. Unless he swept up everything when he left, then things were uncluttered to the point of this workstation having no touch of personality.

How did they handle ushering him out? Did Jason have any last moments alone here to scrub important files into oblivion? Sean decided no. That would have taken too much time to have left behind this innocuous appearance. Did he do his important work off something more portable?

The presence of seven or eight identical flash drives

laying nearby now stood out and drew Sean's attention. It seemed reasonable to take an inventory of them next. He was about to insert one when he noticed a port was already occupied with one of those look-alike flash drives.

A quick scan of the file and directory names in that drive didn't reveal anything notable. There were various executables, script files, and old source code files—if he could believe the date stamps. Sean tucked that flash drive into his pocket and reviewed the other drives. They were all blank. Did Jason have them lined up for a reason?

Sean turned his attention to folder names on Jason's computer. Then he fired up Eclipse, a programmer's development environment. Here a designer could edit source code, compile it, run it, and debug it all in one place. The hierarchical code file associations revealed how the design was layered and linked. But the date stamps revealed they hadn't been touched in months. Eclipse also complained of missing associations. It didn't appear Jason was doing any work at all. At least with what was in his tower.

Sean pushed back from the desk. It was as if the design had frozen long ago, or even died on the vine. There had to be a reason for this. Perhaps all the work had migrated to the office server. But Eclipse would have been using that server as its home directory. If Eclipse were his barometer indicating Jason's work focus, then it appeared Jason was not using this workstation to do any design on a flash drive either.

Unconsciously, Sean's hand patted at the flash drive in his pocket. When he became aware of this, he decided to follow his intuition.

The flash drive must be important beyond his first

impression. It wasn't supposed to be left behind was his second impression. A flash drive needed to be in Jason's computer. This was to return things to the initial conditions.

He reached for one of the blank flash drives sitting idly by. He plugged it in. It should do for a crude honeypot, a trap that gave the appearance of value, but had none.

If it disappeared, his intuition would be validated about the importance of the flash in his pocket. If someone complained about this drive in the tower being blank, then he could move on to what motivated them in Jason's behalf.

It was getting late, now. His back ached from last night's activity. His bus would still be half an hour. Waiting in the rain wasn't high on his list of must-do. He went across the office to the far dark wall where the couch stood. He slumped down onto it, and then stretched out in the low light offered only by computer screens now that the table lamps had been turned off. He counted on an edge of hunger to keep him from falling asleep, but he needed to rest.

Sean mused on the day's events, the struggle he had overcome at Wade's office, and the analysis, such as it was, of Jason's computer. There were still many blanks, and the closer he got to the code, the further he was from the whole of the design. There was also the possibility that sleep might overcome his hunger.

* * *

He was brought out of a fog when something snapped. It must have been the bolt of the lock on the door. Sean rose on one elbow in the dark fold of the couch. The computers had gone to sleep and their glow was gone. He would have dropped back to the couch, but the door opened. It seemed like it was a long time between the lock snapping and the door opening, but that was his fog still clearing away. When a small silhouette came in from the dim hall, it darted quickly to Jason's computer. It moved with purpose, it bent at the table with deliberation and as quickly reversed direction back to and through the door.

Sean now could think clearly, and his first thought was that the intruder didn't lock the door going out. The sum total of time in this was no more than a dozen heart beats. Mom was going to be worried was his second thought. He wanted to call her, but the situation demanded he explore the hall and check the elevator. All of this consumed another dozen heart beats before he rolled out and went to the door.

The hall was empty, the elevator was at ground level. He pressed the call button and waited. After ten or twenty seconds, and no movement of the indicator showing any answer to his call, Sean stepped over to the stairway door. He pulled it open and heard distant, even steps echoing up to him.

The ghost had visited the office and was now leaving without too much concern. He looked at the elevator indicator and found it still showed the car was at ground level. Bill, the night operator, must be a heavy sleeper. However, he hadn't given the buttons any more exercise.

Leave it, he thought.

He walked to the end of the hall and looked out the window into the street far below. There was slim to little chance of seeing anyone on the sidewalk, but someone was crossing to the parking lot across the street. The dark form, at times lit to a dab of gray in the pool of light of a street light, moved to what looked like an expensive roadster. The car's quick maneuvers out of the lot and into the street confirmed his hunch.

"Goodnight Jason. Let's go see if you left anything

behind." But first, he had to call home, just in case.

He flipped on the lights and noticed how late it really was. Too late to call, better to just go home.

He walked over to Jason's computer at the same speed as the ghost, bent over it and then returned to the door. What was that all about?

Returning to the desk, he surveyed it. Nothing different. Just as he had left it … except the honeypot flash drive was missing from the port on the computer.

Sean weighed the situation. Jason had returned for the files Sean confirmed were in his pocket. Jason still had a key to the office. Jason would sooner, or later, discover he had the wrong flash drive—an empty flash. He probably had no idea that Sean had been on the couch. Jason knew the habits of the night man and had taken the stairs up and down so. There would be no witnesses.

Sean stepped back out into the hall and walked to the elevator bank. Only a couple of minutes had passed. The elevator indicator still showed no signs of movement. Bill, the night man, had in all likelihood slept through his call. So, now was the time to dress the stage.

That turn of phrase was something he had learned from his mother's long habit of going to the theater. She had drug him to many productions before he could rebel.

Rebelling was still outside his experience.

There was little Sean could do to secure the building or the office. If the files Jason wanted were on the office server, there wasn't much he could do about that at this moment either. Short of setting up a cot across the door to insure that Jason couldn't return to rummage unnoticed, then doing more was out of the question.

Sean woke Jason's computer, took the flash drive out of his pocket, and put it in one port. He then put a blank flash drive into another port. He copied Jason's files across to the second flash drive. He removed both, returned the first to his pocket, and left the copy among the other scattered, empty drives—a double deep honeypot.

Sean moved to the door and surveyed the office. His mark upon it was slight to the point of that one flash drive back in his pocket. He thought that few of the crew, much less Jason, actually knew how many there were, to miss one. The port that held the original flash drive was empty on Jason's computer. That computer would put itself to sleep soon, and things were as close to typical as anyone would expect.

His exhaustion from the long day and night was lightened by the buzz of this quick coup. It was white hat versus black hat—up close and personal instead of imagined remotely through reading log files. He felt good he was out in front in white this time. The good fight promised more battles ahead when he could dig out the value of the drive in his pocket. But exhaustion couldn't be denied, and he had to get home.

OK, lights off.

He started his mental checklist. He stepped through the door and considered the lock.

Door unlocked. Any real risk in this building was not from the skid road bums that inhabited the alleys nearby. Risk had already arrived with a key, walked through this door, and took what he thought he wanted. Sean closed the door. It took an enormous effort of will to walk away from an unlocked door, but he managed.

It took another effort of will not to press the elevator call button. Dressing the stage, still. Instead, he followed

Jason's lead and took the ghost passage down the stairs.

* * *

It was a lonely number 17 bus home at this time of the morning. Runs out to the end of the line operated infrequently, and Sean had been lucky to catch it coming through town. Seattle wasn't a large city, but compared to Pueblo, there was a stark contrast. His bus home left behind a sterile canyon of empty buildings sitting silently asleep. A few short hours from now and the migration would reverse, filling the downtown alone with the same number of people who live in Pueblo.

On his short walk from the stop near home, through their neighborhood, he saw the ferries in Puget Sound crossing in opposite directions. They slowly merged and then drew apart at the halfway point. Sea lions bellowed from the moorage at the bottom of the cliff of to the southwest. Few houses had any lights showing through windows—except one, his home.

Mom was either still up, or napping on the couch. Sean checked the time. It was going on 2 in the morning. It was only about an hour after Jason's ghost walk, but here, near home, that visit seemed more distant. Now he had to get ahead of his mother's questions. A pain throbbed behind his eyes with each step up the outside stairs.

There was a reckoning ahead.

"Are you alright?" were Melissa's first words as Sean came through the back door. He crossed through the kitchen to find her, as he expected, rising up from her light sleep on the couch in the living room. One lamp burned at the other end of the room.

He sat nearby and rubbed his head. "Fine enough, Mom. Sorry I didn't call. I know you must have been worried."

68

They were starting a familiar dialog, but Sean thought that this time, this one should be different. "I should start with why I was out so late."

His mother accepted this shift in the conversation, but held off the moment as she folded the blanket that she had covered herself with on the couch. "It must have something to do with what you ran off to do this morning."

Sean released his breath slowly. The throbbing turmoil subsided. He sat and composed his thoughts. "You know this fellow, Wade, that I have talked about a few times, right?"

"Yes, dear. He's given you some chores to do. But you have never really said what they were, or who he was."

"They were more than chores. He calls them assignments. I suppose that's more accurate. In the business world, they are called contract work."

"And that is where your money comes from—contract work."

Sean felt good that Mom wasn't pressing him, that she wasn't judging him. It was going well—so far. They didn't usually talk about money. It was a difficult subject after Dad had divorced Mom. She got the house. But this offered mixed prospects.

"I feel like I need to contribute to keeping the house." Now he had laid another card on the table. Mom had never asked him for help, and her SSI seemed to hold things together, along with his minor contributions.

She folded her hands together and nodded. "It's not your responsibility, Sean. But what you have contributed has helped. It's not easy with my fibromyalgia to get out and earn an income."

Sean grasped at a straw. "Why don't we sell? What they call downsize? That would help you, and I could find my own place."

"This is too much, Sean. You find a place? Me downsize?"

Melissa shifted slowly as though her sharp joints were being drawn into an argument. "First, downsizing is a good idea in another economy, Sean. We bought into the wrong side of the housing bubble."

She swung closer with care. "And you finding your own place doesn't seem real in this same economy. After-all, the money you've added from this contract work isn't really enough for you to go out on your own. Isn't that so?"

Her shoulders slumped. "I'm sorry to put it that way. It sounds like you are a prisoner here. The market seems to have bottomed out, and the news says there's some hint of recovery. Given that, I would love to see you make your own way."

Melissa tried to brighten things. "Can you do any better by finishing your schooling and getting a job that pays better? How long do you think that would take?"

This was the moment. Sean decided to come clean and lay out the remaining cards in his hand. This was the first time they had talked about finances and loss so frankly. *Did this turn start earlier in Wade's office?* Perhaps it was forged in Sean's stepping up to his new crew. He pulled back slightly from that realization.

"No, school isn't going to bring me anything. My old friends are busting their backs with studies and debt."

"But they would be going on to better jobs," she countered.

"I already have their jobs and making good money," he said.

It was on the table now. She pursed her lips and looked as though she was trying to sort that last statement out.

"OK. You are going to have to explain that. Contract work, as I think of it, is a glorified phrase for temping. Being a temporary secretary, file clerk, even janitor."

She shook her head. "Sean, I understand things are pretty sad for your generation, but, certainly, you can do better. A college degree still means something to business."

"Mom, you are still thinking of the steel mills of Pueblo where strong backs made good money, and white shirts made more. We left that behind when Dad moved us out here to Stevenson Specialty Steel. Besides, he did that because Pueblo's steel industry rusted through the strike, and the ledge he put himself on here crumbled away too."

"There's other work. Your father tried hard, but got caught without training. You need more than his muscle and luck with the strike settlement that gave us the cash to buy in here. You need school for those jobs that will open up, eventually."

Melissa ran her fingers through her thin hair to straighten out the sleep tied tangles. "Sean, you are very close to becoming trapped in a guilt that is not yours. It wasn't your father's either, but he embraced it in spite of what I said."

Sean could see that this conversation was out of balance, and it was because he hadn't given her any hope. Mom just struck a nerve. His shame of easy money his dad couldn't reach was still there. Tonight another ghost emerged to haunt him. It was more powerful than Jason's simple phantom.

"Mom." Sean's breath ran out. This wasn't a good start.

Wade's interview technique could help now. *Breathe in quickly, and let it out slowly.*

"I have a lot of money."

"A lot of money." Melissa sat up, stiff with anxiety.

"And it came from good work, paid good wages."

She kept her alert posture, but the fear in her eyes settled. "I suppose you will have more to say about that. Does this tie in with Wade, your boss?"

"The short, quick answer is that I work as a hardware designer and programmer. Wade operates a contracting business, placement is what they call it now. It is temporary, but not in the way you think of it.

"Temporary means for the length of a project in developing a product for a company. I have been in several, so far. I have worked my way up from a low level, entry position, into a position that expects several years of experience."

"How did you do that?" She asked this not so much for an explanation, but more for the release of her tension. "Years of experience means going to the job every day—punching the clock in and out. You have rarely been out of the house for more than four or six hours straight during the day. Not the ten to twelve hours that fills a man's life in the mill like your dad."

"You want me to go to school for the new jobs, Mom. The new jobs already exist, and you can do most of that job's work at home. Most nights, I was at work when you would tell me to go to bed and stop tap-tap-taping at the keyboard."

She let her shoulders drop. The new information was going to take some time to sort through. Although Ted, her ex-husband had made good money in the past, good enough to put them into this house, it came through his sweat and muscle, with a liberal amount of smarts. When his muscle and sweat no longer guaranteed their needs, he gave up on his intelligence being enough to bridge the gap. He was still trying to sort it out.

Melissa was torn, "You were working when I called down to stop playing on the internet? I was worried you might be doing porn."

If a blush could have lit up the room … "I did for one contract." Sean's cards were spilling uncontrollably across the table from his hand. "One of my short term entry level assignments from a large job shop. I did data aggregation, designed links, automated setting up accounts, counting advertising clicks," he said in a rush so that he could move the conversation away from the smut that infected his income from those early days before work with Wade.

"Look," she said as if to put more distance in, "It's late, and we both need rest. So far as I can tell, it seems you are doing fine. You seem to have thought about a lot of things lately, can we agree to talk about them later?"

"About this money stuff?" he said tentatively.

"That. Or anything else you've been hording away while you've been down stairs in your cave."

Sean couldn't hold back a yawn. His back ached from having napped uncomfortably back at the office. The conversation had been going well. He wanted to trust in the future. "Sure."

"It's time for me to go to bed, now. Goodnight, Sean."

"G'night Mom."

With that, she rose stiffly and moved across the room to turn out the last light. Sean headed back through the kitchen

Drones Over Seattle

for the basement stairs.

GOING DEEPER

"So, day two. The lights still on?" Jim held the door as Sean joined others in the small car.

He appreciated the banter. This job had its perks with being in a vintage office building instead of one of the several business parks that offered sterile, manicured surroundings. And there was Jim's Old Spice aftershave mixed with the smell of his wool uniform to add to the real sense of venerable work.

"Well, I was in the dark, last night. Bill a heavy sleeper?"

Jim pondered that. "Not especially. Usually, he's doing his rounds and it takes a few calls to get his attention. Why, did you have any trouble?"

"Oh, I walked down. That's fine. Still getting to know the ropes."

On arriving at his floor, Jim added, "Well, just in case Bill isn't at his station to see you through the doors, you will have to lean on that call button a long time too. Also, don't forget your key works on the front doors after hours, if you come in late. Each key use is logged automatically into our security system."

Sean took his key out and inspected it. "It got an RFID chip inside?"

Jim raised his eyebrows. "You're in Seattle's Tech Tower."

"Duh," Sean said to himself as he put his key away. However, he didn't need to check the records to know that Jason was haunting the halls at night.

As Sean approached the office, he thought he'd be the first, or one of the first to get into the office, but in fact he was the last. The crew was busy at their various pursuits, but the mood shifted when he arrived. Did they discover the break-in?

"Wazzup?"

Brandon took this as a cue. "Do you want to pick up from where we left off last night?"

"I suppose so, after I browse Jason's tower a little more to see what's what."

Then Sean fiddled with the office key in his pocket. "But before that, I would like to ask about security here."

Brandon shrugged and the others returned to their work. "Sure. This tower is pretty safe. What's got you bothered?"

Sean was more interested in office security, but Brandon's opening would work as a bridge into it. "Was Jason's separation friendly?" That question caused heads to rise. Their work didn't seem to fully occupy their minds—at least not right now.

Brandon nodded. "Oh ... The usual problems and anxieties on both sides. We didn't have to call anyone to escort him out. Is that what you're asking about?

"I was wondering about re-keying the door, for instance."

Brandon turned his head toward the door to dwell on this. "We took his key, if that is what you mean. And the door was locked when Teodor got here this morning. Wasn't it Teodor? He was directly ahead of me when we both arrived."

Teodor raised his head and looked at the two. "Yep."

Ashley added, "But we sometimes forget to lock up."

Sophia countered, "Not me. I always lock if I'm the last one out."

"And sometimes not. I've been locked in by you," said Ashley.

"I didn't want to leave you unprotected," explained Sophia. Sean noticed something passed between them in their glance.

"Anything else? Like password control or computer virus?" continued Brandon. The others seemed to stiffly shift back to work at this point in the discussion. "We did that too."

Sean shook his head. This locked door was an interesting turn of events. Had the ghost returned, browsed again, and locked out? "Give me an hour with the files, here." He glanced around the workstation. All the flash drives were gone.

The ghost had swept the desk clean thought Sean. Jason had made sure to take the files he was looking for. He automatically felt for the original flash drive in his pocket and found it next to his key. Last night, his first impression was that it was old, unremarkable work. However, to keep ahead in this game, he needed to drill down through the folders of files stored in it. He also needed to do it away from here.

"I've changed my mind," he said. "I'm going out for a coffee. I will be back in a while and then we can pick it up again."

*   *   *

Sean walked past the first bus stop where he and Aurora had dropped off yesterday. This was a brighter day, which is to say only partly overcast and not raining. He thought of Betty, his unusual seat mate that previous morning and then later as a surprise guest at the bakery. It was a long shot that someone's grandmother was an investor in the business he was put in to rescue.

He mused on his self-image as a white knight. Wouldn't an unbiased stranger agree? Last evening the dynamics had shifted toward him. He held something valuable. His assignment was on track. This rushed a thrill through his body.

Jubilation is exciting new work and money sweeping aside old problems.

Did all of this flow from Brandon's chance participation at Sean's *CyberDome* presentation? Brandon was quick to usher him into the circle. The rest seemed only to accept him when the prospects of a new focus pulled them together. It appeared as though their faith in the ghost, Jason, was faint. That was, perhaps, justified given his mixed, but generally poor performance through their last milestones.

Sean felt like he still needed some distance before examining the ghost's legacy he carried in his pocket. The trees lining the avenue's island divider presented emerald tunnel views. Sean scanned the entrances to the buildings that lined the left side of the street. The sidewalks were empty right now in contrast to the small crowds that accompanied the rain on their first day. He could see the entrance to Pribylov, ahead.

As he prepared to turn into that doorway, he caught sight of a small sign out of the corner of his eye. *Snooker.* It was small, and the sign probably dated back before World War Two.

Sean stopped and stood on the sidewalk looking on an angle across the street. The sign announced the pool hall at a doorway that lead immediately to a flight of stairs like the entrance that climbed to Pribylov. He could cross the street to find his distance, he thought. He was tempted to use his invented password "Jack sent me," just to test what that might bring. He smiled at the romantic notion of this dated speakeasy jargon. However, it did fit the neighborhood with its store front missions, cheap hotels, bars, and panhandlers.

In the winter, these buildings varied between muted red brick relics and ash brown derelicts. The upper floors of the west-most of them shouldered against the massive concrete viaduct of Highway 99. They formed the southern, faded margin that stretched blocks east from the water front into the International District. The similar buildings there, relieved only by the grand architecture of the two railroad stations, continued indistinctly up one of Seattle's hills.

None of that was evident during the height of the summer visitor boom. The leafy canopy along the avenue softened the hard edges and masked the grim upper floors. Across from the square, one of the finest office buildings from that past era presented its classic lines framed by the park's trees. Even now, with the sidewalks bare, these blocks remained a lightly colorized version of old newspaper photos used for historical postcards sold in the tourist traps.

He discarded the view, turned, and took the stairs two at a time up to *Pribylov Investment*.

* * *

Sean stood by as Aurora finished up her notes at her computer. He noticed that the reception desk had sprouted a second display. She was about to catch up with him having three back in the tower. In contrast to him, she was putting her two to work while, today, his three were as useful as sundials in the rain.

"Just a minute," she said to the hum in her pocket. She took out her phone, consulted it, returned to her screens, and tapped away on the keyboard.

Sean thought a moment before asking, "two step authorization?"

"Yes. Just a minute."

"Not the normal activity of a receptionist, Aurora."

"Just a minute, Sherlock."

Sean looked at the two doors behind her. Mr. Dearborn's office showed no light shining beneath the bottom crack of the door. The other office, which he presumed was Brandon's, was probably just as vacant.

As Aurora worked both the computer and her phone, he glanced out the windows. He looked for the Snooker sign across the street but it was hidden by trees. He caught a glimpse of the pool hall through the limbs, but a view inside was obscured by the haze of decades of traffic exhaust filming the distant windows.

He mused to himself, "Core samples through that grime could probably carbon date the layered history of smog."

"Gosh, Sean, how absolutely profound," said Aurora.

Sean did not turn to bask in admiration. He knew that bouquet that Aurora tossed was dripping with irony. So, he continued his musing. "You seem to be as busy as Sybil working out a prophecy, yourself." Then he turned.

At that moment, before Sean could open a conversation about why he was there, Mr. Dearborn plunged into the office from the hallway. "That research ready, Aurora?"

He caught sight of Sean with such a start that he stopped in his tracks with enough momentum left to put him into a forward roll. Andrew turned on his heel and put the momentum into half circling Aurora to put her desk between him and Sean.

Aurora reached over to a printer and removed a stack of print-out. She handed it to Andrew silently. Andrew glanced at several pages, took three quick steps, snapped the key in his office door, stepped through, and his brief visit dimmed from memory.

In a hushed voice, Sean said, "Megan says he's OK?"

"Get off it, boy, and exercise your people skills. I'm sure Brandon has his own eccentricities." Aurora was annoyed, but that passed—for the most part. "So, what's with the visit? We aren't paying you to slum."

"We?" He looked around the office with a dramatic gesture. "Do they offer Kool-Aid in the water cooler?"

Aurora shook her auburn hair back at his vague reference and settled to wait for a response that could better inform her.

Sean pulled out the flash drive he had taken the night before. He handed to her, and she examined it for a moment. "I want you," he said, "to do some research for me. Check out what the files on this add up to."

Aurora raised her eyebrows, and then she looked at the flash drive in her hand again. Without raising her glance, she asked, "What's the mystery?"

Sean described the events of the late night intruder.

She offered a half twisted smile. "A ghostly visit, and you think he was after this? I don't see any connection."

"I wouldn't either, until this morning when the trap was sprung and the bait of my honeypot was missing."

Aurora shook her auburn mane again. He knew he had to explain.

"I made a copy of this flash drive, and left that on the desk among the empty drives. I left the computer without any flash drive in its USB port. Just as the ghost had left it. I left the door open. Just as the ghost had left it open."

Aurora lifted her face, but it was impassive.

Sean continued. "When I arrived, everyone was there before me. Brandon and Teodor were the first, and they had to unlock before getting in.

"When I examined the desk and computer, there were no flash drives around."

Aurora emerged from her thoughts. "The ghost returned after you left, swept up all of the flash drives, and then locked the door going out."

She began drumming the table top. "You were expecting something like that to happen, weren't you?" Aurora was now engaged in his report of the events and the flash drive's apparent value. She flipped the flash drive in the air and caught it with a sweeping grasp. "I'm going to crack this."

"I also need something more," he said.

"Yes?"

"Anything on file about our developers—and our clients Andrew, and especially Brandon."

Aurora shrugged again, "They shoot spies, you know." And she flipped the flash drive in the air again and added a conspiratorial smile, "But for you ..."

* * *

Sean made sure to pick up a coffee on his return. No one noticed his prop because the office was empty, and the door unlocked. This triggered Sean's concern about security. It had been difficult enough for him to walk away with the door unlocked last night, but the unlocked door this afternoon brought another, familiar pain.

This wasn't about any present danger or fear. His tight shoulders signaled the beginning of a cascade of anxiety. The group was absent mindedly courting self-destruction and Sean felt like he could get caught with them going down the drain.

He hadn't yet grasped the engineering problem that would soon define the shift in their mission. Sean knew he could solve technical problems that had solutions, but the people problems drained him.

He knew it was more than an occupational hazard. Insecurity appeared in his life when Dad had moved them out here from Colorado. The move was supposed to bring Dad work in the specialty steel industry in Seattle. It didn't quite pan out that way, and soon after Dad was out looking for work in fields he wasn't prepared for.

To cope under this stress, Sean discovered he could bury himself in very intricate work to distract him from his parent's growing desperation. It seemed their problems were out of his reach. It was best to avoid what couldn't be solved was the lesson he learned during this time.

The problems grew and Dad called it quits. Sean heard his dad, one night, describe himself to his mother as a sinking anchor. An anchor threatening to pull everyone down with him. He signed the house over to her as part of the separation agreement, and walked away from what was left of the strike settlement money in the family account.

His dad's plan was to start out all over, from the bottom. As a plan, it was meager, and it worked slowly. Dad would give them updates, but communication was sparse and infrequent.

Sean tried to shake the dark past off be putting his focus on the fascinating puzzle the ghost offered. There had to be a solution hidden in plain sight within the flash drive. The real attraction was that if it was a solution, what was the mystery? He hoped that Aurora could make sense of the files he set her to investigate. If the files had no connection, then it was no more than distracting confusion. His shoulders tightened even more.

Relief was going to be elusive if he chased those thoughts. He returned to Wade's mantra. *Take a quick breath in and let it out slowly.* Sean, over the space of ten minutes, did this over and over.

* * *

Voices filled the hall. One voice was Jim's. The door opened and the whole crew filed in. Sean noticed that no one had paused to unlock it. Anxiety threatened to replace the calm of his last ten minutes, but they drew him into their circle.

Teodor waved at him as he went over to his place. "Too bad you missed lunch with us."

Ashley, unusually open, added, "We were off to this bakery that has good sandwiches."

"I think I know that place. I had coffee with one of the regulars that is an investor." Sean said.

Brandon pulled up short. "Really?"

"That must be Betty," said Sophia. "We've offered to show her around here, but she hasn't dropped in yet. I don't think she's interested in watching us on keyboards."

Teodor brightened again. "We could pull out the robot, and put it through its paces."

Ashley darkened in the same measure as Teodor had lit up in animation.

Sean found this an interesting offer. "I think that would be a good idea all around. I need a reference object to judge my stabilization designs against."

"What do you mean?" asked Sophia. She rubbed one of

her arms, working over her smooth muscles down to the wrist.

"As I understand it, it all started with you, Ashley, and Jason at hackathons. Right?"

"Yes," said Ashley. However, she didn't seem especially interested in Sean's inquiry. Her eyes moved quickly, surveying the others.

Sean continued, "And everyone's work is, in some way, associated with problems of mission, navigation, hardware, and integration?"

Brandon stepped in here. "That's what the money is paying for. Teodor, your suggestion has merit. We need something to invigorate the project. Something tangible as Sean's pointed out. Something that can unmistakeably demonstrate application and achievement." Then he added pointedly, "For progress payments—against the missed milestones."

Brandon throwing his weight in with this blunt goal received everyone's attention and interest.

"Fine," said Sean. "What would it take to ramp this up? This is something I can get my arms around."

Sophia knitted her brow. There was conflict somewhere inside. "You mean I have to talk to the 'bot?" She started to knead the muscles of her other arm.

"You are mission integration, aren't you Sophia?" Sean wondered at her consternation.

Sophia's face hadn't settled. "It's been a long time since I've had to interface to the 'bot. Jason buried it in the closet, over there."

Sean glanced in the direction she indicated to see the door. Behind it was the hardware he could understand.

"Was Jason the only one who knew the inner workings?" The prospects of unraveling Jason's knot was not encouraging with *GyroNautica* in its current drought of funds.

Ashley spoke from behind her dark curl. "Of course not. I had my hands on a soldering iron with Diana more than him."

Teodor turned slowly towards her. "Diana?"

A light laugh sprang out of Sophia and brightened the dimples of her smile. "Really? Was Jason intimidated by too many women around him? Imagine, keeping a prisoner in the closet. What would people think?" Again, another of Sophia's remarks hit a nerve and Ashley shrunk away from the conversation.

Sophia noticed this shift in her, but offered only a curious look before returning to the subject. "You're right, Sean, we need to release her and let her strut her stuff." Her smile recovered.

Sean turned to Teodor for his sign-on. "Teodor, how does firing up -um- Diana fit in with your preference to shift from crawling to flying?"

Teodor, still in an animated mood, sprang up. "I want to fly, if that's still on the table." He spread his big arms high and wide just in case his enthusiasm wasn't apparent. "But for the short-term, crawlin' works for me. I can cope as long as hardware integration and navigation give me the APIs that can get us to where we need to go."

"What do you mean if I can give you an API?" said Sophia —the dimples faded. "Haven't you been white box testing my mission control interface?"

Teodor shifted into a subdued mood and shrank into a chair. "Sorry, Sophia, I was speaking overall. Of course I've been testing the hooks in your code. And Ashley's. Here, of late, it's been rather abstract. So, I guess this is our natural next move."

Brandon hadn't sat down since they arrived, and now he was nervously pacing. To Sean, it looked like an exhilarating nervous movement rather than one of regret or fear. Then Brandon moved directly to the closet and pulled open the door.

Sean expected that his enthusiasm would carry through with Brandon tugging out the robot, Diana. But, instead he stood there staring. Teodor, stood, stepped next to Brandon to look over his shoulder.

He exclaimed, "It's not there!"

* * *

Sean felt the ripple of his phone. He reached into his pocket and looked at the text from Aurora.

GOLD   SEE ME NOW

Sean rose to his feet in the middle of the confusion that was rising in the office. Everyone went to the empty closet as though the sum of their numbers would return the missing robot Diana.

"Ashley," called Sean. She didn't respond. "Ashley!" This time she turned with a dazed look. "Let that go for a moment."

"Let it go," she vaguely echoed.

"Ashley?"

"Yes, yes, yes." Ashley shook something off.

He was beginning to reach through her shock now.

"I want you to scan the project repository and look for the hardware drivers for Diana. Can you do that?"

Ashley threatened to slip back into her shock, but

snapped out when a task was put to her. "Scan the repository for hardware drivers. Why?"

"I have to go over to Pribylov and check something out," said Sean.

"Yes, of course." Ashley was still out of it, and disconnect was growing again as her attention turned to investigating the empty closet.

"Check out the repository," repeated Sean as he headed for the door.

Brandon tried to slow him with a question. "What are you doing at Pribylov?"

Sean turned from his question to gaze at the door. "We need to talk about security before we close up tonight." Brandon accepted this silently.

* * *

Today was something of a yo-yo day. He and Aurora could have as easily gotten together on their phones. But she had texted and she explicitly directed them toward a more private conversation, face to face. It was just as well given the odd turn of events with the missing robot, Diana.

"So, tell me about gold."

Aurora sat back in her chair. She squinted her green eyes as she pressed into her interrogation. "First, what was your impression of the contents of this when you gave it to me. You did look it over, didn't you?"

"Just stuff," he shrugged. "It didn't look like it was related to robotics or platform stabilization for that matter. I wondered about that. Stabilization was Jason's major contribution to the project—and nothing to show. That's why they looped me in to replace him."

"Mmhmm. Well, you didn't look very deep. There are a lot of files full of assembly language design."

"I will have to look at that closer, certainly," he said.

Her point tied in with the robot's design. "Those files must have been buried deep in a file tree. However, the gang has discovered that they are missing some hardware that was stored in the office. Those assembler files are probably interface to the robot's sensors and actuators."

"Perhaps," she said. It didn't look like Aurora was taking off her interrogator's hat. "When did this hardware disappear? Last night when the ghost was wandering the halls?"

"That would be a guess—a bad guess. From the way they took it, you understand, it could have happened anytime."

"Anytime in secret," she said pointedly.

"Yes. Well, if we have to rebuild that robot from the ground up, at least the code interface you found—"

"—We found."

"We found. Then that code would help define what Diana was built from, and what she was supposed to be able to do."

Aurora tipped forward in her chair. "Robot? Diana? One and the same? Sean, your messy world of linear design is populated with certified whackos."

"Word. Well, thanks for the gold. Make me a copy to take back to the tower, and keep that secure somewhere."

Aurora bobbed her head, as if keeping beat with an unheard song. "That wasn't the gold."

"No? So, what did you find that you needed me here for?"

She stopped bobbing her head and slipped into a thoughtful mode. "Well, the assembler files were something you needed in the short term. At first I thought that they may explain the reason for your night visitor."

Aurora ran her fingers through her mane. "But the gold is deeper stuff, you know. There is this executable called Tyche—maybe not gold, but silver or bronze."

"Means nothing to me. Go on," said Sean.

"There was other code—snippets—written in FORTRAN." Aurora her palms over the desk surface as she focused on one of her computer displays. "The snippets looked like they were mined from some other work, because they weren't programmatically related. That is, no calls from one to the other, although with some editing they could be drawn together. Did you look at the timestamps of any of this?"

"Aurora, just go on explaining as if I were that certified whacko standing here."

"Sorry 'bout that. The assembler files were written over a span of months starting last summer. The snippets were put together in the past few weeks. There's a huge gap between them of months."

Sean nodded. "A long time in this development cycle. Unless Jason was digging deep for solutions after hitting the wall last winter."

Aurora shrugged and handed Sean the original after she had made a copy of the flash drive during their conversation. "Well, you have everything now. But more about this being gold."

She turned back to her display. "I did some searches on keywords and phrases from that FORTRAN code and it lead to some pretty dicey sources. Some of it came out of course material posted as homework at one of the Air Force postgraduate schools."

Sean nodded as if this made sense. "Let me guess. Software design for the Predator?"

It was Aurora's turn to be surprised. "Yes, I saw that term, but the coursework was titled Amber/MQ-1B."

"Can you give me anymore on the significance of the initials MQ?"

Aurora nodded. "Multipurpose."

"Sounds innocent enough. Actually, this sounds more like where Teodor wanted to go."

Aurora shook her head. "Multipurpose is the version that carries munitions."

"Oh … Teodor didn't give me that impression, certainly."

"This research material is stuff that goes back 30 years." Aurora tapped her tooth with her finger.

"Hence the availability of some of this code on the web." Sean was trying to put the innocence back into it and resurrect his impression of Teodor's enthusiasm for flying.

Aurora stood up and started walking around nervously. "This still goes deeper than simple access to old code dug out of the museum. I've been able to connect it to Jason's pitch to investors that centered around this technology going into the private sector."

"So, did he pitch a killing platform?" He meant it as a joke.

Aurora shook off his attempt at humor. "As the pitch goes —as I've seen it in Pribylov's files—the law enforcement sector will probably be the first to get airspace authorization from the FAA."

"I see the gold now. And it covers the public service

sector they have consistently aimed at." Sean ran his fingers through his hair.

"There's a disconnect here," Sean pointed out.

"Go on."

"It doesn't seem like anyone in the office is designing for a drone—until now, literally. And even now, no one has really signed on. As I've seen it, anything drone-like is the brain child of Teodor, not Jason."

"Did Jason obscure the goal?" asked Aurora. "Obscured it for both the developers and the investors?"

They both slipped into silence. Sean had become infected by Aurora's nervous pace, and he wandered some himself. He found himself absently gazing out the windows, across the street to the pool hall.

Not knowing where to go with this news, and with Aurora back in her seat brooding over what appeared to be office work, Sean decided to head back to Elliot Tower.

"I'm going to see how this code reconciles with the repository Ashley is investigating." He waved the flash drive at her and dropped it into his pocket. "Bye."

"Before you go—now about gold that we can spend. Specifically, how we are being paid, and how much."

Sean knew from his parents that talk about money, wages, bank account balances, and the rest would lead into dangerous territory. A cold front moved into the office. The temperature plunged through the deep core of his body. Could he take up Aurora's introduction of this topic? How had she come to this knowledge except by snooping through the files much as she had discovered the investment angle for *GyroNautica*?

Aurora, sensing that Sean was not about to leave now,

moved into the topic. "I already know what I am making on this assignment. I also know how much Wade is charging."

The chill deepened. Aurora was painting a frame around Wade, someone who had directed Sean to some very rewarding assignments. "Do you know how much Wade is charging for me?" By carefully dodging her last statement, he avoided in probing how much Aurora was making.

"He's charging *GyroNautica* seventy five an hour for your work."

The room's walls closed in, and he felt like he was in tower's elevator dropping faster than anything he'd experienced before.

"Sit down Sean, and take a breath," said Aurora. "If multipliers are constant for us, both, then you are earning only twenty five of that."

Sean had agreed to that figure going in, and had felt very rewarded by Wade. Now he felt a betrayal. But he needed to paint a happy face on this news. "Even at that, I'm making two to three times the rate of college graduates who've become baristas instead of chemists."

A shudder ran through him and he sat down. He had to bolster Wade's defense. "And I don't have to chase across town to cover time slots between various coffee shops to scrape together 30 to 40 hours of work in a week."

Aurora waited and watched Sean until his color was returned. "There's something even more off about the contract."

"I don't want to hear it until I talk with Wade," he said.

Aurora motioned for Sean to settle down. "This isn't about Wade, its about *GyroNautica*, and we've already heard enough about it. They don't have any money."

Sean took that in slowly. Of course, this was a familiar topic of conversation. "No one in the office has let that fact slip past my attention. And, yet, everyone's showing up for work every day," he offered.

Aurora nodded, "And we have been here only a short time. There won't be that much lost if we just step out now."

Sean got back up. "Let's approach this differently. We need to let Wade connect the dots for us. Right now all I see is pepper scattered across the table, maybe there's a clearer picture with the right lines connecting."

Sean tried to shake Aurora's disturbing news off. "Anyway, I need to get back to the tower. Even if this is the last day, you know, I need to give them value."

Aurora lowered her head, shaking it sadly for a moment and then rose as she took on Sean's resolve. "We'll do that." She stepped around the desk and surprised Sean by stretching her arms out for a hug.

With her embrace, Sean could feel the room stop falling and warmth restored.

"OK, I'm back to work." When he reached the door, he turned and looked back. "Thank you, Aurora."

MISSION SHIFTS

His visit with Aurora was still with him back at the office. Small noises distracted him too easily. Taking a breath helped sweep back the cobwebs, but his fingers tingled. When he glanced furtively around, the others looked lifeless. Then he became aware of the tick of the clock on the wall.

Ridiculous. That clock was an anachronism in the digital age.

Taking a breath helped him return to his self identification with things analog, things linear. The clock was a linear representation of time. Looking at it he could see the past, the present and the future, all at a glance. The flow was connected. Digital clocks were stuck until an unseen moment passed. But to truly clear the cobwebs, he needed something more. Like work.

Sean needed to let work push back the painful discussion that Aurora had introduced about their pay. He got good pay. It could be fantastically better, though. He wished Aurora hadn't tipped the fact that Wade was making double Sean's salary for Sean's work. Conflict sent the tingling further up his arms like a column of ants.

He tried stroking his fingers along the oak grain of the table to edge away the ants. That didn't work well. Was this what he saw Sophia doing? He skirted his fingertips along the table's rim and found cuts and nicks from years of use. Sean's hands explored the table's rail that supported the top. Here, rough mill work had survived unsmoothed from the beginning. The burr of small splinters would have easily found their way to the quick beneath his fingernail.

Work. Focus. This isn't about Wade. This isn't about Wade? Designing a killing platform was his work. When he signed on this was about—he thought—a robot that searched disaster sites. That evoked the image of the rescuer. Now he saw the avenger. Maybe he was wrong and only painting himself into a corner. No one else had a problem. He had to stick with problems he could solve.

Work. Work harder. Dig into these files. What is the mystery of the ghost's visit? Jason isn't connected to Wade's share of Sean's revenue. Jason isn't connected to drone attacks. Sean suddenly realized that no one had even discussed why Jason was booted out.

Work on the files. The answers were in the files in his pocket. These files were valuable to Jason. Demonstrably so. Twice so. Sean was there to discover their value. Value would be found in the files, Sean told himself.

His pulse thumped hard. He thought he could hear it. It had replaced the tick of the anachronism on the wall. The tingling of his skin was like finding money. A giddiness of winning the lottery boiled in his imagination. He flicked through files automatically. His activity spun up like a jet engine. It was approaching a destructive uncontrolled acceleration.

Ashley approached Sean as he nervously browsed the files on Jason's flash drive. The workspace tools, Sean's IDE, now showed the state of Jason's design some weeks before his departure. Sean had forged through a lot of abstractions, skimming through them like a cruise missile. However, that missile hadn't found a target, and was short on fuel. He welcomed the distraction Ashley promised.

Sean let out a breath of exhaustion and asked her, "How's the reconciliation going?"

"There's something odd about it."

Sean waited for the rest of it and let the engine in him wind down.

Ashley held the pause a bit longer and then continued on.

"The repository has shown no remarkable change. What I do see is the steady growth of new units, and revisions of existing ones. Nothing has been deleted, and there are no branches."

Sean nodded, both to express he understood this, and to motivate her to finish. However, in the back of his mind he wondered how the files in the flash drive he was holding onto figured in comparison to this inventory she had finished.

"Yet, something odd too," she repeated blankly.

"So you say. Something outside of the repository?" It seemed like Ashley was still stuck on the missing robot and needed a push. Expanding his reach could lead to finding the value that Jason knew was in the files.

Ashley wrapped the curl around one finger, and then released it. "Have you seen our dashboard, or our model perform? That was Jason's area of focus for the past six or eight weeks."

She hadn't brought anything new, but she had offered him something he hadn't done. Sean reassembled all of Jason's design abstractions in his mind. Yes, they added up to the sense of a model now. However, there seemed to be some short-fall of integration.

"Most of the files I've seen look like facades," he said. The code abstracts he saw were those facades that gave the appearance of the design, without being able to actually do anything.

"I've buried myself in looking further under the hood," he said, "but it seems to be exceptionally spotty there. Was somebody else, Teodor or Sophia fleshing out these abstractions?"

Sean felt the flow of jargon calming him. He was back in familiar space that had insulated him from his parents' frank discussions about their split up. He pushed this recognition aside as others around them moved.

Teodor had apparently overheard this question, and Sophia also was being distracted. Teodor slid heavily over in his chair and chimed in. "Yes, we split the load pretty much equally. We haven't done a demo have we?"

Sophia entered the conversation. "We started with modeling after we put Diana in the closet." Sophia's expression made Ashley shudder which Sophia noticed. "Sorry. When we retired Diana, you know, that's when we switched to building a virtual model rather than focusing on a physical model."

Teodor, fidgeting heavily in his chair, evidently wanted to add something. "At home, I hacked through the night to do a flying mock-up. I want to try it out. It would be rough, but I successfully tied in calls to Ashley's and Sophia's APIs."

Sean was swept up in the ensemble performance that was gathering energy. "Any way we can take a test flight?"

"You're sitting in the cockpit," said Teodor, who clearly enjoyed Sean's acceptance of the model's metaphor. "Jason's 'puter has the most resources, so we would assess code integration there. When you fire up Eclipse, point it at flier on the server."

Sean got out of his chair and waved his hand at the now empty seat. "Teodor, you want to do this?"

Teodor simply slid his chair over, and nudged Sean's seat out of the way. Teodor tapped away on the mouse, closed some applications, and found the icon that suited him. Soon two of the three screens were filled with charts and tables. The third screen showed a wire-frame graphic. This last screen looked like a primitive version of the classic Flight Simulator.

Teodor whipped the mouse across the first two displays and set switches, clicked on radio buttons, and entered field values. With a wave of his hand, he said, "You can see the real-time values coming from the platform's sensors, and reports of its control surface settings."

"Surface settings?" said Sean. "I presume that means flaps, ailerons, and so on."

Teodor nodded vigorously and added, "Rudder, pitch, roll, yaw, lift, air temperature." He pointed at one table with its associated graph. "I can set temperature, here," he waved the mouse over the cell entry, "for instance."

Ashley finally returned to the conversation. "And this is the odd part I mentioned, Sean."

Sean turned to face her. She ducked her chin and avoided his gaze. Sean looked back at Teodor, who was inspecting the screens.

Teodor started humming, and he reached out to tap one screen with the tables. "This looks rather under-populated," he said to himself. When he turned back to speak to everyone, he offered, "There are fewer variables in these tables." He tapped deeper into hidden spreadsheet views. The deeper he went, the more he lost his momentum until he slowed to a full stop. "This is not my recent stuff—it looks stale." He ran his hand through his hair. "What's goin' on here?" he muttered to himself.

Sophia edged Teodor out of the way and began navigating the mouse through the screens. She opened some new data views. "These are sparser than I remember, too. We are missing last month's data fields."

Sean, again, turned to speak to Ashley. "How does this compare to what the repository history suggests?"

Ashley gave a weak shrug and shrank back. "I can see

the abstract classes for those views. But all development after that seems to have fallen off the cliff."

Teodor was twisting in his chair. "I watched Jason implement those interfaces into working classes. We saw the data supported in the views, and that data flowed into the model's simulation."

Meanwhile, in the background, the simulation of the running model revealed a well tuned take off and stable flight. Sean had been watching this while they had been wondering about the missing elements. "Is this model running with a scripted mission?"

Teodor glanced at the displays. "Yes. It's a rather tepid mission. We should be banking toward the exhaust chimneys in Red Square at the University when this flight gets out over Lake Union."

"That's a rather thin description for Hermes, Teodor." Ashley, with new conviction, added, "We have a script, as you asked. It is written in a translation language I call Hermes which is based on Prolog. It looks and reads like Backus Naur Form. Predicate calculus, you know."

Sean shook his head. "No, I don't know." He did know, but he decided not to expose his hand during her sudden surge off from a shaky start. "I'm just a knuckle dragging analog designer. I would like to hear more about your work."

Ashley blushed quickly and turned to hide it. "It would help if you were cross-trained like the others," she said from beneath her long curl. "The minimum amount of understanding isn't that big a leap. Clausal grammars at this level are actually quite readable. Complete programs written in them are short and sweet."

Sean listened as Ashley's expertise kicked into overdrive. The change, her transformation from passive to active, emerged as they moved away from discussing the files, Sean noticed. Their hidden value must be considerable and she must know it.

To prove this advantage of cross training, Sophia offered her own instruction. "Stick to only Ashley's script. Once you learn the parts, it comes together quickly. It is something that we all can edit on the fly and watch the virtual model respond to the new rules."

Teodor, to complete the lesson, also chimed in. "Sean, it got to me too when Ashley introduced it to us a two months ago. It vastly improved everything. Think of it as a chain of rules that have to be met. For example, one rule says that you have to have propulsion before you release the brakes for takeoff. A rule before that is checked is that you have to have sufficient fuel for the mission before you start propulsion."

Sean stirred with the enthusiasm that the others invested in Ashley's work. Was that investment still in the repository? "Ashley?"

"Yes?"

"Are we now running off one of your scripts, or is this simulation running under an older design? There seems to have been something significant that shifted roughly six weeks ago, and your investigation supports something odd about where things are now being, somehow, like a throw back."

Now it was Ashley's turn at the controls. She clicked through several menus and a window popped open. "Hermes is still part of the design. I finished the translator before I ported it into the project, so it is in a separate repository. As mentioned before, the script itself is the simple one we use for a baseline. We have a library of scripts for test regressions."

Sean could see the power in Ashley's work now. The scripts were gold when it came to regressions that could cross test all future changes. Then, on reflection, Sean thought about the word gold coming up again. "Can you show me this, or any script right now?"

Ashley raised her eyebrows, her dark eyes sparkled. "Sure. This simple." And one display filled with a text window that contained less than a hundred lines of structured text.

It looked familiar.

As Sean browsed the entries and noted their format, he recalled seeing the same thing in several of the files he had opened in the flash drive in his pocket.

"You say there is a library of these scripts?"

Ashley nodded her head vigorously.

"In the repository?"

"In one of them. We compartmentalize various aspects of our project. Data is separate from production code. Scripts are data."

"Time to reconcile that repository too, then. And any others," said Sean gravely.

Ashley's jaw dropped. "Damn!" She rushed off to her computer and sat at it, working it intensely.

Teodor saw this and he, too, was affected by Sean's last order. "Those missing live table entries were for hardware driver simulations. Those came from Jason's hardware repository."

Sophia interjected, "It looks like they were unplugged from the simulation."

This was something of a mystery to Sean. "Shouldn't hardware code be in the project code repository?"

Teodor's face reflected his perplexed state. "It would make sense if we were running the simulation through a robot. Diana isn't quite up to the task of flying." His face cleared. "In the simulator, Hermes is also doing the job as being an intelligent stub. We write a script as how we expect the hardware to respond, and Hermes runs the script to give us hardware readings or simulated actuator responses. That was how I quickly hacked this flying simulation last night."

Sean insisted, "That's my point. You run these scripts as part of the project, and yet they are not in the project repository. Any thing to report Ashley?"

Ashley's head was buried in her hands as she bent forward into her display. She sat back slowly, and hammered one key home on her keyboard. "Nothing here. It's as if it never existed." She quickly swiveled in a half circle to another workstation and began to work its keyboard. "Whew! There are still back ups, but they are two weeks old. That means we've lost just a few files. We hadn't written anything new in a long time, except for some slight mods. Those I can re-enter from memory."

Brandon had entered the office half way through Ashley's investigation and looked around with a quizzical expression. "'S'up?"

"We've found a corrupted repository," offered Sophia. "Ashley has to rebuild it, and re-do some work that hadn't been posted to a backup."

Brandon nodded, "Is this serious, or just a hiccup?"

Ashley angrily interjected, "I'm on it, Brandon. We will be back up to speed by this evening."

Brandon pressed on, "Is this a bottleneck?"

Sean felt it was time to set priorities, or this group risked falling back into confusion. "Real hardware needs to be integrated into the code testing. Diana, our robot, is that test platform. Diana is missing. We can try to find it, or rebuild it."

Sean could see they were following him closely, now. "From there, we weigh the performance of code and machine. Without that, everything's just a guess."

Brandon sat at the table and motioned all to join him in conference. They moved to the table, except for Ashley who was busy resurrecting the lost scripts. Brandon noted this, but opened a new round of discussion anyway.

"I was out late to take care of re-keying our locks and notifying Elliot Tower that their main entry is compromised. They took that without too much issue, things like this have a habit of happening. Anyway, we will see new keys before five this evening."

Brandon moved on. "Now, with that out of the way, we need to weigh our options as far as this robot goes. I want to take a poll on how likely is it that we can find it—that is, if it is simply misplaced. If so, how much does it serve our investors to do that?"

Ashley perked up to this. "Sean's right, we've been coasting. We need something." She quickly returned to her work having put in her comments.

Teodor and Sophia simply nodded in agreement, but Teodor said, "Are you fishing for something else, Brandon. I hear you say something about serving our investors. That could mean anything. Aren't we already doing that?"

"Let me put it like this," Brandon balanced back in his chair, "What if we build a flying robot instead of searching for a crawling robot?"

Sean thought about the files in the flash drive in his pocket. They were the legacy of an aircraft that weighed roughly a ton. It would easily fill the office, but then how would they fly it? Was Brandon aware of where his questions might lead? Fortunately, Brandon saved him from revealing this flash drive's secrets—if they were secrets. He knew the closer he held this knowledge to him, the more value it might have later.

Brandon tilted his chair back down, leaned forward, and sat with his arms spread across the table. "How small a package can we get by with that exhibits all the characteristics of the software, and still fly?"

Ashley stopped her work, pushed her self away from her workstation, and joined them. "Good question."

Sophia's dimples returned. "Kewel."

"I'm all for it." Teodor hammered on the table to emphasize this. "I've always been for it. I tried to shift there with Jason, but he snubbed the idea when we were talking together, alone, about locking in the investors."

All heads turned to Sean, the hardware wizard. He now realized exactly why Brandon had selected him. Had Brandon kidnapped the robot to force this choice?

"I suppose it's up to me," said Sean. "We would need a kit. An almost-ready-to-fly RC airplane."

"I know what RC means," said Sophia, "radio controlled. But do we have enough time to build one? Teodor's dad putters with them. As Teodor joked, he spends hours in the garage sanding balsa, and weekends with the club crashing them in the park. We don't need something where we would spend more time fixing a broken wing than patching new code."

Brandon paused to consider Sophia's complaint.

"Teodor? I would like to talk to you about your father's hobby interest later. Meanwhile, how big a plane would you say we need?"

"Wingspan of six feet." Teodor spread his arms wide above the conference table. "Less than this. So that we could carry the additional electronics payloads that support the mission. Can we do it with no more than a pound of hardware, Sophie?"

Sophia seemed interested, but concern showed. "That would take a month to build and a truck to move."

Teodor shook his head. "This isn't my dad's design. Almost-ready-to-fly is quick to assemble and the propulsion is integrated into the frame."

Sean needed to feed out more details. "Our non off-the-shelf concern is with RC telemetry and proprietary control. This will take a lot of radio channels."

Brandon evidently liked the way things were going. "Tell me about actually flying it. Like, we aren't going to hoist it out the window here."

Ashley, who had been listening intently, said "We can fly it by video. We could throw it out the window and fly it were it could go."

Brandon pursed his lips. "Great ideas, like flying, need landing gear. Ashley, where would you land it from here so we could retrieve it for more flights."

Ashley shrugged. "OK, so we don't throw it out the window, but your problem is still the same. Have you any answers?"

Brandon looked at Teodor to direct her question his way.

"We could disguise our work so that it looked like the typical RC activity at a park that has open space for our alpha testing," said Teodor in his smooth baritone.

Brandon liked Teodor's answer, but pushed it. "We will want to fly outside of the confines of a park to really test the mission objectives."

Teodor smiled broadly with a conspiratorial grin. "Some fliers have been known to go way off course. I knew one modeler that rented a helicopter to do a flyover of the area and surrounding neighborhoods to search for his downed experimental kit."

Sophia whistled. "Some boys have too much money."

Brandon looked around the table. "Sounds like things are back on track, there's a new plan, testing is going to be performed in real time and on something that goes one step beyond proof of concept.

"This will rejuvenate funding. Speaking of which, Sean we need to talk about billable hours. However, let's get sign-on, around the table. Ashley?"

Ashley said, "I can do this. The only down-side I see is in the degree of hand crafted hardware and rat's nest wiring." She looked to Sean for comment.

"We can modularize this everywhere," Sean assured her. "We would be using OpenSource makerware components with software tailored by us."

Ashley nodded. "I hoped you would say that. I'm definitely for it."

It wasn't the glimmer so much that Sean noticed, although it certainly exposed a new fire within her. It was more her fixed gaze that was a change from her nervous glances.

Sophia looked fired up with enthusiasm, but she was rubbing her arms again. "I'm for it, but I'm uncertain where my mission integration, the construction side, would tie into this." She was looking to Teodor to fill the gaps.

"I already have a vendor in mind," Teodor said. "We can browse their offerings so you can get your arms around the whole thing."

"OK, I'm in," said Sophia.

Brandon looked at Sean. "That leaves you."

"Not quite, I think we all need to hear from you too. For myself, I do this stuff before breakfast."

Brandon faced his own question handed back by Sean. "As an agent of our investors, I will say that the first missed milestone has been met, checks will be cut, and we will enter onto the next, missed milestone."

Quiet descended and then was disrupted by several releasing their breaths. Self consciously, laughter of relief sang around the table. "Whew," said Teodor.

"OK, then," added Sophia.

They all pushed away from the table and went to their workstations. They left Brandon and Sean still seated at the table. Brandon opened the next line of conversation in lowered tone. "We need to change hats here, and talk money."

"Sure," said Sean with some mild concern. He also noticed the tingling in his arms re-emerge. The flush of work for the past hour, or more, had put it to ease—now it was back.

In a louder tone, Brandon offered, "How about some coffee?"

"Sure."

If the others had been listening, they probably could have been excused for thinking this was a rather flat conversation.

But none lifted their head as Brandon and Sean stood, gathered a few things, and left.

* * *

"Wade forwarded your time accounting cards to us," and Brandon passed them across to Sean. "I know that this kind of work lacks a lot of structure, and sometimes this community does telecommuting."

Sean nodded. They sat nearly alone in a coffee shop that was outside of their normal neighborhood. This was going to be strictly private.

Brandon continued, "This question might sound a bit off tangent. When you're eating at home, traveling on the bus, or, say, stretched out on that couch in the office. How much are you thinking about the project?"

To Sean, this was indeed an odd question, and he felt like he had to unpack it carefully. He noticed Brandon nodding his head slightly. Was this a faint, rhythmic touch of his brother's idiosyncrasy?

"Let me lead here," Brandon offered. "I have down time when my wife or kids come into the picture, but otherwise I am always at work. You've met my brother, Andrew, so you can see how far to the extreme that can go."

"OK, I don't have many family moments that distract me," Sean admitted. "So, yes, this is always chattering like a monkey in my mind." He didn't know where this was going unless it was an indirect pep talk.

Brandon pointed at Sean's time cards. "Then that time should appear on these. We expect you to sleep at least eight hours a night, so you reporting in the neighborhood of sixteen hours a day on the project is not something that would upset us. All we ask is do the right thing."

Brandon relaxed into his chair. "Your addition to the team has been transformative and I feel justified in my assessment in how your presentation at *CyberDome* could bridge to our mission."

Sean said, "OK, I'm finding this work challenging and unique. I like it and the team. I'm a bit leery about this bookkeeping of hours, though."

"Oh?" said Brandon.

Sean searched for words to connect to this leery feeling.

This extravagant gesture was like a honeypot.

"Getting paid to think between munches on my sandwich? Man, that's just—"

"—Just do whatever you think is the right thing," said Brandon. "Anything else you feel we should be talking about right now?"

The "right thing" still felt like he was pushing the button to empty a compromised account.

Sean shrugged his shoulders. "Can't think of anything else."

It now qualified as a second very stressful day with money being skimmed off him, and money being thrown at him. There had to be an explanation, and it better come soon.

As Brandon rose and gathered his things, Sean said, "Wait."

Brandon stood there waiting as asked. "What would you like to talk about?"

Problems over money now lost to problems over mission. "I do have some problems, here, with gaps in the story."

Brandon pursed his lips and slipped back into his chair. This time he sat stiffly. "Like about Jason's departure?"

Sean nervously nodded. "Some of that, yeah. But first about the mission. It's arrived out of the blue, and it seems to have been an old idea."

"Hmm," responded Brandon. "Well, it's all of a piece." He scratched his head, and examined his cold coffee absently. "This does go a long way back. Long being months, if that's not too confusing."

Sean nodded. Brandon's context for this time scale was familiar to techies. "Time I get, the rest needs to be unpacked."

"OK. What I mean by all of a piece. First, even if everyone acts as though the mission has changed—from crawling to flying as most would call it—a drone was where we had been focused on for—well—those same months—or so Andrew and I thought."

Sean could tell that Brandon was entering new territory. As fluent as he normally was, he was fumbling now. Sean found he could connect with that. "Could you explain how could everyone be working on a different mission?"

Brandon nodded. "Yeah. You certainly have the knack for asking a penetrating question. This is where we get to the Jason part. Again, some time ago, Jason had come into Pribylov with a new spin on where the project could go."

"A flier."

"Hmm? Oh, yes, a flier, a drone. His idea was for a commercial drone. It was an edgy idea, but we work with edgy ideas all the time. We look for edgy ideas."

"That doesn't explain the fact that only today that we decided to build a flier." Sean rolled his shoulders to release the knots in them.

"Yes—no, it doesn't—you're right. Andrew and I were

recently becoming concerned over the missed milestones. I moved into the office a few days ago—to monitor activity—to see where the stall in progress was."

Sean had seen a vague picture, but it was getting clearer by the moment. "This has something to do with Teodor? He complained that this drone idea, his, was blown off by Jason."

Brandon acted as if he wanted to explain, but he clutched up. After a reflective pause, he appeared to be readying for a second approach. "I suppose there's no diplomatic way to put this." He held this thought for a moment. "Jason was playing off both sides to fulfill a third agenda."

Sean said, "How?"

"Like I said, we kept our hand out of it for too long," said Brandon. "Some distance is a necessary part of the start-up culture, but we were distracted with our other holdings who have their own growing pains. Aurora's filling in for Megan has proved to be a boon in helping us along." Brandon reached up and scrubbed the back of his neck and head. "I hate to say this, but I hope Megan burns out with her classes and comes back to join her."

Sean had heard enough of the Jason story. "It would seem that Jason's departure has been smoothed over." Brandon nodded without comment. "But what are the investors looking for in a drone? The reputation for them are they are killing machines."

Brandon flinched. "Sean, there is only so much beating I can take, but your question deserves an answer. You—and the group—are going to have to be flexible. There is a market for drones—even in the cities—downtown Seattle no exception. We have to expect the police to be one of our customers."

Sean gulped in air. "Flexible? That's gibberish."

Brandon huddled closer, glancing to check out the nearby empty tables. "The drone we design could save kids in the floods we experience during winter heavy rains. That's part of flexibility."

The offering of generous pay was cranking up the heat under the pressure cooker. The Jason story clamped the lid tighter. The mission shifts in all the troubled companies before, were rehearsals for this main performance.

"I'm going to have to think," Sean said in a tone that indicated a close to their discussion.

"So. No go?" said Brandon.

Sean released his held breath. "There's a lot of change going on. The work is the easy part of it—difficult as it might be." He looked at Brandon waiting for a clearer answer. "I'm signed on."

"OK. Your reservations are OK with me as long as we keep in touch about them," said Brandon.

"Thanks," said Sean.

Brandon gathered his things, once again, and this time departed without Sean calling him back.

* * *

Once again, Sean was out of sync with the others in the office. When he returned, they were out. And, again, the door had been unlocked. How much could changing locks be a solution?

Rather than staring at a blank display at his workstation, he decided to wander over to the window and unplug his mind. The day looked inviting with white clouds drifting in a blue expanse. As much as he was trying to disconnect, his mind buzzed. Sophia should be in the preliminaries of chasing down the vendor for cost, availability, and delivery specifics for the proposed RC flier. Teodor and Ashley should be working out navigation issues.

These thoughts propelled him away from the window to seek out some neutral corner of the room. Perhaps if he hid himself in the closet.

He pulled the door open and looked inside. The closet was deeper than he expected. From the back, in the dark, he could see activity lights flickering from a server rack. As big as the rack was, and it was big, the closet was bigger still. There was enough room for a 1950's sci-fi movie robot to have parked there.

He fumbled around and found a switch. Labels revealed that this rack was the central hub for all the overhead cabling that ran in the trays in the office's semi-exposed ceiling.

Most of the cables spanned out to other offices, serving the capacity of the main feed coming into this floor. Sean did a quick estimate for what that capacity could be. It had to be quite a big pipe connected in the back.

"Interesting." And then Sean was aware that he still had the meter running. Brandon was right.

Brandon might know how to pay for Sean's mind running like a power meter, but there was still Aurora's questions about how Wade took his cut. If only there were others there at work to distract him from facing this issue.

He flicked off the light and closed the closet door. He crossed the office, went through the door, and locked it behind him.

* * *

Sean waited for Aurora outside on the street at the steps

that lead up to the offices of *Pribylov Investment*. She had let him know she could be late. She would text him when she planned to get down. He was content to stand there anyway, he didn't want to visit the office.

He had already been there quite a while, but the day was pleasant enough. If he was determined to disconnect, to stop the meter for even a short while, then he needed something different, something more distracting than standing there. But what would do that?

Snooker. The small sign, across the street, reminded him that there was another world with a longer continuity than that of the internet age. The internet must have already spanned his whole life and most of his parent's adult life.

He was going to go off the grid.

The climb up the stairs from the street was similar to the climb up to Pribylov—with a major exception. There was no dark, carpeted hallway of paneled doors. Sean found himself immersed in an alternate reality with islands of pool tables lit with hanging lamps filling a dark sea.

The room was neither bright, nor dark, but the tables were each distinctly illuminated, and their traditional green baize absorbed it evenly like the moss of the Olympic peninsula's rain forests. Sean mentally shifted into a glade surrounded by the trees.

Figures moved and then crouched. The thrum of the cue strike resonated like a wood guitar string. Then came the cascade of clicking collisions like a crystalline rock slide in the distance. Player's occasional murmurs merged as though they were the sound of a shallow brook.

Sean's heart rippled. The second sensation was his phone vibrating—a text arrived.

`where r u?`

When Sean glanced at the time stamp on Aurora's text, he was surprised to find it was twenty minutes after he had crossed the street.

* * *

They matched notes about pay on their walk from the bus stop to the Roosevelt Courtyard. Aurora offered her story about how Andrew had conducted the same pep talk that Sean heard from Brandon. There were similarities about how much time should be billed for a day at Pribylov for Aurora. Andrew appeared to be trimming his extravagance by suggesting that Aurora should get something closer to twelve hours of sleep a night. "How old does he think I am? Nine?"

Sean smiled. "And you thought he was—"

"Shut up."

* * *

"OK, I hear you. Both of you. It is an odd situation, the nature of their business relationship with me, and the economics of it." Wade was remarkably settled in the face of their torrent of questions about the accounting, as Aurora put it.

Sean and Aurora had taken their usual places on the rugs near Wade's low tea table. They weren't comfortable, however. Aurora had taken the lead again and Sean was glad to sit in the background while she vented.

"Sounds like nothing I've ever heard of," said Aurora.

"Wade, you are making more money off our work than we are," said Sean.

"That is the appearance, the reality is far different."

Aurora folded her arms and was about to release another

cataract of statements, questions, and demands—and not so subtle hints about getting ripped off.

"Aurora, before you go there again, let me ask you one question." Wade tried to offer her some tea.

Aurora declined his gesture and simply said, "Go."

"Are you getting a good wage? You saw the numbers, the split. That's real."

Aurora's arms unfolded and then she forced them up again. "Yes, but—"

"—Whoa, let's try another question seeing that that answer was positive beyond your expectation. Do you understand risk and investment?"

Aurora tightened her crossed arms. "I'm getting an education at Pribylov, but I'm not particularly interested in taking on any risk."

Sean peeled himself away from the wallpaper of this conversation. "Why are we moving to this topic, Wade?"

"Before I cover that, Sean, a third question that either of you can feel free to field.

"How's the finances of *GyroNautica* been through the recent past? Surely, you've researched this as deeply, Aurora."

Aurora ducked her gaze, and answered toward the floor with, "Times have been hard. No money. No pay. But they are there because it's theirs."

"You are working in their company, but do you expect to observe their same pay-out?"

Sean blurted out, "Is this twenty questions now? Let me ask one. Will we see a paycheck? Soon, rather than at the end of the rainbow?"

Wade laughed at his turn of expression, but not so hard as to bring them to an explosion. He covered this quickly with, "Your pay will be every Friday at close, just as you expect. It will be for the hours Brandon and Andrew have suggested, if you accept their generosity—such as you put it. This will continue for the duration of your contract."

Aurora's arms dropped, and she moved in her chair as if she had feeling returning to her legs that had fallen asleep. Sean could tell she was still processing. He asked, "So, let's talk about the elephant in the room."

"Fine, what Aurora calls my billing multiplier. Right?"

"Yes."

Wade settled back and took a sip from his tea. He glanced at the darkening sky as evening drew in upon them. "The multiplier, as we are calling it now, is an industry staple. It is my income, it is their cost for me finding talent to place with them."

Sean nodded, but this was not enough. "But double or triple our wage? Wade, this is slavery."

Wade waved to calm Sean. "True, from your perspectives. However the multiplier also covers my costs when I have to pay my crew, such as you and Aurora, if the client fails to come through." Wade noticed that Sean was not satisfied even here, and he continued, "And, yes, double or triple your rate is far above the realm of a normal charge -um- multiplier."

Wade paused before shifting the discussion. "This brings us to the culture of start-ups, appearance, and reality. The reality is that there will be no money coming into this office from anyone—neither *GyroNautica*, nor Pribylov."

Aurora emerged from her brooding. "That doesn't make sense."

"Well, we've already established that neither of you are investor savvy. At your ages, not unusual. You kind of see the outlines of it like a cartoon figure."

Wade took a sip and looked at the two. "For the purposes of your contract, I'm the investor backing your wages. That, and the multiplier, is my equity investment into their company. And it is also my faith in you two pulling Pribylov's chestnut out of the fire. Those boys are accepting the rate as an unsecured bond—"

"—Too much information, Wade. I get it. I get it. OK. Sorry for the trouble I've been giving you." Aurora's arms were now more open. Her face was slightly flushed.

"Does unsecured bond," Sean kept that line open, "mean they simply pay you, instead of giving you a part of the company?"

Wade nodded. "You catch on too. For investors, debt is cheap. However, their bond to me being redeemed only happens if things turn out well. Unsecured means I could end up with pennies on the dollar—or empty-handed."

Aurora stirred, stood up, and almost began to dance slowly around her chair. She was drawing a thought out as she moved. "Our pay is coming out of your pocket." She snapped her fingers. "If they fail, you lose it all."

Sean wondered how it took her so long to assimilate what Wade had said.

Then she stopped and pointed her finger at Wade. "You know something we don't!"

Wade's eyebrows rose. "And so we move to a new level. Have you noticed how your perception shifts once you get out of yourselves?"

Sean was surprised at Wade's question, and noticed that

it held Aurora in suspension.

"OK, maybe now's not the time for the Zen of this moment," suggested Wade. "I'm not without my resources. Carrying your costs is hitting me in the wallet, but, as I've said, most of that is factored into my margin."

Again, Wade made a gesture of offering tea. This time they accepted.

"Even when they inflate your time, this adds to my investment. You are my leverage in more ways than one." Wade's mood then shifted as it appeared that the wages, charges, and costs had all been laid on the table.

"Yes, undoubtedly, neither of you know the back story of Jason. He brought value to the boys at Pribylov, and he took it away—or at least the most productive developments of it recently. There are two revenue streams somewhere in here."

Aurora perked up. "There's something I've heard before from Megan."

Wade showed interest in her statement. "What did she have to say?"

Aurora's bright mood dimmed somewhat. "Just those two words in association with *GyroNautica*—no explanation, and I didn't ask."

"Too bad. We need more information on this second stream. Right now it is only a hint, a rumor about knowledge discovery. A seemingly off-the-wall suggestion from Jason, now departed. Maybe its buried somewhere in the project."

"I've got some material in for Aurora—and Megan I suppose—that may bear on that," said Sean.

"Any ideas?" Wade said to both of them. They shook their heads.

"Now's my turn to rain on your parade," said Sean. "This project they're developing has been done before. They are called drones. No one is going to think *GyroNautica* is coming up with something new."

Wade nodded. "They don't have to. *GyroNautica* just needs to deliver a stable surveillance platform at a mid-entry point. Sean, you've gotten them out of the ditch, and the rest of the team will soon accelerate development."

"However, to protect my investment, I need to re-emphasize that I need more information," added Wade.

Aurora picked up his inference. "We got it. I'll get busy on Sean's file trove."

"With Megan," said Wade. He caught Aurora's skeptical look, "Oh, yes. I have the inside dope on that. You two are to put your heads together and find all the pieces."

BUILDING ICARUS

It didn't take very long, less than two weeks, for the last of the flier components to come in. Over that time, Sophia was in her element in both chasing down the various modules, and assembling Sean's tailored hardware modifications into their new prototype called Icarus.

Icarus stood in its own dedicated space of the conference table. It's smooth surface and sleek lines gave the appearance of motion. The propulsion unit sitting on top suggested a smooth, strong hum of a jet would lift it into the sky. Icarus had its long, graceful sport wing installed. Its span reached beyond the edges of the table.

However, there was no hum of propulsion. Quiet filled the office, aside from the occasional keyboard entry. The smooth surface of Icarus added the slight odor of plasticizers. It was something akin to new car smell that Teodor suggested when they first unpacked it.

Teodor offered that if they could tolerate the plasticizers for a short while, then they would enjoy how their choice for battery power would pay off. There would be no gas to store, seep out, or spill. Also, at the end of the day they wouldn't fill the room with spent exhaust products from their workouts on the field.

Away from the rest, Sean had lost himself in his linear designs. Icarus had a suite of sensors that no RC airplanes carried. He crafted them for precision, dynamic range, and low noise. Those sensors were going to expand Icarus' intelligence gathering capacity.

It was as if Icarus had a dozen or more senses. Sight was among them with two cameras. Icarus' voice and hearing in the form of data streams was channeled through expanded radio circuits for telemetry. They had taken a slice of radio spectrum that was outside of the usual RC control band.

Icarus' sensation of feeling arrived from a multitude of flight control surfaces. Icarus' sense of its relative place in space came through a compass, proximity sensor, ambient light sensor, and magnetometer. Its sense of balance came from its gyrometer and accelerometers. Its sense of absolute place was through its GPS module.

To lighten the technical side of project reviews, Teodor wryly suggested that they shouldn't use wax to hold Icarus' wings on. The crew groaned at his ancient joke.

When Brandon, trying to be clever, over-played Teodor's joke with, "There'll be no problem of sun overexposure in Seattle." This was met by the humiliation of silence in response.

Sean pondered Brandon's oracle when he gazed at the skies outside. It was the second or third time he had seen the blue sky from their tower perch in two weeks. The sun streamed into the office from the west. It lit the fine details of Icarus. This helped Sophia as she and Teodor inserted micro-modules into the hogged-out interior of the airframe. They managed to create a cavity that could hold all the new components and that didn't violate weight loading limits, nor unbalance the craft. Teodor had experience with those failures and carefully shepherded them through.

Sophia sat back with satisfaction. "It all seems to look good, Ted. I wouldn't have had the courage to just start carving out that much material."

"Thanks, Soph," murmured Teodor.

They were at the end of a long process, and Icarus was still in one piece. Outwardly, it looked like it did when it arrived.

Teodor stood and stepped back to admire their work.

"When we take it out, it will draw notice, but only as a new craft on the runway."

Brandon smiled. "It works for us all to maintain just that appearance of our being ..."

"RC Nerds," offered Teodor slyly.

Ashley bridled. "You just want to show off. You know what they say about boys and flashy cars."

Teodor kept quiet.

Sean was glad at this turn in restraint. He wanted to keep the conversation moving along the design path instead of following the parade of personality. "So, we're on for this weekend with a static test of the flight system?"

All in the office nodded or flashed thumbs-up.

Brandon nodded his head, tallying the count as he surveyed everyone's positive feelings. He focused his attention on Sean. "How soon before we are going out for a test flight?"

Sean, instead of answering, turned his gaze to Teodor. Teodor fielded the question. "Sophie's mocked up an RC remote, but our navigation system and up link down link will be in the van doing the work. But, we need the static tests to confirm all sensor driven channels and controls are active."

"But will it fly—out of the box?" asked Brandon.

Teodor gritted his teeth. "Brandon, you've been sitting in the same design reviews. Why don't you tell us what you've heard?"

Brandon was uncomfortable with that when he had been seeking reassurance. "I don't want to see this plunge and burn."

"It's electric powered, not gas," Sophia reminded him.

Building Icarus

"OK, so Teodor's descriptions of his father's RC models haunt me," Brandon pushed back.

Teodor took this as a pass back to him. "I kind of liked those crash and burns. Dad never let me at the controls, so the only fun was waiting for something to go wrong. Is that what you mean about a haunting, Brandon?"

"Just don't burn me, man."

Sean ignored this escalating tension by reinforcing the context of their progression of design. "It will happen. We want failure to happen soon, and in front of us. Get used to the idea Brandon, we've already talked this one to death. Let's just get through the static checks first, OK?"

Sean gathered some things for his next move. To no one in particular, he announced, "I'm off to see Megan and Aurora at the office." The only response was Ashley's wondering glance and Brandon's shrug.

* * *

Before Sean dropped in at Pribylov, he veered off to the bakery for something to nibble on. The weather continued nice, and the sidewalks were filling with tourists. He doubted that the Underground tours would absorb enough of them for him to find a seat at the bakery.

He was nearly right. The bakery was crowded. But timing was such that when he left the till with his food, he found a small, empty table. He had barely taken his seat when someone behind him asked, "Willing to share your table? I mean, if you're alone, you know."

He was shorter than Sean by half a foot, but older, somewhere in his late twenties. As he stood there waiting for Sean to respond, this fellow swept his long straw colored hair back over his thin shoulders, adjusted his owl frame glasses, and gave an unbalanced grin.

"Sure," said Sean.

Like Sean, this fellow carried a computer bag slung over one shoulder. Their similar dress also spoke of them being coders in the neighborhood of coders who were transforming this 19th century saloon district.

He expected nothing more from his seat mate. Sean was there to rummage through thoughts and shift gears. He did that where projects were a mix of hardware design and software design. If he tried to shift his thinking between these two activities too quickly, then gears would clash.

His seat mate swept his long hair back with a flick again that got Sean's attention. With eye contact re-established, his table companion plunged right in. "Platform stabilization going well up there?"

Sean didn't, at first, feel he really heard this. Then the significance of a stranger asking this very specific question soaked in. Sean looked at this newcomer in the eyes. "It's going very well, Jason."

Jason shared a thin smile. "I thought that would make introductions unnecessary." His brows merged into the heavy owl frames.

"So, you know me then?" said Sean.

"Sean. I was with Teodor and Brandon when we saw your presentation."

Sean was caught. Not only was Jason at the presentation, but Teodor was as well. He could recall Brandon's use of *we*, but Sean never connected it to anyone else from the group. Jason had to do that, and that was the shock. But Sean had to push through, beyond it.

"I didn't know I was such a rock star," he said.

Jason shrugged that metaphor off. Sean could tell that he wasn't held in as high esteem with Jason as he was in others'. "So, this appears to be a meeting that you wanted," said Sean.

"I have something of high value—a proposition that could generate a lot of revenue," came Jason's low hiss across the table. "What I want to know is can you get the investors to redeem it?" There was no inflection to the question. Jason was not asking for a favor.

"Or, this could mean a good deal of cash money to you for doing what you do best with solving problems." Jason slipped this in casually like he already knew where things would end up.

Something he can do well, and a good deal of cash money for doing it?

There was a jarring thrill and Sean began to stir with heat. He couldn't distinguish if it was a good or bad feeling—yet. If Jason's overture wasn't about Wade's question of a second revenue stream, then this could mean a second source of cash to Sean. Sean needed to straighten that out.

Sean prepared to draw him out, but Jason surprised him by rising, taking up his bag, and stepping aside.

"There's more to be said, but there's the ground work," said Jason. He turned and twisted his way through the lunch crowd. The swell of heat Sean felt faded with Jason's departure. A chill followed.

Sean tried to draw together his thoughts on Jason's sudden appearance—and disappearance—and the irony of a ghost fitting into things again, when another voice asked, "Could I share your table?"

This time a couple, a guy and a girl around his age, again with all the trappings of coders, were standing at his elbow with their food. The girl who asked, smiled disarmingly. Sean took his sandwich, stood and offered, "Go ahead, it's yours."

The girl's expression changed to embarrassment. "I didn't mean to chase you away. We can fit. We won't take up any room at all!"

Sean continued to step aside, he smiled at the fellow behind her, and then returned his smile to her. "Something's come up at work. My buddy, who just left, has motivated me to get back."

Why was he so jubilant? Jubilation, cash money, and work spun together. It could be Jason's unexpected lead that seemingly confirmed Wade's suspicion of something of hidden value being built into the project. Heat erupted within him again—and as suddenly cooled. Or was it the prospects of cash money as Jason had tempted deliciously?

* * *

The door to *Pribylov Investment* was locked. Aurora and Megan were, no doubt, out at lunch themselves. So, Sean decided to visit the snooker hall. The sun, mild temperature, and it being Friday had tourists from the cruise ships milling around every shop window on the avenue.

When Sean came up to the sign announcing snooker, he slipped through the small doorway and up the flight of stairs. Again, he was met with an overall quiet penetrated only by the cue strikes and ball collisions. There seemed to be less commentary coming from what lies were left for the other player. Sean considered that, perhaps, this small group was more intent on the money than on the banter.

He wasn't sure there was any money in these games, but if he trusted Betty, then something was being payed beneath the table.

Building Icarus

If he trusted Betty—Sean thought—there was a curious idea. He had only seen her twice. Perhaps he elevated her significance through her association with Megan as her god mother.

Now, as for Megan … Sean glanced off into the distance and let his mind settle on the hanging lights. They were bright, but subdued outside of the field of play. They illuminated the action, and brought a soft glow to the rest of the hall.

He knew Megan only in the context of the pair of Aurora and Megan, given they now worked together at Pribylov. If he took the pair, subtracted Aurora, he would have Megan, wouldn't he? Aurora has sharp edges, but he counted on her in a pinch. If he could take away those edges, would he find Megan equally dependable? He wanted to fill that blank in to her favor.

In the last week, Megan lit up when he visited to check their progress with Jason's ghost files. He hadn't trusted her on their first introduction. Her spark, as he thought of it then, seemed artificially bright. However, since she had returned, her ever present spark was now comfortably bright.

His thoughts drifted back to the unoccupied tables with their soothing emerald green. The green was as deep as any mossy path through the forests. Time slipped away as he stood there, mesmerized by the view, the low voices, and the caroming balls. When he glanced at the time, twenty minutes had slipped away as it had in his last visit.

Sean drifted down the stairs back into the hustle on the sidewalk. Some tourists parting around him glanced at the sign above him—*Snooker*—and not recognizing it as a tourist attraction, they moved on in search of a compelling distraction.

Traffic was thin. Sean took a chance and loped across the tree lined divide in the avenue to the entry of Pribylov's offices.

* * *

Megan's face lifted when Sean came through the door. Aurora glanced up, and brushed her auburn flare back. "Hi." She went back to browsing the computer display. Megan had joined Aurora's shift of attention, but did not return to their work. Instead she silently waited.

Megan was dressed with a black and white striped top as part of a dark outfit, a black tight cap on the back of her head over dark metallic red hair, and dark cherry lipstick.

"Hello." Sean carefully answered Aurora's greeting to both of them. As long as Aurora wasn't paying much attention, he returned Megan's gaze.

"Got it up yet?" asked Megan.

"Hmm? Oh, Icarus. Not yet," said Sean.

"Who chose the name Icarus?" Megan gave a coy smile to encourage Sean into longer conversation.

"Who knows—I mean, I don't know. Must've been Ashley, is my guess, or Sophia, certainly not Teodor."

"Certainly not Teodor," echoed Megan with a nod.

This was like a private joke between them, but he wasn't comfortable with their private jokes. Yet. What was next?

"Could you two stop chattering and someone give me a hand here? Sean, you've been coming here for this, so come 'round." Aurora emphasized this with a wave of her hand, her finger tracing a route around the table she and Megan sat at.

She continued. "There's still that odd executable we

found last week called Tyche that doesn't reside back in the tower office. I don't know what to do with that loner, so we are going to focus on scripts."

When Sean took in what they were studying, it looked like a phone log in table format, but there was something more to it than that. "What do you have here?"

Megan took up the question. She slid up alongside Sean and pointed to one display. "Using a brute force search with grep, we have a candidate file on that flash drive you discovered, and we are comparing it to a similar file in Aurora's private network view of your office's development system."

"Say what?" said Sean. "You can see our repository?"

"Megan and I built a Virtual Private Network before lunch," said Aurora.

"She's being generous," said Megan. Her bobbed hair swayed as she turned her head to Sean to explain. "I just took notes on how to do it again."

Sean was impressed with Aurora's talent at building this VPN and bringing all her tools to bear on the problem. Megan sounded savvy too. She wasn't fumbling the words and the concepts of advanced networking. Sean felt like the ghost's files, once a wall of impenetrable dullness were buckling under Aurora and Megan's efforts.

"The red text entries are the ones that didn't match the copy in the drive you brought in," added Aurora. She looked up for Sean's response, and she caught his gaze still lingering on Megan after her answer. "So, whaddayathink?"

Sean shifted his attention to the display, examined the entries, the differences, the similarities, and he tried to draw something out of it. "Looks like structured statements, or XML."

"Really," came Megan's quick affirmation.

"Indeed," added Aurora rather more flatly.

"Was it originally this way?" asked Sean. "There's no reason for a simple text file to be in table format."

"You're right, Sean," said Megan. "We did that to find a pattern. The cmp, compare, command is being piped into a formatter."

"Is there a pattern?" He asked them both while admiring Megan's continued ease with this work. Sean slowly turned his attention to the screen, bent closer, but nothing revealed itself. "You two have been at this longer—tell me."

Aurora heaved back from the table and sighed. "No, no pattern."

Megan cocked her head back again and offered a half shrug.

Sean sat down and continued to examine their table formatted results. Was there some pattern other than what was original and what was discovered? Soon he discarded that line of thought and simply read the originals.

Was there a story here? In either file, the lines read as complete sentences, even if they were somewhat awkward.

"You say the development system already had a file like the one discovered on the flash drive I brought in," he said. They nodded. "Any thoughts about its purpose—its intent?"

This was part of Megan's turf. "It, or both versions, rather, are outliers. I found the version I have using grep."

"grep, as you've said before," said Sean.

"I taught her how to use it," explained Aurora. "She was trying to do it with that crapola search that MS offers. You know, the thing with the cartoon paper clip."

"They changed it to a cute doggie," Megan said, but wrinkled her nose. "Aurora knows these awesome command line tools that I used to pull the file out fast."

Aurora had UNIX skills that he was now becoming more aware of. Megan was her quick student. "But this still doesn't tell me where these statements tie into. Weren't they in some sort of directory tree?"

"Just a shallow one three deep," said Megan, "Specifically in a folder called happy valley with the file name place.hrm, and located a folder called course, in turn located at the root within a folder called play."

Sean nodded. "Yes, I recall something like that, but skipped over it. There were several unusual names there, but the folders, themselves, were empty. How about in your files?"

"Just as sparse," said Aurora. "Altogether three folders called data, course, pay, and the one file we have in comparison."

Megan continued, "The development system copy of the folder play didn't have the folders data, or pay. When we compared date stamps, the development copies were a month older. You brought files that were newer. There were only two files total. Of those two, you only had one that we shared called place. What we are looking at are the combined contents of place.hrm. The other file is an executable."

Sean nodded. "Intriguing, the other file, that executable that you say I was missing, what is it called?"

Megan began to lift her closed hand up and down as if to stir her memory about something she held. With her eyes shut she struggled out with, "That Grace Kelly bag."

Aurora smiled. It must have been some shared joke,

Sean thought.

Aurora took Megan off the hook. "Hermes. Girl—Sean wouldn't have any idea about a high fashion French purse maker."

"Really," responded Megan in a conspiratorial tone. She pouted her dark cherry lips at him.

Sean took this in, and refused to notice their effort to mock him. "Hermes," he said in a half whisper to himself. He bent back toward the computer display and re-read the entries there.

Megan looked peeved. "You aren't going to ask about Grace Kelly?"

Unusual for Aurora, she chimed in with a more conversation tone, "Megan's god-mother showed us clips from a film Grace Kelly was in."

Sean, still immersed in the content on the display, offered a neutral comment. "You two socializing, then?"

"Betty then showed us these pictures, you know, of her with that bag when Princess Grace was pregnant." Aurora waited for Sean to comment, but shrugged at his indifference.

"Nice," he said absently. Sean drew his finger along the entries. "I can see something here now."

Megan looked over his shoulder. "What?"

Sean was troubled by what he saw. Neither Aurora nor Megan were aware of the significance of the Hermes program. They had no reason to be, yet. And it was with that thought that Sean connected two dots. Both Hermes and now Icarus were names drawn from Greek mythology. Two connected dots didn't give him a shape, or outline. They hardly suggested a line.

Megan repeated, "What?"

Sean explained, "This longer version of the file you've been comparing, actually both versions, this is a script. Aurora, you're up on UNIX tools, you know what I mean by script."

"I know what a script is too," pouted Megan. She lowered her head to peer at him from beneath her dark bangs.

Aurora considered Sean's comment for a moment. "You mean that Hermes is a script language? Or, rather, Hermes is a translator of this script file?" She joined Sean and scanned the display. "If you say ..." She took the keyboard and opened a shell into the operating system.

"Let's see what this does." She typed in the command.

```
hermes place.hrm
>
```

The cursor in the shell blinked for several seconds, and then returned to a system prompt.

"Hmm. That wasn't very productive," said Aurora.

Megan offered, "But it did function. There were no system error messages, so you did something right."

Aurora swept back the auburn tangle of her hair. "Good point." She began browsing through the file system. "Nothing new here."

"Try it again," said Megan.

"I don't think so. We need to check the logs." Aurora turned her browsing to the system's internal tools. Sean and Megan sat silently while she clicked through the layers of menus to get to the deep activity reports. "Strange ... Maybe ..."

After several minutes of browsing, she found what she

was looking for. "Yeah. Slippery little devil."

Sean was about to say something, but Aurora held him off, "I need to set something up, and then we are going to try it again." She opened other tools that Sean recognized as being network oriented. She also opened another shell and designed a script file of her own and named it after one of the system files.

"Can you do that?" asked Sean. He knew what she was doing. His black hat days informed him she was deep into the security layers of the system.

"You can't, but I've already given myself permissions to do anything." Aurora closed up some of the tools and returned to the first shell that held Hermes. She repeated the command. They watched the cursor blink once again. Then the shell flowed with data. When it ran to completion, several readable lines were tagged onto the end of what was apparently a data dump.

Sean read a proclaimed error, "Looks like Hermes crashed on that run. Got anything else from it, Aurora?"

Aurora pointed at a single line entry of 12 digits. "There's the internet pointer where the data was transmitted."

"Anyway that you can put a name on that IP address?" asked Sean.

"I have my suspicions, given the crude way the tracks were covered up as part of the run of the code." Aurora submerged herself into threading her way through the web this time.

"You going to put it into the address bar of your browser?" suggested Megan.

"No, I don't want our first run of Hermes' cross-load to be tagged with a repeat, probing visit." She pasted the address into a field on a technical web page. It flickered and offered a report. Aurora glanced at it briefly and the spun around to Sean and Megan. "It's an anonymous proxy website address." She looked back at the end of the data dump she had left open. "Yeah, there's the account number. Probably a one-time cypher good for a couple of hours or a day. Untraceable at this layer of the game."

Sean pondered if he had run across Aurora in a security chat group sometime in the past. Her talents at tracing an intruder were quick and efficient. Her instincts were well developed.

Had they cracked heads in the past while he was hacking?

Everyone sat silent for a while. They knew that something had happened that was outside of the scope of either *GyroNautica* or *Pribylov Investment*. Occasionally, each would glance at the data dump, and then return to musing over the sequence of events.

Sean shook his head. The others noticed and looked on, waiting. "We've probably tipped our hand."

"To Jason?" asked Megan.

"To whomever," was Sean's response. "When we fired off Hermes with that particular script that was on the flash drive I found; it performed its work and sent a message, or data on to the script's author."

"Being halfway sure to cover its tracks, too," added Aurora. She swung to the computer and started to copy the complete transaction that she had captured.

Sean watched her. "I hope that didn't go out too. Did you redirect that stream?" Sean knew it did, but his question would serve to cloak his past.

Megan looked back and forth between Aurora and Sean. "Are you asking if Aurora kept this last operation to ourselves?"

Aurora nodded to Megan. "Yes to both. This dump," she indicated with a wave of her hand toward the display, "this time, went no further than here."

"Hopefully, we still have some edge," said Sean.

"Aurora gave us some edge?"

"A thin one, Megan. If we think of it this way, our unknown script author got a data dump, independent of that author having launched the script. A one time run would suggest to them that we tried and gave up when, apparently, nothing happened."

Megan offered, "It's thin. I think the author would probably wonder why we didn't try it over and over—the usual fumbling with something that is unknown."

Sean reflected on her challenge of his decision.

Megan looked back at the display. "Aurora, please save all of that. I want to analyze it." Aurora nodded, and Megan continued, "Do we repeat the run to give that impression of fumbling around?"

Sean shook his head and then added, "It is what it is. We've already tipped our hand that we were aware that the file was a Hermes script when the report was sent to the offsite respondent."

Megan nodded her head. "The author also knows that we have the most up to date script, one he must've thought he had recovered from the tower."

"Exactly," admitted Sean. "The author now knows we have a copy of the flash drive he thought was solely his."

Aurora had been following their conversation thoughtfully.

"I've heard a shift in the tone of this, Sean."

"A shift?" he said.

"You've deliberately called our ghost the author, the respondent, and specifically a him," said Aurora. "Jason. Why not put his name to all of this, instead of carefully framing everything with fuzzy words?"

Was it time to mention Jason's approach earlier at lunch?

Jubilation, cash money, and work.

Sean chewed on this for a while as they waited for him to say something. Their launch of Hermes with the extended script had been a loss. Jason, the author, the ghost, whomever, now knew the balance. If he mentioned Jason's lunch time visit, then there was danger that this information would dilute his advantage more.

"Just my way, I guess." There, that capped the dialog by saying nothing. If he didn't name Jason, then the ghost would be suitable as a target without a known purpose.

"So, where do we go from here?" Aurora had been copying the data dump and passed it to Megan and Sean. She shut down the computer as if to put an amen to a closed grave.

Sean summoned up an earlier statement he had heard from the pair. It had him wondering. "What was this thing about seeing a movie with Betty?"

"Megan invited me over to their apartment. Guess what? It's in the Roosevelt Courtyard where Wade keeps his office."

Megan brightened and offered, "Why don't we duck out of here and drop by?"

Aurora took this up enthusiastically. "You go girl!"

Sean was caught in his moral dilemma where this was still

only early afternoon in the workday. On the other hand, Megan's offer was something he wanted to accept. But it, too, was clouded with Aurora and Betty being in the picture.

Aurora prodded, "C'mon, Sean, you can afford to go off the clock."

That stung. They were making good money on top of inflated charges that all seemed to be leverage for an investment. Sean was troubled that nothing was clean, and now his desire felt the same way.

What did he want? The girls beckoned, but his priorities were to build up a bank account to cover costs at home. He didn't ordinarily think of it in such glaring terms. He rarely thought of it at all. Now his choices were in competition.

Sean released his breath heavily. "I need the money, Aurora."

Aurora could see Sean slump. "Yeah. Sorry about that crack. What I meant was take a break. The others won't have Icarus ready for your tests until tomorrow, right?"

"Please?" said Megan. She laced her fingers together and held her arms down to produce a pleading gesture.

Sean didn't want to dwell on his personal problems, and Megan's pose moved him in a new direction. "OK, let's go."

* * *

Sean and Aurora waited on the sidewalk as Megan locked the office, upstairs. To keep from talk about money, Sean attempted a bland line of conversation. "Don't Andrew and Brandon come into their office much?"

Aurora pursed her lips as a bookmark to a serious observation. "Brandon much prefers the high rent district of the tower. Andrew is always on the hustle."

"Him, Mr. Personality, on the hustle?" Sean didn't much care about the distinction, but it kept the silence away.

"Hustle as in run around," Aurora offered. "He isn't schmoozing, if that was what you thought you heard."

"Just what is it that you two do, these days?"

Megan came lightly down the stairs, her metallic bob bouncing, and stepped into the conversation. "We would like to think we were the glue that held things together."

Aurora, in another out of character move, broke into a stage introduction. She waved her hands and declared "Aurora does the research, and—"

Megan followed suit with the theatrics. "—Megan does the analysis."

Sean laughed in surprise. "What?"

Aurora and Megan exchanged smiles and replayed their routine with a variation.

Megan did a pirouette and proclaimed "I do the research, and—" She raised her hand in presentation.

Aurora turned in place. "—I do the analysis."

"Betty taught us that," Aurora said with an hint of pride.

Sean was beginning to see that Betty was truly active in their life, even at a distance. "She was a dancer?"

Aurora made a rude noise. "No! Well maybe. It doesn't make any difference! She's a remarkable woman who thinks we work together well."

Sean put his hands up and shrugged in mock surrender. "I have to agree."

* * *

Betty's apartment was laid out in the same pattern of

rooms as was Wade's office. They were both in suites on high floors. With Betty's apartment as an example, then each had two separate entrances. One door connected from the corridor into the foyer that lead them into Betty's living room. Betty's other door connected from the same corridor at the back into Megan's bedroom. Sean thought about his usual business visits to Wade.

As he re-imagined them, Wade's office had the same arrangement as Megan's bedroom with Wade's far door to the corridor. Aurora had, more than once, pushed Sean to consider connecting the dots. The dots created a picture of Wade working out of his apartment.

It was upsetting how quickly those dots connected to his anxiety. It reminded him how his dad was now trying to reinvent himself in his own bachelor apartment? The prospects of that were slim. A man who worked with his brawn now trying to set up a home office? What was Sean doing here that could help his and his mother's situation?

Sean looked at Megan and Aurora chatting at the coffee table and anger in him surged unexpectedly. They were both comfortable daughters. Aurora came from a stable family, and Megan lived securely with her god mother. Anxiety, in place of prayers, nightly reminded Sean about the mortgage on their home before he could find sleep.

Megan came across the living room to Sean in his isolated chair. "Show me a smile, Mr. Grumpy."

Sean shrouded his feelings with a wan lift of the corners of his mouth.

Megan did a mock examination, and shrugged. "That'll do, I suppose." She quickly leaned forward and pecked him on the cheek.

"Thank you for trying. Come and join us over here."

Her words were suddenly muffled. Aurora may have said something. It might have been supportive. That was an impression that lifted him out of his chair. He walked carefully.

Each step felt deliberate. The ottoman, the coffee table, each were hazards to progress. Did it take him long to cross the room?

"Welcome, stranger," said Aurora.

"Um—Thanks," was the best he could mumble.

Aurora looked at Megan. "What did you do to him?"

Sean smiled at this. "Sorry, I must've stood up too fast."

"You OK now?" said Megan.

"Sure. Whassup?"

"You're still whacked out, Sean." Aurora didn't allow his feint in conversation to pass.

"I'll get you something to drink." Megan rushed off to the kitchen. Glasses clattered. Water ran. Ice clinked. A bottle opened and then gurgled as it was poured.

Soon, Megan arrived with three bucket sized glasses on an ornate silver platter. She put it down on the coffee table and then distributed the drinks.

Sean took one. It had a rich amber color. The taste of molasses was surprisingly light and the sweetness lingered beneath something else less familiar. "What is this?" is what he asked after he drained the glass.

"Would you like another?" asked Megan, eager to hear him say yes.

"Yes. What is it?"

"Betty's Choice."

Aurora tasted hers. "Is that the name of the drink, or

simply a statement?"

"It's what Betty calls it. The bottle's label says Blackstrap Rum." She returned to the kitchen with Sean's glass, and the familiar sounds repeated.

When she returned with Sean's refill, Aurora asked another question. "Betty likes rum?" The question carried a hint of a moralistic tone.

Megan smiled at the inquiry. "It's a learned taste, she says. She picked it up from Wade. Sailor's drink and all that."

Sean and Aurora were both surprised by this revelation. Sean reacted first. "She knows Wade so well that they drink together?"

Megan looked at them as though this was certainly no mystery. "Duh."

Aurora laughed. "Duh? C'mon, girlfriend, some facts behind that."

"You mean that you don't know ... She's his aunt."

Megan sat down nearby, next to Sean on the couch. "He moved into the Roosevelt Courtyard a couple years ago when she had a small stroke."

Sean noticed that Megan's hand was close to him on the couch. Her news had its element of surprise. It also explained one of his questions about Wade working out of his apartment. Those answers drifted through his mind unimpeded to allow him to focus on her hand. He sipped his refreshed drink now. "Wade was in the Navy?" He knew this, of course, but he asked anyway to keep himself in the conversation.

Megan turned to him, and shifted closer as if to tell a secret. "Yes. A long, long time ago," came in a half whisper.

Building Icarus

Sean looked out the windows. Just like Wade's view. A view of the water? Perhaps, Lake Union would be in view, perhaps, if he stood to see it. Then a reflex took hold of him and he laughed.

They looked at him with their own bemused smiles.

"At our age," Sean said, "everything is a long, long time ago." He went on to add to himself, "even a month ago."

Megan reached out and caressed his cheek. "Yes, you are right."

Aurora raised her eyebrows. "Perhaps I should find myself a room." When Megan turned to her comment, Aurora added a wink. "Time for me to head home. One's my limit, even if it is Betty's Choice."

STATIC TESTING

The flier Icarus and the conference table were in the center of the office. Workstations had been moved around it into a nearly full circle so that everyone could gaze on it as if it were their idol on the alter. They still had views of their own computer displays—their more personal deities. The circle also spoke to the inclusive shift that came with Sean's integration.

The sky outside, cluttered with a few clouds, cast a veil behind Seattle's new towers where lawyers sat looking over them. The obscured sun indirectly filled the office with an even flat lighting. This was enough to remove shadows and allow for a detailed view of Icarus from any angle.

The office maintained its quiet and composure. It was cleaner too. Gone were the stacked cups with their lingering scent of stale coffee. There seemed to be a correlation between the earlier fretting and grumbling, and the stress that proceeded their shift in mission. Now, as they were about to enter into testing the practical and real application of their design, the team was calmly subdued by focus.

Sean sat at his workstation. It was his now, no longer Jason's, especially when they rearranged the layout. Sean had donated one of the displays to Ashley. Her work was increasing in complexity and productive benefit as her design of Hermes ran more scripts to control the flight, and to perform the mission. Hermes was being tailored to be aware of its vast assembly of sensors. Sean hoped their tests would prove this.

He surveyed the rest of the office, and glanced at the closet. It was a mystery. It held far more computational horsepower than all of them together demanded. And yet it hummed unnoticed in the background of their activity. At some point, he was going to have to recruit Aurora to come over and give her appraisal about it.

Teodor was playing with the RC controller that Sophia had refashioned. He pressed some buttons to no effect. He flipped the unit end-over-end and found what appeared to Sean to be the on-off button. Teodor switched it regardless of its purpose, and then he righted the controller to re-press the same buttons. Again, his effort came to no effect. He, again, flipped the unit end-over-end. Sean thought Teodor could go on like that forever, so he looked back at the flier Icarus.

It was a large flier for its price range, but as it sat on the table, now this set of wings didn't reach over the edge. Icarus came with a set of two wings for differing applications. One configuration was marketed as the sport model, and the larger wing was marketed as the glider model. Earlier, the glider wing reached across the table top to lap across the aisles on either side.

Sophia had assembled it slowly, not because it pressed her capability, but more out of her reverence for good design that attracted her admiration for its details. She was still checking out the fit of the conventional servo control linkages as Teodor fumbled with the controller. As she worked, her dimples revealed her confidence. Her eyes danced as they scanned over the wiring.

"Sophie? What gives with this useless POS?" He put it down rather hard on the table.

Sophia glanced at it and then turned her attention back to the flier. "Did you put the batteries in, Teddy Bear?"

Teodor brusquely retrieved the controller and began his end-over-end examination, apparently searching for the battery compartment. He popped open a cover, muttered and oath, and went to a box. He rummaged for a while and withdrew a battery pack, put it in, and then snapped the lid shut.

Again came the end-over-end roll of the controller in his hands. He looked at the flier and pressed a button to no effect. Having gone down this path several times, he could now find the on-off switch. Pressing the controller button, however, still yielded no effect. "So, what is this for?"

Sophia raised her head to see Teodor handling the controller with increasing frustration. "Icarus needs its batteries installed too." She flexed her wrists before returning to her work.

"Mmm." Some of Teodor's frustration was defused, but an edge of agitation remained. "Does this do anything?" He pawed the surface of the controller.

"So far it has only one function. That button that you've been pressing is a dead man's switch. The other buttons and the joy stick don't do anything at all," she said.

Sophia went to the battery box and drew out a battery pack for the flier. She installed that quickly and smoothly, and closed the flier up. "OK. We're ready to rock'n'roll."

"Should I start the script for testing?" said Brandon. He clambered up from the sofa against the wall, and walked into the circle.

Sean nodded. Ashley waved her OK with that idea and bent close to her display as she put Hermes to work. Occasionally she would whip her long curl away—it would fall back unnoticed.

Nothing happened. Brandon looked at the flier. In a puzzled tone he offered "OK, so now what?"

Teodor interjected, "This isn't good."

Ashley whipped back from her console. "No RF Feed."

Sophia swung in her chair to face Teodor. "Teodor, now's the time for you to hold down that dead man's switch. Good. Ashley, we're ready, Girl, start the test script again."

As they watched, Icarus' rudder swung both ways to their limits. The movements were subtle, but obvious, and their repetition proved that their movement was not accidental. Then the elevators lifted and depressed. This was followed by similar movements of the wing's ailerons.

Time passed with nothing else happening. Brandon looked at his copy of Ashley's console display and nodded. "The reports are all in. Such as they are without our followers hooked up yet."

"Teodor?" said Sophia.

"Yes?"

"Are you still pressing that button?"

Teodor fumbled for a moment and said, "Yes."

"OK, Brandon. This time, instead of Ashley, you run the next script."

Icarus' rudder, elevators and ailerons all moved to specific positions. Brandon, still keeping most of his attention on his display reported, "We are in the loop right now. The report says OK, but there are several dozen warnings. Ashley, what's that about?"

"Icarus' sensors indicate that its attitude doesn't match its flight characteristics," she said.

"Its attitude. You mean like Icarus is expressing its contempt?" Brandon was further puzzled.

"No, silly. With Icarus in a loop, several of its sensors are reporting that it is actually in a level position. Instead of contempt, let's call that confusion. These warnings come from cross checks that in a more sophisticated script would call for action from Mission control, us in the downstream end of telemetry."

Brandon showed some consternation about this. "This is new to me, Ashley. Teodor, is it new to you too?"

"Sounds like the design we have taken into consideration in the advance stage scripts, Brandon," Teodor said.

Sophia stepped in, "Let's get the rest of this done before we talk the batteries to death. OK, Ted, release the button."

The control surfaces changed configuration. Brandon moved at his display and then glanced at the flier. "This is part of the plan." Then he added a plaintive question to Sophia, "Right?"

Sophia nodded. "The dead man switch works. The surfaces are set to glide in a descending spiral without power."

Sean now came into the conversation. "We don't have power to the propulsion for obvious reasons. So we don't know for sure if that power has been killed—just in case."

Brandon checked in again. "That means we kill power to the propulsion just in case of something going wrong with our custom control, right?"

Sean nodded. "That dead man's switch control goes over the conventional RC channel right now. And that is a single point of failure that we should consider and change in the future. That command should come through three different paths into a voting system."

Ashley, who had been working on script changes at her computer while watching, asked, "We use this dead man switch just in case of failure, and it is also a—what did you call it?—a single point of failure?"

"Well, it is a safe single point of failure. We share radio

space with all the other -um- amateurs on the field. If one of them accidentally sends a signal on our channel, then Icarus takes a dive regardless of our ability to control," said Sean.

"What I mean by safe, is that this switch, or someone else's control of this switch, puts Icarus into a defined shut down and it comes to ground in the most advantageous way."

Teodor laughed, "And thus we pay you the big bucks for platform stabilization—nose planted snuggly into the ground."

Sean joined with Teodor's laughter and found he was surprised that he hadn't taken the comment about money so deeply this time. Things were working well, they were ahead of schedule and the next set of tests promised equally good results. They were getting value for his charges, clearly, and he could tell that was the intent of Teodor's observation couched with a laugh.

Brandon pulled back from his workstation. "Well, sooner or later we have to light off the propulsion. Are we going to throw Icarus into the air and see if it flies?"

Sean considered this. "Ashley, is that how we are going to do this?"

Ashley pushed back from her workstation too. "We can. But I'm not sure we want to."

Brandon nodded. "But to test your platform stabilization routines, Icarus has to be in the air, right?"

Sean nodded and offered a wan smile at the investment account manager. "Teodor will have his thumb on the dead man's switch. Things won't get out of control for very long if tests prove to be negative."

Brandon shook his head. "There's nothing better?"

Sean smiled more firmly this time. "That's what you tell us. We could spend more money with university engineers sitting at mainframes running expensive simulations ... If you have more money to plug into this investment."

"Ouch!" came Brandon's answer. "Take your thumb out of my eye, will you? I just don't like the idea of planting roughly $5000 into the dirt the first time out."

Teodor made a dramatic gesture of removing his thumb from the button on the RC controller. "Brandon, it won't be a total loss." In an impish mood, Teodor lifted his hand high, and pantomimed Icarus spiraling down into the ground. To this perverse drama, he added a raspy whistle.

"Maybe a couple hundred bucks worst case, and that would have to be from a height of several hundred feet. If we could get it that high, then something must be working right." Teodor looked at Sean and smiled at him too. "This dead man's switch is great insurance." He looked at Brandon, "and cheap, too. Besides, even, say, $500 a week is negligible to our burn rate."

Brandon put his head in his hands. "Burn rate, don't remind me." He looked up and whistled out slowly before realizing its similarity to Teodor's crash simulation. "OK— let's get our failures done quickly and out of the way."

Teodor, with a slam-dunk gesture said, "Let's go for it!"

* * *

It was late in the afternoon when the sun had managed to find its way out from behind the occasional cloud and fill the office with unexpected color. The dark stain in the oak trim around the windows, in the door frames, and in the door panels flamed in ancient gold tones. However, this deep amber light made the darkness of the closet interior even darker in spite of its hanging lamp.

152

Sean drifted in thought about this lamp. It was one of those bare filament types. It cast shadows with harsh, hard edges. His thoughts diverted to how he was alone, and the rest of the group were off to catch something to eat, and that worked out just fine. Sean had begged off so that he and Aurora could do some investigation with this closeted computer rack without attracting attention.

Behind him, he heard the elevator open out in the corridor. Soon after, Ashley stepped into the frame of the open door, the sun brilliantly lit her figure in silhouette, with her mane burning.

Fine looking woman, Sean thought, but he would have liked to have seen Megan spotlit alongside of her. He tried to imagine Megan's metallic touches in her dark hair lit by the sun. But she wasn't there, and his wish would have to wait until another sunny day when they were outside. The odds of that were dreadfully slim, but he could bask in imagining the opportunity.

Aurora sloshed her coffee cup toward him in a gesture of greeting. "You riding high?" The aroma from her cup reminded Sean of his sacrifice of lunch and the pang woke him out of his day dream.

Sean considered her greeting—riding high—for a while before the subtle message clicked into place. It could have been about work, but not from her. Aurora was trying to make something out of Megan and him.

A thrill trembled across his shoulders. Heat from his core rose and brought a sweat to his forehead. Her probe had found him out. "Get real, Aurora. I left right after you did last night."

Aurora shrugged her shoulders and pressed on. "I didn't ask if you went home, but I guess I will have to take your word for it."

Sean swallowed hard. Pursuing her sly logic could take him places he wasn't prepared to visit yet. "We don't have much time to look at this." His voice felt sandy. Would she take this lead? Then he pointed at the closet rather late to make it seem natural.

Aurora glanced into the closet and strode in. She passed her hands over the rack's equipment and then she ducked around behind it where an old keyboard and display sat in the cobwebbed recess. "Yuck, its dusty back here. Do you have any cloths and spray?"

"Aurora, let's just get it done, can we?" Sean's voice now had the edge of whining, and he regretted he had said anything.

"Sean, this is going to be my office for an hour or so, and I want it clean. Get me a chair too."

Sean mechanically turned and searched out a simple kitchen chair they had. It was the only one that would fit behind the rack where the keyboard sat on its tray. Then he went down the hall to get a handful of wet paper towels from the rest room.

Aurora waited for his return, and then turned her efforts to cleaning the chair, the keyboard tray, the keyboard, and then the display—on every side of each of these. In all, from the time Sean drew the chair in, until she sat, it was very few minutes, but to Sean the time seemed to telescope out dangerously. Sean was too anxious to appreciate her fluid and economical motions.

When Aurora finally sat down, she looked like a pianist at a concert flexing her fingers before starting the first movement of a symphony. There was a sly smile on her face. "Still thinking of Megan?" She didn't wait for his response, being satisfied with his visible consternation. She turned her attention to the display as she entered commands.

Now Sean was thinking about Megan. The hanging lamp's glare was somewhat hidden by the rack. The sun's remote, lingering amber glow softened and filled the sharp shadows. Aurora's typing, clicking away, reminded him of those moments standing at peace in the pool hall. Megan was across the street from that pool hall. The hypnotic clicking slowly ushered her over to him. The heat of Aurora's sly jabs were renewed by his memory of the sweep of Megan's lips brushing his cheek. A ripple of excitement ran through him and his back arched slightly.

"The bandwidth on this is enormous!" Aurora's statement snapped him back to the present of the musty closet and the purpose of their clandestine meeting.

"Is that all you've found?" he asked.

"Half an hour has brought some interesting things into view, and the bandwidth is just frosting on the cake. I thought I would let you have the frosting first. Sweetie."

"Give me a break, Aurora."

"Oh let me enjoy myself. You two were so cute."

Aurora let the moment pass quickly and returned to her work. "This high speed switch is driving optical feeds for this floor. Oddly enough, this office doesn't use but, perhaps, one percent of its portion of the total feed."

"What's that mean? One percent of something like ten percent with ninety percent to nine other offices on this floor?"

"Something like that. At a guess, this office uses no more than 0.1% full capacity."

Sean did the math. "That all?"

"For hardware developers? That would seem to be excessive, but the logs reveal more," she said.

"More consumption? How much demand has been served to this office?"

Aurora weighed his question against her view of the logs. "Four months ago, about half the total capacity of this rack was handling traffic back and forth across the Pacific."

As Aurora closed down her network tools, Sean put this new fact into the mystery of Jason's activities. "This might be a lead into the second revenue stream that Wade asked us to look into."

Aurora shrugged. "Not much in the logs to tell us that."

Sean felt he had to risk something here. "Anyway those logs could have been edited to remove traces?"

Aurora looked at him quizzically, and then browsed the system some more. She hovered the mouse cursor over re-opening her tools, but stopped short. "That's pretty deep, Sean."

He could feel a flush move over him. "How's that?"

"If someone removed traces of their activity, then, by definition, we wouldn't see traces of their activity."

"I suppose not."

Aurora flicked the mouse. "I could dig some more, I suppose. If we have time. It sounds like hardware man might have an idea where to look."

"No, let's get this buttoned up." Sean wanted to hustle her out before her questions outran his and led to his hidden life.

Aurora stood up and started to shift the chair so they could take it out of the closet. "Such a shade of red you're wearing! If you're worried about appearances, like us being alone together in a dark closet before the others come back …"

"Aurora, where is your mind?" Sean fought her innuendo, but curiously enjoyed the inferences. Had he always been a romantic cipher to her before?

She wove the chair past him as it seemed he was stuck on the spot there. "Outside, Bucko."

Just as they finished straightening things, the team began to drift in from the corridor.

* * *

"Dude! That is really dark," said Teodor. "That can't be Jason. He was a loner, but that doesn't mean he is going to rip us off." Teodor wasn't taking this well, thought Sean. But news like this wasn't pleasant.

Sean had decided to tell the story of the ghost's visit on Sean's first night in the office. Perhaps telling it after the initial flush of their first tests on the static model wasn't well timed. However, there seemed to be no better time, and waiting wouldn't brighten prospects.

Perhaps he shouldn't have doubled down. Sean added the story of their second meeting in the bakery. He mentioned that Jason made a vague offering about something of value. However, he said nothing of the remainder of the deal where Jason was going to cut him in, alone.

Ashley thrashed out of her chair, to her feet. "You met him, but Jason, according to you, didn't say much."

Was there something else there in her protest?

Ashley stopped short and failed to follow through. There was more than enough steam behind her complaint that

Sean could see was corked up tight.

Sophia tried to fill in Ashley's gap. "All he did was offer to help. What is wrong with that?"

"Ashley," said Sean. "He was cutting a deal, not volunteering." He was beginning to recognize how this doubling down and his holding back Jason's offer to him had backed him into a corner.

"You say that like it was a drug deal." Ashley showed her wound, but her conviction was strangely absent.

Sean looked around the office. Teodor and Brandon had drifted away. They disconnected themselves from the discussion, but they still followed what was being said. Aurora was acting like a silent referee while standing off to the side.

Teodor sought to derail the tension. "Who's your friend?" he said indicating Aurora.

Brandon took this question. "This is Aurora who is helping Megan in our office in the square."

Teodor's attitude shifted. "You and Megan work together? Whowouldathought."

Aurora lifted her eyebrows. "Who wouldn't have thought? Why?"

Teodor tried to shrink his big shoulders and ducked his head. "Megan is -um- very, you know, kind of private." His face started to flush.

Aurora picked up on his embarrassment and bit her lip as she weighed what to say. "We do well together."

Brandon stepped in. "I should say so! Together, they've managed to help me and Andrew sort out some conflicting technical claims that are made by our teams in our portfolio."

"Brandon, that investment stuff is pretty dense," said Sophia. "Can you unpack what you just said?"

"That was the explanation for an investment term," sighed Brandon. "Aurora, sorry for the sloppy intro."

Aurora smiled at him and turned to the rest. "I help Megan. We have this pile of business plans. The best of the worst of them, make claims about their inventiveness. We fact-check, basically."

"Like Googling them?" suggested Sophia.

"Frequently. And just as often we rush over to the library to check with the reference librarians."

Sophia accepted that, and then added, "You say the best of the worst. How about the rest?"

"We check them too. When they have something to offer. You never know. Sometimes we discover that a group is unaware that they are sitting on a gold mine."

"Together, they go through three times as much as Megan did alone," Brandon beamed.

"This is all nice and well, but it has nothing to do with Jason," injected Ashley.

Sean wondered about her doggedness without passion. She seemed to be struggling for air in her sulk.

Brandon pressed Ashley on her focus. "You know something about Jason that would help?" When Ashley averted her face he added, "Has he been in contact with you," and he scanned the rest of them, "or anyone here?"

Ashley nodded, "Yes."

This apparently surprised everyone and they gave this their full attention.

"This is cards on the table time," said Brandon sternly, "It affects our investment in intellectual property."

Ashley thought about this deeply, and the time began to draw out. "Ashley?" prodded Brandon after a long interval.

"What?" her response was vague, her attention was uncentered.

Brandon said softly, "What's going on?"

"I didn't do anything wrong!" she answered.

Brandon kept his voice soft and asked, "Are you OK?"

Ashley still held her gaze low. She shrugged quickly. "Why are you asking me these things? Jason is gone."

"But you have talked recently? That's fine. We would like to know what it was about. If that isn't personal. You know. If it's about work."

Ashley shook her head.

"It's not about work?"

"It was about work. It's personal," came her conflicted response.

Brandon sat back. "Well, let's take this off the table for the time being." He turned to Sean and ran off a check list.

"So, what we have is Sean's visit late at night. He seems to have visited more than once. His visits seem tied to him acquiring a flash drive. We are missing half a dozen, or so. We are also missing our old robot, Diana. He still had access to a key until we re-keyed. There are these files that went missing from our repositories. There are these same files on the flash drive that Sean picked up in advance of Jason's visits."

Brandon took a breath to allow the facts to sink in. "According to Sean, he set up a honeypot sting for Jason's second visit, and he caught him buzzing around—rather quickly, too."

"Please," cried Ashley.

Brandon drew up short. "Do you have something to remove or add to this list, Ashley? Do you want to reopen your visit with him?"

"That buzzing around the honeypot is disgusting," cried Ashley.

Brandon considered this, and let her objection lie there.

"Maybe we should plan for tomorrow," offered Teodor.

Again, thought Sean, Teodor's contribution to the conversation seemed to be to defuse the tension. However, as things stood, it wasn't a bad suggestion. So he took it up and asked, "You ready to take to the air?"

* * *

Teodor's shift of topic and Sean's followup were held off until everyone got some coffee outside of the office. This quarter hour off helped make the transition. Still, there was some sense of everyone walking on eggs.

Ashley seemed to have regained her composure. There was a chance, Sean thought, that she and Brandon had squared the details of her meeting with Jason.

The crew stood around Icarus in a subdued mood. No one was ready to step into the vacuum except for Brandon.

"Are we ready to take to the air?" he said.

It should have been an easy opener. Everyone was slow to nod, shrug, or grunt—but they eventually came to agreement. What was needed was some enthusiasm. Again, Brandon took on the task of pumping them up.

"Teodor? How do we actually fly this if the RC controller is simply a brake with that dead man's switch?"

"We'll have joystick control, actually a mouse, in the van. It will connect through telemetry on a non-RC frequency."

Brandon already knew this. Everyone knew he knew it. Everyone was used to his form of project meetings where he played the dummy. Dumbing it down was what he needed in order to frame their work in terms suited for investors. The crew had even thanked him for his dense headed questions that forced them to re-examine the design choices they had made. Not many changes came of this form of review. Perhaps one in twenty questions forced a reboot. The reboots lifted the boats on a new tide.

"Who's the pilot here?"

Ashley took in a deep breath and sat upright. "Sophia is the one with the mouse and the video feed from Icarus. However, her control is an override to an autopilot that engages from the time Icarus is on the runway."

"What do you mean by autopilot, Ashley?" Brandon's voice had softened for her.

"Script. Hermes is operating a script that describes the mission as a set of objectives."

"And that is our secret sauce, isn't it?" asked Brandon.

Ashley stiffened, and then resumed her role in this familiar drill of project review. "Yes, we are striking for a completely human free drone navigation system."

Brandon turned to Sophia to ask a question, and to also take that last spike of pressure off of Ashley. "Sophia?"

"Yes Brandon?"

"Have we got our down-looking camera on board?"

Sophia nodded. "Only for testing weight distribution—balance, you know—and total wing load."

"So, it is not operational for navigation I take it."

"No, that integration will come with our more frequent static testing here in the office after the first fly-off. Provided that our first test doesn't have Icarus flying off to Canada."

Teodor chuckled at that, as did Sean and Aurora. Ashley smiled. It looked to Sean that the ice had thawed. Taking this natural pause, Aurora offered her goodbyes and shifted towards the door. Sean followed to her slight tip of the head.

* * *

"She's got a thing going on with Jason," explained Aurora.

They stood near the elevator. The marbled glass door panels up and down the corridor were glowing with various hues of color coming from the sky outside as the sun's final light shifted in and out of the clouds.

"Am I hearing you right?" Sean suspected he was, but this was something that was unexpected. Then he thought about Megan's overture. "Talk about out of the blue."

"Seems like you answered your own question, Sean. However, you've been up close and personal with Jason. What do you think?"

"I find him … unlovable." Sean added a weak grin and searched for other words in a struggle to close down her question. "Stiff, hard to approach, arrogant, difficult—"

"—I get it. I get it." Aurora weighed his response to offer, "Who are we talking about?" Without waiting, she shifted. "Sorry. By the way, that is quite a crew you have here at *GyroNautica*. Everyone's tight. You handled yourself quite well."

Then Aurora shifted again. "Back to Jason. What's his hold? We can guess that, even if it doesn't make sense. Maybe events will break the hold. Poor Ashley."

163

Sean nodded sadly. Indeed, for relationships that derail, Sean already knew that agony and had lived with it for several years now. It reminded him of his mother's pain, and what drove him to take Brandon's offer of inflating his time-sheets.

He acknowledged to himself that he, indeed, was always on the clock in his head with this project. However, there was his father's old fashioned cultural bias of clock punching and never bringing work home. This gave him push back.

Aurora, breaking Sean's reflective mood, returned to their current interest. "Ashley needs to work it out for herself. I think she'll ask for help at some point."

Aurora's face revealed something emerged that was more complex. "I wonder whose trust she thinks she's violating?"

Sean now recognized Aurora's radar was engaged. Trust was certainly a hot button for her. He knew that Aurora was now on the right path of examination.

She continued with, "Did you catch how Brandon called Hermes their secret sauce? Running that executable has led us to grief back at the office."

Sean nodded. "And there must be some significance in Jason trying to reclaim the more complete script."

"Really," signified Aurora.

"The secret sauce is equal parts Hermes and the script. One is the engine, the other is the fuel." Sean explained.

Aurora wasn't entirely convinced. "Hermes seems to be a substantial component to an otherwise pedestrian flying robot. On one hand, the script we ran didn't give me the impression of anything even remotely connected to that mission. On the other hand, what's in the script must be a key to something."

Sean nodded to that, but he nervously wanted to keep his distance here. His hand was in many scripts in the past that he just as soon wished never emerged again.

"If that key isn't immediately obvious, we will have insight through the script writer's style," he said. And he realized he may have said too much for a simple hardware engineer.

Aurora latched onto this. "Style," she said, "where did that come from?"

"Just babbling on," he said. "Somehow scripts and plays I've gone to sort of mashed up here."

"Makes you something of an expert, then," said Aurora. "Sean, why do I get the feeling you're hedging?"

He knew she was calling him out. To move forward meant he had to tip his hand.

"I think you, Megan, and I should revisit Jason's flash drive and follow any relationships we can discover in his script files," He said. "Scripts are tops for that. Especially where we found relationships between rather obscure atoms —those curious phrases that defied us."

"Curious phrases, yes, but atoms?" she echoed. "Calling them atoms sounds like we're way beyond my skills with Linux shell scripts."

"It's the most elemental part of the script that is not an abstraction," he said. "It is literal. An atom is complete and when a translator hits one, the translator triggers an action— a computer command that is tailored with all the adverbs and adjectives that had been encoded in the script phrases before that atom fired."

"I thought you flunked English," she said. "Atoms, adjectives … This talk is like looking through the wrong end of a telescope."

He searched for a metaphor. "I can see all the relationships in a script written in, let's say, Greek. However, I don't need to know a word of Greek to follow the flow of the script."

"Hermes, Icarus, Greek," she said. "We seem to be following a theme here."

Sean nodded. "It's like we're watching a Greek tragedy in the original language."

"Not my idea of a fun evening," said Aurora.

Sean had to back his way out and start over. "The script defines the actors, time, and setting. The actors reveal their relationships through script triggered actions. The actions give shape to the story. Style offers uniquely plotted patterns in the story."

"Where do you get all that stuff?" she said. "This comes from all those plays your mother insisted you go to with her."

"Back when I couldn't say no," he said. "Doesn't my theatrical analogy make sense?"

"You certainly answered my question about style," she said. "And the next time I hear about atoms in scripts—talk about style—I will be sure the speaker is as spooky as you."

Aurora walked away from the windows they had stood near, and to the elevator. She pressed the call button and straightened herself out in preparation for leaving.

"Well, thanks for the fun in the closet, the party with your friends, and the lesson in drama," joked Aurora. "I've got to do some actual work. Want to follow me back to Pribylov's?" She added a knowing wink to prod him along.

Sean wanted to see Megan again … "I don't think so." Duty stood in his way.

Aurora furrowed her brow so tight that her auburn

eyebrows merged. "Do the right thing, Sean."

"What do you mean?"

"Take yourself off the clock. Just get your hat and hit the road with me. C'mon."

"No. No. I've got tomorrow to prepare for. Help Sophia with the tie-in of feedback system. And stuff like that."

Aurora sighed as the elevator door whispered opened. She stepped into it and left Sean to return to his office.

* * *

"You've got me flying high and wide," sang Sophia in a quiet voice along with Ella Fitzgerald playing on her mobile. She was bent over Icarus. Her hands were unnaturally twisted into a void within the flier that she had hogged out earlier.

She looked up as Sean came into the office from the corridor. "Just in time. Help hold this, would you?"

Sean helped her feed a cable deep into the interior and mate the connectors between the radio and a sensor.

"Couldn't you build these with longer leads?" she complained. "Look at your own hands. You could never have got them into here to hook things up."

"Extra length is extra weight, and the sensor is where it is to help balance the load. Sorry, Sophia, Teodor has been on me about there being a lot of weight variables to consider."

"So, in a sense, your engineering is a matter of conflict management, hmm?" Sophia looked up to impress this point, so it seemed that, perhaps, this was a wry joke.

"Never thought of it in those terms, but, yes." Sean considered that his specialty there as the platform stabilization designer was to reduce conflicting messages from the constellation of sensors that describe Icarus' place in space. As the design progressed, there would be more sensors tied in. At this time, many were being carried as dead weight.

Sophia held her gaze on him. "So that's what floats your boat?"

"Sophia, you certainly are a font of reductions this afternoon." Sean wondered what was going on. What seemed a joke had taken a strange turn.

"Odd things going on today. Remember, you stirred up the mud, and now the water is cloudy."

The others in the office were lost in their own work, and this seemed to be a private conversation between him and Sophia. This indicated a new level of intensity had risen. No doubt the thoughts that filled the team's minds varied from excitement through to dread.

Brandon clearly was watching the budget's bottom line if they crashed. That was a rather ordinary dread. Ashley seemed to have a dread that reached deeper. Teodor and Sophia were mission oriented, and both were jazzed up with thoughts of flight. Sean could identify with them, but when he thought about Jason's offer, somehow Ashley's mix of reactions tracked in him.

What would be the net sum of these tensions expressed in Icarus? To Sean, Icarus' flight could follow a varying compass of emotions and escape their planned course.

Fitting Icarus' tragedy, were they already skirting too close to the sun? Sean tried to shake off this ancient metaphor, but there was no denying that things were edgy.

"Conflict management, conflict avoidance. Have you any circuits designed for anxiety?" Sophia seemed to be reading Sean's thoughts.

Sean laughed with a bark. "Don't I wish!" It caught the attention of the others, but they quickly submerged into their activities.

"Don't I wish," he repeated with the lowered voice of prayer. Then, pensively, he added "Sophia, that is a good question. Technically, that is."

"I'm sure we were both thinking—technically," mocked Sophia.

Sophia had been finishing up installation of all of Sean's peripheral sensors. "So, do we move on to round two of static testing?"

"Yes, let's do that." Sean reached out for the battery pack for Icarus and slid it into the compartment. This was in front of the new void now housing telemetry and some of his sensor support card designs. At the same time, he unhooked one connector. "We won't need the dead man's switch for this."

Sophia went to the master workstation where telemetry was connected to. Sean motioned for Sophia to hold up. He crossed the office and got their field lap-top that was going to be in the van and returned with it.

"Hook up to this."

Sophia nodded. "Good idea, test things as close to actual as we can." When she finished making the transfer of new telemetry scripts to the lap-top she booted up. "OK, we are on the air."

"We have power. Icarus should be giving you a feed."

"I've got raw feed here in the console."

Sean then went through his mental checklist. "Start up the emulator."

"Emulator running."

"How are the platform readings? Any outliers?"

Sophia carefully observed all the online sensor settings, the online sensor readings, and the warning indicators. "Readings agree with settings, and indicators are all green."

Sean stood with his feet shoulder width apart. "OK, we are going to do a slight dynamic test." He bent at the waist and took the fuselage ends in his hands. "Any change in readings?"

"None."

"OK, Icarus can climb fast, but I don't know the metrics. However, I do know it will climb nearly vertical with its glider wing. Something we will be using. Make sure to have it in the van, Sophia. But for now, get ready. Turn on the charting too."

"Charts are running. OK."

Sean lifted the front of the flier and then lifted it quickly above his head. "Shut down charting." He put Icarus back on the table and joined Sophia.

Together, they studied the charts generated from Sean's sensor test feed. Sean mused over them, muttering about what they could see. "All accelerometer axis readings are consistent with a steep climb from the initial level. The gyro shows the change in attitude."

Sophia nodded and added, "The spike of your sudden speed change is aligned with the G spike. Trim looks good."

Then Sean pushed back from the lap-top. "We need to see a sustained flight to assess the whole package."

Sophia was now being joined by Teodor and Ashley. Ashley's mood was still subdued. They looked over the charted data from Sean's sensors. Teodor stroked his chin and then rubbed his nose. "Are we going to be able to fly by wire, Sean? Sophia?"

"It's all there on the screen," indicated Sophia.

Teodor took this in and hesitated before asking, "Ashley, I see this noise here." He pointed it out on the display. "Think Hermes can cope with this?"

Ashley's face showed pain from an unknown source. "We are using the fastest laptop we have. Telemetry only manages the broad scope of sending commands and looking at stability to update commands.

"There's no way to check that loop in static, or Sean's limited dynamic tests."

Teodor was not satisfied. "Just tell me about coping with this noise."

Ashley took that criticism poorly. "Who can account for Sean's trying to model a shaky climb for a quarter second?"

"Ashley, the point is something's got to be prepared for this stretch of data from any source of shaking."

"Isn't that Sean's job?" objected Ashley.

Brandon, who had been hanging in the background, offered a grim smile in response to Ashley's abrasive performance.

Sean was pacing around to reduce his own tension, but it wasn't enough. "OK. Let's button up Icarus for tomorrow's flight. I gotta take a break."

* * *

Sean closed the office door behind him as he entered the corridor. He felt the hot flush that erupted with Ashley's criticism. In the few paces to the elevator he tried to smooth his ragged breath.

The jubilation was fading. He was standing on a

ledge crumbling with Ashley's anger.

Jim opened the car door. It was empty of passengers. Sean stepped in without his usual greeting. Jim closed the door and pushed the lever to lower them to the tower foyer. The floors slipped by quickly.

"How's things?" Jim asked.

"That covers a lot of life … Jim."

"That's what I meant."

Sean weighed his anxieties. "Where do I start … on this short flight?"

Jim smiled, knowing that the *GyroNautica* crew was increasingly using flying metaphors. "Where do you hurt?"

"My breath … is hard to come by."

Jim gave a quick shift to the lever short of the first floor, and the car bobbed unexpectedly. Sean reached out for balance and gasped, "Are you crazy, Jim?"

"I see you've found your breath, Sean."

Jim opened the car door to a small group seeking their way upstairs. Sean wove between them. Through the foyer, he pressed forward in anxious strides. Somehow, he had been deeply affected by Ashley's emotional reaction. He had to escape.

Outside, the day was uncharacteristically warm. The breeze of a downdraft from the building's shadowed side calmed the heat of Ashley's blame. Sean stepped out of the doorway and to the side to let it soak in. Soon, he could bring his senses to bear, but hazily he considered his path toward the Pioneer Square district.

Where was he going? Why?

Autopilot would have him heading for *Pribylov Investment.*

His usual agenda when he went there was to ask questions and get answers. The nervous drama in the tower would unlikely find answers there.

Unless Aurora or Megan had the back story on Ashley's descent into darkness, what could he achieve going there? That, of course, simply suggested that answers for her were not going to be found. Aurora had her spin on it. But that seemed to be contrived from a Harlequin romance.

He decided, as he had already announced, that he needed a break. Perhaps a walk would do that. And with that he meandered in a direction that loosely suggested its way to Pribylov.

SNOOKER

The brick buildings of the Pioneer Square district were a rag-tag mix. Some had interesting architectural features. Sean especially enjoyed the bay windows. Some buildings offered several floors of turreted nooks, something more elaborate than bay windows, rising up their flat fronts. There were arches capped on rustic columns bracing the main entrances. Other buildings were small store fronts with a neighboring doorway to a floor of rented rooms above them.

Along the avenue was the State Hotel with a neon sign that advertised rooms for 75¢. The sign offered a cultural companion to the plain Snooker sign that was only a short distance from that. If he needed a break, the pool hall had been an oasis from bother. Sean turned his path toward it.

He reached his usual spot of seclusion among the low hanging lights. The click of ball strikes and hushed voices brought a familiar relaxation. However, there was an occasional cheer; but that occurred infrequently, and within this familiar space, it didn't interrupt Sean's meditation.

"You looking for a game?" A familiar voice took Sean out of his reverie. He found Megan standing at the nearest table with a cue stick. "Or did you come to see the money game over there?" She tipped her cue toward the group of people in the back.

Megan didn't wait for him to answer, but instead started to rack up on the table between them. She looked at him for some response. "Cues are on the wall. They aren't very good. You take what you can." Again she tipped her cue, one of fine wood, toward the line of careworn cues that were as old as the building.

"Strange to find you here," said Sean.

"Oh, I don't know. I've been coming here for years with

Betty." Megan smiled at his mild surprise. "However, finding you here is a first for all my visits. This place isn't on the tourist maps, but it has a far more interesting history than the saloons nearby. You didn't simply cross the street in the wrong direction, did you?"

"What if I said Jack sent me?" Sean drew this cliche out for a second time since his bus ride with Betty.

Megan leaned back on the table behind her and shrugged. "That recommendation's likely to find you out on the sidewalk."

He focused on the pout she made, her dark cherry lips contrasting against her smooth white cheeks. "Yeah, I heard that somewhere," he said. "How about Betty sent me?"

Megan smiled, "Ah! Yes, you have been warned." She stood up to her full five foot two and wagged her head at him. Her thick and bobbed hair captured the table's light. Its metallic red danced with life.

Sean drew in the effect of her move and then returned to the stale line of conversation he began. "Yeah. Betty did send me, or, at least, she is why I decided to visit here several times now."

Megan tipped her cue to those on the walls to silently repeat her earlier question. "So, do you want to play together?"

He so needed to do that.

Sean walked to the wall and took down a cue. He knew a little about how to check it. He rolled it on the table to see if it was warped. It was, but likely as not no worse than the rest. Meanwhile, Megan racked the balls and set up the cue for lagging.

"What shall we play?" she asked.

"Eight ball is the only game I've played."

She nodded and then struck the cue ball lightly and they watched it rebound against the foot rail and settle to a stop short of the head rail.

"Let's see if I can do better," said Sean. He struck the cue ball harder and it rebounded off both rails, stopping further away from the head rail. "Mmm. Looks like lady's choice."

"You have manners, I see," toyed Megan. "I think I'll break."

She snapped the cue ball hard into the pack with a crack, scattering the balls across the table with one striped ball sinking. Sean would have allowed that to the luck of her power, but then she shifted her energy into gliding around the table light and silently like a deer hunter moving through mountain pines.

As she stood before a shot, she checked the tip of her cue with a glance. With a smooth fluid motion, she drew her cue stick into position, tapped the cue ball hard enough to sink another striped ball into a pocket but leave the cue in that ball's place.

Megan swung around the table to take another shot in the opposite direction, but it failed to sink any balls. The cue ball was also left in a poor position for Sean. She smiled at her leave for him and said, "Snookered."

He was not going to make a great impression from here, thought Sean. And he fulfilled his prophecy as he struggled through his shot. She recouped with another stripe sunk, but the following one missed. Sean then began a strategy of no strategy. He slammed the cue ball into the dense center of balls on the table, hoping for the best of outcomes. He achieved one solid being sunk, but also sunk one of hers in the process.

"Your god-mother, Betty, can probably do better than I can," muttered Sean to the green baize of the table.

Megan sunk another stripe and paused once she found another opportunity. "I doubt that she could. I've never seen her pick up a cue. However, she does have the capacity to surprise people, including me." Megan sent another stripe home. As she shifted to another position, Megan appraised her lay and then started ducking all the balls into the pockets with her hands. "This isn't any fun for us. It's time to go to work."

"Let's sit down first," suggested Sean. "There's some chairs over there."

"Sure." Megan took her cue apart and put it into its case. She grabbed her purse from beneath the table and followed Sean to the seats across the hall.

Sean took in a breath and surveyed the room. He could smell the room's combination of mustiness, the suggestion of a century's smoke from men departed, and Megan's light scent. He shifted closer to her and she reduced the distance even more.

The players in the distance were still surrounded by a mute crowd. The sound of the balls striking weren't as violent as his impression of Megan's last run. However, the room seemed to soak up the far sounds and lights to give them an intimate space together in their dark corner.

"What's up?" she said into his ear. She swept her hair aside, with her hand brushing against his shoulder doing it.

Sean bided his time in responding to her question. Clearly, Megan had identified a line they were about to cross as going from fun to work. It didn't seem he was ready for fun, however. With that failed attempt behind them, Sean regrettably faced the poorer choice.

"About work," came his introduction to their shift in activity.

"About work," she echoed. Her finger traced a pattern on his arm.

"About your work, to some degree," he said, "I know about that through Aurora." His mind was drifting, following the arc she drew.

"I like her. We cleared up one line I don't like getting crossed. As for work, I don't generally get along well sharing things, but that's worked out fine between us too."

Sean weighed that statement. Sharing what things? This was like a strange beacon in the fog where there was supposed to be no coast or rocks. However, the warning of lines being crossed was on the charts now.

Apparently, Megan sensed his examining her last response. "Sharing a task. Sharing responsibility for my job. Stuff like that. Andrew and Brandon can certainly pass a load of work over to me. I want to please them."

"So do we all."

"And then there's Betty."

"Betty," echoed Sean.

"She's got some money in their schemes."

"Is that bad? You certainly have a front row seat at Pribylov to see how things lie. And if I'm any judge of how you know how to appraise a lie, like our game at the table, you've got the knack."

Megan shook her head. "No, nothing wrong that isn't ordinarily part of the game."

"And yet you use the word ... schemes," said Sean.

"I'm not a gambler like Betty."

"What worries you about Betty, and Andrew, and

178

Brandon?"

"I'm not worried about her, except that I might not be able to protect her investments." Megan became agitated. She flustered through more explanation with false starts that died quickly.

"Something strange going on?" said Sean.

"Aurora told me about Ashley getting upset."

"Do you know anything behind that? Aurora suggest that …" He closed that statement with a shrug.

"Aurora is right, if that is what you mean. She doesn't know Ashley, but she recognized Ashley's problem."

"Can you fill in the blanks for me, Megan?" Sean was struggling. "I'm only picking up the vibes."

"Aurora already told you, Sean. Ashley and Jason had this thing going on. And for a long time."

"When did it stop?" he said. "I presume it wasn't a clean break." And with that comment it suddenly struck Sean how much he was invested with this turn of events, as if though it were something between his parents.

Perhaps if he could get things to fit together. Then he could … *That's clearly a fantasy heading towards grief,* he thought.

"I'm not that close to the group," she said. "I talk with Teodor a bit, and he gave me the news. As best as I can make it, they split up a couple of weeks before Brandon ushered Jason out of the company."

"Brandon has said nothing about this angle?"

"Not him, but I doubt if their relationship was lost on him." Megan patted his hand. "But guys don't always get it."

"Like, I don't get it?" he said. "I'm at the beginning of that list. Is there something else?"

Megan pressed against him. "You already know the answer to that. You just need to ask about the elephant in the room for yourself."

"Elephant ..." Sean muttered. "Yeah—you did say something about a line. Must be important to you,"

"It's important to who?" she said.

Sean was afraid of all the possible outcomes to what was important. But why be afraid? Megan was close. He enjoyed that. He wanted that. That was important.

So, it wasn't a line he had crossed, he thought. And he knew what she was prompting him for. All that was left was to believe it, say it, and act on it.

"It is important for both of us."

"And for Ashley and Jason, too," she said.

This shocked Sean. He was unprepared for their inclusion. "Crossing a line involves them—and us?"

"Sean?" she said. "You are great at making connections —up to a point. At least you remembered about crossed lines. I'm glad you said that."

"This is getting too much for me," he said. "I need some help with this."

Megan looped her arm into his. "Remember when you and Aurora came in, the first time?"

"Yeah."

Megan tugged at his arm to draw his ear close. "I was bad."

"Bad." A shiver ran through him.

"I was treating Aurora like a competitor."

"For work?" he said without believing it. It didn't make sense, for one. And then her and Aurora quickly coming to terms, and being so close for another. "You must've thought that Aurora and I—"

"—Were a thing." She strained closer to his ear. "I was acting like Aurora had what I wanted. I hope I don't have to explain more. That part wasn't easy to say."

Sean could now attest to that. Her grip on his arm was numbing it. She had been pulling his shoulder out of shape. She squirmed up to one knee to gain height, climbing his arm. He wanted to hold her, but this was awkward. He managed to say, "So, it was like Aurora crossed … the line before we came in."

"And?" she asked, her lips warm against the lobe of his ear.

"I like it."

"What?"

"I like the way it is now," he said. He turned his head to add something else, but she gave him a kiss. They enjoyed that for too brief a time.

"Mmm, good." Megan bounced out of her seat.

This snapped Sean out of it. He knew he didn't want to change anything now, but Megan clearly had something on her agenda.

"Remember work?" she said.

"Do I have to? When there is so much that could be better?"

"But more comfortably somewhere else. Time to cross the street, Sean."

They gathered up their things and headed out.

On the sidewalk they were out of the sun. They were where the street was draped in dense green, but it was brighter than they were used to. As they stood to let their eyes adjust, Sean recalled something that still stuck in his mind. Something he didn't want to cloud their growing closeness, but still needed to be aired.

"I'd like to ask about crossing the line some more," he said.

"We're safe," she said.

"It's about Ashley and Jason."

"Oh. Yeah. What I said, before. Just a feeling, you know." Megan gathered her words slowly. "Those two— someone crossed a line somewhere. It's not a nice place for me. It must be a bad place for others, too."

Megan and Sean went to the sidewalk's edge and she lead them across, weaving through the traffic standing at the light, bounding over the tree lined median and then across the open lane to Pribylov.

* * *

"Sean, there's not much I can add," said Megan. "You might find out more from Teodor."

Aurora was uncharacteristically bristling against Sean's pressing the topic. "Sean, cool it. The simple fact of it is a failed love. Life goes on. Come to terms with it."

This stung Sean. It was too close to his family experience. Surely, Aurora must be aware of his own pain. Possibly not. His family was stoic. It was a perverse balance they played at home. In the end, Dad saw the shame of self proclaimed failure as better than the shame in asking for help.

But what problem connected failure to abandonment was

the solution? Sean knew Dad's moral equation had to be just as unclear to others. Friends, sometimes, acted as if they were walking on eggs near Sean. *Was he as injured as Ashley?*

"This needs to be sorted out," said Sean.

Aurora shook her head. "And how far is that going to go with three people, here," she pointed down with both hands, "who know next to nothing beyond a guess?"

Sean needed to put the brakes on pressing them for an explanation. They acted as if it were a part of human nature that was inaccessible to him. This made him angry.

Megan stepped in with a suggestion. "There are only two people who know the answer, Sean. I don't suppose Jason is going to open up—if you could sit him down in front of you. And one thing that hasn't been said here is what does it matter?"

Sean found that this was a question he couldn't answer out loud. It was important, he was sure. And it was important beyond his personal need.

"There is something elemental about all the curious problems that surround *GyroNautica*. Ashley and Jason seem to be pivotal."

Aurora and Megan listened without comment. However, their silence suggested that they were weighing his point. No one could appreciate the warm, soft sunlight filtering through the trees and into the office. Small motes of dust danced in some of the sharper beams that penetrated the green leafed curtain. Even the noise of traffic had calmed to mark the moment lost on them.

Megan said, "Well, it seems that only time will tell. The missing parts of this story will come out sooner or later."

"Sean?" said Aurora. "You want me to drop in on your first flight tomorrow? I can try to mix in and pick up some of the story."

Sean relaxed with their helpful comments. "Yes, thanks. Come out and watch. Make a picnic of it."

Megan brightened with that. "Now there's a suggestion I can get my arms around. What do you say to a picnic, Aurora?"

"Let's do it. I can bring a summer salad."

Once again, the world had slipped off its axis with them planning a picnic at his offhand suggestion. Still, they were on his side, working hard to be there, and it had been his suggestion—however offhand it was.

He surrendered. "OK, but bring umbrellas too."

Aurora and Megan plunged further into their picnic plans. Sean left them to this and decided he needed the quiet comfort of his familiar cave at home.

* * *

Sean spent the bulk of Friday afternoon, evening, and night smoothing out his design that integrated the sensors placed throughout Icarus. His cave, downstairs, was remote from both sun and rain. Through the years, its temperature would hold steady around 65. It was warm enough to keep the musty threat of mildew suppressed. It was also not so hot as to feel too close—but only when he didn't work through the night like he had last night.

He pushed back from his work when he felt air flood down from upstairs. Mom must have gone out to get the morning paper. When an outside door was opened, the stairwell acted like a chimney, lifting out last night's air, and filling his cave with a new breath.

Sean, at this hour, was finishing up using Ashley's high level script design. He groggily imagined the needs of the flier, and anticipated the instabilities that could come from many sources.

This he over-worked into a scenario with the classic butterfly effect. Could his design anticipate how the beat of a butterfly's wings in Japan might initiate a catastrophic chain of events capped off with a typhoon boiling down Puget Sound to whip Icarus out over Mount Rainier?

It was just such a strained fantasy that played out in his fogged mind as he awoke after nodding off at his computer. What was amusing going to sleep was disturbing on waking. How much was he influenced by omen, augury, or divination?

This was a question that was not far from his current designs. There were many staid and risk avoiding coders who drew back when he talked about Fuzzy Logic. They were often the few college scholars that vaguely knew what he was talking about. The scholars had encountered this field in only one class that was an omnibus of mismatched topics. That is, they had a vague introduction which they quickly left behind.

Sean's Fuzzy Logic design solutions made his designs shine at the various presentations he had done at *Beyond the CyberDome*. Instead of the conventional 1s and 0s of binary design, Fuzzy Logic worked with fractions of 1 that offered more flexibility. Many in the audience caught his analogies quickly.

He taught them that a binary yes or no might be fuzzily expressed as probable or unlikely. Framing his talks in terms of Dr Who's *TARDIS* played to the fringe element that flocked there. The could immediately recognize that the

Doctor often got close enough without having to be exact.

The *TARDIS* Stabilization Problem was an example of insider humor that played well at these group events; especially when they all appreciated how little stability the *TARDIS* offered in any program episode. Was this humor going to haunt him in this afternoon's flight?

"You coming up for breakfast?" said his mother.

"Coming!"

Sean put together his own breakfast from an assortment of grains, dried fruits, and nuts. His mother had already poured some orange juice for him and put it at his place on the table.

She was waiting for his company before she began eating her own oatmeal. The scent of its cinnamon gave the morning's air a flourish.

"How are things this morning?" she said.

"I dreamt of butterflies again," he said simply.

"And wind storms?" continued Melissa.

"All part of a project that is going on this afternoon."

"Are you going to spend a rare nice day indoors again?" she said.

Sean smiled and let his spoon clatter down. "No, we will be outside for all of this."

"That's a nice change. With your new friends?"

Sean shrugged noncommittally.

"Sean, you need to open up more," said Melissa.

"How?"

"At least admit you have some friends."

"This is work, mother."

"Even at work, I presume this is work through your friend Wade, there must be some form of friendship about it."

Sean thought about his mother tying Wade into an association of friendship. He wasn't about to deny it, but neither did he want to express it. Saying it would bring bad luck. Where did he stand on omen, augury, or divination?

Then he thought about Megan. "There could be some friends."

"Any interesting girls at work?"

Sean often wondered if his mother were a mind reader, or perhaps an extraterrestrial. "Mom, sometimes I think that my success in designing things came invested with your ability to drill down with questions."

"You're welcome. Does that include evading some?"

Sean knew that she was going to keep him pinned down on this until he gave an honest answer. She could measure that to infinite precision too. She and Aurora shared that talent, and with that thought, he sensed a safe, neutral out. "There's Aurora."

"That's nice. Do you two have something going on?"

His mother shocked him at several levels. Her question echoed with the back story of Ashley, and traced around the edges of his desire for Megan. "Mom, is there anything at the table that isn't off limits?" Having said this, he knew he was only squirming in a trap that tightens.

"Hmm?" came her feigned innocent response.

"No!" He felt himself struggling, still—this wasn't going to pay off.

Melissa took another spoon of her breakfast, and she ate it slowly while waiting for him to continue.

He decided to wait her out. But he was going to have to fill the void in conversation. He also had to try to deflect the point of her questions. "I've got to rush. We are going to be testing an RC model airplane out at the park."

"How many of your friends are going to be there?"

"I would suspect the whole lot of them—and more. I made the mistake of cynically suggesting it was going to be a picnic. You know, like instead it was actually going to be hard work? They took my picnic quip literally, and now it's getting out of hand."

"I can bring some buns and cooked hot dogs," she volunteered.

Sean's attempt at steering his mother's conversation away from heading toward Megan had blown up. Instead, he had turned his mother from a remote bystander into a participant. This came from working too hard to control the situation.

Surrender was the only option. "That would probably go down well, Mom."

"Don't worry, Sean. I won't cramp your style with your special friend. She won't even notice me."

"I don't believe that for a moment, Mom." Sean cringed at her use of special friend. "All I ask is that you don't start drilling down there. Know what I mean?"

His mother crossed her heart, "It will be a picnic."

Sean wondered how many ways that could go.

A PICNIC

Their choice for the first flight of Icarus wasn't well planned, it was simply one step that followed the last. Further, this being a rare nice weekend, club attendance at the airfield was high. Failure wouldn't be inconspicuous.

Sean found *GyroNautica*'s own complement had ballooned through the additional participation of friends and relatives. Many from the office had arrived in the van, a throwback to the 70's with shag carpeting and airliner passenger seats that Teodor's father had obtained from Boeing surplus. As Sean took stock of their ad hoc fan club, he noticed Betty had arrived with Megan. There was also his mother who was spreading a picnic on a large, patterned, light blanket.

"Sean! I would like you to meet my father," said Teodor.

How Sean had missed them in his head count surprised him. If Teodor was large by any account, his dad was taller and heavier yet—like a retired fullback.

"I bet Brandon didn't tell you about my dad's participation in this with us, beyond our using his van." Teodor gestured to Sean, "Dad, this is Sean. Sean, my dad, Zak. You two should get on well, he did this talk about platform stabilization for the *TARDIS* at *Beyond the CyberDome*."

Sean found his hand lost in Zak's large grip. Zak's pressure was respectful and his greeting came with a genuine smile. "Glad to meet you. Teodor mentioned that *TARDIS* thing some months ago. I'm sorry I missed it, if only because Dr Who and I go way back."

"Sean?" said his mother. "Excuse me, Zak? I overheard. I wanted to see if my son was ready for lunch. Would you like to join us?"

A mixture of anger and fear rose in Sean. Their alpha

flight test was now a full fledged picnic. Metaphors flooded his thoughts about inmates running the asylum, clowns taking over the circus, cheerleaders stealing the show from the game. Teodor had slipped away, abandoning him to play host.

Zak was gracious. "Why thank you ..."

"Melissa."

Zak continued, "Melissa, nice to meet you, but I think we need to get my membership card in the slot for our radio frequency."

"I hope that you might join us after," said Melissa.

"I will try," said Zak, and he departed towards the pit area where fliers were being set up by others.

Once again, events had washed over Sean with his mother taking the initiative, and Zak, Teodor's dad appearing to be a key player for this flight. "I'll be with you in a moment, too, Mom, as soon as I talk with Brandon. Or Teodor, or anyone who knows what's going on here."

"Sean, you can't control everything," he heard as he raced off.

Zak seemed nice enough, but Sean found his temper rising in response to his introduction. He found Brandon next to the ancient van. "Brandon? What's going on here?"

Brandon raised his eyebrows and gave a faint smile to disarm Sean. "Going on?" He turned to look at the van. "Things are just about ready." He peered through the tinted windows. "Ashley is inside doing a dry run on static checks while Teodor and Sophia are handling Icarus in the pit. You mean that going on?"

Sean was about to sputter out his next question if he didn't tamp it down. "Teodor's dad seems to be the ringmaster here."

Brandon tried to smooth things out by holding his hands out, palm down. "Ringmaster is a bit extreme, Sean. I know how you use language precisely, I get your drift, but take it easy. Zak is here at my request once Teodor told us about him being into RC models."

"What? As a groupie? An extra man at the table for supper?" Sean's exasperation spilled out.

"Again, watch your words, Sean. We need him to get on the field, and to get into the air." Brandon added a sweep to indicated the general area of the park. "We can't simply toss Icarus into the air and go unnoticed. Zak has a membership. He's known here on the field. He knows the ropes."

Sean still simmered but things sounded like they had a rational basis. "Tell me more."

Brandon relaxed some. "Sean, the first thing we are going to do is break the rules. Icarus is an illegal design for this airfield. They don't allow autonomous or first person view flights. Zak has agreed to take the heat if we are found out."

"Take the heat? That's for me," said Zak as he stepped into their close conversation, "I'm the original bad boy here."

"Hi, Zak, thanks for taking part with this test," said Brandon. "Are we in the line-up?"

"We got our frequency." He then took out a membership badge, and pinned it to his hat. "This makes it official."

"Fine." Brandon opened one door, reached in, and pulled out the controller. "Teodor has put you through the drill on this. You want to take it to the pit for testing?"

Zak hefted the controller and smiled at the irony. "Dead Man's switch. Got it." He put a Bluetooth earpiece into his ear and pressed it. He waited a moment. "Ashley? Yes, I hear you too." Then turning to Brandon and Sean, he said, "Well, things are warming up. See you on the flight line where I will premier my RC pantomime act."

Sean knew that Zak understood his part of pretending to control Icarus while it was flying under program control. His anger slipped away further in the face of Zak's natural friendliness. "Make it an Oscar performance, please."

Zak snorted a laugh, "You bet, there will be some folks here waiting for me to pull a blunder. I hope to bore them."

Just as Zak moved off towards the pit, Megan and Betty joined them. Megan was sporting a black T shirt with a goth pixie printed on it. It worked for him. Her dark bangs framing her bright eyes and plum red lipstick attracted him like a new source of gravity. Megan went into a tight orbit around their group. There was a skip in her step as she became absorbed in the blue of the sky and the green of the grass. Her gaze took it all in and then settled on Sean. She drew up next to him. Their arms touched at the sides as they stood together facing Betty and Brandon.

"Megan said that things were happening here today, Brandon." Betty was dressed in a more casual outfit than when Sean first met her. "What are the odds?" she asked Brandon.

Brandon, without missing a beat offered "Still one chance out of ten, Betty. Even if we could fly to Hawaii, we still have to prove we can land."

Betty looked out to where Zak was working with Sophia and Teodor in the pit with Icarus. "How's Ashley?"

Sean became alert to Betty's unexpected question. At the same time, he felt Megan's hand take his. With her hand exploring his, Betty and Brandon's conversation began to slip beneath his imagination's sound of rain in the forest.

Brandon glanced at Sean as if there might be some issue about sharing this discussion with him. But then he returned his attention to Betty. "Things have been stirred up. You must be aware of that to ask, Betty."

"Poor girl," was Betty's only response.

"She's taken up the controls inside the van." He indicated this with his thumb over his shoulder. "Most of the pain has gone from the last flare-up." With this he glanced briefly at Sean.

Sean struggled to keep the conversation in the front of his mind. Megan's finger tracing light patterns along his wrist brought his imagined rain fall to a torrent. He was like the Tin Man rusting in the rain. Would Dorothy, at his side, remember his oil can sitting nearby?

It had been a long time since he had thought of that old movie, The Wizard of Oz. There was something eerily similar there with Ashley about to control their first flight from behind the curtain. His attention was beginning to wander, as was his focus. He could dimly see his mother beyond the van, on the picnic blanket. There was a smile dawning on her face as she looked at him and Megan together.

Time was distorted too. He had the curious feeling that it flowed quickly at the edges, and slow in the middle. It twisted like a whirlpool. The rain became a rush of water circling him in the vortex. Megan's palm was now against his.

"Someone is going to have to explain this," Sean said. Questioning eyes met his outburst. "About Ashley." He darted a glance at the van as if she might emerge in reaction to his voice. Megan's fingers laced into his and the tidal rush was threatening to drown out his own voice. "Aurora suggests ... there was something going on between Ashley and Jason."

Brandon took a deep breath as if he were about to submerge with Sean into that whirlpool. "Aurora is perceptive. Sean, it was just an office romance. Ashley didn't take the breakup particularly well."

"I didn't notice anything about her performance in the office that was affected by this," said Sean.

"It was her performance in the office that showed the most," answered Brandon. Betty stood aside and followed their conversation with interest. "Her best design work has emerged in the month before you came in, including right up to this week."

Sean stood there, silent and questionless. Megan had added a small swing to their paired hands. Was Dorothy limbering up the Tin Man's arm? He glanced, once again, out to that picnic blanket and found his mother's smile had broadened.

Betty snapped him out of his reverie with, "Sean, did you catch the implication of what Brandon said?"

"Hmm? No."

Betty sighed, and then slowly said "Ashley has buried her pain with an immersion in work. Your friend, Aurora, caught the problem when it reemerged recently."

"We're up in the next few minutes," called Zak from the pits.

Betty, and Brandon too, glanced toward the pits, and she continued, "Let her take her own time on this. She already knows that her and Jason's split has become an open secret."

Sean nodded and as he scanned past the van towards

A Picnic

the pits again, he caught a movement in the van's opened window as Ashley settled back into a chair inside a pocket of dimly glowing terminals. From the corner of his eye, he noticed that Megan's own glance had been taking the same scan, and the same pause at the movement. He squeezed her hand and she turned her face to him.

"Don't focus on pain," she said in a low voice, and she dropped his hand with a slow sensual release. Her plum red lips parted slightly, and then she returned her attention to the others. "Are we here for fun?" She hooked Sean and Betty's arms and drew them toward the spectator area.

Zak was already on the runway placing Icarus into take-off position. In the sky beyond, in the flying area, there were other models circling. One RC Helicopter hovering nearby was rocking in place like a school playground swing.

This was Sean's first real opportunity to appraise the other fliers that had gathered in the pits. Icarus seemed to be a large flier in the office, but here on the field it was simply average to unremarkable—in size. It still attracted glances.

"Sean?" asked Megan, "what is it about these airplanes that you like?"

"In the scheme of things here, our flier is an inexpensive model," he said, "but it is still an engineering leader."

"How's that? Because of our control system? Our IP?"

"IP?" asked Sean.

"Intellectual Property. The secret sauce. What turns an idea into dollars."

Sean shook his head, "No. I hadn't even thought about that much."

"No?"

"Well, it includes our work, certainly. But look at it. That is a high-performance ducted fan power pod above the wings and body."

"Like a jet?"

"It does look like a jet," he mused. "There's a fan inside that acts something like a jet compressor. I don't think they allow jets, however." He considered this technical aspect, mentally fitting it into their mission's equation. "We are, according to Zak, already breaking most of their prohibitions here at this field."

Megan smiled and rocked up on her toes to his guilty admission. She quickly turned her head to face Zak on the runway, and her page boy cut swirled out like a dancer's skirt. "I can hear it now!" She hugged closer to Sean and he held her briefly at her waist before guiltily dropping his arm. Icarus was picking up speed going down the runway, and in its short, sport wing it rose quickly.

Something about that didn't seem right.

Then it came to Sean with a sickening rush. He hadn't fitted Icarus with the longer, soaring wing that would make control easier. That had been his principle job to perform for the day, and he had forgotten.

Zak moved back from the runway to the pilot's station to join Teodor. Sophia had already dropped back and rejoined Ashley in the van.

Sean felt he was about to lose sight of Icarus, but he followed Megan's gaze upward to where their flier was still climbing high. A glance back to Zak revealed him holding one hand to his Bluetooth.

Megan offered, "Somehow, that doesn't seem to be part of the script. Anything wrong?"

From behind them, Sean heard Betty. "Anything wrong?

It looks wonderful, impressive. It has leveled off. Whoops! It looks like a roller coaster now."

Icarus was bobbing up then down in what should have been its leveled off flight path. To stay within the perimeter of the flying area, Icarus was going to have to bank soon.

Icarus rolled to perform the bank. Sean ticked that maneuver off on his mental check list. The GPS was working fine. That satisfied the next tick on his list. But there was the same erratic tendency cropping up in this maneuver. He looked down and saw Zak tilting and weaving the controller in sync with Icarus' bob and weave. These were not on the list to tick—one way or the other.

In response to Megan and Betty's observations, Sean offered, "Things go wrong." He appraised the flight and watched it bank again at the other end of the field. "The bobbing and weaving, Betty's roller coaster, is not a deal killer."

"No?" came Betty's surprised question.

"Notice that it never gets worse."

"Until it has to land," added Megan wryly.

Sean laughed at that. "We won't focus on pain now, will we?"

Megan pursed her dark lips, danced close to him, and dug her elbow into his side. "That will be the worst of your pain," she forecast. Her hair settled around her bright face as she held his gaze.

Sean buried the impulse to search for his mother's knowing grin, they were still in their alpha test. A glance up found Icarus in its third bank. The bob and weave was still part of the dance, he saw. In a way, that was comforting. They had a problem, but it was stable. He then smiled at the irony of his current description of stability. It reinforced his own self-appraisal where he was giving *GyroNautica* their money's worth in design. Then he noticed that Megan hadn't shifted her focus from him.

"You're really plugged in, aren't you?" she said. She lightly bit her lower lip and tipped her head slightly.

"Every sensor is feeding though me," he said with his gaze locked on her now. "It's like the nerves of my skin are up there."

Megan tried to look aside, but her eyes automatically tracked back. "What happens next?"

"A smooth landing, or a hard bounce." He let that thought linger before adding, "It's all in Zak's hands, literally, if he hasn't already figured that out."

As they held their gaze, Betty said, "Here it comes. Look kids."

Their attention moved in response to the low flying Icarus approaching the runway. They stood in silent fascination as Icarus' bobbing became more dramatic against the scale of its low altitude. The variation in its climb and fall threatened to plant it into the ground on one downward plunge or the next.

Sean focused on Zak at his single button controller. Zak was really a one armed puppeteer in this theater they were putting on. Still, he was doing a great job of pantomime as he had promised. As Icarus dropped again, on its approach, Zak squatted slightly, then extended as Icarus began to climb into its oscillation. Then, he pushed the controller away from his chest where he had been holding it close, and the drone of the propulsion unit cut out, Icarus leveled out and then dropped with a steep curling glide to ground where several wild hops followed its first hard hit.

A Picnic

"Goodness!" Betty let out a deeply held breath, replaced it, and sent up a whoop of excitement. "You guys are as exciting as making a three rail shot."

"Congratulations, Sean!" said Megan. She stepped around lightly in front of him and took his hands in hers. Her shoulders wagged, her chin lifted, and she rose on her toes to give him a peck on the cheek. "I wish we had some of Betty's Choice to celebrate—and things." There was something intense about her now, but the press of people joining them flooded over that fire.

Teodor had passed Icarus over to Sophia who had just clambered out of the van. Ashley followed. Zak was conferring with Brandon nearby, but out of earshot. They were soon joined by club members, which was intriguing, but Sean's attention was slated for inspecting Icarus.

Someone had unmounted the wing, and this brought to mind how he had fallen short of his morning's duty. He examined the body for damage.

"The landing gear is gone," said Teodor, "That's for sure. But if that's the worst of it, we came off with a success."

"Sean?" said Melissa, "Is it broken? What's wrong with the wing?"

Now his mother was part of the mix. "No, the wing can be removed. When it landed hard, it broke the landing gear."

Teodor added, "Cheap and easy to replace parts is all." He then extended his hand. "My name's Teodor, and my dad, Zak was the pilot." This was embroidered with a knowing wink that Melissa had difficulty understanding.

"Something going on?" she asked.

Megan stepped forward with her own hand extended. "Zak was standing there on the flight line only for show. Hi,

I'm Megan. Icarus, their airplane, was flying by itself."

Melissa returned her handshake too. "I'm Sean's mother, Melissa."

"That's a nice name, Melissa," said Megan.

Sean's mother responded, "Thank you," while looking at Sean's flushed face.

"Now wait a minute here," came Zak's voice as he approached with Brandon. "Icarus was flying itself? I was here for show, little lady? What am I? A plotted plant?" Then he laughed. "I guess I was a plotted plant for the sake of others around us."

Brandon nodded. "Those that joined us, Zak's flying buddies, all cheered his accomplishment with that wild ride."

"That wasn't our fault!" cried Ashley.

"You didn't see how we were rewriting scripts to keep up with that insane climb," added Sophia.

Zak nodded. "Yes, we were heading into a classic hammerhead stall. It would have been more than a broken landing gear at the end of that."

"It was that bad," said Brandon, more seeking confirmation than asking a question.

"It was that bad because I couldn't pilot it out of it," answered Zak. "You might want to add a way out of that maneuver to your scripts."

Teodor offered "That constant up and down got my heart up in my throat."

Zak brushed that off with, "Luckily I got that bounce timing down on the approach where I could release the Dead Man's brake and let it -um- glide to a landing, but everything turned out well."

Zak smiled at everyone. "Still and all, it was fairly stable." He turned to Ashley and Sophia. "Our pilots seemed to manage the turns and the descent without panic. Yes, I would also say things were a success. My hat's off to you for your hidden performance."

* * *

Melissa recruited Megan, Betty, and Ashley to join her and Sean at her spread picnic blanket. Sean noted that they had all arrived ready with baskets of food and drink. Betty had brought her own folding chair that Megan was lugging from her small car. Melissa tipped her head toward Megan's struggle to motivate Sean. In response, he hustled out to her.

"Here, let me get that for you," he said.

"Thank you, and if you could unfold it for Betty too, that would be nice," said Megan.

Setting up the chair presented no particular problem, but it was ironic. Even though he should be a central figure at this test, he was acting like a drone to the queen bees. Sean asked, "Anything else in the car you want over here?"

"Check with Sophia," suggested Melisa.

Growing irritated with his diminished role, Sean approached Sophia sitting on the edge of the blanket, sipping one of his mother's drinks. "Anything I could help you with?"

Sophia smiled and shook her head. "Thank you, Sean."

Melissa kept Sean on the move, "Why don't you see if Ashley would like to join us?"

His anger with his mother's steering him through manners started fading with Sophia's smile, and he could see Megan's. Ashley needed support too.

Sean noticed that hunger was beginning to rise in him as he viewed the food being passed around. He looked around to find Ashley. Others in the pit area and those going to and from the runway were a constant traffic, but she was not among them with their flier.

He went over to the van, opened the door and checked its interior. There were still instruments active and he thought it best not to interfere there as some of that was ongoing telemetry. That data would have been of no interest, but he didn't know how to shut down the links. Icarus was sitting in one of the modified airliner seats that looked like it came out of first class.

Sean looked out to the parking lot. In the distance, he thought he saw Ashley bent at the side of an expensive car. She was having an animated conversation with the driver of a BMW roadster. Should he walk over? He thought it was her, even if he could only see her back. The driver's face was obscured by the head rest and roll bar.

No, he thought, she was too deeply engaged for him to break in. Instead, he started back to the growing crowd that clustered around his mother's picnic setting. Teodor and his father had settled in, with Teodor's dad talking with his mother, and Teodor and Sophia listening to Betty. He saw Megan coming out to meet him with two hotdogs, but he was uncomfortably split between joining her and watching his mom and Zak.

"Want to go for a walk?" she asked. She handed him a hotdog.

"Mmm, a chili dog with all the fixings." The sharp bite of onions and mustard took his attention away from his mother. "Let's take this trail over to the shade of those trees."

They walked side by side while eating their food. Megan

offered Sean a napkin when he finished. When they got to shade, she looked around for a grassy spot and sat down in the cool, out of the warming day in the sun. Sean joined her and distracted himself by watching the ongoing flights being managed by several pilots behind the runway in the distance. However, it was as if the shade were too cool for him, or their silence weighed heavily on him.

"The flight went well." He summoned up courage to turn to her. "Thanks for the hot dog. I was getting a little low on fuel, myself."

Megan, with her head slightly lowered, peered from beneath her dark bangs. She carefully dabbed her plum red lips with her napkin. "You're welcome."

"I like you." The cool of the deep shadows was brushed away by heat that swept into his chest and face.

Megan took his hand. "I like you too. I was worried about —well … The last few times your hands were so cold, and now they are warm."

They scooted closer together and he put an arm around her. "I don't know what you see in me," he said, and immediately there was the jab of her elbow.

"Your hand was cooling back down. But I think my nudge, there, fixed your circulation." She tipped her head onto his shoulder. He pressed his cheek into her hair.

"I liked you coming in through the door the first time at the office," she said. "Remember how I said I was a bit rough on Aurora?"

Sean recalled her explanation, but he still felt guilt for his impression of her first bright greeting being fake. That remorse faded with her nestling closer. "I don't feel like a rock star."

"That's not how we got here." She turned her head up and her lips pouted. "First impressions are great, but how you later acted with Aurora and treated us both showed me something sweet and strong."

Sean was perplexed in how he was going to return her loving compliment. "I—uh—was," he wanted to kiss her, but fumbling for words added to that frustration. Before he could act on either, Megan rolled out of their embrace and stood up.

"C'mon," she said with her hands extended to help him up, "Time to get something to drink."

Sean's fumbling continued by nearly toppling her in his uncoordinated attempt to get up with her help. They laughed, nearly tumbling. As he focused on his balance, Megan's lips found his on his way up. That sweet surprise punctuated his rising motion.

Clamboring to his full height brought a dark pool shrouding his vision. His knees felt wobbly. Blood pounded in his ears until he remembered to breath. Soon after, the darkness receded and he found his fingers searching his lips.

"You steady now?" she asked. Her smile brightened as she took out her napkin from her pocket. She wet it with her tongue. He paid more attention to that than he would have been comfortable doing just minutes before. There was wonder in his eyes as he watched. "Hold still," she said and she dabbed his lips. "I don't want to embarrass you." The damp napkin came away with faint traces of dark red.

"I came by it respectably, didn't I?"

Megan brightened with his comment, and she looked like she want to add to it, but she simply tucked the napkin back into her pocket. She touched one finger to his lips. He closed his eyes lightly. "Everything's fine."

On their return to the group at the picnic, they came into the parking lot the long way around. Sean noticed the Beamer was still parked in the same spot, but unoccupied. Megan noticed too and said, "With the top down, the steering wheel and the seats are going to be scorching." Then she looked ahead and asked, "Isn't that Jason coming this way?"

They met steps later. Jason stopped and stood there appraising their approach. With a staged sweep of one hand, Jason brushed his long hair back as he lifted his chin to stare down his nose.

As Jason was so much shorter than Sean, he emphasized his gesture further. "Well, what do we have here?" He turned away from Sean as if to dismiss him. "Hello, Megan, I see you still favor Vampire's Kiss lipstick."

Megan glanced back at the Beamer, and then returned her penetrating gaze to Jason. "Burberry Burgundy," she corrected. "You may drive in style, Jason, but your taste still runs to Walgreen's price discount bin."

Jason shook that off haughtily with a contemptuous sneer. He threw his thin shoulders back as if this could claim more height.

"You last said something about having something of value for sale?" said Sean. The words caught in his throat. His breath was lost in a vast cavern. Why had he stepped into a conversational quagmire? Jason had him trapped with his suggestions of quick rewards.

Once again, Jason flipped his hair back and combined that motion into pointing out the group behind him at the picnic. "You were supposed to pass that message on to bean counters. But you still have the chance to become a major stakeholder. Your work could make you wealthy."

The ground trembled beneath Sean. He could sense a form of tunnel vision collapsing around Jason and darkening the day. This feeling was a loathsome bookend to his earlier surrender to Megan in the glade.

When Sean failed to respond to him, Jason pressed on. "Yeah, something of value. A proposition. This test flight was a great opportunity to get past Brandon and Andrew to her grandmother. I asked her if she wanted to invest in a money machine."

Megan laughed. "She wouldn't give you money if you came to the door saying you were selling magazine subscriptions to get through school. And that would have been your best chance." Her eyes glared and she bared her teeth behind a tightly curled smile of contempt.

Sean thought that he was watching this fight open up on TV. Megan might go too far. He wanted to warn her, but words wouldn't come. He could see that Jason was getting agitated.

"Look, you little …" Jason backed off.

Megan taunted him by flipping her hair in the same way Jason had. Sean moved slightly to the side to put his shoulder in front of her. She took hold of his arm.

"So, I haven't heard any value proposition." Sean had to say something, but it was bad to stay with this focus.

What had him teasing out Jason's veiled promise?

"Value proposition. You been learning investment from the twins?" said Jason. He twisted to one side and then the next in apparent indecision. With some effort he managed his annoyance.

"You want a value proposition?" Jason took several moments to move to the next statement. "Twenty percent

ROI compounded monthly on any dollar amount." Jason caught himself, "No, I'm not interested in pikers. On any amount starting at ten thousand. Does two thou in return on investment make a value proposition?"

Jason was way ahead of him. Sean struggled to recall the numbers suggested by Wade's gamble, or Betty's big game matches. "I would think the investors you are trying to pitch to expect 1000% for their stake. Not twenty." Even through the fog Sean was finding himself in, this sounded clear enough.

Jason shook his mane. "You don't get it!" Jason adjusted his owl framed glasses like a professor. "Compounded, not simple return. In a year, I could return that 1000% without the downside of a gambler's ruin risk at 90%."

Sean nodded as he listened. "Gambler's ruin," he echoed vaguely. Jason was lapping him on the second turn. Jason's numbers were overwhelmingly against him.

Jason threw back his hair again. "You don't have to pass on that message." He imperiously looked back over his shoulder at the picnic. "I delivered it myself."

"So, if you don't need us," said Megan. "What's with all this strutting?"

Sean could feel her grip tighten on his arm. She was beginning to press them both forward into greater confrontation.

Jason matched her motion, initially, but forced himself into composure. "Girlie, you could remind your grandmother that this isn't anything to sneer at. She didn't object when she heard it. The twins, however …"

Somehow, Sean's mind cleared. "What's in it for us? You haven't the gift of cool to close a sale."

Sean considered that if Betty was interested, then there was something to Jason's gambit. However, all he had was Jason's read of Betty. Jason could be as ill suited for people reading as Sean was, however.

Jason smiled as though he held the advantage and then sauntered past them to his car. He added over his shoulder, "Sean, it takes something that you uniquely do—for what you're paid now, you can triple it."

It took some time before Sean became aware of Megan's hand pulling slightly at his. Her swings increased along with the beat of his heart. Jason's parting words faded slowly, and he began to respond to Megan's attention.

"Sean?" she asked. "You falling for his line?"

His forehead wrinkled in thought. "I can feel the barbs of a hook." Sean wanted to shake like a dog shedding water. Jason had some insight into him about his work that went beyond the *CyberDome* presentation.

It was something he could uniquely do.

Sean and Megan returned to the group. Melissa's picnic had become the center for the full complement of *GyroNautica* now immersed in conversation. His mother smiled as she saw Sean and Megan joining them. However, Sean saw her smile fade when Zak said something to her. Sean noticed, as they got closer, that Jason's visit must have instilled a tension that they hadn't yet shaken loose. However, that feeling was clouded with his apprehension over Zak's obvious attention towards his mother.

Ashley was muted and remote. Sophia and Teodor were quietly finishing the last of their hotdogs and intently listening. Betty was explaining a point to Brandon. She said, "Brandon, it's not all that complex." Zak nodded in agreement.

A Picnic

"But most of what he said was half investment terms, and the rest sounded like gambling babble from an old copy of *Beat the Dealer*," said Brandon.

"It sounded like it was complete babble," said Teodor. Then he turned from the others. "Ashley? You going to be OK?"

Ashley nodded. "It's nothing. Don't listen to Jason."

Teodor accepted this and shrugged.

"Betty, did Jason tip the love boat over?" asked Megan.

"Oh, Ashley's right," Betty said. "This fellow thought he could place a sucker bet. Here! Of all places." She turned to Brandon to complete her explanation. "In the old days, really old, far older than I am, it was called the Martingale system. You mentioned the book *Beat the Dealer*, similar; but this young man doesn't really understand Thorp."

"You lost me," said Brandon. "In what way does he miss … Why are we even talking about this?" Brandon was becoming uncharacteristically frayed. "Here's Sean, and we need to discuss today's alpha test."

"Went quite well, I think," said Sean as he and Megan settled near the picnic blanket with the rest. His mother slid some food over their way. Sean noticed she moved back, near to Zak.

"Someone said their heart was in their throat, Sean. That hardly qualifies as going well," continued Brandon in his frayed manner.

"That was me," offered Teodor. "Things did go quite well, Brandon."

This appeared to upset Brandon further. "Ashley and Sophia said they were re-writing scripts in a mad scramble during the assent."

"We weren't sure what happened there," said Sophia.

"It was suppose to be a gentle climb," added Ashley. "At least that was what my custom script for Sean's optimizations was for. During the flight, I had to hack together some odds and ends in a rush."

Brandon took up their comments and carried the theme further. "And then that roller coaster performance throughout the entire remainder of the flight. Sean, we brought you in for stabilizing the flight, and it looked like a fish thrashing on a pier."

Sean nodded. "Just the word, Brandon. Thrashing was, in fact, exactly what was going on."

"And that leads to things going well?"

"I'm sorry, Brandon, if it was upsetting, but to me, it all made sense. However, I do have to take some blame for your feelings. It all boils down to Icarus flying with the wrong wing."

It was as if something shifted in Ashley. She suddenly dropped her morose demeanor and became animated. "The wrong wing," she echoed. She scrambled through the few pages of paper that she had in front of her. "Sean, you mean all I had to do was switch from this," she snapped one paper, "to this?" which she waved dramatically in her other hand.

Sean had no idea what she was waving, but if it made sense to Ashley, then he was going to let her carry the ball. "Perhaps if you explained them to us, Ashley," he suggested.

Ashley took a breath and re-examined the two pages she held. "Each of these are wing dependent. They contain custom control surface routines for each wing configuration you assigned settings for."

A Picnic

"Can I see those?" asked Sean. Ashley handed them over and waited for his review. He examined the top of each page. "I see the file names correspond to—"

"—The part number for the wing set," she said.

"Mmhmm. And which wing set routine was Hermes running?"

Ashley took both scripts and examined them, she then handed back one to Sean. "Here, this one."

"And according to our file naming, this is for the sport wing that was mounted?" said Sean.

Ashley snatched back the page from Sean's hand and examined it. "No, it's for the soaring glider wing, see? It ends in the number 2."

Sean shook his head. "Is there a way you can confirm that from this script's contents?"

Ashley scanned the page. "Yes, at these points," she pointed onto the page, "the atomic values for ..." She then took up the other page and compared. "No, Hermes was running the sport wing custom routine. Maybe that is why things were erratic."

Brandon had listened long enough. "So, we were running the wrong script?"

Sean motioned for Brandon to hold his questions. "What values were you changing, Ashley?"

"Oh, that." She mused as she scanned the paper once again. She bent across to show him the assignments with the scribbled changes. "Here, up and down. And the same for this value over here. Just these two parameters—or atoms. These are the only values that make either routine custom designed for a wing set."

Ashley now compared the two originals to the edited script

she had cobbled together during the chaos that Icarus was flying through. "The atoms on the re-write are roughly correct—if ..." She looked again at the numbers on all three pages of code. "Yes, the atoms on the rewrite are for the wing we were flying. Then things should have gone—"

"—clearly it went south on my settings," Sean said. "To answer your question, Brandon, the script eventually matched the wing through rewrites during the flight."

Brandon took this as a cue to re-enter the conversation. "It seemed to be in the same thrash throughout." Apparently, others agreed as no one offered anything new to the discussion.

Sean nodded his head again. "Then, the upshot is that stabilization is not obtainable through program control. At least, not in its current state." Before Brandon could step into this, Sean continued. "And it doesn't need to be. This is all manageable through hardware. My first-pass hardware design was optimized for the soaring wing and I should have set up Icarus with that wing. I got distracted."

Teodor chuckled, as did several others. "So, what you are saying is that Icarus, if it was wearing its soaring wing, would have flown perfectly well."

Sean shook his head. "Possibly. But there's every chance we return to Brandon's use of the word thrash to describe the flight characteristics. It was a perfectly suitable word that is frequently found in control system design."

Brandon was not so easily soothed. "What I hear is that program control did squat little for performance. What I also hear is that hardware has to be tailored for the wing. If the hardware solution goes south, then there is no save from software. I don't like this single point of failure, Sean."

Sophia stepped in. "Sean, how many variables in your

212

hardware take care of the wing selection?"

Sean pondered this. "Well, it is a network of components, but to change that network to adjust between wings, I would adjust four values."

"Could we make those adjustments program accessible?" asked Sophia.

"Like programmable resistors? I can adapt the design to use digital potentiometers in place of the trimmed parts. And that would reduce the part count by two." Sophia was on an interesting tangent, he thought.

Brandon was still far from satisfaction. "Let's not introduce new problems before we've solved the old one."

"You are right, Brandon," said Sean. "We know how Icarus will perform with known values. If we make this design change and script those values into the programmable resistors, then it should fly the same."

"I'm not sure that is any advance over the thrashing we saw this morning." Brandon crossed his arms.

"No, and that is his point," said Ashley. "It shouldn't be an improvement, but I can swap out scripts for Icarus that Hermes is running so we can test alternatives in real time against a known failure."

Sean saw they were not convincing Brandon. "We fly with original values, see it thrash, then switch to a script that uses corrected values and see it smooth out. This would also fulfill Ashley's expectation of using program control through script set values to solve the problem we saw."

Sophia and Ashley both nodded.

Sean was grateful for their support. "Here's what's going on, here. Too many layers between Hermes, Telemetry, the hardware, and the flight control surfaces. Sophia caught that one. We promote the hardware into Hermes. We will get faster reaction times with hardware built into the script through the programmable resistors she suggested."

Sophia smiled at Sean's quick encapsulation. "Thanks for the bouquet, Sean."

Brandon was still unsettled. "All this is shooting from the hip. Is there another way?"

"What's the downside?" asked Teodor.

"We could bury Icarus into the field," answered Brandon.

"Brandon, if you had been paying attention, during our long discussion here, two models have done exactly that behind us," Zak laughed. "Look, I won't be able to keep up with you through all this shooting from the hip, but I've arranged for Teodor to be your pilot for your next tests. Our flight together was enough to renew his membership. Folks around here already know him."

"Thanks, Dad," said Teodor. "Brandon, there's no two ways about this. Do we have to ask you about buying university engineers to run this on their super computer? When we've paid that bill, we still have to fly their numbers to prove we got our money's worth."

"Teodor," asked Brandon, "did Zak teach you upward delegation?" Zak laughed as if Brandon had uncovered a life's lesson. "Well," Brandon added, "you put me over the barrel to get us this far." He let out a sigh. "And it did turn out pretty good. Better than the two that planted themselves behind us." Brandon took another breath and finally settled down. "How long before we are on the field again?"

Sean, Sophia, and Ashley exchanged glances. Sean offered, "one-two days?" and they nodded.

A Picnic

* * *

Their plans were set, a new flight would find Icarus in the air with new hardware and software soon. They were, perhaps, a month away from a flight that would be farther ranging than the short field within this park.

As the picnic broke up, Melissa took Betty back to her apartment at the Roosevelt Courtyard. Zak joined some of his RC buddies and was back on his own. The distance between Mom and Zak suited Sean. He was beginning to realize that he had been close to becoming a little too strange about their socializing.

So far, no one had noticed. His jitters over them had melted away under the discussion of design changes. In his cooler frame of mind, Sean could see he was trying to prop up the idea that Mom was still with Dad. That was a fantasy. He glumly knew better, and he had to fight to hold onto that admission.

Brandon, Sophia, and Teodor were set to carpool back in the van. Megan, Sean, and Ashley would make up the second carpool in Megan's car. However, before they split up for the day, Brandon held them back for another review of the implications of their tests and what lay ahead.

"You've had some down-time," Brandon said. "This should have let ideas percolate. Let's go around the circle. Ashley?"

"So, it looks like we're going to be breaking rules and laws, helter-skelter," said Ashley. In her clipped summary, she didn't appear to be interested in rehashing events.

Teodor, shrugged his shoulders at her concern. "You've managed quite well to this point," he observed. "We were flying under program control from the start. Ashley, there's only one problem we have to worry about—will Hermes'

215

control stand up, or will Icarus crash?"

Ashley still seemed hurt by Jason's recent visit, but she stood up against Teodor's push. "Icarus can fly. We performed three major exercises under Hermes' control of take-off, sustained level flight, and landing. In the next month, we can build out Hermes' repertoire to vary all three."

"Sophie?" said Teodor, turning to a new topic, "How much range can we get from a battery charge?"

Sophia scanned her telemetry data. "It will take some number crunching, Ted, but as a guess with no more fancy flying than we did—fifteen minutes."

"Is that with the soaring wing, or the sport wing?" asked Brandon.

"Well, as I said, as we have the data only for the sport wing—it is still fifteen minutes. Teodor, you should be a better judge of the capacities and limitations than I am."

Teodor took in this acknowledgment of his flight captain status that he had inherited from his father. "Well, we don't need that Space Shuttle launch straight up that burns our capacity. The soaring wing should stretch your estimate out by a quarter. So twenty or twenty two minutes to absolute battery drain."

"We need a safety factor," said Brandon.

"I was getting to that," answered Teodor. "Let's roll back to fifteen minutes so that we have a couple minutes of reserve."

"How much mission can we test in fifteen minutes?" said Brandon.

Teodor said, "How much mission would satisfy you?"

Brandon looked up into the sky. "OK, we need to put our heads together on that while Icarus is being readied for the next flight. I want these tests added to our library of scripts."

Then, as if struck by some greater importance in his statement, Brandon turned to ask, "Ashley? What are we doing to see that both our scripts and Hermes' design is secure?"

Ashley's face drained to white, she gulped to regain some composure and stumbled through her reply. "We've already tightened up security some time ago. We have off-site backups, and redundant backups in the cloud." Her response was easily observed by everyone as being mechanical. However, she got through it and it satisfied Brandon.

Brandon then turned to Sean. "Hardware going to be any problem?"

Sean shook his head. "Strictly linear hardware design would be a snap, as I said. We are taking a risk by digitizing the control feedback loop, but even there I can design in belts and suspenders."

"Do that!" emphasized Brandon. "What is the downside of this shift in design?"

Sophia scrunched her face. "Software could invert all signals, and pitch Icarus straight down."

Sean shook that off. "No, the worst of it would never be an inversion of commands. Software will only be in control of degree of sensitivity. The thrashing that you noticed, Brandon, is called hunting in the old designs that came out of World War Two navy gun control."

"Gun control?" said Sophia.

Sean could see his explanation was too elaborate right now. "Let's just call it overreacting. On the level, when Icarus sensed it was beginning to lose altitude, then it climbed too hard in response."

Sophia nodded. "Yeah, we saw that from the beginning."

"Correct." Sean paused to consider how to keep it simple. "And going further, when Icarus sensed it was climbing too fast, it dropped too fast to compensate. Problem was that it was always behind the curve, and over compensating both ways."

"And this because of the wrong wing?" asked Brandon.

"Yes, my hardware settings for sensitivity were tailored for the slow and mushy response of the soaring wing."

Brandon shook his head. "I thought Ashley was using the right software for that wing. You both made the same mistake. Didn't that nullify it as a mistake of wing selection?"

"The hardware corrections were tailored to quickly maintain level flight with snap changes that would overcome the soaring wing's slow reaction. We were flying with the snappier sport wing, and ground control commands came too late."

Brandon's face lit up. "So, the hardware optimizations for the wrong wing drove hard and that played out harsh when paired with the sport wing." He stroked his chin. "And telemetry was too slow. Always behind."

"Exactly," said Sean.

Brandon clouded up again. "We can't have that. This is all too clumsy. Basically, there are three out of four ways that can go wrong, here."

"Sophia's ask for a digital potentiometer in the feedback loop, and my setting limits on that new design's ability to shift dynamics will unify this."

"Or, so we suppose, barring any surprises on the next alpha flight test," corrected Brandon.

A Picnic

"Barring the unexpected," agreed Sean.

With that and lingering small talk, Teodor, Sophia, and Brandon soon drifted toward the van and departed.

* * *

"Would you like to help clear up Melissa's picnic blanket?" Megan asked Ashley.

Ashley looked up from her clouded reverie. "Certainly." It took no more than moments to fold it between them as Sean picked up the remaining disposable cups and plates.

"Want to go home right away, Ashley?" said Megan.

"Not really. Could we sit under the trees over there. That place where you and Sean were sitting about an hour ago?"

"How about it, Sean?" Megan asked.

Sean had no particular desire to let things come to an end. He had no plan on how he was going to say good bye to Megan when the time came. Their lingering would delay that quite nicely. However, Ashley was a complication he didn't particularly desire. She threatened to muddy up a good thing. However, he was not being offered a third choice.

"Sure, it would get us out of this heat."

"It would seem that the moss on Sean's back is beginning to dry out," joked Ashley. Her turn toward humor as they wandered off to the trees was a good sign.

"Megan?" asked Ashley as they settled in the grass under a tree. "Know any good places to hang out near work?"

"Depends. For me, I just go across the street to a place Betty has been taking me since I was small."

"Really, that close? Is she your grandmother?"

"No, my god-mother. She's been taking care of me since

219

my parents divorced and Mom wasn't up to ...   let's skip that.   Jason was wrong about our relationship, and that wasn't all he was wrong about when he tried to hit her up for money with his scheme."

Ashley smiled grimly.   "Yes, that is what I want to talk about. I need some help and you seem to be close to her. I envy you. I hope you can help me."

Megan reached out and took her hand reassuringly. "Certainly, Ashley. What's going on? How can we help?"

Sean was suddenly engaged through Megan's inclusive we. Up to then it was like so much girl talk that he heard from his room downstairs when his mother's girlfriends came over for supportive visits. What was he supposed to do to help? However, the conversation demanded nothing from him for the moment.

"Did Jason make any sense to you?" ask Ashley.

Sean caught that they looked at him for a response. "I wasn't there," he said, trying to keep his distance from being connected to Jason.

"You know what she means," pointed out Megan.

"No, I don't."

"But you can guess," pressed Megan. Ashley watched expectantly.

Sean let a small growl escape.

How could he described it without saying jubilation, cash money, and work only he could do?

He submitted. "He has this deal on the table. He offers riches if it is accepted. He's so wrapped up in himself he's impenetrable."

"What's the deal? Do you understand that much?" asked Ashley.

A Picnic

Sean wondered at her sudden focus, but he was glad she asked a question he could definitively answer. "There, I haven't got the faintest clue. He is offering this package that is wrapped in gift paper and tied with ribbon and bows."

"Ashley, from what we heard, nearly everyone outside of Betty drew a blank on his offer, too," said Megan. "But the way you ask this, it seems you already know the answers."

Ashley nodded. "All too well, and it makes me ashamed."

Megan reached out and touched her again, "I'm sorry. We're here for you. Do you want to talk about this?"

"Jason is playing out his cards until someone gets hooked." Ashley brooded over this before her hesitating close. "There's more to be said, but I don't know how to begin."

She jarred Sean out of his drifting—*more to be said*—an expression he associated with Jason. Was Ashley trying to open up a new topic?

"Does it relate to various losses we discovered in the office after I arrived?" Sean now felt fully engaged with her pain. He could feel that her slow steps toward disclosure were difficult for her.

Ashley shook her head, and then nodded. There was confusion in her distracted, nervous movements. "Jason was working on a side project for months."

"We became aware of that," said Megan. "That's why Brandon moved into the team."

Ashley nodded. "There's more."

"Go on. Sorry I interrupted you."

"I was helping him," she said with a catch in her voice.

Megan and Sean let that admission sit for a while as

Ashley caught her breath. Megan handed her a tissue.

"Thank you." After she wiped her eyes, she continued. "You probably want to know why I would go there."

"Only what you want to tell us," said Sean. "What would you like to do? What do you need?"

Ashley smiled at him, but her face still revealed discomfort. "This is the most difficult. We were …"

Sean sat back, as did Megan. Were they thinking the same thing? Sean didn't want to be the one to fill in that blank.

Megan approached it, however. "Did he hurt you?"

Ashley lifted her chin high and shook loose the tears clinging in her eyes. Taking another breath as she lowered her head, she offered, "It was partly my fault. It was mostly my fault. He encouraged my design work and that felt so, so very good. Brandon and Andrew also showed considerable interest in it too, but I would have never been able to do it without him."

"I don't see his touch in your design—" Sean stopped as Megan held up her hand to Sean's response to Ashley.

"Mmm." Ashley shrugged. They left her to sort things out without further comment. "But he was responsible. And that meant I might fail without him."

Sean strained to push further, quicker, but Megan took his hand and her squeeze was one of support for him, not to warn him off. Ashley took note and nodded again.

"Today, during our flight, I felt so out of it. My patches didn't work. Things were out of control. Isn't that so, Sean? You can tell us the truth, here, alone."

There were times when his mother made similar appeals when her Fibromyalgia was making her miserable. She wanted support, but on unreasonable assumptions. Sean knew there were right answers that didn't help for being right. There were wrong answers that didn't help for any reason. There never seemed to be any help that he could arrive at rationally. But he had to say something.

"Ashley, you couldn't have written anything to change the course of the flight. Analog circuits are always going to win the speed challenge." Sean tried the flat, unadorned engineering answer, and Ashley took it without any gain. "What Sophia suggested, the digital potentiometers as an analog hook into Hermes, is exactly our solution."

"So?" Ashley wasn't asking for confirmation, it seemed.

"Our next flight with those new controls in place will give you a feel for your contribution. I don't know how that will turn out. Our next flight might be straight into the ground. It might rocket to the moon and hit it. It could surprise us by doing what I expect it to do."

Ashley brushed the last of her tears away. "Thank you for that."

"You feeling better?" asked Megan.

Ashley, again, took some time with her question. "Better," she confirmed with some conviction. "But I side stepped your question. You're both being so kind, and its so ugly."

Megan slid across the grass to her side to hug her shoulder. "We can go home now."

Ashley shook her head. "No, there's more to be said."

Sean caught Jason's second echo. As minimal as Jason's verbal contribution had been, that phrase snapped out. From Jason it was a whip, from Ashley, it was a wound.

"He did hurt me. And it wasn't simply because he left— well, it was when he left, but that was between us, not from the office. No, he cut me loose rather coldly, and then acted as if nothing mattered for the next month or so. He tortured me."

Megan took out a tissue for herself and dabbed at her own eyes. This triggered some weeping with Ashley. She wrapped an arm around Megan and rocked.

"Was he still expecting you to ..." Megan drifted off.

"Some, when he wanted to see new improvements in Hermes. It wasn't like before. It was dirty now. And then I saw how dirty it was before. And there's more to be said."

Sean felt a sting like Jason's whip against him in her place. Things were getting really bent. "Is this about his offer?"

Ashley nodded. "That's the part that it seems most people have very little grasp on, except Betty."

Megan offered a rare question. "Does that include you? With you in the dark with the rest, that is?"

She swung her long dark curl to one side. "I want to know what you thought it was about. Jason left me in the dark, but he manipulated my design changes and enhancements for Hermes with obscure goals that drove me crazy."

Ashley drew her slim legs up and hugged them against her. "I couldn't make any connection to how well my work was performing, but that is when he would ... come on to me. His praise sounded genuine too. I needed that. It worked for a while, then what he wrapped it in became distasteful, he would ask for more, and then he tied it into our brief times together. I couldn't say no."

"Honey, find your voice. Use your voice. If Betty understands anything that is part of us all, she taught me that," said Megan. "What would you like to ask from us?"

Ashley shrugged and took a moment to respond. "You've done a lot just to sit here with me, Megan. And, Sean, I will let our next flight with the new controls show me how much is my own in this. Now that I've unloaded a lot of this pain, I want to feel some excitement about our project." She smiled at Sean.

Still, Sean felt inadequate about what he had to do to support Ashley. Megan had given him plenty of cues and direction. It was like he stumbled over boulders when he encountered pebbles in the path. It was a hauntingly familiar feeling with his mother's issues. But, he reflected, Mom had shown absolutely no problems during the day and this picnic. Her condition could be like that, sometimes it was her stoicism. Trying to guess which was which frustrated the control engineer in him.

"So," he offered, "it seems we are still in the dark about Jason's cryptic offer."

Megan shrugged her shoulders. "We could ask Betty."

* * *

"Of course I knew what he was talking about," said Betty. "I told you that at the park this afternoon."

The day continued with its promise of summer weather, but clouds low in the southwest suggested that promise could be broken. Megan had driven Sean and Ashley back to the Roosevelt Courtyard in the University district. On leaving the park, they had returned through the appendix of the highway that split the software capital just above Redmond. None of them noted nor commented on this because the manicured campus on either side bore little resemblance to their own rustic settings where start-ups were born in a coffee shop, cultivated in an apartment, and brought to investor awareness at hackathons or incubators.

225

Such was their own story and association with Betty, an unpretentious, frequently anonymous angel investor.

"I guess I didn't catch what you said," said Sean. Megan and Ashley waited for Betty to explain.

"You came in late," said Betty. "Both you and Megan." She looked at Ashley and Betty hesitated to include her. "However, Megan should have a glimmer of this from what she heard."

"Betty, I've long learned from you to never play a hunch. So I'm not going to parlay what you call a glimmer."

"Honey, you are so hunch driven that it's spooky. If I ever taught you not to do that, which I doubt, then you never learned it. No one would ever call you a slow learner. So, what does that leave?"

Megan shrugged and gave Betty a hug. "It leaves me with you. Let's skip the lesson through one of your inductions, and you just tell them about this cloudy deal from Jason."

Betty smiled wryly at Sean, "What can I do about her?"

"Spank her," Sean offered coyly—and then he quickly shifted the conversation. "When we encountered Jason after his visit to you at the picnic, he was making grandiose promises of wealth."

"And where was that wealth going to come from?" asked Betty. "Ashley, you aren't saying much." Betty rose from her chair and walked toward the kitchen.

Ashley nodded but lowered her eyes as if to find the answer in the parquet tiles of the floor. "It's a mystery to me too."

Megan turned and reached to her. "Ashley, you asked to come so you could say things here."

Ashley nodded again. The silence that followed was filled only with Betty returning with drinks. Outside her windows, the sky was clouding over quickly. There was no small talk about this, it was so common. When Ashley finished some of her drink and calmed down, then she opened up.

She retold her story she had shared with Megan and Sean earlier in the park. Sometimes Megan would offer a clarifying touch for Betty's sake. Sean stood back and once again had the feeling of his mother's visitors talking upstairs. Now he was in that circle, upstairs, exposed to raw feelings, and no longer numbed by work in his cave of the basement apartment. Much to his surprise, he didn't have that trapped feeling that he was anxious about.

Betty asked Ashley nothing during her recount of her experiences with Jason. Now that Ashley's story seemed to have run its course, Betty summoned up something from her own story.

"Sounds like Jason has some of that infernal I-want-to-slap-his-face quality that my Jack had. So, you aren't going to catch me faulting you for that, Dear."

Ashley groaned.

"However, I can sense a difference between Jason and Jack that may be telling."

"What's that?" Ashley took her comment like it was grace extended to her, personally.

"Jack got slapped," said Betty. "Those were different times, mind you. He got slapped by many, including me. But with me, he didn't grumble or go for revenge, he got better."

"Did he go for … revenge, with others?" asked Ashley. The color had faded from her face and she leaned forward to listen.

"No, and that may be the other difference. The other girls that slapped Jack were like so many rain drops in a cloudburst. He just lifted his face for another drop with the hopes of catching it cool on his lips instead of hot on his cheek. He used to brag about that before he settled down with me."

"Tell more about Jack, Betty," pleaded Megan. "This is new!"

"Goodness child. You know I can't deny you, and I can't resist talking about him. But we have to stop this silliness and clear this problem up." Megan drew a cloud over her face as dark as those outside. Ashley shared her disappointment.

"OK," submitted Betty. "This is a bit vulgar. Not something you tell your children, mind you." She took stock of her expression and her face opened with a smile. "Vulgar. That was Jack—when he was in his element. You kids know one, the pool hall."

Ashley drew a blank on that and looked to Megan and Sean to fill in. Megan nodded, giving the implication that Ashley would be informed of that later. Megan was intent on hearing the story.

"He was such a gambler—he claimed—and he could back that claim. When he was on liberty while he was in the Navy during the war, he could pick up at least two girls a day."

"Does pick up mean something different today, than back then?" asked Megan with an impish grin.

"Megan, we aren't going there. Where was I? Oh, yes. Like I said vulgar. At noon, he would stand outside the YWCA and asked each girl that came out the door if she would like to go on a date later."

"I can see how that rained slaps on him," offered Ashley.

"You mentioned two girls a day." Then her face shifted to express every shade of disgust. "Both girls at the same door of the YWCA? I can't imagine that."

"This was wartime. He was in uniform. Many men were somewhere else. You didn't get a date unless you were asked."

Betty paused to let the scene sit with them. "No, Dear, not at the same door. What he did was to vary his routine. Later that day, at work's end in the offices, he would stand at bus stops and ask the same question to secretaries waiting there."

Ashley shook her head with disapproval. "But to be successful twice a day, meant that he had two dates that evening. How'd that work?"

"When we were living at the Y," said Betty, "we had curfew. They locked the door after nine at night. If you wanted to stay at the Y, you had to be on the right side of that door. My guess is that Jack's success at the bus stop offered later dates where he would pick up a secretary from her apartment—usually shared with other girls—around nine thirty, in time to catch a band at a nearby hotel."

"Goodness! How did we get here? Oh, yes, revenge. Jason's a frightened, angry young man. That adds up to revenge. You see, as often as Jack got slapped, he put his failure behind him and let the odds hand him success. You can't find success if you are plotting revenge."

"I wish I could accept that," said Ashley tearfully. "I've been stuck in my own revenge. I think that is why Jason came by. And why he didn't make sense to anyone. He was there to bully me, and I want to make him pay for that."

"Dear, you can accept it if you need it. Jack could make things clear about where the true odds stood with his vulgarity."

"You heard my story. How vulgar could that be?" Ashley implored.

"Not the same thing, Honey. I'm sorry for your pain, but there is a clear line between vulgar and ugly. Life is vulgar, it is up to us to make it pleasant like Jack did for me, or make it ugly like Jason did for you."

"What about being not vulgar?" asked Sean.

"Jack would have said It's tiring to go through life constipated. Honey, I've heard all the excuses for avoiding chance," she looked significantly at Sean. "I've seen some who took every chance—as an addiction," she looked significantly at Megan.

Megan put on a rebellious face. "Betty, watch your home-spun psychoanalysis."

Betty shrugged. "You're right, you need to pay for it. The odds will catch up sooner or later.

"So, as I said, all silliness. Not discounting your grief, Ashley, but accept life without revenge. Now back to the problem." Betty paused in spite of having said this. She looked around to see if any wanted something more to drink. Only when they declined did she go on.

"What you all seemed to miss was Jason was offering a betting system. It's plainly there in his language. He was looking for someone, like me, to back him. Problem was he was playing me for a sucker."

"How do you know?" asked Ashley.

"Dear, I was fending off sucker bets when his granddad was a boy. What I find unusual was that none of you can spot it when he puts it in your face."

"Betty," moaned Megan. "What did we miss?"

"Like that car he drives?" she offered. "Hasn't it occurred to you that there's something odd there? That's called putting up a front. So transparent you could read a newspaper through it."

"Transparent?" queried Ashley. "He told me he was using Hermes to make money, and it paid for his Beamer."

Sean caught this scrap of surprising information and tucked it away. Is this how money and work tie together? Then he took it to the next round. What did he uniquely do that would improve … It was that second revenue stream.

Betty nodded sagely, "Dear, it covers lease payments. Jason lacks depth for all his cocky flair. Strictly shallow pockets."

Ashley nodded darkly. "About revenge. Like I said, he was getting back at me for having gotten to him. Perhaps you are right about revenge, it was beginning to feel like I was going to stay trapped in a dark well."

Megan leaned forward, "You have something else?"

Ashley nodded.

"He wasn't responsible for our lost files or robot?" asked Sean with some astonishment.

"Like I said." Ashley had more animation and color had returned to her face. "Yes and no. He put everything into motion, but I was the one who stole Diana, and I removed the files from the repository."

Megan shook her head in disbelief. "What did you want a robot for?"

"It was silly revenge. I wanted to tweak his arrogant nose. But changing out the files that were our shared work, that was to protect us. There were backups of robot code around as you saw." Ashley twirled her long curl around her finger.

"Things began to move so suddenly—with Jason's firing, so to speak—that I fumbled some of that."

Sean gave that some thought. Ashley had recovered nearly everything with only a couple of days' work lost, according to everyone in the office. But if Ashley made backups of their side work, why had he come back for the flash drive?

"I was making sure he couldn't scrub our system. I had Sophia install some firewall blacklists logged with his IP address at his home. We examined the logs and saw that he had been keeping copies of everyone's work, but then he wandered off into something else for the last two months. We made sure he couldn't come back in. However, there was still sneaker-net."

Betty raised her eyebrows. "Sneaker net? How can you kids expect me to follow you?"

"It means he copied files onto a portable drive and walked out the office with them," explained Megan.

Ashley nodded. "When things were getting rough between Jason and Brandon, I noticed a lot of flash drives he had sitting at his workstation. The same day, I immediately rolled back our work to several months before. It was premature, and unnecessary. Brandon showed him the door before he got back to his workstation to pick up anything."

Sean skimmed through his story of Jason's night visits to the ladies. He was vaguely suggestive about the contents of the flash drive to hold that card back. Ashley's face passed from shock to relief when she connected the dots.

She tapped her lips in a reflective mood. "That means I did get my revenge. That was old work he took home that night—or the next morning, according to you." Then a wicked smile came. "Ooh! His first take was a blank drive. And then he came back for a decoy. How tasty." She basked in how it played out as if it were her personal triumph.

Sean watched Betty shake her head. This was about revenge as an addiction, he thought. He could see how Betty's lesson played in front of them. Would Ashley be able to break out of it? Then he felt an enormous wave sweep over him. Betty had offered him lessons too. The heat that penetrated him proved he was just as susceptible to ignoring lessons offered.

With Ashley adrift in her own thoughts, Sean continued his story about how he and Aurora had executed the Hermes design from that older version. "Actually, we did it twice . The second time we broke the network connection and caught the upload."

Ashley snapped out of her mood as his new story assembled in her mind. "Strange. That version of Hermes doesn't have web connectivity."

Sean shifted in his chair. It was probably a mistake to have continued, he thought. She had a glimpse of the corner of the card he held back moments before.

"You need to get together with Aurora in my office," said Megan. "She has a lot of data among the other files that is senseless to her."

"How many?" asked Ashley.

Megan raised her eyebrows over her drawn face as if thinking for that answer was likely to lead nowhere. "Files. How many? Who knows. More than two, or even two dozen." Megan took out her phone.

Sean nodded. He wanted to keep out front of this. Ashley was one too many interested parties. "Probably far more than two dozen. I would suspect more than that number just in folders."

"Yeah, it's me," said Megan into her phone, and then she listened. "We've got a situation in the office that needs re-examining ... Yeah, the files. You got it." Megan looked up at Sean and Ashley, and then was drawn back into conversation. "You did? Well, maybe fresh eyes will help. You going to be around? Good. We might be around." She looked up to catch Sean's nod, this provoked a similar nod from Ashley. "Yes, we're on our way. I will drive us down, so it won't be long."

"So my party is breaking up?" asked Betty with a smile. "The Nancy Drews and their Hardy Boy are on a case, I can see."

"Betty, that's not fair, you know you raised me on Nancy Drew."

Betty hugged Megan cheerfully, "I'm just joking, Dear. I hope you find what you are looking for. Call me if you find the odds too good to be true."

Megan smiled and hugged Betty harder, "Sure."

Betty held her gaze, "Listen to me! If the odds sound too good to be true. Hear me?"

"Yes."

"And what are you going to do?"

"Call you."

MISDIRECTIONS

There should have been more light in the sky for this time of year, but the uniform leaden cloud cover and the fine drizzle typical of Seattle dominated. For Sean, this made the traffic lights more vivid as they encountered them in their ride downtown and through it to the Pioneer Square district.

Umbrellas weren't carried, yet, for many. Hoods were up, however. No one on the sidewalks seemed particularly concerned about the weather. Even Megan was tolerating the light rain without turning on the wipers. Sean wondered about this Seattle driving culture that was so lax in contrast to his Colorado driving. He had to allow that afternoon showers there were rather more intense than this. He then took an informal survey of those cars driving in the opposite direction. Only three of the last fifteen or so cars had their wipers going.

He was about to refine his survey to do a correlation with out-of-state license plates when Megan reached to the radio to flick it on. She punched one of the presets and the car was filled with a jump blues dance tune.

"Is this a big band station?" asked Sean.

Megan smiled at the windshield. "Lavay Smith playing *And Her Tears Flowed Like Wine*." Her smile was like a window into another time. "From KCMU, Dead City Radio."

"Girl,"said Ashley, "that was a long time ago. They changed their name, probably when you were only five or six years old."

Megan brushed a tear away and turned on the wipers. "Yes, I know. My mother used to listen to KCMU a lot. She liked Jump Blues. She always listened to *Swing Years and Beyond* on KUOW." They listened to the music play.

When the song ended, and another indie tune started up,

Megan leaned forward and lowered the volume. "Lavay has also played at *Jazz Alley.* What a show." She started to reminisce again. "Betty tells me that *Jazz Alley* used to have its club in Pioneer Square a long time ago before it moved."

"Betty went to clubs?" asked Ashley.

Megan shook her head, "When didn't she? She knows the scene."

She slowed the car as they drew nearer to the district. She pulled into the car lot across from tower that housed *GyroNautica.* As he clambered out of Megan's small car, he recalled the last time he focused on the cars here from far above when the ghost left in a sporty model. Glancing around, he found one. It looked like Jason's Beamer.

Ashley stood behind him. "It's his car," she said flatly.

What was Jason doing here? They had new security at the office. Surely, Jason couldn't slip in there. Sean thought about the next move. On to Pribylov's, or up the tower?

Either way could find Jason lingering nearby, and that would lead to a showdown. At some point, Jason had to connect the dots to all his claims. The way Jason shadowed him, he must be one of those dots. They would be meeting again.

Why was he looking forward to that?

He knew what he had to do. Hermes was wealth. "I'm going up to check things," he told the two. "You go on ahead and catch up with Aurora."

Ashley lifted her hand to stop him. "Please, don't." Her fear had reappeared. The revenge she had tasted hadn't diminished the power of something still hidden within her.

Megan said soothingly, "Everything's re-keyed. Sean just needs to twist the doorknobs."

236

Ashley nodded without a word and they went to the pay station for parking as Sean walked across the deserted street to the front doors.

They were locked, as they should be, and he pressed the night call button. Minutes passed slowly and while he waited, he backed away from the doors to look up at their office's windows. The sky was dark, and the rain deepened that further, but not dark enough to reveal if the office lights were on, or not.

Finally he saw Bill, the night man open the door and look out. It took him a moment before he recognized Sean, and then he waved him in. "Hi Bill, busy tonight?"

"You're the first. Want a lift up, or you taking the stairs for exercise?"

Sean had to think about that. "How long have you been on duty?"

"Since four. The building's only open until midnight—to get in, that is. You dot.commers are like fungus in the dark here when you hunker down over your keyboards through the night."

Sean shifted in place. Should he go up and rattle the doorknob? Megan sure had him pegged right about that particular obsession. "Can you take me up and bring me right back down? I just feel antsy about having left the office unlocked."

Bill waved him into the elevator car. "Sure."

Sean wasn't so fixated on Jason that he didn't let the view of floors sweeping down the glass door of the elevator distract him with its hypnotic rhythm. When they arrived at his floor, Bill drew the doors open with a smooth, practiced motion. Sean leapt out and bounded to the office. The marbled glass panel in the door revealed it was quite dark inside, except for what light the dark skies could contribute through the windows.

When he returned to Bill waiting patiently, he said, "I should have let you return. I've decided to walk down."

Bill nodded. "No problem. I was happy to have your company."

It was some time later that he arrived at the front doors again. Bill was no where to be seen, but that was normal. Sean walked back across to the parking lot, and found the Beamer was gone.

There were several explanations for that. One obvious one is that the Beamer was not Jason's, but he wasn't going to let that end his speculation.

Another possibility was that Jason left the office in the minutes before Sean arrived at the door, and Jason walked down. Sean held onto that notion when he walked down in the off chance that Jason was in the stairway. Had he flushed him out of the building? Sean felt that if he pursued that bad dream too far, he would be faced with a problem. Did Jason have a way in?

Another option was that Jason had been at Pribylov's. If that were so, then the girls were probably stressed from that unfortunate visit. Sean started to hustle. One thing about the rain was that street people in this part of town were unlikely to hassle him. Everyone was in their own space as if private thoughts repelled the weather.

The trees along the avenue darkened the district buildings even further. Few windows were lit to give the impression of warmth or humanity. The transient hotels' occupants would be at the cheap bars. Sean tried to think about how *Jazz Alley* could have operated here nearly three decades ago. It had been only been since roughly 2000 that start-ups had taken advantage of the cheap space. Their taking residence had shifted the culture away from tourism that existed only during the light of day.

As he plunged through the door to Pribylov's, the girls turned to his entrance, and then returned to their examination of Megan's display.

"Hi Sean." Megan turned again to him with a bright smile.

He returned her smile, but his thoughts of Jason were not dimmed enough to miss asking, "Any visitors?"

Megan's eyebrows raised, "You're the first." Inspired, she jumped out of her chair, danced around the table and embraced him. "Welcome!" She kissed him, and then reversed her dance back to her seat. Ashley and Aurora traded glances.

As Sean came around to look, Aurora offered, "We can look at it all night and it isn't going to change."

"Nothing new?" asked Sean.

"Zip, zilch, nada," responded Aurora as she pushed back in frustration.

"It's my turn then," Megan said aggressively.

"Go girl," was Aurora's answer punctuated with a weary sigh.

"Ashley? Can you bring me up to speed?" asked Sean.

Ashley shrugged. "I don't know how he did it, but his copy of Hermes was as current as my last when he was fired."

"Current to the same day?"

"Yes, even to the other files on this flash drive. However, there are other files, scripts, that are absolutely not our work in the office. Megan and Aurora already found one called Tyche, earlier."

"How recent are they?"

"Within a day of his departure," said Ashley "He was scripting for Hermes pretty heavily, and he was using the most recent features. But that makes sense."

"How so?"

"He convinced me to build those features." Ashley began to fade from them.

Sean didn't have to throw in his last card. Everything now showed on the displays. Put Ashley to work was his thought. He tried to draw her back by putting her on a task. "What script was he using most, or working on most?"

Ashley leaned forward, out of the dark, and scanned the display. "That one there. At least by the time stamp on it and its apparently large size. It's composed from several other scripts that look like small exercises."

Megan offered, "Aurora says that the scripts read like Greek to her."

"Sounds reasonable," said Ashley. "I said he left me in the dark as to the purpose of those features."

In the silence that followed, Sean reflected on Ashley's contributions. They were vague. They followed on observations that either Aurora or Megan had already offered. Jason had the most recent version of Hermes, her area of focus. Ashley hadn't actually said she didn't know what he was using Hermes for, she simply agreed his intentions were obscure.

Megan tapped her finger to a tooth. "You know, there are some very curious phrases here."

"So?" asked Aurora.

"A curious phrase makes for a very good search term, especially when I can pair it up with another curious phrase."

"Can you find another 'curious phrase?'"

"Oh, goodness. There are nothing here but curious phrases. Let's see … Sha Tin Vase appears to be an important word group."

"Curious, indeed," said Aurora. "Are you sure we just didn't find something garbled? Ashley, any chance that this was something left behind by Jason to misdirect us?"

Ashley gave a weak smile. "We could fantasize a lot of demons to describe Jason. I don't need any help with that. But I don't know. Sha Tin Vase is simply one more thing that I haven't a clue of."

"OK, something else then." Megan scanned the display, "Curious phrase two: Charles the Great, and," she scanned down the page, "Curious phrase three: Frederick Engels."

"Megan, the first was curious," said Sean. "The others seemed to be lifted from history."

"But the association is curious," she said.

Sean nodded, but not with encouragement. "Yes, the association is curious. Does it make a good search?"

Megan took that challenge and shifted those terms to a search engine. "Too many hits." She began to follow offered links and quickly abandoned them in turn.

Sean drew back from her work to offer, "Bump up the heat, Megan. Find something truly outrageous in that script."

Megan went back to that source and began sifting through it. The scroll went deep. "El Zonda, and Taknam. Not exactly phrases, but certainly original. I'll tie those two in with just Sha Tin and see what happens."

She entered those terms into the engine and sat back to wait for results. "Hmm, 1200 hits. Not exactly a tireless search result, but the leading links offered all seem to support Betty's understanding of Jason. Look. Race form guide for the second. Race form guide for the third. And The Hong Kong Jockey Club for both and others."

"Betty would probably tell us that we shouldn't have been expecting anything else," muttered Sean. "Aurora?"

"Yes, Sean?"

"Remember our last run of Hermes with this script? Let's run it again and see if the anonymizer website gives us the same results, or anything new."

"Sure, I can do that." Aurora was opening a shell and beginning to enter her script when Sean held her hand."

"Wait. Can you rewrite your script to capture all transactions?"

"Oh," said Aurora. "You want to run wide open? Sure, that would be simpler. I just remove the traps and off we go." It took her a short while to rewrite the script as a new command. When she ran it, there was the same screen activity, but it was probably running longer with the additional content.

Aurora turned from the display and asked, "So what do we do with this?"

"Just look for machine-to-machine communications," said Sean.

"I'm looking." She scanned the massive dump to the display. "I need to put this into a text editor that will color both sides of the exchange." She copied the entire dump and opened a tool where she pasted it. The color popped up immediately, and all was more apparent where there was very little response from the distant server. "Better."

"What do you see?" he said.

"The initial handshakes, certainly. But it would be easier if you asked for what you want, Sean."

"I want to know if the anonymizer site accepted this data to forward it on, or if it bounced it."

"Well, then, that simplifies things. That would come toward the end." She scrolled down through the colored content. "It got kicked back, as you guessed. But that wouldn't seem to be unusual."

"Why?" Sean's hopes dimmed in trying to get his arms around this.

"A site like this probably uses one-time keys. Just a minute." She scanned back to the top of the listing. "Here's something suitably hashed. We've already used it once. Jason would have to change the script every time he used it so that it contained the new key."

"Damn!" said Sean.

"What's the matter?" asked Megan with some concern.

"I want Jason to know that we are running his script to put some heat on him."

Ashley lit up on this note of revenge. "If you have run it before, he may have pre-loaded the key into the script, but hadn't run it before Brandon ushered him out."

Sean shook his head sadly. "That would only be a guess about something that happened back then. We are stuck in the here and now."

"Not so, Amigo," said Aurora as she opened a network console. She hummed as she searched the menus and selected a function. "Here we go." She smiled with satisfaction. "From the ancient dawn of our earlier experiment ..." She opened another file into the editor that colored the transactions.

"What are you doing?"

"When you asked me to make changes with the script, the parts you were interested were already logged both back then and now. That's why I ask you to be more in touch with what you want and share that," said Aurora.

Megan raised her eyebrows, "That's good advice, Sean."

"Hmm."

Aurora smiled at that clipped response. "Which is more frightening, Sean. Not getting what you want? Or getting what you want?"

Sean stood up straight. "Where's this going?" The two were harping on him like his mother would.

Aurora's smile faded only slightly as she turned to the display. "Right here is your answer." She pointed to the text displayed in the server's color. "Ashley was right, our first test went right through. We caught the second one before it went out, so our third bounced because to the server it appeared to be a second request without a new key."

"I hope it brought shivers to Jason," said Ashley grimly.

Sean and the rest accepted her wish and took a collective breath to move on to the next stage. "I don't see what else we can cull out of this material. We had, what, 95 to 99 percent of it in the script already."

"No! Wait," said Ashley. "Aurora, does this older log of data show anything coming back from the server? It should have been a two way link."

Aurora's head bobbed as she ran the data dump to its end. The last screen on the display was rich with server content. "Well, you were right, Ashley. None of this went into its own dedicated file, and we only looked for dedicated new files last time. None existed and we left it at that."

"Save that to a file for me to compare with the script.

Now, are we at the end of the log dump?"

Aurora scrolled past the server return and found a short data transmission out, followed with a short response before the connection closed. "I will include this in your file too."

"OK, that's enough," said Sean. "I'm shot. We've doubled our workload with a new flight coming up and this data analysis. Ashley?"

"Yes, Sean?"

"Focus on the flight scripts and let this simmer for a while. Don't burn out."

"I need the challenges to keep the pain away," she explained. To Sean, this was a louder echo than Jason's catch phrases.

"Come here, Honey," said Megan.

Ashley rose and they hugged. Aurora joined them silently and they stayed there for several minutes until their breathes were in synchrony.

As they broke up, Megan offered "Sean? You want a lift home? Ballard from here isn't too much out of my way back to the Roosevelt Courtyard."

Sean stiffened. He lived in a daylight basement apartment under his mother. Mom would be up and eager to talk. He didn't look forward to it, even though he was always surprised how well those things turned out. "No thanks, Megan. It is really well out of your way. I need some alone time on the bus to put the events into place in my mind."

"Sean? Really?"

"I walk one flight down to the street, over a block, and catch the 17 straight home, then two blocks on."

Aurora looked at Megan and tipped her head. "Strictly

logical."

"Strictly logical. And how long before the next bus?"

"Don't know. Don't care."

Aurora pursed her lips. "Don't care, illogical."

"Illogical," echoed Megan.

"This is beginning to sound like one of my scripts caught in a forever loop," said Ashley.

Sean lifted his eyes toward the ceiling. Megan slid over to him and ran her fingers through his hair. "It's early. We could go park at Golden Gardens. It's a nice night."

If anyone cared to look out a nearby window, thought Sean, nature would have put a lie to her description, but Megan was nuanced and flexible. This is exactly what frightened Sean. His designs in control engineering needed things defined and specified. The three ladies were haunting him with their exploration around his walls.

"Look, I gotta find my space and put things together," said Sean finally.

This didn't disappoint Megan—too much—she stepped back and allowed him to gather his things to go. "Another time will come," she promised.

Sean lowered the wall a bit. "Another time would be nice. I would like that." The trace of disappointment Megan had evaporated.

"Attaboy," came Aurora's only comment.

Ashley, removed from her dark mood, smiled and added, "The script with your like edited in is becoming more human readable." She reflected on her comment and added, "Boy, that was clumsy. Like Aurora said—attaboy!"

With all his things gathered, and the girls closing down the office to go their ways as well, Sean found the separation beginning to weigh on him. This was not what he wanted. Working against that was the earlier momentum of his shame about living in a boy's space. Their collective acceptance with its probing thread of play threatened his dignified stability. However, it was a curiously exciting balance.

As he wandered away from their good nights and Megan's parting embrace, his steps slapped through puddles on the sidewalk. His hair, still tousled by Megan, was getting very wet.

He wanted her fingers running through it again. Then he hoped she would let her hands drift down to the buttons on his shirt as his slipped his around her lower back. He found himself facing up into the rain as he walked. It ran down his face. He enjoyed tasting the slight brine it offered as it traced between his lips.

His walking on automatic worked too well, he thought. And it was exactly this thought that broke the spell to have him search an internal map to answer *Where am I?* Events outran his search and answered with the characteristic growl of a decelerating diesel, the screech of brakes and a whoosh as a bus door opened for a single passenger in front of him. He had arrived at the bus stop, and he had to make a decision: get on, or go back.

He got on.

* * *

Distracted, Sean missed his bus stop and got off at the more distant one beyond. This meant he approached home from the other side. The street facing side of their house that they rarely entered from. It also meant he could see the blue light of the TV dancing on the curtains.

It was early, still, and that thought echoed with Megan's similar observation when she invited him to Golden Gardens, the popular beach front two or three hundred feet down the hill to the west.

He mechanically checked the mail box. Empty. He climbed the steps from the street corner and ducked slightly under the low hanging branch from the massive Cherry tree with its thirty foot wide, low crown.

"Hello, Sean," his mother called out as he came through the front door. "How was the rest of your day with your friends?" She raised a remote and clicked off the TV. Silence replaced the reality show she had been watching, and he became aware of the distant barks from the sea lions taking refuge on the breakwater a half mile south of Golden Gardens.

He closed the door on them and dropped into a chair nearby. His mother waited until he settled himself. She lifted her eyebrows to re-express her question. When he offered nothing, as though searching for something to grab hold of, she tried another approach. "There were certainly a lot of your friends at the park today. Are they all part of the club?"

"The club?" echoed Sean vaguely.

"The park's RC model flying club—they have posters all around. Guidelines, rules, that kind of stuff."

"Yes. The club. No, they were not part of the club. Except Teodor and his father Zak."

"OK." Melissa waited for more.

Sean shifted uncomfortably. "We were testing a design."

"Sean?"

"Yes, Mom."

"This seems more than just you with a group of friends.

There was pressure that comes from work, not play. And there was that fellow that disturbed everyone. What was he talking about … Oh, yes, you weren't there."

"I don't know where to start."

Melissa waited for a moment, and then suggested, "Tell me about the people. Fill in the gaps for me."

"That's not what I meant," Sean fumbled. "About work that is. Yes, they are part of it. OK, so about the people." Sean was sorting things out and stalled again.

"Like, what is your girlfriend's name?" Melissa prompted.

"Megan," came his immediate reply. He was shocked how easily he said it.

"Nice name, Megan," Melissa offered. "She introduced herself, of course, and Betty."

"Betty is Megan's god-mother."

"That's nice."

"Then there's Brandon. He's kind of the boss, but not the boss."

"About late 30s?" she asked.

"I would suppose. I am working at a startup, and he is an account manager for an investment firm."

"I don't know about those things, investment firms that is," she said.

"Betty is one of the investors," added Sean.

Melissa nodded. "I got the impression that she's a risk taker. Did she buy some shares in this company?"

"I don't know how things are set up between her and everything else. Startups are high risk—often meaning high failure. This isn't the time to go into finance."

"Thank you for that. How about the older man who was flying your airplane?"

"That's Zak. His son Teodor—who is the team leader and was at his side—is his son." Sean thought about her question. "Surely, he introduced himself."

"Yes, he did. Zak seems nice," said Melissa.

Sean was not sure what that meant, and then he tried to push back on unsettling feelings. He could not imagine his mother showing interest in men other than Dad. But that had been gone for ... two years, or more? Couldn't they work it out?

"Anyone else? There were two young lady's in Zak's van, I noticed," said Melissa.

Sean stirred out of his thoughts to answer. "Um. Ashley and Sophia. Ashley does ..." Sean paused as he realized he was going to have to explain a lot about their work to make sense of his introduction. "They do programming for the flier. It was actually flying itself—sort of. We had some snarls, but nothing fatal."

"It was exciting while I watched it. I liked the acrobatics. Was that hard for Ashley or Sophia to program?"

"It was hard for them, but mostly because they couldn't fix those acrobatics, as you call them. That had been my fault."

"And it wasn't a fatal flaw," Melissa offered kindly. "Maybe a hard bounce at the end."

She noticed that Sean wasn't picking up on her support, so she moved into a new realm. "This job that you have is a far cry from what I imagined you doing."

"Oh," was his only response.

"What do you do?"

"Platform stabilization."

Melissa smiled. "I'm afraid that tells me as much as investing finance."

"Sorry. I'm a hardware engineer for them. They were in a bind and called me in on contract."

Melissa took this in silently.

"Mom, you know I make pretty good money. I've wanted to help you out with something more than what comes from a barista's tips."

"Why, thank you Sean. I have checked, and things are slightly better than when we last talked about this. We can make it. And someday, as you said then, you will move on. Downsizing soon may not be too much problem. The housing market is beginning to improve."

"Mom, then that would barely be breakeven."

"Breakeven is good. Breakeven means as much money as it took to get into this nice house. Breakeven means we lived here cheaper than if we rented. Breakeven works."

Their place was well situated. It enjoyed what the real estate agents called a keyhole view north into Puget Sound. A glance into the distance could reveal the Edmonds Ferry crossing in the night—the keyhole view being between the two houses opposite them. Their home was a 1940s Cape Cod with dormers upstairs where Melissa's bedroom was. Sean occupied a non-code mother-in-law apartment downstairs, and it suited him fine.

Theirs was possibly the smallest house on the block. But from his experience of life in Colorado, having four decent sized bedrooms didn't seem small at all. That, of course, said nothing of the surrounding homes that might sell for twice what Melissa could have asked. One advantage they enjoyed was that they had trees that cooled them in the summer, and warmed them in the winter. They were the perfect buffer to weather. The old cherry tree out front was the envy of the neighborhood when it blossomed in the spring.

"I've been building up a bank account so I could help, Mom."

"Let's talk about your girlfriend."

"Mom, don't change the subject. It has taken me a lot of thinking and courage to do this."

"How could I help you, dear?"

"Do you need any money?" pleaded Sean. "I've saved up thirty thousand."

"Goodness! You do make good money with your work. And in these times. Does all this come from your hobbies downstairs?"

Mom understands my jubilation.

"Long before we moved here," he said. "Dad and you were very helpful with buying me all those electronics kits when I was in junior high."

"Who could have known?" mused Melissa. "Your dad never thought much of them, but he didn't have any interest in that kind of thing, either."

"Why'd he buy them, then?"

Melissa smiled at his question. "Because you had an interest in that kind of thing. We've always had a difficult time trying to get an answer from you about what you want. The kits were the only things you ever asked for."

"It was quite a reach for Dad, this high-tech stuff," Sean said in a subdued voice.

"He could tell that jobs were moving toward tech. He's doing quite well, by the way."

"Really? I haven't heard."

"Talk to him more, Sean. He would like to hear from you."

Sean shrugged to push that idea away. Things were strictly out of kilter if he had to balance between Dad and Zak. Mom had offered a suggestion that sounded like he should call up Mr. Brophy his old chemistry teacher back in Pueblo.

"Now, maybe we can get around to Megan. How did you two get together?"

Sean wanted to surprise her. "In a pool hall." It was reasonably accurate, at least to his being sure where Megan was coming from.

Melissa's eyebrows sprang up and she tilted her head. "Stop hiding behind humor, Sean. You really need to say more."

"Yeah, I've heard that often just today."

"Good that you are getting support from several people, Honey. Do something about that, please?"

"How do you feel about her?" she said.

A wave of heat flooded through him. Sweat broke out along his brow and he hesitated to wipe it.

"Would you like something to drink? You look flushed."

"I'm OK," then he shifted. "Yes, please." His mother was going to be long in the kitchen. She never did something simply. It gave Sean time to think. How did he feel about Megan? He loved her. Then a second wave of heat ran through him.

"Goodness, what a day. Here, take this and drink it down,

Honey."

The tide of heat retreated as he drank the cool drink. It was a mix of fresh fruit in a slushy that his mother must have had in the fridge.

"OK," said Melissa. "Maybe my question was too much right now. I can wait for you to sort through things if you want."

"I want to ..." Sean fumbled for words for fleeting ideas. Emotions caught those words on hooks. "She's something special, Mom."

"I thought so. Just a word of advice."

"Yes, Mom?"

"Let her choose the pace."

"That's been at a run so far," he said.

"OK, two words of advice. Make sure you know where the brakes are when you see a curve coming up."

Sean thought, that applied to nearly everything everyday since he'd signed on with *GyroNautica*. "Talk about hiding behind humor, Mom."

"Fair enough," she said. "Does it translate to something we can both agree on?" She looked at him closely. "It must, it isn't a flush, more a blush."

"Geez, Mom. Back off for tonight. We both know where you were going."

"Her nice curves, and where that could—"

"—Got it." Sean waved goodnight as he stood. He was surprised by his mom's direction in the conversation. He saw Zak, in his memory of the afternoon, slipping closer to her. Then he tried to replace that image with Icarus' bounce on landing.

DYNAMIC TESTING

The week passed quickly. Sophia's contribution was in replacing hardware components. She swapped the fixed resistors with the digitized versions that would now be under program control. Scripts now could trim the analog circuits to suit wing changes and possibly other more subtle but potentially important control attributes.

Ashley, on her side of the flight design, added her new layer of sophistication to the language of Hermes. She had buried herself in work for the entire week, running spreadsheets to do software validation from the telemetry data they acquired during the last flight. Ashley acknowledged that Sean's acceptance of failure had given her useful data.

What remained was to prove it would all work together. What was hoped was that there would be no surprises. Sean refused to offer guarantees. Flying Icarus would reveal where the design needed to go.

Their second time on the flight line was quite different with the park pressed by a light mist threatening to grow in drama. Clouds scudded by low in the sky. They were barely distinguishable from the general light overcast with their varying shades of dark gray. For Sean, in Colorado, clouds were either fluffy white, bleak black, or missing.

He squished through the former marsh, now soggy park lawn, toward the pit area to join Teodor as he went through the flight checklist with Ashley and Sophia in the van. Teodor would occasionally cup his hand over the Bluetooth they used for a team voice channel.

Teodor, while talking, gave him a nod as he approached. Sean waited until he was finished and then asked, "Is the runway slow in this weather?"

"Dad used to talk about that years back, but not much recently. Must not be an issue, now."

"How did the checklist and yesterday's static checks go?"

"Brandon liked the static checks." Teodor craned his head to look around. "Funny he's not here now for this flight." He shrugged that off. "It's not exactly picnic weather, is it? You here to act as the spotter?"

Sean nodded, and drops of moisture ran down his forehead as he looked up. "The white wings should be visible against this dingy cover."

"Yes, indeed," said Teodor, brushing water off his face. "But don't you think you should have put on those great big soaring wings this time?"

Sean shook his head. "We'll do two flights with a wing change to the soaring wing for the second flight."

"Good idea. We'll see how well Ashley's scripts handle your design changes."

Teodor then cupped his hand over his ear again and his attention was back in the van. "OK, three scripts." He then added for Sean's benefit, "Ashley reports that there will be a suite of script tests."

"A suite of tests?" said Sean.

Teodor cupped his ear. "Yeah, Ashley." He looked at Sean. "The original flight test, and variations."

As the last model flier cleared the runway and began its climb, Teodor carried Icarus out and set it at the end for takeoff. Teodor was walking back when the engine in Icarus began to build up thrust. He turned awkwardly with the controller in one hand, and his other cupping his ear. He backed up to the pilot area as Icarus took off.

"Hey, Teodor!" came a call from far away. "You trying to

prove you can fly blind?" Laughter followed from the occupants of a car in the lot, behind.

Teodor waved and smiled, but as he approached Sean, his grin faded and in a low voice the anonymous audience couldn't hear he said, "I think this dead man's brake is going to kill my thumb."

Sean who kept his attention on the climbing Icarus responded, "How's that?"

Teodor, was also focused on the flight. "It's the tension of keeping the button down. I'm pressing it harder than I need. I know this, but then I press even harder."

Sean glanced sideways. "Well, you better start acting like you're in control. Put some English into your body."

"English?"

"Sway your body to match where you want to fly—English."

"Where did you learn that, Sean? Going to the theater?"

"In the pool hall. It means you put a spin on your shot to steer the ball it hits."

Teodor threatened to pay more attention to Sean than his job. "I don't get it."

"Act like your dad did when he was at the controller last week," said Sean.

"Got it."

As they watched, Icarus pulled out of its climb. It was roughly done at the same speed as last weekend, but Sean wasn't sure. The overcast weather gave a different experience with all other things being equal. Telemetry would tell, so there was no reason to linger with doubt.

The level flight phase started smooth, but then Icarus

snapped down and leveled off at a new height twenty or thirty feet below. Then Icarus quickly snapped back up above its original height and settled into a level flight. Sean could feel the hair on the back of his neck raise. He noticed Teodor uncomfortably cup his ear and then give up listening so he could maintain the facade of using the controller to fly Icarus. Given they had an audience in the parking lot, this act was strictly necessary.

"Sophie reports that these altitude corrections are part of the script." Neither Teodor nor Sean took their eyes off of Icarus as it went into a turn at the end of the flying area. It was a wide turn, and Icarus slipped to a lower altitude during the maneuver. "Sophie reports this is planned too."

Just as Icarus found a new level to fly, it went into a barrel roll over the length of the field. It banked at the end, and then reversed the barrel roll coming back. Icarus banked again at the end of the course. As Icarus leveled out, it went into an outside loop coming down into a landing.

This surprised them both, and Sean had to keep his eye on Teodor's finger straining on the dead man's switch. What would happen, he began to wonder if Teodor released it, and killed the propulsion? Could they reattain thrust if he pushed back down on it? Before he could think that through. Icarus had landed smoothly. A car horn honked behind them in celebration.

Sean turned to wave with a smile, but it faded when he noticed the honk came from a Beamer and not from Teodor's acquaintances. The Beamer's emergency flashers were on.

What to do? The story was pretty much that Jason had a scheme he was trying to pitch, and no one really cared. That scheme, thought Sean, was miles from flying a robot. There was nothing here of value for Jason. But what was going to make him go away?

More so, what to do? Sean stood there, frozen in indecision. Teodor bumped into him as he turned to go get the flier on the runway. This broke his paralysis, and Sean went to the van, but kept the Beamer's flashing lights in the corner of his eye. No one emerged from it before he climbed in to find Ashley and Sophia sifting through the telemetry.

Sophia looked up with a smile. "Bet you were surprised. Ashley has been working with Zak on aerobatics."

"Teodor didn't mention that," said Sean, but with his attention focused on the Beamer visible outside the tinted windows.

"Zak thought it would be a hoot, as he called it, to surprise you both."

"The bad boy of the field, if you will recall," Ashley added. "What are you looking at?" She bent forward and followed his gaze. "Uh, oh."

Sophia joined in and shook her head. "What's next, Sean?"

"Contact Teodor on Bluetooth and tell him about our visitor. Ask him what he wants to do."

Sophia cupped her hand to a Bluetooth and nodded. "He's already gotten the drift of the situation. He says you should change to the soaring wing, change batteries, and we will go on with the next test. Here he comes now."

The van door slid open again, and Teodor lifted in their wet flier. There wasn't much room left to make the changes and hold all four of them in the back, so he stood in the doorway opening the battery compartment.

The weather shifted during their preparation. Sean looked out the other window to observe fliers that were abandoning the pit area and the pilot stations. Rain began to drum lightly against the van's roof as the sky darkened even more. Teodor finished his work and Sean removed the wing. "Teodor?"

"Yeah."

"I wanna try something about Jason. We're going to put on an act, and you need to get in."

Teodor put one foot up onto the lip of the doorway and was leaning in when Sean stopped him. "No. Close the door with a bang, and then climb into the driver's seat. We are staging a play for our unwanted audience."

Teodor did exactly that, if perhaps with more force on the bang of the door. Sean focused on the Beamer as Teodor hefted his weight around in making a production of climbing into the driver's seat.

"So, what now?" said Teodor.

Sean kept his attention on the blinking lights. "We give it five minutes. Do the brake lights light when you touch the pedal now?"

"Sure. They will with the key in accessory. You want me to do that?" said Teodor.

"Act like you are getting ready to pull out. Use the brake lights to give some sort of stage dressing."

"Yeah, kewel." Teodor shifted in his seat and began reaching around with dramatic sweeps to adjust the mirrors, especially the outside one, and the sun visors.

The flashers went out.

"OK," said Sean. "You know, Teodor? You're going to give your old man competition for the runway Oscar with your acting."

"Thanks," said Teodor. "I'm a quick study of my dad. I can pick up quick on his quirks, but I'm not one to be flashy."

"Not entirely, Ted," said Sophia.

Sean glanced at her and then looked around. "Full brakes set and start the van."

"We going already?" asked Ashley.

"No, just idling."

Headlights lit up.

Teodor gunned the engine twice to clear up its cold sputtering. "Anything going on with Jason?" he said to Sean.

"Not yet. Hop out and run around to our door fake a job that needed to be finished, and then hustle to get back to your seat."

Teodor, with perhaps too much of his father's flair, did as he was directed. He closed the sliding door again, with a dramatic bang, and the Beamer pulled away as Teodor came around to the driver's door. He clambered in and stalled the engine trying to move the van.

"I still have the parking brake set," Teodor said while peering at the outside rear view mirror. "We weren't going anywhere, anyway. Yeah, he's definitely going—Gone. So, you got the soaring wing on, Sean?"

"Got it, but not on yet. That'll be simple. How about you, Teodor? Any problems with flying in the rain?"

"There are problems even in blue sky," said Teodor. "Why don't we just see what happens? You playing Brandon's worry game?"

"Just sayin'."

The rain drumming on the roof hadn't lightened up by any means, and the windows were beginning to fog. Sophia noticed this too and began to crack windows open. "We are ready for another flight here," she said. "You need a bumbershoot?"

"What is with this bumbershoot thing?" asked Sean. "My mother uses that term too."

Sophia just shrugged her shoulders and passed an umbrella his way.

Handling an umbrella and Icarus with the soaring wing was quite daunting until Teodor caught up to him and helped guide things through the doorway.

"Probably a good thing to start up the van," Teodor said. "Battery kinda goes flat under even the lightest load. The charge will help us through the next trial."

They started out toward the now deserted field. Even the parking lot had become vacant—except for their van. The trees in the distance were leaning away from a fairly strong wind. The marine layer was uniformly dark granite, but with very close attention, one could see the lower barely lighter clouds scudding along below the higher layer.

"I think I'm going to have to hand launch this," said Teodor. "Are you girls ready?" He cupped his ear and nodded. "OK, we are going to skip the runway. Start 'er up." Icarus began to hum. "Put the pedal to the metal," he added, and as the propulsion unit began to wind up Teodor ran a few steps and threw Icarus like a javelin.

Teodor backed away as Icarus lurched somewhat, rolled slightly and then settled into a gentle climb. Sean could see the effects of the wind in the settings of Icarus' control surfaces. However, as Icarus climbed, it gained speed and those visible details were lost to both distance and the haze of rain.

"Yow!" yelled Teodor, and he whisked the controller off the

ground. He pirouetted, holding the controller like a serving tray. "Almost—Not almost—Did forget the act." He began to bend and sway in concert with Icarus' climb and turn at the end of the field. He looked around the field to confirm that, yes, they were still alone there. "Wait!" came his second exclamation. "How could we be flying if the dead man's switch wasn't being held during take off?"

Sean came over and reviewed the situation. "We don't want to experiment with that on top of flying in this wicked weather."

Teodor, still stuck in his dad's bad-boy persona, ignored that as he pressed and released the button several times. "Nothing happening there." He looked over at Sean and shrugged and then returned to continue his dance.

Icarus was attempting to do the barrel roll from the previous run's program, and the rolls were slower, but that stood to reason, thought Sean. The combination of the propulsion unit's available power and the wings were going to impose a natural limit to that exercise. Then Icarus got caught upside-down in a roll. All too quickly it was flying out beyond the periphery of the field.

Teodor began stabbing the dead man's brake button, but this effort was blind faith in the face of the failure that he had joked over just moments before. "Water must've soaked the control system," he muttered. He was shocked when Sean snatched the unit from his hands.

Sean flipped it over and found the power button. It was in the off position. "The unit was never on to be able to engage the brake." He held down the brake and turned on the unit. Icarus was still flying away, and for whatever reason—which might include being out of range for telemetry control—they were doomed to watch it disappear. "What the hell." He released the button and Icarus began to swoop down in a languid spiral before the weather sent it into a slow cartwheel.

"Sean? Push the button down," said Teodor.

Sean did and Icarus responded by leveling out into a low altitude return. "I wondered about if pushing the button after setting the brake would return it to normal flight."

"Do you suppose?" said Teodor.

"I suppose so. Sophia? Ashley?" Sean yelled to get through to them on Teodor's Bluetooth connection. "Can we get Icarus back here and down safely?"

Teodor flashed an OK.

Just as Teodor had the foresight to hand launch Icarus, this was proven by Icarus' bumpy return. Still, they had flown under trying circumstance and returned relatively safely from an intermittent failure.

* * *

The office smelt of damp grass. A glance out the window would have reinforced more the sense of wet pavement. Still, spirits were high and they clustered around Icarus sitting on their conference table. Ashley and Sophia at the edge of the table were huddled over the van laptop to examine the telemetry data.

Brandon, on occasion, glanced over their shoulders when they turned the numbers into graphs. "Sorry, but Andrew and I were engaged with investors for one of our holdings. I can see that Icarus is in one piece. That is a success of a kind, so I will just sit here to pick up the story while you all sort things out."

Teodor swabbed up the small pools of water that were draining from the interior of Icarus. He glanced at Sean with a grin. "Icarus' bane—he flew too close to the clouds."

Sophia looked up. "Do you think that was the problem on the second flight?"

Teodor lifted the tail and more water drained from the void behind the battery compartment. "Do you think?" He mopped it up. "I think it was the radio link that went south. What does the telemetry data show? Any gaps?"

Ashley nodded. "Serious gaps."

Sophia looked from her to Teodor. "But both radio links? The Dead Man switch wasn't working either."

Teodor shrugged with a touch of embarrassment in his grim grin. "Never turned on the unit."

Sean added, "There's something of a hardware and software perfect storm about that. Software didn't see the absence of the Dead Man signal as a Dead Man event."

"It goes beyond that," said Teodor. Clearly he had an idea about how things should be and he stood to emphasize his authority as the mission leader. "We need to restructure and use today's alpha field tests as gifts."

Ashley looked worried at the seeming criticism. "What went wrong?"

Teodor pursed his lips and raised his eyebrows. "Well, in a sense, nothing went wrong."

"So?"

"Then everything went wrong. Flying off over the rainbow wasn't in your script, was it?"

"I wish you wouldn't put it that way," said Ashley with some pain. She pushed her small frame into the corner.

"Sorry, but Icarus did threaten to go off on its own," said Teodor.

Ashley sprang forward. "That was because Hermes' commands weren't coming in to Icarus through telemetry." Ashley's black eyes glinted. "This problem was not about my scripts, but about Sophia and Sean's hardware. You didn't handle the controller very well either. None of this is script driven."

"Point well made, Ashley. I don't think anyone, even me, can fault you there." Teodor's admission soothed Ashley's wounds.

"But we are still left with the several incidents," continued Teodor. "Way back, there was the initial mismatch of hardware platform stabilization to the wrong wing."

"We solved that," said Sophia. "The first flight data, today, is bullet proof. Our change that allows Hermes to set the hardware control loop is rock solid."

"You are right there," admitted Teodor. "It was even weather proof for both wings' flights. The rain and wind were not very upsetting until it soaked inside. But this underlines what I am talking about and where I want to take us. These initial designs have been good in their own way. But they are too rigid, unable to offer flexibility. Your and Sean's solution brought some of that needed flexibility. We need to increase flexibility."

"Hermes is about the most flexible flight control system there is," retorted Ashley who was, again, on alert.

Teodor tried to calm her. "But it needs to be able to talk to, and to listen to Icarus over a radio link and pass control data through its telemetry."

"Well?" demanded Ashley.

"That is too rigid," said Teodor. "We need to more tightly integrate Hermes into Icarus. I mean that literally."

Brandon was alert. "And this means what?"

Teodor rocked heels to toes. "We promoted hardware into Hermes. That worked fine until telemetry got drowned."

"Yeah?" prompted Brandon.

"I say we demote Hermes' Navigation control."

"And that means?"

Brandon stopped rocking. "We add another system board inside Icarus with Hermes' Navigation control running on it."

Brandon stirred and then jolted. "This sounds dangerous, Teodor. Where is this leading as far as Navigation control being put into the sky, instead of from a ground console as it is?"

"And in that question, Brandon, lies the answer. Or at least a large part of the answer. We have already been through this analogue."

"Teodor, that sounds like English. The words are English, but what you've just said doesn't make sense to an Englishman. What is this analogue stuff?"

"Analogue as in analogy, one thing like another. We experienced platform stabilization problems that were cured —"

"—OK," Brandon held up a hand to slow Teodor. "One thing at a time here. Sophia and Sean's fix is the analogy were working on here?"

"Exactly."

"OK, so button that up tighter so that when you shift to the new analogue, then details don't fall through the cracks."

"Can do," assured Teodor. "First to Sean's point that hardware, as in linear, not digital hardware, is eminently faster at finding a solution."

Brandon turned to Sean. "Is that what you are saying?"

"At the time, it was," said Sean. "And it still is. You can throw processor cycles and boost clock speed to your heart's content, but my analog designs will always outrun them to solutions of greater resolution and stability."

Brandon was dumbfounded. "That kind of goes against the grain of everyone's understanding."

"Then everyone's understanding is wrong," countered Sean. "You've already seen the evidence, so the census count of everyone's understanding has fallen by at least one, yourself."

Brandon was getting a little heated. "Sean, I've backed a lot of hardware designs."

"I'm sure they did well enough in a marketplace satisfied with mediocre performance."

This time, it was Teodor's turn to step into Brandon's usual role of mediator. "OK, before this becomes a slugfest, let me anticipate your objection, Brandon, and ask Sean a question that will close this up."

Brandon nodded and his composure returned. Sean waited expectantly.

"Let's see," Teodor seemed to summon up Brandon's persona to ask the next question. "We have access to small processors with clock speeds that grow faster every year. Likewise, memory gets cheaper. We have chips that can convert linear signals into digital ones for fast processing. Why do your linear designs, as you say, outrun them?"

"Can we do this in a dialog?" asked Sean.

"Certainly."

"You said nothing of the program that was running in this fast processor with cheap memory."

"I can see how you tick people off, Sean. No, I didn't. Your point?" said Teodor.

"It takes some time to execute that program that steals from the raw clock rate, doesn't it?"

"Yes," conceded Teodor.

"And this program runs within another program that, in turn, steals from the robbed clock rate. Right?"

"Yes. And I will concede that even at this point, these two programs run under others and they also steal clock rate. But, Sean, let's get on with it."

"What is the elemental purpose of the base program that does the controlling?"

"It runs an algorithm, and applies a signal that closes the control loop," said Teodor.

"And there you have it!" said Sean exultantly. "At the base of it, this program is trying its hardest to simulate what I can already design with a hand full of components."

Brandon flared up again. "Oh c'mon. That's a sophistry."

"A simple example. Would you replace your $100 analog foot brake in your car with a $1000 digital processor brake?"

"It's being done right now," came Brandon's reply.

Sean shook his head. "What they are doing and your veiled choice seem to be worlds apart. Brandon, you could have said yes more simply if it was such a great choice. You must've heard the story of our malfunctioning brake."

Brandon was miffed and unmoved. "OK, so your linear designs are better performers. Why do I feel this is a side bet and not the main round of competition?"

"That returns us to the analogue," responded Teodor, glad that they were moving on. "Sean's design has a digital hook in it. The program doesn't have to run a simulation simply to control the only variable it was concerned with."

"Sounds reasonable," said Brandon with composure returning again.

"Sean's design is running optimally to maintain a very restricted criteria. It's response time to sudden changes with complex outcomes is instantaneous when we need instant corrections."

Sean stepped in. "However, there are big picture demands that need to over-ride even the best presumptions. My design doesn't have that built in, because that would lead to introducing unacceptable noise through increased inputs."

Brandon nodded, "I presume this is where the digital potentiometers arrived in our story here."

"Indeed," said Sean.

"But where does this argument about fast and furious go when you slip in the digital baby sitter?" Brandon folded his arms and sat back triumphantly.

"Again, this touches on the heart of the matter, and gets closer to answering your objection."

Brandon's face screwed up for a moment before dawn came. "Yes. Why do we want Hermes running on Icarus?"

Sean could sense where Teodor was leading. "The digital baby sitter, as you put it most excellently, is a low speed surrogate of the parents. The baby sitter can handle most common problems, and knows how to get hold of Mother or Father in an emergency. Even until then, the baby sitter will be working with the best solution available."

Brandon appeared to be relaxing. "Am I going to have to watch my language? Brother, a simple thing like baby sitter … OK, it makes sense with the digital potentiometers that you and Sophia added. And I have to admit it was a rock solid addition to the overall design."

Teodor continued his pitch. "Well, we bump that up by putting Hermes' Navigation control aboard Icarus. This has nothing to do with Sean's linear hardware, but with Hermes working in the proximity of the digital potentiometers."

Brandon took a breath and whistled lightly. "We have some hooks in Hermes that is like the baby sitter calling the parents when baby Brandon throws a uncontrollable fit?"

"Um," Teodor looked like he was juggling that thought. "Uh, let's unpack that to see if we are both on the same page. Yes, there are hooks in Hermes. Those hooks engage when trouble goes outside of Hermes' script solutions on board. Those troubles come slowly without hysteria. Like long range navigation issues. Hermes phones home, so to speak, to ask where it should be going. Until home phones Hermes back, Icarus flies on in its own calm."

"Nice catch," smiled Ashley. "Even I got that analogy."

Teodor bowed to her which provoked Sophia to give a polite opera applause.

Teodor was on a roll. "We have to go here, or we have to close shop. Icarus is supposed to be autonomous. This shift of Hermes on board brings automatic flight."

Brandon was completely on board, himself. "We need to consider other marketplace traits, like visual recognition systems."

"Whoa," said Teodor. "You're right, but this has to be done in layers so that there is a hierarchical sense of design. We are just only entering into these issues right now."

Ashley stepped in. "That means hooks at each level for

shifting platform, flight, and mission agendas. The spread of command, control, and communication would fit perfectly into Hermes."

Brandon broke into a nervous pace around the room, throwing out questions as he went. "I like it. I hate it. I have a problem with it."

"What's that?" said Teodor.

"Does this mean a total redesign? I mean—I mean you have control from a van moving into Icarus. Do we stop using the van? What happens to … How does Icarus phone home? Tell me, Ashley."

Ashley flipped her long curl back, it immediately returned to hang over her eye. "The design is Object Oriented. We simply use a facade—wrapper or interface, whatever—called Navigation to pass data through."

"Sorry, Ashley, but that jargon is above my pay grade," said Brandon. "Assist, anyone?"

Sophia stepped in. "The critical data will be passing between objects in Icarus, and the slower data between Mom 'n' Dad and the babysitter will go through the slower telemetry."

Brandon stirred some. "That I get."

Sophia mused on Brandon's slow uptake. "Teodor wants to move significant portions of Mission and Navigation control to the other side of telemetry to cure our schizophrenia."

"So rad, girlfriend," said Ashley.

"Wow!" exclaimed Brandon. "A split mind. This is beginning to light up like a Christmas tree." Brandon's eyes lost their focus and he appeared that he was soon lost in his thoughts.

"What about our ghost problem and Jason's visit in the rain?" Sean asked.

Brandon apparently didn't hear this. Ashley, however, started in response.

When Teodor noticed this shift in Ashley, he turned to Sean. "You sure know how to spill the punch bowl at a party. Let's just wait for him to be a real problem instead of a supposed problem. We're secure here, aren't we?"

Ashley didn't brighten with Teodor's confidence.

JASON'S CHALLENGE

There was progress on design changes that Teodor mandated. However, Sean's participation was plunging and his billable hours followed that down. His specialty in hardware design was very tangible. The customer could look at Sean's work, feel it, give it a heft, and quickly decide when it was complete. Sean's end in the design's life cycle came with a clear demarcation. He knew they would commend him. He would hear that he had done exactly what they asked ... and that would be the end of it.

So when Brandon asked to see him at Pribylov's instead of *GyroNautica*, then that was the familiar fulfillment of Sean's work script. The setting had its familiar trappings of the final ritual. The dialog coming up was sure to wrap up the plot. Then the curtain would fall. He didn't need a program to explain anything.

They settled stiffly into chairs on opposite sides of a desk in Brandon's investment office. The dead air and filmy window spoke of infrequent visits. Sean focused on such inconsequential details in times of stress. An ache grew in his chest from loneliness.

Megan wasn't in the front office when they arrived. He missed seeing her, but maybe it was better this way. He searched for a reason how that could be true, and he found conflict. He wanted to be near her, but not with this going on.

He was being turned out, and shame painted itself into his picture. He didn't want Megan to see him playing out his version of Dad's shattered work life. In exit interviews, Sean had sat at desks like this many times now, but Megan made a difference he hadn't felt before.

Things were more intense. Being cut loose made him bitter. Anger burned in him. He wanted to erupt. If he erupted, he didn't want Megan nearby. He had to smother the eruption so that Megan wouldn't see how ugly he could get.

Sean felt cornered. He may never see Megan again, if he couldn't control his conflict. But there was only one outcome. Sean's end was coming like Icarus suspended at 10,000 feet with the battery drained. Had they designed a script for that situation? That was absurd.

He heard some words, lines of dialog, being mumbled across the desk to him.

"… and we appreciate how you helped turn things around," said Brandon. That was Sean's cue.

"I simply did what was necessary," Sean said to the dust on the table. His gaze wandered further to the floor, as he felt the last of his battery drain—his propulsion dying.

Brandon's side of the conversation still came to him through the fog. Sean muttered polite responses sensibly when the dialog demanded. There were no future prospects, or so it would seem, with *GyroNautica*, unless they got into real venture capital rounds of investment. Sean had little idea of the reality of that, and it certainly didn't meet his immediate needs. He thanked Brandon in the right places with the proper modulation of voice. He could tell it was a good performance, because he was watching himself from a third row seat in the theater.

The curtain fell. Sean joined with his imaginary audience as they wrestled into coats. He merged into the anonymous crowd's shuffle out into the street. He stood there, lost without a role. Sean needed refuge.

He crossed the street and climbed the steps to his familiar pool hall. Inside, competitors in the distance hovered over tables while their small audience mingled nearby.

Unfortunately, calm didn't come to Sean.

He could sense that those shooting pool, the real people, not the ones of his imagination, were doing serious work. Without care for the battered hall, the indifference of tourists who wandered outside, or the new hustle of start-ups being started, two players competed alone on the 50 by 100 inch field of green. They were occupied in their roles as either hustlers, or road players.

A flicker of Betty's story from Sean's bus ride with her reminded him that sometimes a considerable amount of money could trade hands here—in a moment.

They must find jubilation in their work and in the reward from their bets.

He needed to find income. Expenses at home never stopped. Sean then thought about the circumstances of Jason having been cut loose too. Given the vague picture of that offered by those at *GyroNautica*—Ashley, Sophia, Teodor—his own picture seemed just as indistinct.

Jason must have needed an income too, but that Beamer he drove spoke of a creative solution. Jason had captured much larger fortunes, if Sean accepted the bravado of his performances. Betty had warned everyone not to be drawn into that illusion.

It wasn't working like it had before. The magic of Snooker had dimmed. The numbing trance was gone. Here he was still stuck in the ditch thinking about money, when he had sought quiet reflection.

What was it about money? The gang at *GyroNautica* were working for starvation wages on the hopes that their sweat equity would pay off through an eventual buy-out. In contrast, Sean had been taking home fat paychecks covered by Wade. Heavily inflated paychecks. The thought of his boon submerged beneath shame.

He struggled with Brandon's observation that Sean's work continued outside the office. This was unlike Dad's work in the steel mills. Was Dad experiencing a new reality where he was bringing his new job home each evening? Sean couldn't see that in the picture.

Sean had made more money over this stretch of time than he had made in the last two assignments. It went into the bank. Mom refused to take anything but a pittance. That small sum was not even what the mother-in-law apartment could bring in if she rented it out to strangers.

The contradictions were unsustainable. He left the pool hall to search for a new calm.

Out in the dark street he was met with the familiar soothing mist. Walking helped even more until he realized his path was taking him back to the tower where he was no longer part of the gang. At future alpha tests out on the flight line, he could be a rubbernecking tourist watching with fascination, but the problems were strictly theirs, and they had moved on from solutions he could offer. With each step he saw the tower loom higher above him.

He wondered if he should turn back to First Avenue for his bus, or just wander aimlessly until what ever held him could be shrugged off. Lost in indecision, he continued along the front of the parking lot opposite the tower. Then movement drew his gaze to a car door opening and a short form unfolding from the low driver's seat. Recognition kicked in when the fellow flicked his hair off his shoulder with a backward wave.

What did Jason want with him?

* * *

How did they find themselves in this dive? Sean sat there ready for confrontation, and Jason promised to be a willing target. A worn out, indifferent waitress finished serving them a couple of equally indifferent beers in the gloom of their booth buried at the back of this ancient tunnel of a bar. Grimy windows nearby looked out on walls of dirty whitewashed brick.   The open lid of a dumpster in the alley partially blocked that miserable picture.

When Sean was through taking in the local atmosphere, he hunkered down expecting to hear yet another con story from Jason. Instead, Jason led with a feint.

"You look like I felt when they showed me the door."

This was beyond belief. Did Jason have an inside lead to both *GyroNautica* and Pribylov? With Jason sitting in his car, at that particular time, and Sean just happening past was so coincidental that it exceeded reasonable odds.

"I haven't a clue as to how you feel, dude," said Sean.

"Enough sparring, Sean.   My message is the same, you've shown interest, you're here. But it seems I haven't sugared it enough."

"Look, dude, I'm only here to drain your steam. If you think you haven't sugared things enough, well that's your look out. Saying so doesn't sweeten the deal. Look, do you have something to offer? Even something to say? It'll be hard enough to stomach this lousy beer if you don't bring some life to your pitch." A flush ran through Sean leaving behind a sweat in spite of the clammy surroundings. He was caught in the wrong role from a bad play.

Jason leaned over to his computer bag and drew out an envelope that looked like it held a curiously narrow paperback inside.   He slapped it down on the table,

278

splashing the small puddle of beer spilt by the waitress.

"Here's $10,000 of sugar if you want sweetening," said Jason in a voice too loud for this neighborhood. However, the barflies seemed undisturbed as they lazed over their drinks. Jason shoved it across the table trailing a oily sheen of beer behind it.

Sean looked at Jason with a blank face. What was Jason asking for? What did $10,000 have to do with it? These were questions that Jason promised to hedge with drama, bombast, and bravado.

The greater question was why was Sean there sitting through it? In Jason's gloat was a leering hint of darkly intriguing assignments and extravagant rewards that had Sean hooked. The cloying, respectable version was that they were there to talk about challenges and opportunity.

Cloying talk had been unproductive for him an hour ago when Pribylov cut him loose from work. So the question echoed again, why was Sean here? He was hedging as deceptively as Jason. With his fresh wound of separation, maybe he wanted to punch someone without guilt or regret. And yet here they were sitting muffled in the stale dampness of this skid road coffin with two untouched beers and this envelope. They both exhibited the inertia of moss on a fallen tree trunk deep in a dark forest.

Sean pressed the envelope and felt its firmness. "So, what's with this?"

"It's yours if you can put things together for me. Look, here it is. I've seen your run of Hermes with my script. That network report to me lit up like a beacon. Nice touch. You must've copied my files before I could retrieve them. That was fast, man. Within hours of me being boosted out the door."

Jason fiddled with his owl frame glasses and watched Sean for a moment. "I figured that flash drive would have sat there in my system untouched for days when I showed up that night. And to top it off, you left me a copy like a honeypot for my second visit." Jason smiled ruefully. "I thought I had misplaced it there on the desk where I found it, but when that network run report came—whew! Busted."

Sean didn't know what to do with Jason's appreciation. Sean was thinking fast at that time of Jason's ghostly visit, and Sean had figured it correctly. And, apparently, he had played it out well, too.

Jason continued, "What I've seen of you, aside from your presentation at CyberDome, is that you are a quick study. You ran Hermes once and you must've realized it notified me. The others would have fumbled along running it several times before they gave up clueless. I bet you've examined a ton of logs to figure out what it was doing."

Sean nodded at Jason and thought of the adage that the best defense is a quick offense. "Pretty crummy betting system."

"Crummy pays very well," came Jason's dead pan response. "So, would you like to buy a BMW to tool around in?" He nodded towards the soaked envelope that was beginning to stain. "There's the down payment."

The stain bothered Sean, and he flipped the package over, feeling its heft of bills inside. "For what? You got tired of beating up Ashley? I'm not interested in taking any punches."

"So sentimental," came Jason's cold dismissal. He slid his glass of beer to one side.

"Dude, cut the crap and fill in the blanks." Sean felt he was already a willing victim of that game that was igniting his desire to throw a punch across the table. The anger inside wanted out. Certainly, in a place like this, it would be no strange scene. He ratcheted that urge down so hard his lungs clamped against his heart.

"Hmm, seems like we're close to a deal."

With a shock of recognition, Sean saw familiar contradictions returning. He wasn't against Jason's idea, even if he didn't know it completely. He was through arguing terms of employment. He hadn't objected to the compensation. What he wanted to hear was the design specification.

Right now, he thought, no other time, don't wait for anything, he should walk out.

He sat there frozen to Jason's grin.

It was like the smile of the cobra before it struck. Sean sat immobilized between fascination and anger. Safety was nothing more than a step away from the table, a step out the door, and a walk down the street. But there was the stained money envelope that would inflate his bankroll considerably. But not enough. What were the prospects for more if this much simply fell into his lap? And then there was the question that kept Sean there. What was Jason buying?

Was this the trap that Ashley described? Certainly her bargain with this devil wasn't struck here on this escalator to the drunk tank. Sean could feel the dankness that Ashley felt. He felt that the pit in her soul was as dark as this hole. He shuddered at the degradation she must have submitted to. And this all went through his mind as he focused on that envelope that was beginning to dissolve. The ink within was becoming visible revealing the vague portrait of a solemn Andrew Jackson recognized everywhere.

Jason slid a flash drive across the table to him. "You

probably recognize this."

At first, Sean wasn't sure what he meant. And then it dawned on him that Jason was recalling his late night visit at the office to gather up the files that he left behind. He looked at the flash drive next to the soggy envelope.

"What's it to me?" he asked.

"Take everything here on the table if you think you can improve on my revision of Hermes." Jason chuckled to himself and offered an explanation. "You will find an executable program in this called Tyche—more importantly, its source code." He offered a sardonic grin. "You already had the most recent copy of the executable, but it appears you simply cruised right past it."

Jason played it out. "Tyche was the love child of Hermes and Aphrodite." When Sean still betrayed no interest, Jason shrugged it off. "Inside joke. OK, let's cut to the chase."

Sean smothered his mixed emotions. The muscles of his jaw were set so rigidly they hurt. He got Jason's perverse joke about a love child and it cut close to home. Jason was probing Sean's attachment to Ashley, and possibly his feelings for Megan.

It was a relief when Jason decided to move on, but Sean needed to propel him. "So cut to the chase, dude."

Jason's smile set like concrete. Sean still hadn't gotten up and walked out on him. "Tyche extends the design of Hermes by integrating the primitive control loop into the higher levels of abstraction. You should recognize where this is going."

Sean felt himself buy in. "It's taken a long detour, but, yes, you've finally identified my connection to what's on the table."

Jason took this in without comment. "This higher level of abstraction is very necessary for improving my advantage in placing orders."

"Mmhmm." Sean could see things coming together with what Betty had characterized as a gambling scheme. But orders? Stock orders? Was this the familiar gambling Jason expected to interest Betty?

"These connections I've added feel organic to what could be done, but I don't have the chops for keeping Tyche from trashing my edge and burning my profits. Tyche is borderline stable, but that won't do when, out of the blue, it crashes hard."

"And you trust me to take this and help you?" Sean was buying in further.

Jason sat back in silence for a while. "This is just the start —not a knock off assignment that you must be used to." He glanced around the dive and weighed his next words. "I can see us doing enhancements once a month, same deal, in better surroundings."

Strange excitement quivered through Sean. Indeed, the offer had sweetened with stability, work that begged for his skill, and a more than generous amount of money. Both their needs fit together in Jason's puzzle—just as Jason must have figured.

Once he got Jason drawn out, the scheme was clear enough. It was barefaced gambling. Tyche was working out the odds in horse racing. Jason's picnic visit was for him to make a pitch to Betty's background in betting, not investing. Betty had said it was a gambling scheme doomed to failure, but he and others had simply read that as the standard jargon for risk with start-ups.

This project for Sean was Jason's own form of a honeypot

trap, he thought. "How do I know this is good for me?" he said. But he knew his question was inconsequential, a thin veneer of respectability.

Jason's mood darkened. "You see the money in front of you before you do this, right? How do you know? I'm the one holding the bag. I'm betting $10,000 that your design tricks will make that up in spades." Jason leaned forward and his long hair fell over his thin shoulders toward Sean. "What do you want?"

More challenge, more money, more ... Sean was already being offered all that for the taking. He tried to hide in a corner by dumbing down.

"What if I need help from someone else? Hermes is in a higher language that I am only familiar with on casual basis."

Jason flipped his hair back and peered through his owl frames. "You've got more savvy than that. You understand where this is going and how to get there."

Jason cooled down to offer a compromise. "If you need someone to hold your hand, like that cute Megan, then you pay her out of your pocket. Just keep her out of the loop of what's going on between us. And no one is to have a clue about the horse tracks."

Sean realized that Jason had already anticipated his objections. This was dangerous, but there was the money. He tried to think of another way to put him off. "Can I think about this?"

Jason tightened his lips together. "Guy, you been thinkin' of this for longer than us just sittin' here." He picked up his beer and pounded it down. "Take the money, or take a walk."

JASON'S OPPORTUNITY

The envelope sat nearby on his desk at home. It was dry now, but wrinkled and stained, offering the stale aroma of cheap beer. Sean couldn't open it—yet—but he felt more interest in the baton passed his way from Jason.

Sean had Jason's new flash drive in his computer. First, he had carefully scanned it for virus and infections. Then he opened it to examine the source code for Tyche. He placed both designs on his display, side by side. Within half an hour, he found Tyche was very much like Hermes, the original design it descended from.

Both designs sought solutions from complex, problematic data rich environments. However, this was still on a fundamental level for Hermes. Jason's Tyche had a rich layer of language enhancements over Hermes' basic offerings. Sean was going to have to dig into the design to find out why Jason thought he had insights worth $10,000.

Jason and Ashley had worked shoulder to shoulder on Tyche in the months before Jason's departure. This picture was now much clearer after reading the code. Sean wondered how Ashley described her contributions as being driven by obscure goals. Jason's hand was in the gambling, certainly. But Ashley's hand was in optimizing that outcome.

He could see that Ashley was a digitized version of his analog self. This was probably a reason for their not getting along too well with each other. When he had challenged that linear designs could always beat digitized ones, he was close to lighting a very short fuse. It was remarkable that she hadn't gone ballistic.

Some of Ashley's new Hermes flight script commands added in the week before their second flight came out of her work on Tyche. That was now obvious. He skipped past what motivated Ashley to support Jason even to this point.

The envelope in front of him reminded him that he wasn't eager to examine his own motivation.

Stick with the problems that had solutions in reach.

Another half hour's examination revealed how Tyche combined input from a wide array of sources. It's data came not from robot sensors, but from race tout handicap reports. Where the robot's Hermes would predict moves past obstacles, Jason's Tyche sought to optimize a bet given track conditions, jockey's ability, other horses' standings, and so on. How well that performed remained to be tested.

How did this shift from one to the other happen? Sean pushed back from his display of the two designs on his monitor to give him room to think. Side by side, they revealed their commonality. Tyche's added features were apparent, but not dominating the basic design. He stood up and began to wander back, further away from the display.

Sean stood far enough back that he couldn't see any design element distinctly. The robot and the race track had disappeared. What could he remember about the designs when these were removed? Hermes and Tyche were both problem solving languages. Each shared a dictionary of shared commands. Each had their own specific dictionary of commands.

Sean went back to his desk and looked closer into the specific dictionaries to sort out the significant differences. Ashley had designed a natural language interpreter that looked almost like English in its syntax. Sean knew it better as the clausal grammar of an artificial intelligence programming language.

He mused on the irony of having picked that up in an AI online course offered for free by Stanford University. His mother would've been proud to know he was studying. But that pursuit had been to further black hat challenges he had taken up in the chat rooms. Sean shook off that disturbing memory to refocus on the sense of both designs being interpreters.

In Sean and Ashley's world, interpreter design was done using UNIX tools called lex and yacc. When he dug into the directory structure of the flash drive, he found a folder holding the lex and yacc files he expected.

Everything was coming together. Sean knew enough to fill in for Ashley. Jason had tapped the right person. However, as far as he knew Jason's appraisal of him came largely from his presentations at *Beyond the CyberDome*. He hadn't discussed his language designs there. That skill wasn't revealed outside of the anonymous black hat chat rooms. Jason was either very lucky or had hidden insights.

Sean thought back to their last meeting. When he tried to slough off Jason by acting dumb, Jason had blown past that cover. Jason not only expected him to see stability issues in the new design, he expected Sean could fix them in the new language of Tyche. However, he still needed to exercise Tyche with Jason's scripts.

The jubilation of this challenge is what motivated him, not the sticky envelope of bills. If he didn't open the envelope, he was still OK. If he opened the files, well, that was OK too.

Sean reflected on his own contributions after Jason's departure from *GyroNautica*. Was he very different from being a Jason in his own way? At Sean's prompt to jettison the robot and go for the flier, the group moved in his direction. Shortly after, *GyroNautica*'s mission quickly shifted from rescue 'bots to surveillance drones. This twist in his character crouched into the back of his mind while he browsed the new design. It slipped further back as he felt

Jason's scheme stirring him across many levels.

Sean scanned all the script names throughout Jason's new flash drive. They were far more extensive and usefully explicit than the few he had discovered in Jason's first flash drive. Together, those names could outline a story about gambling. The scripts fleshed in the outline with a complete story. They were action oriented with drama and exciting, rewarding climaxes.

Their time stamps revealed they were contemporaries of the first flash drive, some were newer. Jason must have been taking only a sub-set of scripts and executables to the office. This tool-kit could have been used for testing through the high capacity servers in the back room. It was time to pick a starting point.

One curious script file name, and it had been curious names that Megan had caught, was the Hong Kong Jockey Club. Sean read through it and found tokens for track names, owner names, trainer names, horse names, and true to the file name, jockey names. It was very abstract, and it was missing what Ashley called atoms. He knew that if he cross referenced some terms within the script, that they would point into other scripts. There was a tree like structure, then, in Tyche where some scripts were branches of the tree, that might call other branch script files, or eventually leaf files—the atomic level of scripting.

He felt a deeper rush of discovery.

The script he had chosen echoed with Ashley's first lessons with Hermes to the group, and how Icarus acted them out on the stage of aerial maneuvers. What he was reading contained significant elements of Teodor's future design goals for integration of the various layers of mission, navigation, and cruise control. Jason and Ashley had already gone where the group was just now exploring.

However, in both Hermes and Tyche there was the problem of thrashing, of over correction, of a latent hyper sensitivity. Sean discovered this was built in, and not an obscure bug. He had already patched together a solution once, but he had not solved the problem.

He could now fix the underlying problem for Hermes, but Tyche demanded real-time debugging—it's own flight tests, as it were. If he could hold Tyche in his mind as a control platform for a flier, then he could drill down to the instability that, as Jason put it, burned through the profits.

Was this going to be a $10,000 walkaway? The patch to Hermes to add connectivity from it into the control loops was basically very simple. Hermes would suffer, eventually. The patch would fail somewhere. Now that Sean had seen the full picture and possibilities in Tyche, could he, in fact, replace a few calls, adjust several values, and turn both Hermes eventual failure and Tyche's emerging chaos into placidity?

How could Jason afford to spend so much for something that appeared to be so simple? The only thing that Sean could think of was that Jason was making far more money on the existing design, than he would be losing if Sean couldn't carry this off.

This realization came in all of the second hour, and the prospects of making $5,000 an hour were perverse. Sean pushed back from his desk to guiltily indulge this fantasy. Then he pulled back to his keyboard and began to explore the files again. He had to prove these changes to himself. Jason must have an exercise routine that wouldn't expose Tyche to the bet takers. It was as simple as finding the folder called Test and he plunged into it.

Drones Over Seattle

* * *

"Sean?"

The last of his parallel test runs were now finishing at Happy Valley racecourse in Hong Kong. Sean compared Jason's original Tyche design against Sean's modified version. The Jason's original revealed mild thrashing that Jason had called borderline stability. Running alongside was Sean's patched-up Tyche using the same script. His patched code was rock solid.

"Sean?" called Melissa, "you coming up? Your breakfast is turning into lunch."

"Yeah," he called back automatically.

He scanned the spreadsheet charts and dashboard that Tyche used in a familiar nod to Hermes' flight telemetry readout. Sean smiled at the similarities with take off and landing. Each of the nine races revealed a similar progression, but in a shorter span of time. The main difference was Tyche's representation of a landing was done at full speed—consistent with the end of the race, of course.

"Sean?" There was the faint drumming of music behind her call.

"OK."

Last night, the first races using Jason's original code compared to his patched code brought him wild swings, but Sean was prepared for that. He needed some error in the system to get a feel for how much tuning was needed. The last three race bets—after a dozen changes through the early hours of morning—improved so that the noise had been put to rest.

He pushed away from the desk after a last glance at the bottom line for the last race that morning. Jason's design of

Tyche would have taken in $5,650 as written and run. Sean's patched version of Tyche would have taken in $6,050. If Jason had and ran this new version, that is.

Sean re-ran the scripts with the archived race data to do a final comparison. His improvements were really seen in the aggregate of many races, not simply the last. The ever widening swings in forecasts was a growth problem that spanned a season, not for the 57 seconds of a race.

As he climbed the stairs, he did the bookkeeping. Jason's outlay of $10,000 would be returned in three days of racing. Sean proudly observed that he had accrued the same return in one day. Even more, he was ahead with cash in hand compared to Jason having to place bets—illegal bets.

Between his old work at *GyroNautica* and now with Jason, there seemed to be something similar in the moral balance. Where did drones lead? His steps slowed to a trudge as he weighed this. The group at *GyroNautica* had hammered the ethics of that out, but their arguments were hollow. On the other hand, Jason's scheme was something that announced itself, full and foursquare—he was there to tease money out of someone else's pocket.

All gamblers shared that goal, thought Sean. Even Betty, surely, couldn't dispute that. He squirmed against what would have been her response. She would have pointed out that both bettors were matching their shooting skills in competition. Sean could sneer that her livelihood was based on side bets, just as were Jason's.

Sean stopped midway up the stairs. How did he come to think of it as a sneer? He hadn't put in more than a night's work for him, and Sean was already shifting towards Jason's unpleasant side.

At this point, both *GyroNautica* and Jason paid Sean well

—Jason's assignment paid quicker. *GyroNautica* was nice, but getting cut adrift was painful. Jason promised more work to follow. Probably an illusion, he admitted, but getting cut adrift from him wouldn't be a pain at all—except for losing excellent money. Could he call it $10,000 a day? Even if it took him a month to do the same thing, it was excellent money.

From above him, an old hit played over the radio.

Reach out, for me.

I'll be there to love and comfort you;

I'll be there with the love;

I'll see you through.

Sean thought about his mother's moods for playing loud music from the 60s, or whenever, in the mornings. Then his thoughts returned to his toying with the scripts and Tyche through the night with the Hong Kong races that had just finished.

He sat down mechanically to breakfast as his mother busied around the kitchen. What would $10,000 break down to for a per-hour rate? Roughly $1000 an hour? What was that a minute?

"Sean?" asked his mother from her seat across the table.

"Mmhmm," he answered automatically as he thought in dollar terms of seconds in a minute.

"You OK?" she asked. "You don't seem to be here. Something happened about work?"

"Work?" came his absent echo.

"Your routine has shifted."

His mother's attempt at conversation began to penetrate Sean's focus on Tyche. The high of a mesmerizing, industrious night was fading. As it faded, then he felt its weight.

"Are you tired?" she asked with concern.

Sean hazily scratched himself as his mind tried to submerge back into to the per-second rate that $10,000 broke down to. Then he bobbed back to the surface. "Yeah, tired. At it all night."

"Eat something, and get some rest."

It took monumental effort to pick up a spoon for the cereal. Lifting the glass of orange juice would have to wait for real strength. The spoon in his hand balanced like a rock on a ledge. It could sit there for eons, or fall in a moment. What would his mother think about his windfall? What if he could do this every night?

That thought sought its own balance with Jason. How important where their relative contributions? It was Jason's hungry edge that tapped into a sure revenue stream. But Sean smugly knew it was his sober groundwork that mastered Tyche's growing instability that over the long run would become catastrophic.

It had been only through the accident of timing that Tyche appeared to be doing moderately well. In the long term, the original version would take the system beyond the event horizon to … What was the term Betty used? It seemed so appropriate. No, it had been Jason who first called it. The system would run to gambler's ruin. Sean had pulled Jason back from that cliff.

As Sean scratched himself with the spoon's handle, Melissa stopped eating and bent forward. "Sean, I've seen this before."

"You've seen what before?"

"You are acting like your father did when he lost his job." Melissa waited while he squirmed in his chair.

Sean tried to deflect her. "What did happen was that my contract came to an end. No big deal. I was making good money."

"Some of what you say is what your father said too."

"But I've found more work—so to speak."

"Then what's going on?" she insisted softly.

Sean took a deep breath and let it out in a ragged explanation. "You remember Jason's visit at the picnic? Well, we are working together on this idea."

"I didn't get the impression from him that he had any money to hire you. He talked like he was looking for money."

"He's got his problems," he said. "But there's this idea that is a real money maker." His story felt muffled.

"Hmm," said his mother. "It doesn't sound like much more than a con job."

"But I've worked with it," he protested through a yawn.

His mother shrugged and sat back. "Perhaps you should consult someone who has experience with money makers. You are surrounded with people like that, you know."

Sean was now hearing her through his fog of exhaustion. The words dimly made sense. He thought of Ashley, of Megan, and of Aurora. "People like who?"

His mother took little time to present him with a list of names. "Betty certainly comes to mind. She saw through Jason where others were baffled by him."

"Betty," echoed Sean in numbness.

"The fellows, those investors, you know them."

"Yes, the investors." Sean could see the pattern his

mother was making, but it dimmed quickly.

"And certainly your boss," she added to his surprise.

"Wade? How do you get that?"

"Didn't you say he was backing your salary in return of it being an investment in the place you've been working at?"

"Was working at," he corrected. "They dumped me."

"I'm sorry you feel bad about that, Sean. You really should talk to Wade. Look, you aren't eating now, and it looks like you are about to drop to sleep in your chair."

"Yeah."

"Go down and get to bed for some rest. And Sean?"

"Yes?" he said as he rose from his place. The spoon clattered from his hand.

"Leave that," Melissa told Sean as he fumbled to recover it. "I think you should talk to Wade. Can you at least do that for me?"

"I'll try," Sean said as he drifted toward the stairs.

* * *

At the Roosevelt Courtyard, Sean paused to consider his next step. There were several possibilities, even here with nothing more than a punch of the floor selection button on the elevator. Ostensibly, he was here to talk with Wade about his conflicts about taking Jason's money to work on his gambling scheme. There was the problem, however, that he didn't want to talk about this so much as he needed to.

He stood there, what to do? The other options were to stop off and visit Betty who could illuminate the entire gambling side of things. The last option was to visit Megan, but that was a slim chance. She was, no doubt, at work. He wished she wasn't.

So Sean unwound these options and selected the floor that Wade was on. Both Betty and, more, Megan would have been a distraction to facing this issue. How was he going to start? This was not one of Wade's assignments, Sean had gone into it without asking him. How could he expect Wade to help?

He stepped out of the elevator car into the hallway. He could have followed the carpet's pattern to Wade's door automatically, but he made an effort to find his grounding as Wade had instructed him before. This was part of Wade's drill for approaching an interview.

There was a small table in front of him. It stood between two etched glass mirrors in their frames. The mirrors, he noticed, were a repeated motif along the hallways to add light and space. The etched pattern was repeated in the printed pattern of the wallpaper. He bent forward to trace his finger over the etching of the mirror. Was this a modern reproduction that was matched to a modern wallpaper? It was hard to imagine that they could have survived the decades, nearly a century without suffering wear and abuse.

Then he realized he had checked out. His grounding had been hijacked by simple distractions. Sean took some deep breaths to bring him back to what needed to be done. He was nervous about using Wade's interview techniques to meet with him.

Wade didn't seemed surprised with his arrival. Wade sat on his small cushion with a cup of tea nearby. He rose and waved Sean in. As Sean drew closer Wade greeted him with a bear hug. "Let's talk about things."

"Like some tea?" he asked, and without waiting for Sean to answer, he poured him a cup and handing it over. "Sorry, no milk, cream, sugar, or whatever. I never seem to stock those things even though I would like some lemon, on occasion."

"Thanks, this will be good for me." Sean appreciated the bitter tea. The ceremony let him search for a way to step into his problem. Small talk was never a strong suit for either of them. And then it occurred to him that Wade's offer of tea and mention of the lack of cream amounted to small talk. Did Wade shift to suit Sean's temperaments?

"Glad to hear you can use it." Wade looked at him without inspecting him. His gaze wandered out the window to view the best weather that they had had in days. The drifting clouds varied the general lighting in his office.

Sean looked around and noted, again, how it was the second bedroom of Betty's matching apartment. The other door, he could imagine, led to a short hall, other rooms and then an L shaped living room.

Wade followed Sean's gaze with a glance over his shoulder to the same door. Then he returned his attention to Sean. "So, what brings you here? Looking for another assignment?"

Sean grasped at the word assignment. "Well, yes, assignment, assignments in general I mean." It wasn't starting out well. "I've dropped out of some work that you are probably aware of. I've picked up some work that you're unaware of."

"Yes, on the first. I hope that wasn't a rough separation for you."

Sean felt an obligation to cover for Brandon's goodbye. "I've no problem with Pribylov, but, still, it hurts to be cut loose from the project."

Wade nodded in sympathy. "Problem solving can help with pain, and sometimes it can cover up pain."

Sean tried to take that statement in, but it was elliptical. Wade noticed his confusion. He said, "We engineers are considered to be a cold bunch—thinking machines." He tipped back against his low tea table and mused over the blank of the ceiling. "Sean, you, like others, take my assignments like a drug to kill pain."

Sean was surprised. Was this a complaint? "Did Brandon have problems with my—"

Wade, still focused on the white expanse above, held up his hand. "That's your pain shaping things in your mind, Sean. Pribylov has gotten everything they wanted from you, and more."

This pleased Sean, at first. Then his mind, as Wade warned, began to draw out a brooding angle of his having been used up and discarded. "Thanks for trying to cheer me up."

"But you haven't cheered up," said Wade. He drew his gaze back down to Sean. "If it wasn't Pribylov, then let's get to what is troubling you."

"A project for Jason," said Sean.

Wade did nothing other than nod to encourage him to go on.

"Jason. I still don't know what was going on, but I do know what he was doing."

Again, Wade simply nodded.

"He has, on times, visited us at *GyroNautica* or at our flight tests for one reason or another. At the picnic he tried to pitch a proposition to Pribylov—Betty, actually."

Wade shook his head sadly at this. "Betty and your mother told me about that episode. He's been a problem."

"They visited you?" said Sean.

Wade nodded and then refilled Sean's tea. "Betty recognized him. She keeps tabs on her investments. I should probably ask her if she keeps handicaps on players like Jason."

Sean only nodded. "How long did they visit?"

"Betty and Melissa?" Wade mused. "Half an hour, I suppose. Later, your mother gave me a lift out to Green Lake for my afternoon walk. She joined me."

Sean's mind went back to the picnic and Zak's attentions. He was getting unsettled about how his mother's life was getting tangled into his.

Wade shifted back to gaze at the ceiling. "We, you and I, were talking about Jason. There's something going on there?"

He waited for Sean to fill that out. When nothing more came, he carefully introduced an idea. "Jason's a nuisance in general, certainly. But Sean, he affects you more than the others."

"That's not true," protested Sean with too much drama. "He's absolute poison to Ashley."

Wade nodded at being corrected. "Poison for both of you, then. I can tell you feel for her problem. There seems to be a considerable amount of pain attached to her and Jason. I suspect there is an equal amount of pain attached to you."

"Yes, pain."

"Can you put a name on that pain?"

"Jason—"

"—No, something deeper. Between a manipulative individual as I suspect Jason to be, and Ashley, who Betty suggests is fragile—there's something physical that has been confused with emotional."

"You know about … You've heard of this with—through Betty while she and my mom were here?"

Wade nodded. "Then, and over drinks on other occasions. Not much more than chit-chat, then, Megan sometimes keeps company with us on our weekly get-togethers. Office talk is only a small part of our discussion."

"So, do you think I've got a physical/emotional issue going on with Jason?" asked Sean with outraged injury.

"Sean, we are all fragile to some degree. You are being played if you are here to work through something inspired by Jason."

Sean struggled through unexpected turmoil to put this all together. Wade seemed to know where this was all going before Sean had even lifted his head from the pillow early this afternoon.

"You need to release something," said Wade softly.

With his breathing coming ragged, he searched the floor around him for his bag. Through blurred vision, he recognized the vague outline of it behind his chair. He snatched up the bag, ripped open the zipper, plunged his hand in, pulled out the package, and slammed it on the floor.

The force of this split the envelope at the beer stain that weakened the paper. Bills spilled out. Sean's breathe became more regular and color returned to his face.

"Money!" said Sean with some emphasis. "There's a name to put to the pain."

"That would seem to be a lot of pain," noted Wade as he gazed at the burst package of bills. He looked up at Sean and tipped his head to one side. "Still, there's something that goes back. Isn't there? Jason is an easy victim to beat up in the privacy of the office, here."

"I said money," insisted Sean.

"What does it solve?"

"We need it. Mom needs it."

"Did your mother ask for it?"

Sean couldn't add this all up. Of course he hadn't said anything about this money at his feet to her. She certainly had never asked for anything when he had offered to help her before this money came into the picture. "There are all these things going on," came his reply.

"You've certainly revealed the two most stressful problems that everyone suffers," said Wade.

"Rejection."

"How's that?" asked Wade.

"Putting another name to the pain." Sean began to nod on reflection over his statement. "Just like Ashley, I suppose. There must have been painful rejection tied up in her reactions."

"Good catch, Sean. You two share a pain that bonds you. How are you doing?"

"Better." Sean's breath was coming more slowly, evenly, and deeply.

"Good." When some time had passed, Wade bridged from the old topic to a new one. He pointed at the burst package. "First, do what you need to do with that. And, second, you appear to have missed an important element in your last discussion with Brandon."

Sean scooped up the bills in the disintegrating envelope. "You're going back," he said as he stuffed it into his bag.

Wade continued, "The boys at Pribylov want you on a retainer basis."

"What's that mean?"

"Well, what it doesn't mean is any money. However, they want to cut you in for a piece of the action if you will do on-call work."

"On-call work? I don't recall that being mentioned, but I wasn't exactly all together at the time. What kind of on-call work? And for what?"

"First, this has nothing to do with me. It is strictly between you and the boys in general. If you agree to be available to them on one week out of a month for any of their investments in trouble, then you will get $7,000 equity for each of those months."

"It's a gamble then," noted Sean ironically.

"Not like Jason's, would you agree?"

Sean took in a breathe to revive his spirit. Wade noticed and nodded.

"No, this wasn't a side bet. What about other work you may send my way? That might interfere," said Sean.

"Sean, that sounds like a problem you could handle without too much grief," Wade noted dryly.

"Yeah, I guess so." He looked around, down at his bag, and then back to Wade who was smiling at him. He smiled back and then took another sip of tea.

"So," said Wade, "anything else? Like to talk about Megan and you?"

A sudden flush erupted in him. "Um, I don't know where to go with that," he flustered.

Wade raised his hand, "Betty would probably be the better audience. You might want to include your mother, too."

Sean smiled sheepishly. "She doesn't wait for invitations

to go there, Wade."

"Glad to hear that. By-the-by, one thing that you probably haven't heard, they called me just before you arrived. Do you have your phone in airplane mode?" Wade broke out in a smile as the irony in his question connected with Sean. "They couldn't reach you."

Wade continued as Sean checked his phone. "They are having another flight this afternoon and as part of your on-call nature of business, they would like to see you there."

"Sounds great." This lifted Sean's spirit immensely.

CONVERGENCE

This time the weather split the difference between the last two outings. There was a high thin layer of dingy pearl so uniform that it refused to offer any feature. The flight field was still in the distance. Sean looked up to spot any flights already in the sky. As he noticed on their last flight, a flier would need a paint job that would contrast with this sky to make it visible. Icarus was still good to go in that respect.

He was riding in with Wade. For Wade, this must have been a rare outing, but, then, Sean didn't really know Wade's life outside of work. It had been a surprise to him that he and Betty were related.

"You get out much?" he asked.

"Half any day, it seems I'm out," said Wade.

There it was, thought Sean. He had that pegged wrong too. "So this isn't cutting into your time at the office. Is it?"

"Well," said Wade while he navigated the car through the park. "I can tell this isn't going to be a picnic, but I could say this is still work. I'm usually out checking in with others working on assignments around this time, too."

They must have been the first to arrive, because the van was not there—and neither was there an idling Beamer. Sean directed Wade to a spot near where he imagined the van would park.

"This the right time?" asked Sean.

Wade glanced at an old heavy automatic watch, an Omega Seamaster. "Close." He scanned the pilot area and mused on their activities. "What's the drill, here?"

"For our flying with Icarus?" said Sean. "Unassisted take off, usually. Climb to altitude. Level off. Acrobatics to check out stability issues. This usually pushes the limits. Then

304

descent and landing."

"All under program control? No human intervention?"

"That's right. We watch the numbers streaming back through telemetry. Ashley will modify the script on the run, so there is a form of human intervention."

"Sounds as it should be," Wade said. "And, no doubt, breaking every rule in the book here."

Sean nodded. "Teodor acts as our host for flight privileges. He and his father, Zak, have been flying here for years. Teodor is also our avatar."

"Avatar. Uh-huh. How's that?"

"Yeah, he holds a mock controller and acts like he is controlling Icarus during flight."

"Got it," Wade acknowledged with a nod. "A fellow named Zak. Hmm. Knew a fellow in the Navy called Zak."

They sat there in silence and waited. Sean considered he might be off a day. "The right date?" asked Sean.

Wade glanced at his watch again. "Close."

"Maybe the same Zak?"

Wade shifted in his seat. "Unlikely, unless Teodor's last name is Zakopyko."

"Oh?" Sean tried to draw him out.

"Quite a character, smart as a whip, part of the crew that I worked with." Wade shifted into another time that long vanished as far as Sean was able to grasp.

"You think he's still around?"

Wade turned in his seat with a half smile. "Don't push me into the grave, yet. It's only three steps away for all of us."

"Not what I meant," Sean said immediately.

Wade returned to look vaguely at the flight line. His gaze went somewhere else, Sean thought.

"Zak, a Destroyer man. Pretty rough duty, but we didn't work below decks, thankfully." He shuddered. "Some worked in the asbestos lagging locker. Even then they knew that stuff would eventually kill you. Most of them smokers too." Wade looked sideways to Sean. "Not the same kind of smoke as you might think now. Tobacco. If Zak or I had been in that division, then, yeah, your question ..." Wade sighed. "It was a crazy time." He looked into the rear view mirror. "Looks like time and date were close enough."

Sean turned in his seat and saw the van approaching. When he turned back, he caught a view of Megan's car already parked. He saw a wave from the driver's side. He waved back as his heart picked up several quick beats. As the doors to that car opened, three women got out. Megan first, Betty, and then his mother.

"Oh, jeeze, another picnic," he muttered.

Wade smiled. "How nice of the ladies to join us." He clambered out of his low slung car, and Sean followed more nimbly.

* * *

"Take these," said Teodor as he handed Sean some low power binoculars. "Check out the fine movements we have scripted when Icarus gets up there."

"Shouldn't you be testing the original script to confirm Icarus is flying much as it had on our last time out?"

Teodor nodded, and then shook his head. "The script has roughly the same moves. Ashley's added some elaborations. Fine movements."

"How can you add a fine movement to a loop or barrel

roll?"

"Well, not exactly the same script, then. The fine movements are when we are on the level. It will come first after the climb. Level out and back, then the same routine as last time." Teodor rolled the controller over and turned it on. "Not the same as last time here however," he smiled. "But I wish there was another way to sense the dead man switch, this makes my finger ache, I press it down so hard."

"You should've bought the premium controller with the prosthetic finger attachment," Sean joked. They laughed.

Wade, who stood slightly behind them with Megan on his arm, gazed at the sky. "Is Icarus up for rough weather?"

Teodor turned to Wade, and then turned again to follow his gaze. There was just a hint of darkness in a patch that was drifting their way.

Wade noted, "Squall. Should be over us in ten minutes." He looked at Megan. "Hon? Do you have an umbrella in your ride?"

Megan smiled brightly, and nodded. "Sure do." She released his arm. "Be right back."

Wade smiled at Sean. "She should be on your arm," he sighed with a false concern.

Sean balanced the binoculars clumsily in his hand just to do something. He looked back at Megan chasing down the umbrella. Next to her car he noticed two camp chairs set up with Betty and his mother in them, chatting. When Megan brought out the umbrella, this stirred a new conversation. Megan seemed conflicted. If rain was coming this way, Sean thought, then she was probably giving them warning, and then weighing where the umbrella would be best put to use.

His mother and Betty huddled their chairs together and

took the umbrella. So, his intuition read that correctly. Megan came dancing back and threw Sean a warm smile as she hugged up next to Wade. How could he be jealous, but how could he do his job and enjoy her nearness too?

Wade smiled at him again. "They also serve who only stand and wait." Megan punctuated that with a small wave.

Sophia was approaching them with Icarus and its soaring wing attached. There was some slight trace of rework around the access panel that suggested weather proofing. She handed it directly to Sean who juggled the binoculars until he realized there was a purpose for its strap.

"Got it?" she asked. "You can take it out to the runway." She handed him an earbud. "Use this Bluetooth to give us your visual reports."

"I've been meaning to ask. Isn't the range rather long from the van to us out here for Bluetooth?"

Sophia smiled at the opportunity to shine. "I've rigged up yagi gain antennas that can keep us linked out as far as three hundred meters."

"Really! That's ten times as far as they are specified and they generally don't do that well even then."

"Indeed," she smiled. "Don't forget we can hear everything—if you are prone to saying something you shouldn't ..."

"I won't forget," he promised.

"Oh, yes you will," she promised in reply, and then she turned to hustle back to Ashley in the van.

Teodor nodded to this. "Now we're streaming in stereo." He pointed to the bud in his ear.

"And we heard that in stereo," came Ashley's voice over the connection.

Teodor shrugged and added a wry grin as if to say, you were told so. "Time to get Icarus out on the runway. We're up next."

As Sean placed Icarus, he noticed that Wade's prediction of rain was becoming more evident as the field darkened. They had already flown through heavy rain with gusts quite comfortably. Barring any script induced issues, the weather shouldn't be a problem. Acting as a spotter with the binoculars might be another thing, however.

With occasional glances over his shoulder, Sean walked backwards so that he could keep his attention fully on the movements of Icarus. The propulsion unit spun up and Icarus smoothly pulled forward with an increasing speed. It took very little time for it to lift off and go into a steady climb. Sean would need the binoculars soon.

He was back with Teodor, who performed a pantomime, again, much like his father had to give the appearance of being in control when Icarus pulled out of the climb and went into level flight.

"Got it in view?" asked Teodor.

Sean adjusted the focus, "yeah, got it. What am I looking for—" He broke off as he watched closely.

Over the Bluetooth came Ashley's voice, "We're getting some rough numbers, here."

"Yeah, and I can see it," he said back.

"So can I," added Teodor. "This is disappointing."

"Can you describe it?" asked Sophia.

"Ratty, ragged, nervous," offered Teodor.

"We can see that in the numbers," said Ashley. "Got anything more descriptive of flying?"

"I'm looking at it closely," said Sean. "How long before the turn?"

"Coming up right now."

Sean intended to wait for the turn completion, but performance suffered. "OK, this isn't very smooth either. Out of it and back to a shaky level. Icarus is flying according to the control surface settings, but they are pulsating."

"Pulsating," echoed Sophia.

"See it here, too, in the telemetry data," added Ashley. "I thought something was faulty in the transmission, but you see it."

"The pulsating is rather fast," continued Sean. "Does that bear out in the data?"

"Yes. We are coming up on the next turn and aerobatic move."

"Barrel Roll?"

"Sorry, yes, everything is our former script running."

Sean followed the progress of the roll, but Icarus always managed to fly off in a direction he would not have expected. He lowered the glasses to get the overall view. At a glance he could see the barrel of the roll was shrinking in diameter. The roll turned in a screw thread that was getting tighter. It was so tight now that he brought up his binoculars again and could see Icarus was …

"It's getting quite agitated," said Teodor. "The barrel roll is tightening up and starting to curl down. Not enough lift."

Sean dropped the binoculars again, and saw that Teodor was right. Icarus was going into tight rolling dive. He took up the binoculars again. "The control surfaces, the elevators, flaps, rudder, are all still—well you know the word for it—thrashing."

310

Convergence

Overall, the flight was going as planned, but the fine control had become erratic forcing a growing instability. With that, Sean came to a realization. It was Jason's problem with Tyche that he had already solved.

However, if this was the same problem, then Icarus was closer to Sean's forecast of catastrophe for Jason's betting scripts. Icarus was playing out Gambler's Ruin in minutes where Jason had the leisure of a race season before catastrophic thrashing accumulated.

"Teodor," Sean began to warn.

"Yeah?"

"You are coming up on an opportunity to let go of the dead man's brake."

"So it seems."

"Can you recover from this?"

"I just have to anticipate the moment."

"The moment?" came the question over Bluetooth.

"Like," Teodor lifted his finger, "right now."

"Flat-line," Bluetooth responded.

"Sophia?" called Sean.

"Yes Sean?"

"Do we kill power to all systems with the dead man's switch?"

"No, control can be recovered just like last time. Nothing in scripting has changed there since the last flight."

Sean watch Icarus dropping in a lazy corkscrew like a fast swan. Teodor's moment to release the dead man's brake still had Icarus in a bad attitude. It was going to hit the ground too hard and at the wrong angle.

"Ashley?" asked Teodor.

"Yeah."

"Can you swap in a short script that is just about landing? Landing from a poor position like this?"

Ashley must have been thinking as there was no response. Then, she said, "I'm editing something right now. There it goes over the air to Icarus. Ready."

Teodor put his finger back down on the dead man's switch. They could hear Icarus' propulsion unit wind up again, and the flight leveled out of its precarious descent. However, the thrashing returned. Right now it was a mild, nervous twitch, but experience had demonstrated that would grow if they didn't get Icarus down first.

On the last turn, Icarus was in a position for a descent that wasn't too steep or fast. As it dropped, they could see the control surfaces quickly changing.

"Sean," asked Teodor. "How could it still be doing a relatively successful descent with all that chattering going on?"

"The soaring wing is more forgiving of the sudden changes," said Sean.

Teodor bumped into him while watching the flier. He hunched his big shoulders as if they could lift Icarus. "I thought we moved the wing characteristic into program control through the hardware connection."

Sean dodged Teodor's next sway. "The large wing still absorbs some of the positional noise. In effect, its normal mushiness is a natural filter that smooths out the rapid thrashing. We are lucky that our script links to the feedback system are holding the flight together."

"Yeah, but the chattering isn't set for glide descent,"

protested Teodor.

"We are set for a glide descent in the script, Teodor," emphasized Ashley.

Sean jumped in. "You are both right—to a degree. The script says glide descend, and the controls are thrashing on that average. It is a very poorly applied version of what is called pulse width modulation."

"Which means?" asked Ashley.

"It means that Icarus is for a very, very short while trying to fly up, and then for a very, very short while it is trying to fly down," interjected Sophia. "The very, very short time for down is slightly more time than the very, very short time for up. Thus on an average it is flying down."

"There's something else at work, here, too," said Sean. "What Sophia says is correct, but we also have a problem of degree. I've seen this before on a slower scale where it's the amplitude of the correction swings get larger and larger."

"Like early in this flight?" said Ashley.

"Hold on, everyone," said Teodor. Icarus was getting dangerously close to plunging as the errors grew. He let go of the dead man's switch. Icarus' propulsion went silent, but when the controls went neutral, Icarus' attitude was still too radical for a smooth landing. They were in the same position as last time, but lower.

Teodor pressed down on the dead man's switch again and the propulsion unit kicked in. The control surfaces resumed their thrashing, they could see that now from ground level. The lower altitude was to their time advantage, now. Icarus took up the glide descent.

Teodor held the controller out as if to ward off disaster. "We won't have another chance for this style of reboot—so we'll let the chips fall where they may."

The chips fell hard. Icarus busted the landing gear in a hop and snapped off the tip of the wing as it did a cartwheel into a high flip.

"I wonder if Brandon's wallet felt that through ESP," joked Teodor.

Ashley and Sophia emerged from the van and joined Teodor at the edge of the field. They gathered the parts of Icarus and carried them back while Sean wandered off to the group, behind. He found Wade talking with Betty and his mother.

He wondered if Wade and Mom had watched the flight, because they seemed distracted now. That was annoying. However, he let that thought slip below his mental re-runs of the flight. His concentration on the problem was like a salve on a mosquito bite's irritation.

"Looked quite good," said Melissa.

"Good save," added Betty.

"Couldn't you see we were in trouble?" said Sean, more to his mother than to them both.

"From the beginning. Picked up on that right away," said Betty.

"Hmm," said Sean as he plunged back into the knots of the problem, again.

"Good eye, Betty," said Megan.

"Comes from watching the players line up their shot, how they take a practice stroke, and what comes of it."

Wade laughed. "Betty, isn't there anything that doesn't eventually boil down to the game?"

Megan jumped in on that one. "Not when there's money

on the line."

Betty arched one eyebrow. "Did you see what was going on?"

Megan brightened. "Who could miss that bounce and flip and things?"

Betty patted her on the hand. "You keep away from bets involving people shooting pool, Dear."

Wade translated, "Keep your day job, that is. On the other hand, there's a world of investment that your god-mother shouldn't wander into simply because she can sniff out a bet. Megan, you've been able to keep her from some crazy investments that Pribylov backs."

Talk had wandered off the flight and onto other topics. Sean ceased to pay attention to their picnic chatter. Focused on the problem, he could see the parallels between last nights work and today's flight emerge more clearly.

Wade then shifted the conversation. "I've got a proposition to make." As his focus was on Betty and Melissa, they nodded in encouragement. "I'd like to take you two to lunch so we can continue our conversation." Megan pouted at this and Wade noticed. "Megan, why don't you give Sean a lift to the office?"

"If he wants a lift," she said while turning the pout into a lure for Sean.

This branch in the conversation drew him back in. They were already taking it as a given that Sean and Megan were going to leave together. Without further discussion, Wade and the ladies headed for Wade's car. There, they paused to consider the feat of getting into his sporty car. His distracted gaze was caught on them.

Megan tapped along his arm like she was playing an

arpeggio on a piano keyboard. "Let Wade figure out how to get them to lunch." She looked up at the threatening sky. She tugged at his sleeve. "Let's go."

Sean stumbled along. He needed to keep with the fascination of today's problems, but the picnic atmosphere was derailing that. The appearance of Wade abandoning him to flirt with his mother was difficult to sort out.

This triggered something inside that competed with a strange brew of feelings. One feeling was being pleasantly alone with Megan, but he found other men's attentions with his mother as troubling. As they drew closer to Megan's car, he still took glances back at the group clustered around Wade's car.

"It's their problem to figure out, Sean," she said. "Take off your engineer's hat so we can talk."

Sean stiffened.

We need to talk, Sean, was what Mom said when she and Dad decided to split.

In a nervous glance back that he tried to hide from Megan, he saw Wade's departure. The van was also moving slowly off. Jason's Beamer surprisingly joined the queue. A heavy mist fell like a curtain over their retreat.

"Yeah," said Megan, she had caught his glance back. "He showed up late. I would guess he caught Icarus taking the thump on the ground."

Megan took his arm. "OK, we need to hop in before we get soaked out here."

Sean struggled for enough air to say something. "You said something about talking. We need to do that. We need to talk." The words tumbled out poorly. What was he going to say?

Megan lost color. "OK, but let's get in out of the rain." Her short hair was becoming plastered close to her head.

The parking lot began to drain cars. Fair weather fliers had been long gone, other more intrepid ones were departing. As they settled inside her car, they were among a dwindling few still parked there, the others might have been the last of flying hopefuls.

Megan wore a serious, pale face. "You wanted to say something."

There it was, he thought. His invitation to talk was more a defensive reaction to smother her suggestion to do the same thing. But now that he had taken control, he didn't want it. He noticed that Megan was closing up. He had over-reacted, and it had been a shabby move.

"I'm glad to see you here," he said. "I was hoping you would show up."

Her color began to return. "I was afraid you wanted to … That you wanted—that you didn't—that it didn't matter. If I was here, that is, you know."

"Megan," he began, "I probably come off cold. The unfeeling engineer, you know. I get caught up in solving problems that help me feel better."

"What feels bad?" she asked with care.

"I don't always know." Sean swallowed hard. "Right now, some of it has to do with Jason's scheme … and me."

"Some of it?" she probed delicately.

"Some of it … Other stuff. Mom, Wade, us." He sought another breath. "About us. When you said something about us talking—needing to talk. That kind of invitation sort of brought up bad things for me. Like you wanted to cool things off."

Sean looked nervously her way. "That's not where I want things between us to go."

"Oh, Sean," she reached across the seat to lift his hand off his lap and take it in her hands. "I want to see more of you, not less. I want there to be warmth between us, not to cool things down. I wish I used another phrase." She drew his hand up and kissed it. "I feel better hearing you talk about this."

His stress melted. With a new breath he felt he could go further. "I also mentioned a scheme."

"Yes, and Jason. What's going on there?" she asked with concern.

He gave her a brief, monotone outline of their deal and fell silent. The dry recitation made his chest tight again. His gaze focused on the air controls on the car's dash. Isolated drops of rain splashed against the windshield.

"OK, those are the facts," Megan said when his pause drew out too long. "What took you there to that dive?"

"Money," was his simple reply.

"What about money?"

He tried to shrug, but it was a meager, insincere effort to communicate. "I need money."

"Are you sure that's what you need?" she asked with concern.

The question shocked him when it came from her. Mom or Wade usually approached it from the direction of what did he want? He searched for words.

"I want love more, but the lack of money seems to poison the future." He shifted uncomfortably. "I'm afraid. Afraid of losing both. My parents split." His chest flooded with air. "Losing everything."

"I can see you now."

"I don't understand how. None of this makes any sense." He rolled his shoulders with new energy.

"Not the sense that you are used to, perhaps." She pressed his hand harder and then rolled down her window slightly. The rain falling against the earth could be heard more distinctly. "The air is nice, isn't it?"

The rain cooled air filled his lungs. Her hand was warm. He could hear her breath. There was a scent, more than rain and damp earth, he could tell was hers. "I need more courage."

"I hope you find it in yourself. How is this about Jason's scheme?"

Sean nodded. He pointed to his bag between his legs in the foot well. "The money's there. I've been carrying it like a curse."

"When I was younger, Betty had me read one of her favorite stories. It sounds like your curse. The story is called *The Monkey's Paw*."

Sean shrugged at that. "Strange name for a book."

"I just loved horror books then," she said with a wistful smile.

"Really," said Sean.

"For real. Just ate them up." She shook her hair out, and some of the wetness slung drops into Sean's face. He lifted his chin as if he were braving the storm.

She daubed two or three drops off his cheek. "Anyway, to make it short, anyone who used this talisman, the monkey's paw, to make a wish, soon found that wish coming true and seriously upsetting all their other plans." Then, with a smile, she nodded to emphasize, "Delicious, really wicked stuff, but

I was 13. I've graduated to more courses at the banquet."

"I would like a taste," Sean said, moistening his lips and leaning closer to her.

They kissed. The rain continued. The windows fogged.

ICARUS' AUTOPSY

As Megan pulled into the parking lot opposite the tower, Sean caught sight of Jason's BMW. Even though the rain continued to obscure things, it was very obvious Jason was inside because the brake lights showed the pressure of his foot using that pedal as a rest.

"It's time to exorcise this spook," Sean said to Megan.

Megan took the space that put Sean's door next to Jason's. It was uncomfortably close.

"Megan, you sure can take me to the edge."

"Mmm." Megan held a thought. "Well, I suppose you're not talking about our banquet together." She glanced over at Jason's vague portrait in his rain scored window and Sean saw her wrinkle her nose.

She turned to him. "Let Jason drift and you snuggle up to our edge over here."

"That can be a long way down," he protested slightly.

She pouted. "Oh, you've put your toes over and wiggled them before."

A tremor rippled through him—then he got out. Only two choices, and he had to do this first. He could see Jason rolling down his window in concert with this.

Indifferent to the rain, Sean stood there and challenged him. "What's with this hangin' 'round thing with you?"

Jason was not perturbed by the challenge. "Things happen on the cusp."

"Sounds like a vulture."

"A very successful species," said Jason. "You got something for me more than vibrating the air?"

Sean nodded that he had Jason's work with him. "You're

321

used to waiting in parking lots and I have business to do in the tower first. We'll meet, but no dives this time."

"Choose your own."

"McDougal's."

Jason bent forward theatrically to look past Sean to Megan seated in her car. "I will meet you where they serve minors."

Sean looked back to where Jason's gaze went, there, Megan smiled out to him through the windshield. Without an invitation, she assembled her things, hopped out, snapped open her umbrella, locked her car, and danced around it to join him. Together, they trotted across the street and into the tower's foyer.

Jim greeted them, especially Megan. "I'm sorry that this ride is going to be so quick with you."

"Take us above the clouds to the Chinese room, then."

"I'd like to, pretty lady," Jim said with a smile in return. "Problem is those clouds go up 'n up." He shifted the lever, "but I'll do what I can for two lovers."

Sean put his hand on her arm. "We've got to get this review out of the way."

"You didn't worry about the time in the parking lot," she reminded him. "Besides, we sort of worked through lunch. Don't worry, our side trip will be short, just a peek. Up, up, and away, Jim."

"We are doin' it Megan."

When they arrived at the ornate observation lounge, Jim cast the vendor a warning. "They're guests. Look the other way, Andy." Andy showed he understood this with an amused smile, and continued reading his paper.

322

Megan danced across the carpet to one of the several ancient Chinese chairs in this lounge. Jim pulled close to Sean to whisper "If she sits in that, it means marriage within the year."

Sean looked at him, wondering.

"Old custom," explained Jim with a wink.

Sean noticed that Andy was watching, too. The three of them, together, held their breath as if they were at a coronation.

Megan let her hand trail along the back and one arm of the ornate oriental chair. She looked back mischievously. Then she danced back. "We'll visit again, Jim," she poked Sean in the ribs, "when we don't have work gettin' in the way."

"Maybe the gentleman would like to check out the—"

"The lady and gent need to get to work, Andy," said Jim. "Let's preserve custom for their next, longer visit."

"There we have it," said Andy, "This lackey of heartless capitalism says you gotta go to work. Quelle bummer." He picked up his newspaper and snapped the pages open.

* * *

Megan was half right. Icarus lay on the table with its broken, wet wing. The half not right was that no one else was there. A design review seemed remote. Sean wondered if lax security was part of their DNA. He and Megan had simply walked in. No locked door. Jason hovering like a hungry specter downstairs.

"It's like some things never change," he muttered to himself.

Megan came up with a paper towel from a roll nearby.

She patted down the flier with attention and care. The wing had been removed, but it sat across the fuselage top near its mount. When she finished drying it, she handed it over to Sean who examined the break, and then the landing carriage. Satisfied with his cursory inspection, he continued with minute scrutiny for the fuselage.

At that point Teodor wandered in. Ashley and Sophia could be heard behind him talking in the hall as they came closer. "The wing mount has been torqued too much for Brandon's comfort," he said. "The fuselage—the whole shebang—may be a write off."

Brandon heard this over the girls as he entered behind them and responded. "And, yes, my wallet's ESP twinged with grief." He noticed Sean and Megan already inside. "Thanks, Sean, for showing up on short notice."

They put away their things, finished conversations, drew up chairs, and settled around the table where Sean and Megan had been examining Icarus. The table was lit by a single table lamp, a period fixture that had been meant to be part of the office décor. The pool of light illuminated their faces set against the mottled sky framed by the windows. It was an intimate scene not unlike Sean's first view of the pool hall's interior across the street from Pribylov's.

Brandon opened the meeting. "So, Sean. Today's flight, as I understand it, was a near disaster. And by the descriptions I've heard, it seems some of the past instability has returned." He looked around the table. "Do I have this right? Or am I being hysterical?"

Sophia rolled her eyes. "The words Brandon and hysterical don't fit together in any sentence here. However, I will give you credit for getting edgy."

Teodor ignored that and went to the heart of the matter.

"What you say is largely true. We managed to pull it off through human intervention, and that goes against our mission."

"What say you, Ashley?" asked Brandon.

"Wait a minute," objected Sophia, "I haven't finished."

Brandon tilted his head to her. "Please."

"This last flight wasn't really like any of the other ones at all."

"Sounds the same," said Brandon. He shoved his hands into his pockets as if to say *show me*.

"Sean reported, and we observed the flight control surfaces," Sophia glanced at Sean for support, "thrashing. This was not at all from the same symptoms that got ironed out."

Brandon caught her glimpse toward Sean and repeated, "Seems we've been here before, and perhaps I've misunderstood the term. Want to fill me in on the significance of thrashing?"

"It is the response to sensors with over-correction being applied to the ailerons, elevators, rudder—our control surfaces," said Sean. Then he backed out of the conversation to let Brandon put this information together for himself.

Ashley coughed. "It would seem that our scripted equivalents to the digital potentiometers to the hardware were a little ... Off."

"Expand on that, please."

Teodor took this up. "I tasked Ashley and Sophia to put some script changes into both Hermes and the scripts to hook into control surface sensors and the functions that Sean's digital potentiometers offered."

Brandon's brow lifted. "My understanding was that we discovered a solid stabilization with the digital potentiometers the first time. But that control was at the lowest level of the design. Remind me, especially in the way you thought of it, what lowest level means."

Ashley took this. "If we were to liken Icarus to a human." Brandon nodded, and she continued, "Then lowest level is like how your leg bobs when the doctor thumps you just below the knee. The reaction is automatic—or autonomous as both we and the doctor would think of it. It is an unconscious muscular reaction to new conditions."

Brandon slumped forward on his elbows with his face into hands. He pulled back slowly. "Yeah. I get it. But we aren't talking about our earlier goals."

Teodor gave him a quizzical look. "No?"

"It was in terms of demoting Hermes into its own, on-board processor board. Moving Hermes to the other side of telemetry. Now the conversation is talking about lowest levels."

"Sorry," said Teodor. "We had to shift our thinking, too. That demotion was disruptive to the old patterns."

Brandon calmed. "So, did new patterns emerge? You all have a plan behind this, I hope."

"Boundaries shifted too," said Ashley. "But all this change has brought us to a tight design. We added a facade—"

"—let me dig deep, here." Brandon took a breath as he rose from his chair. "OK. Facade. Something to help you think of Hermes living inside the flier. Is that like a wrapper?" He threatened to begin pacing.

Ashley swept her hand across the table as if to brush away Brandon's question. "Something like that. Wrapper, facade, a new design concept we call Cruise control. Hermes spans Cruise control, Mission control and Navigation control. Sean's hardware can be monitored, poked, prodded, and set by them through scripts."

"And the hardware integration worked excellently there." Said Teodor. "And I wanted it to migrate up into the high level of—"

"—You wanted what it?" asked Brandon. "This unconscious reaction we were talking about before this Cruise control appeared in the discussion?"

"OK," said Teodor. "You're going to have to stay with me for this. The terms I have to talk about are like a strand of pearls."

"I'll try to follow." Brandon removed his hands from his pockets, sat back down in his chair, and crossed one leg. He was in it for the long haul.

Teodor took a breath. "I wanted the low level, autonomous control to migrate up into the mid level of the design pattern we now call Cruise. Just like your car's cruise control, it senses slowing or speeding and adjusts things back. Got that so far?"

Brandon nodded and was about to say something. Teodor shook his head and continued. "And then I wanted to migrate Navigation closer to Cruise control where you, the driver as navigator, have to set the speed to hold, and that becomes automatic."

Brandon nodded again, and Teodor finished. "We continue on with Mission control on top where you, the driver as navigator, are listening to your GPS describe your way to your mission's goal."

Teodor smiled. "There's a lot of control systems linked together, there. They are coordinated through Hermes with

Cruise, Navigation, and Mission as those pearls in the strand of design. "Things get more sophisticated as you move along this strand."

Megan surprised everyone by asking a question. "Is this really like a strand of pearls, one after the other, no jumping from a low one over a middle one to a higher one?" Sean watched her inspect everyone's reaction. The metallic highlights in her hair were picked up nicely in this lighting, he thought. Then he joined her in waiting for an answer.

Teodor gaped like a beached fish for a moment. Ashley and Sophia had answers, it seemed. Sean noticed that they didn't act like they were secure with sharing them. Instead, they joined everyone else in waiting for Teodor.

"Megan," Teodor said, "you sure can test a designer."

Megan nodded. Sean wondered if her nod meant she knew she could test him, or that she knew that he needed testing. Either way, her question went to the heart of the matter, but he would let them play that out until they got cornered. Megan, he thought, might have seen that corner they were backing into.

"Well," said Teodor, "I described it as a linear strand. A lower level control routine doesn't normally skip over a higher level to get to the highest."

Teodor opened it up to include Ashley and Sophia. "Right?"

"Mostly," said Ashley. Sophia nodded. "Sometimes, Navigation wants to know something from the low level Cruise controller," said Ashley.

"Yeah," Teodor waved that away. "Mission can make a command that has to be served by Navigation, which needs to be served by Cruise. Sometimes Navigation skips over Navigation and asks Cruise directly for status."

Ashley and Sophia relaxed enough to look at Megan to see if that satisfied her question. Teodor looked at Brandon to see how he felt about the design review. Sean knew from last night's work that this wasn't the end of it.

Brandon shrugged his shoulders and his mouth set tightly for a moment. "Rather ambitious, but we are here to be ambitious." Then he swung his crossed leg back down to lean closer to the table. "That leads to what do we make of this failure?"

Ashley's brow knitted over the problem. When Brandon turned to her, he waited for her to surface out of her reverie. Her brow smoothed and she offered, "Yes, it is the same problem. We forgot Sean's lesson."

"What do you mean, Ashley?" said Teodor.

"The Navigation's script was out of timing with the needed changes." She had the van's telemetry data open in front of her, and was browsing it. "When I compare the sensor data with the control application data, there's a huge gap in time between the two."

Teodor was becoming frustrated. "How much is huge? What are we talking about here, minutes? Seconds?"

Ashley fussed with her hair. "Maybe a quarter second."

"I got what I asked for, I guess. A quarter second, but what does that mean to us?"

Sean waved to get her attention. "Ashley, would you slide that laptop over here to me?"

He could tell that they were about to embrace a tar baby. Ashley's attempts at real time analysis was wandering the field. He knew last night's lessons would serve them.

Ashley passed the laptop over, and he browsed the data from several files he opened. As he submerged into more files, the group left Sean in his element. Some drifted over to look at what had gotten his attention, but soon returned to the general discussion.

If Sean had bothered to listen, he would have heard about their second-guessing the source of Icarus' flying problems. For the next half hour, he browsed the telemetry data in parallel with scripts that were supposed be in control of their ill performance.

* * *

Sean had gone deep. Conversation around him failed to penetrate his focus. The drug of work subdued his knots of tension. His future meeting with Jason was forgotten.

Looping through the data, the scripts, and Hermes' design, Sean found a familiar thread he could follow through the tangle. He scrabbled around for a sheet of paper and took notes.

Brandon watched Sean as if an answer would appear suddenly.

When it didn't, he focused on Sophia's pacing. Her nervousness reinforced the concern showing in Brandon's face. Brandon then sought relief from Teodor.

Teodor, responding to Brandon's nervous attention, offered, "I have to leave this to the experts. My hunch is that moving to the new design patterns is the right path to take. But we are getting hammered in the learning curve."

Brandon took this without showing any relief. "Maybe I'm too close right now."

Sean typed away with occasional glances at his notes. Sophia's pacing had settled to where she was standing behind him and looking over his shoulder.

"Of course!" she exclaimed and heads turned to them.

She then took Icarus and the wing off the table and parked it nearby. After that, she snatched up one of the displays that sat idle at Sean's former workstation. She attached it to the laptop he was working at and spun it around so others could follow his work.

Teodor and Brandon looked, but they had problems of trying to find the focus of Sean's effort. Ashley, on the other hand, ungraciously swiveled the screen towards herself.

"What are you doing to Hermes, Sean?" she asked with a wounded pride. "You shouldn't be editing this," she added with resurgent authority.

Sophia shook off Ashley's objections. "He's hot, Girlfriend. Look at the script changes too."

Ashley did this, and her concern shifted into interest as her tight shoulders fell back into a restful, but attentive posture. Over the next twenty minutes she remained close to Sean. She watched as he made changes to the script and to Hermes in tandem. She gazed at his notes and then crossed over to her own workstation to view her design.

"Oh," said Brandon who had recently been hovering over Sean's shoulder.

"Do you get it?" Sophia asked him.

"Well, no," he said. "I just see how the two are working off of each other." He stepped back slightly to expand on his admission. "I've never really gotten this Hermes business in my head, but now I can see something going on. How they fit, the script and Hermes that is. Can you give me a print-out of the Mission script?"

Sean lifted his eyes, took this in, and then turned his attention back to his work. Soon the printer was humming in the distance as he continued his edits. Sophia went over and got the copy. She handed it off to Brandon and then joined Ashley back next to Sean again.

"Look at that," Sophia said to her. "We were making corrections in the wrong loop."

"Not even wrong loop," said Ashley. "This is his own loop —no, not a loop, a recursion. I haven't seen that style of design since school."

"Recursion?" Teodor was puzzled. "This is not in my pay grade. Do we need a PhD for this, Sean?"

"Tell that to my mom," said Sean. "She thinks I should still be going to school. What I'm doing is making sure the numbers you are using don't change halfway through your calculations is all. It happens here." He made a vague gesture to one of the open views of code.

"Is that what he's doing?" Sophia asked Ashley.

Ashley pulled the display even closer. "Yes. We've been stepping on our own data. Keep going, Sean."

Sean saved his work and then backed away from the laptop. "I've seen this problem before. Just last night in fact. Spooky."

"How spooky?" said Teodor.

Sean was about to take a step off the edge. This was not the time to be talking about certain specifics of last night's design lessons. He looked for something in the code in front of him to stay on course with this project. "Um—all the calls to Cruise from Mission and Navigation. Those calls were injecting a lot of computational noise into Cruise. I've got patches installed there, and Cruise has been hardened."

"Are you finished?" asked Brandon.

"No. There's a lot more to be done. Probably another four or five hours, but that is mostly testing and tailoring."

"Is that how long it will take you?"

"When do you want it?"

"By tomorrow morning for another test flight."

Teodor sat upright. "Icarus? I thought you said we busted it up too much."

Brandon bit his cheek. "Means there's less to lose. You can make it fly, right?"

Teodor looked agonizingly up at the ceiling as if the answer to that were printed there.

When Brandon looked for his sign-on, Sean shook his head and glanced over toward Megan. "I've got other things on my plate, next." She gave a slight nod. He returned his attention to Brandon. "There's enough done, right now, for Ashley and Sophia to put together the rest."

Teodor turned to the two, "Is that so?"

They nodded. Ashley added, "It's actually a problem that is very fundamental. We've been dodging the bullet so far, but it nailed us today. Cruise, as Sean was saying, was getting pounded and passed that pain on to the flaps and rudder."

Brandon was shifting back to agonizing because of the padded answers. "So, promotion of programmable potentiometers may have given the skittish flight surfaces too much exposure to slower program control. Moving that control into the Icarus is what got us here."

Brandon summoned up a breath. "We can't take a step back, but I need to hear some love."

"You know programming is not my strength," said Sophia, "but this reads well, and I've heard of the problem that Ashley is talking about. It gets very pronounced where computations are distributed."

"That wasn't the message of love I wanted to hear," said Brandon.

Ashley nodded sympathetically. "It's subtle but vicious. When Hermes was working with a sensor reading, that reading was replaced halfway through the computation. Hermes—Cruise that is—was making control surface changes based on unsynchronized sensor events."

"OK, so no love sonnets," said Brandon. He slumped into a chair. "Tell me how you see it without going heavy on me."

"Maybe this will help," said Sophia. "Think about a computation you do in the office on a regular basis. Something weekly or monthly. You use a spreadsheet you share with someone. Got it?"

"Um, sure."

"How's that?" said Sophia.

"Oh? You want me to go on?" said Brandon.

Sophia nodded.

Brandon folded his arms and thought for a moment. "I do a slope intercept problem to find burn rates. You know—how fast cash is being used?"

Sophia nodded. "That's a painful memory right here."

"Of course," said Brandon. "We do this for a number of our holdings so we can closely watch those that don't have much runway left—you know—available funds—so that a group reaches a buy-out or venture capital investment before we run out of seed money."

"We must have been bouncing through the weeds way beyond the end of the runway," said Ashley.

"Um—well ..." Brandon faded out.

Sophia picked back up. "So, let's get back to your

method. To do a slope intercept, you need two sets of numbers. Cash available, and time available. You take weekly readings of cash on hand. And you are doing this for several outfits like us."

"Yeah, but, so far, none of this seems even remotely close to explaining thrashing," said Brandon.

"One last question, then. The burn rate—how much money is drawn, or paid out, or whatever—that is held as a constant I would presume."

Brandon's face contorted. "It does if me and my brother keep each other informed."

Teodor became animated. "I can see where this is going. You just looked like your puppy died when she asked that question."

Brandon nodded, sadly. "Andrew, once, only once was enough, did a draw to buy supercomputer time for a group that was on the ropes, but this was for a side project for their paying customer."

Teodor nodded. "I still see it. Andrew took a draw—unknown by you. Later, you read numbers that suddenly showed that their runway disappeared. You had to tell them you were going to pull their plug. Over-correction number one."

"What an understatement." Brandon nervously crossed and uncrossed his arms.

"Then the customer pays off for this side project where they needed the supercomputer time through them," said Teodor. "I bet Andrew made that as a deposit and the group was flush with money. Suddenly, in your numbers, there was a mile of runway in front of them. Then you had to rush back to plug life support back in. Over-correction number two."

Brandon bent forward with his head in his hands. "Gad, that was such a—thrash." He sat up with a start. "Yeah, a thrash. I whipsawed them twice within a week when normally I can spot these catastrophic signals a month ahead."

"And," said Sophia, "it appears, Cruise was reading and setting hardware about ten or twenty times a second but stepping on slower Navigation's four per second hardware calls for its own computations. The two were way out of sync, like you and Andrew."

"Yeah, yeah, yeah," said Brandon. But he slumped. "OK, I know my problems, but I still need to see this in connection with Icarus."

Teodor took his question. "Let's say Hermes has set Navigation to fly on a level, but sensors tell Navigation that Icarus is dropping. A gust of wind from behind will do that."

"Why?" said Brandon.

"We lose lift. But only for the duration of the gust. Faster Cruise notices at the same time as Navigation's call, and adjusts to compensate. It also knows when the gust has passed and adjusts for that too. That was seen in the successful half of our previous flight test."

Brandon struggled out, "Then, why didn't that work—"

"—Unfortunately," said Ashley, "halfway through Navigation's computation, its rate of change value changed direction in the background. Navigation thought Icarus was still in trouble and flipped the direction."

Brandon nodded. "And it has already returned to level flight when Navigation sends its own command. Yeah, then it climbs as commanded. This upsets Cruise which commands it to descend. But that should correct it, shouldn't it?" He looked at Sean for an explanation.

Sean shrugged. "It should. But it over-corrected for the unknown loss of lift and Icarus plunges. The next cycle, as you guessed, has to compensate with a new climb command to return to level."

"And that should take care of it," said Brandon.

"But it didn't," said Ashley. "Brandon, get with it. Look at Icarus over there. Does it look like things cleared up?"

Ashley's former enthusiasm for Sean's changes had faded. She nervously twirled her long curl around her finger as her dark eyes fixed on him. "Sean, you have more explaining to do."

"The recursion will satisfy the blind changes if Cruise is updating on just the sensor reading it took last," said Sean. He was going to have to step through this discussion carefully, but everyone would be pushing, soon. Ashley was going to get irritated by his own highly qualified answers.

"Meaning we were looking too closely?" said Ashley.

"Yeah. In a nutshell. The first-order solution would be to do a box-car average on all sensor readings, but that would hide the real problem."

"I saw that—what you call first-order solution—in the code changes," said Sophia.

Sean nodded. "That solution helps build precision and smooth the noise."

Ashley was still combative. "What about the thrashing? Is that solved by using recursion?"

Sean shrugged again. To answer this would have him describing his work for Jason. But he had to fold it carefully into the discussion, somehow. "The thrashing is the system, Icarus, in a natural resonance that is initiated by a jolt of noise—a gust. Gusts are commonplace."

"Sean," countered Ashley, "that's tech-mumble."

"Recursion is the second-order solution," he said. "It masks out hyper reaction by sub-sampling the sensors at a rate that is more suited to the needs of control."

"C'mon," said Ashley.

Sean searched for a way to translate his horse racing corrections into flight control. "Navigation doesn't need to know where things stand every quarter second. In the current design, if sensors get called too frequently where their numbers go into slow computations, then Icarus' reaction will build into an oscillation—thrashing."

"That," said Brandon, "should be simply solved by slowing calls."

"Simply patched," said Sean. "Not simply solved."

"Word," said Teodor.

"The problem," said Sean, "is old sensor readings in Navigation are being substituted by newer readings for Cruise before a Navigation computation is finished. The noise you are suffering from isn't so much a gust of wind as it is data being stepped on."

Ashley looked pale, and she moved slowly into her read of the analysis. "My expectation was that those Navigation numbers for rate of change would remain steady through the computation. Damn! This never happened for robots."

Sean caught her last statement like a slap. Robots and horse models, both, needed more time to build up to thrashing.

This is why Jason came to him. Sean had Icarus as a crucible to separate out problems more quickly.

Ashley cast an imploring look at Sean. "What if my Navigation routines held a local copy of the initial sensor data?"

Sean shook his head. "That's a field of landmines. It depends on the compiler that built Hermes. This goes deep when your compiler optimizes variables' assignments."

Ashley slumped. "Then only Cruise will get trusted results. And the trash will build for Navigation and the rest."

Brandon looked at them trying to find his anchor. "So, it's not the digital potentiometers. This is about the other sensors."

"About the size of it," said Teodor. "Sean, were you reviewing the work with the potentiometers for these changes you've made?"

"Right now, the potentiometers are set and forget kind of numbers in this operation." Sean looked at the code for a moment. "Yup, the pre-flight routines call those settings once, and never look back. No, this instability is about computations running on shifting data."

Sophia swept the printed telemetry data out over the table. She bent over them, arranged the pages and started bouncing a finger over key entries. "There, there, there, and Whack!"

Ashley joined her, and then so did Teodor and Brandon. They watched Sophia point out the data again. Ashley sat back down with a surprising amount of composure. She had shifted significantly. She smiled at Sophia, and Sophia straightened up to offer a summary.

"Thus the quarter second whiplash in our control changes." Sophia's head was bobbing to that quick rhythm. This motion bordered on a cartoonish punctuation to the discussion. The group began to laugh. "Knowing this, and fleshing out Sean's changes should put us on the map tomorrow."

Teodor joined their enthusiasm and hefted the fuselage and wing. "I'll super glue these if that's what it takes to fly." Teodor looked back at Sean. "And you recommend ..."

"In the long term, move to Functional Programming for Hermes' construction. For the mid term, follow the leads I've left there. For now, use recursion," he said.

"I like it," said Brandon. "I like it. Teodor, your inspiration of extending this—design pattern?—could be our competitive edge in the market. This is golden. This is money."

Sean straightened up and Megan grabbed his arm. "Money?" he said.

"Certainly," answered Brandon. "In the future, that is. This project is climbing the curve faster than many we've backed in the past.

Brandon began to cooly toy with Sophia's print-outs. "Now, I don't want you guys going wild, or anything. Let's solidify our gains with tomorrow's flight test. If that goes like we're talkin' right now, then I want you to do something that pushes out of your comfort zone for the next test."

Teodor smiled. "Sounds like where I get to inherit my dad's reputation of being the bad boy on the flight line."

Brandon continued his comment to Sean. "Money, here, means your investment in time as equity instead of drawing charges is going to compound. Your skin is in the game just as much as the rest of us."

PROJECT DELIVERY

"Do you think Jason's still waiting for us?" asked Megan.

Sean checked the time. It had been a couple of hours now, or more, since they had gone up to the office. He hefted his bag and felt the envelope with its weight of cash thump inside. "He'll be there."

The sun broke through the clouds. Stark shadows retreated into the alleys. The sidewalk dried in front of them. Foot traffic had picked up as well. People ambled alongside. The few blocks they had to go quickly fell behind.

As they climbed the few stairs into the restaurant, they were cloaked in such a darkness that they had to pause to let their vision adjust. At a distant booth, Jason rose and waved—or was it him brushing his hair back over his shoulder again?

Was it that dark? Sean felt his gut roil. He reached out to his side and found Megan's hand for momentary support. She gave it a squeeze and let it go. For that last dozen paces, he took a deep breath and let it out slowly as he approached Jason.

"We have business to finish," Sean said.

Jason stared through his owl frame glasses. He leaned forward with his elbows on the table, and the thin fingers of his hands laced together. "I hope this means what I hope it means."

Sean slid into the opposite side of the booth first. Megan slipped in next beside him. His put bag open between her and him. "You aren't generally that oblique," said Sean. "This is going to be as short as it was long in you waiting here."

"Cryptic is as cryptic does," Jason replied to Sean's comment. "Why don't you try drawing out your conversation, developing your socialization skills?"

This rocked Sean. It had nothing to do with the business between them. However, it proved that Jason was in control. He had to challenge that. "Small talk? Trivial stuff? The weather? How about why is it we always find you nearby? You camp in your Beamer?"

Jason sat back with a smile. "Ah! My timely visits? Ashley tells me when things are right. Good choice for discussion. You're a quick study, Sean."

Megan broke in, "Ashley?"

Jason pursed his lips and shrugged. "Pillow talk—you know." He shifted forward. "Great conversation openers, kids, but let's get to business."

He was stunned again. Sean took this news in, but it wouldn't fit. He had chosen the topic, and Jason had pinned him on it.

Megan wouldn't let Jason's vulgarity go. "You're baiting us."

"It's my talent—my sparkling repartee—and it sparkles plenty," said Jason. He shifted away from his original goal to toy with them some more. "I can guess why you think this is my solo act, but Ashley's the boss."

Sean shuffled this new piece into the puzzle. If he examined Jason's disclosure for value, there were clues littered over the many weeks to support it. Even though this muddied up what they were here for, Sean felt trapped to press further.

"Why wasn't she working on what you passed my way? It's her specialty."

Jason's face lit up, his thin smile curling open. "You passed her audition." He glanced at his phone, opened the message application, and flashed Ashley's text at him. "Seems like this afternoon you swept the finals too."

Jason looked at the screen's text and smiled again. "Yes, indeed. She needed someone disruptive like you to make our betting code solid."

Sean shook his head. "I was called in to replace you for robotics platform stabilization."

"One and the same." Jason turned the palms of his hands up. "The coach signaled me to do a sacrifice bunt for the team. I made room for you." Jason arched one eyebrow high over his glasses' frame. "But only at the office."

"Ashley was ready to … sweeten the deal …" Jason looked at Megan as he continued, "Motivation, if you get what I mean." Jason's gaze went somewhere else for a moment. "Something wild."

"This is twisted," said Sean.

"You mean us sitting together here, across the same table?" Jason gave them a twisted smile. "Or something else? Sean, we've crossed paths online some time ago when your interests ran along the lines of what we have to finish here."

Sean felt a shiver run through him. Back in his black hat days, Jason, or Ashley, or both must have been close enough to identify him. Was his work during that time an earlier audition to the one that Jason coyly mentioned? Sean tried to remain passive to close this line of discussion.

"How do you ever expect anyone to work with you like that?" said Megan.

"I suppose it would be due to my generous, sharing nature. Wouldn't you agree, Sean?"

"You have been very generous," said Sean. They had

moved back to the present where he was prepared to go. He reached into his bag and withdrew the envelope, and dropped it on the table between them. That was followed by a flash drive that clattered next to it.

Jason took off his glasses and with a mannered exhibition he cleaned them. He reached across, ignored the stained envelope, and picked up the flash drive. "Anything of usefulness here for me?"

"If your exercise script at the Hong Kong tracks are any indication, you should see an increase in revenue."

"Give me a number. How much is your work going to bring us?"

His gut knotted. Sean remembered to take a breath before going there. It was money they were talking about. It was as close as the shrouded bills between them.

He started slowly. "Where you would have taken about $5000 in a race, the changes I've done should bring you $5500, or thereabouts, now."

Sean could imagine the calculations Jason was performing in the heavy silence. Sean weighed how the lead had passed from Ashley to him. He hadn't gotten his arms around how she still fit into the picture, but it wasn't going to shake his resolve.

"As much and as quick as that?" Jason examined the flash drive as if it would affirm this. "OK. And what's with this?" he said, pointing to the stained and broken package patched with tape.

Sean's arm quaked, but he did manage to push the money across, away from him and toward Jason who watched suspiciously.

"OK, another cryptic message." He looked at Megan.

"Why don't you go check your lipstick so we can talk strait here?"

"Do you remember what shade I use?" came her challenge.

Jason let his tongue trace the edge of his closed lips. "More messages from Western Union."

"Cryptic is …" repeated Sean from Jason's earlier expression. Then he abandoned the posing. "Take the money back, this is the first and last of my work for you."

"This is what I gave you?"

"All of it, all 10,000."

"And this flash drive has—what?"

"What you want. Or as much as I've done and will ever do. It will perform to your own test as I described. Beyond that I have nothing to add."

Jason nodded and added a twisted smile. He tapped the table top with the flash drive and then thrust it into his shirt pocket. As he reached for the envelope, Megan grabbed it unexpectedly and ripped off one end of the beer colored wrapping.

Jason shrugged with a hint of completing a Faustian bargain. "By your boyfriend's account, I will make that up," he pointed to the money in her hand, "in a couple of days."

Megan listened indifferently, as though his comment was no more than the clatter of glasses at the distant bar. "Sean has a standard contract rate of $2000 a day, four hours minimum." She drew out a stack of sticky bills, and dropped them into Sean's bag. "That should cover it. If you have any problem with it, consult your bed partner."

Sean laughed as she tossed the loose envelope back onto the table. "Sound's like the end of the discussion," he said. With this, Megan slipped lightly out of the booth and Sean pushed his bag along and climbed out after her. However, he stopped short and turned back.

Jason watched with detached curiosity. Then he revealed his distrust by patting the flash drive in his shirt pocket to check its security. Satisfied it was still there, he adjusted his glasses and waited for whatever was going to develop.

Sean reached into his bag. He withdrew the clump of bills. He could see a question in Megan's eyes, *What are you doing?* He was sure she had more to say like *That's yours.* Jason had that *whatever* look that fit with his cynical smile.

Sean wondered what expression was crossing his face as he methodically ripped the bills; half onto the table and half into his bag. No one said anything. Jason scooped them up indifferently.

Sean and Megan left Jason at the table and went back outside. Sean's pace was automatic. He realized he wasn't thinking of a destination. Megan was there, walking alongside, but he didn't appreciate her until she took his arm. Now, he felt compelled to say something, to explain.

"I know what you were thinking."

Megan said nothing, but gripped him slightly tighter.

Sean looked inside. "I couldn't take that money. It wasn't his to give. It wasn't mine to take."

"You haven't said what you got out of it," said Megan. "If you didn't want the money, why did you take his job?"

Her question drew him back into last night's work. The adrenalin of discovery returned suddenly and cleared his head. "This rush of the aha when I corner a problem and smack it down." The adrenalin just as quickly disappeared, leaving him feeling drained of energy. "But afterward I felt trapped."

"Afraid?" she said.

Sean stopped walking and Megan turned to listen to him. "Afraid," he offered in a vague echo. It wasn't a confirmation, nor a question. Sean looked past her, he didn't feel connected to anything. He saw a piece of torn paper in the gutter, still plastered there from the last rain, and not yet released by the sun's drying power.

"Sean?"

Sean heard her call. "Uh-huh?" He needed to focus on what was going on between them. He juggled his bag to the other side, took her hand, and started back along the sidewalk.

"You said trapped," said Megan, following at his side and moving her hand to take his arm once again. "Like you were forced to do it?"

Sean thought about Ashley—the waif brutalized by Jason. Those thoughts were roiling. "Aurora once warned me about my people reading skills. Forced? I wish I could say yes."

The adrenalin's high returned. "I was in top form when I smacked down Tyche's problems last night. This afternoon, the sweet surge of aha rushed through me when I recognized the roots of Icarus' last flight problem were also in Tyche. Those highs brushed away all concerns about gambling schemes and surveillance drones. Both offered buckets of money. How's that for being trapped?"

Megan's brow wrinkled with concern. The corners of her mouth withheld her familiar smile. She held her thoughts for a moment before she offered another question.

"You put Jason's money behind you. That took courage,"

she said. "You did it twice. I don't think Jason has the same hold over you—unless you are looking for revenge."

"No revenge needed." That summoned up Ashley's drama. Her complexities and Jason's innuendos had Sean tied up. "But what explains Ashley?"

Megan gasped and took another moment to respond. "The explanation is there is no explanation."

They walked along while the sun moved behind and then emerged from the clouds. Their path was a new one that lead into the highrises of downtown. Traffic flowed alongside. Those on the sidewalk with them were office workers instead of tourists.

"So," said Megan. "Where do you stand with *GyroNautica*? I mean if you weren't going to be distracted with your aha thing."

"That's difficult." As the paces fell behind, he became calmer, not from the drug of work, but from having let his demons out. He could tell there was more to do in that regard.

"I have a problem with their mission, and yet the problems I solve go places that few get to explore."

"If you think you understand their mission," said Megan, "then you are probably wrong."

Sean lifted his head up as though he heard her statement come out of the sky. "Wrong? I thought Brandon was dancing with joy about cornering the mid-entry level drone marketplace."

"Yes, I caught that too. In our office, I've heard Brandon spin angles at every milestone in a project's life. That wasn't the mission you signed up for, was it?"

Sean stopped and turned. "Megan, that is annoying." He

caught her smile fading with his retort barely said. "No. Sorry. That's the part of me feeling trapped coming out."

"Tell me more about that, then." Her soft smile returned. Her grip of his arm slipped down to hold his hand.

Sean tried to keep his bag from slipping while he ran his fingers over his brow and through his hair. "You were right about the shift in mission. It started out as a humanitarian rescue robot. Now it's about drone surveillance."

"Today," she said.

"I suppose that's significant," he said. "Tomorrow may bring a new mission. Could be an armed drone for handling conflicts in Seattle's neighborhoods."

Megan shook her head. "I've gotten into a trap like that before, and Betty has told me that I was doubling down."

Sean thought about that, and their visit with Jason just behind them. Had he left his resolve on the table? "I still need the aha."

"I can see that's not going to change," she said.

"I just uncoupled it from money."

She nodded.

"But it was Jason's money."

Megan waited.

Sean grew apprehensive through the quiet.

What hadn't he said? What did he need to say?

"If the drone mission becomes armed … That's too dramatic. If it becomes surveillance … If, if, if." He shook his head. "If I were faced with Jason's proposal—again …"

Megan waited.

The sun warmed the back of his ears. "If an armed

drone? No. If a surveillance drone? Probably no. If Jason's proposal? Probably. But that sounds shabby."

She took both his hands. He let his bag slip to the crook of his elbow. "I want you to try something that Betty made me do. Would you do that?"

He offered an uncomfortable chuckle. "What did you ask?"

"Do this." Megan hopped, springing up from her toes several times. "That's all."

Sean began to stoop for a high leap.

"No. Like this." She repeated her move.

Sean barely lifted his body an inch and nearly tottered off to one side.

"Good start. Let's do that again." She prompted him by springing up again several times in place.

Sean sought his balance by lifting up on his toes first. The next time he lifted, he felt the tension in his calves. He bounced lightly on his toes while his tendons stretched and recoiled. He repeated this until his muscles and tendons slipped into tune. The on contact bounces turned to hops and his feet cleared the sidewalk's surface with each spring. The rest of his body began to resonate with this new rhythm. Muscles up from his calves linked in harmony. His stomach and chest relaxed at the peak of each spring. His breath flowed.

Then he stopped when it felt like it was time to stop.

Megan took up his arm again, and returned them to their walk.

Something had shifted, thought Sean. "Well, that was fun. Thank you."

Project Delivery

Megan looked at him, "You're welcome."

GRATITUDE

"Gave back all the money, did you?" Wade leaned back against his tea table and swept his prayer beads up. He wrapped them loosely around his left wrist.

"Yeah, even the money Megan held back," said Sean.

"So you said. Nice chunk of change she held in your behalf. Do you recognize the value?"

Sean reached behind for his bag, pulled it around, and spilled the torn bills onto the carpet between them. "A lot of money."

Wade didn't pay much attention to Sean's gesture. "More than money."

"It is cursed money." Sean shifted nervously on his small cushion like Wade's.

"That's not what I'm talking about, Sean. But what you say is revealing, too."

This was like a grilling from his mother under similar circumstances. Then the idea of pairing Wade with his mother struck a discordant note. He needed to fast-forward out of this.

"The guys have called me out for the next flight."

"And I have some prospects coming up in the months ahead for you," said Wade. "An assignment in Georgetown that you may find interesting. But let's leave the future to another day."

Wade slipped his prayer beads off his wrist and jostled them in his cupped hands like coins in a beggar's bowl. "More than money. Let's talk about that."

"I just did—a curse."

Wade sighed. "Instead of money, talk to me about the value, or worth in what Megan did."

Sean couldn't grasp the significance of Wade's statement. He looked at the pile of torn bills littering the carpet. They were worth nothing to him, and Jason's share were worth nothing to Jason.

Tearing them in half had been his own touch of revenge, and ironically, a value he and Ashley could share.

Sean didn't think this private evaluation would pass Wade's muster. It didn't feel particularly eloquent, so he shrugged.

"Megan expressed your worth, and you didn't acknowledge it in your story to me, to her, or to yourself."

Sean closed his eyes to erase the image of the bills on the floor. "I can see Megan. By me. With me. I can hear her quiet acceptance while I worked through my grief with assignments." Sean noticed something else. "Jason is now as faint as a ghost." He opened his eyes.

Wade waited, sipped some of his tea, and then glanced out at the late Spring's uncharacteristic weather with white clouds dotting the sky. "Can you give me a list of those who have acknowledged your value?"

Sean opened his eyes. "Megan."

"How about Megan? What's going on there?"

"I think I love her."

"Nice. Anyone else?"

"You mean, like, love?"

Wade smiled, tipped his head to one side, and shrugged.

"Mom." He waited for Wade to fill in the pause, but nothing came but his smile. "Brandon, Teodor, Ashley, Sophia," he recited quickly. "Andrew, too." Wade held his smile. "Even Jason."

"Even Jason," said Wade. "Even Jason. Hold onto that list so that it's handy. Write it down to keep it near you. Don't digitized it, don't stuff it away into some database."

Sean felt a weight was gone. "There's also Betty and you."

"Thank you. But can you own your worth?"

Sean didn't have to struggle to find the meaning of that. All he had to do was add his name to the list. It was a simple thing. Then he noticed Wade was waiting.

"Uh ..." How was he going to do this simple thing? "Uh, I guess ..." A thrill ran through him. It was pronounced enough for Wade to notice.

"Yes," said Sean, "I go on that list—I suppose."

"This needs to be ramped up." Wade looked at him for a while. "Write out this list to make it real."

"OK"

"That's not all. I want you to write out your contribution to GyroNautica."

Sean wondered about that. "How could I—"

"—You've done an oral presentation of much of this material at *Beyond the CyberDome*, right? Put what you've learned into a white paper and publish it for the same audience."

Sean could see where Wade was going with this. He could write a white paper, true, but there were other obstacles. "Who'd publish me?"

Wade smiled. "Do an eBook. Sean, use your own generation's tools and self publish."

Sean smiled back. It was as simple as that. "I'll call it *Solutions to the Tardis Stabilization Problem*. Yeah. Got it.

This makes the values list exercise more real."

"Revisit your list with thankfulness. Go home and share it with your mother. Same with the others. When you are next with Megan—well you can elaborate."

* * *

Sean and Megan stepped out of the offices of *Pribylov Investment* into the bright day. Not taking the usual path along the avenue, they turned up a side street and walked a couple of blocks without talking. They took a moment to stand and view the architecture of the railroad terminal at the end of the street.

"Ever taken a train anywhere?" Megan said.

"Not many trains in Colorado, at least in Pueblo. I know I would have to go to Denver to catch the train to Chicago or San Francisco or maybe here."

"Betty took me on a long ride when I was small," she said. "I loved it. I could run up and down the aisles, go to the club car, things like that, and no one was bothered by it."

"Wanna do that again sometime with me?" he asked.

"That would be so kewel," she said. "Where?"

"Denver to Ogden?"

"There's a curiously specific choice, Sean, but I thought you hadn't taken a train."

"I said there weren't many. I took one once as a kid too. Went to visit Mom's sister in Salt Lake City."

"So, what recommends this particular ride?" she said.

Sean slipped into a reverie as they ambled along. Six or a dozen paces later he came back to explain. "One hundred tunnels, one of them used to be the longest in the world."

"Spent a lot of time in the dark, hmm?"

"The conductor came through the dome car when we approaching the Moffat tunnel. I was in there with a bunch of high school students on their way to a dude ranch. Lot of couples, I just hung back alone."

"Mmhmm."

"He asked if everyone was OK. Some came back with a roar, others ignored him."

"Yeah."

"As we entered the tunnel, it was like being pushed into a piston because the air pressure increased. That's what I noticed. Then the conductor leaned to the switch panel, cut out all the lights, and walked away. Some of the girls gave a scream."

"I bet. An old cupid, eh?"

"For those next ten minutes, at least."

Megan squeezed his hand. "That would be fun."

www.ingramcontent.com/pod-product-compliance
Lightning Source LLC
Chambersburg PA
CBHW070405260626
47161CB00001B/280